Lindsay Buroker's

Forged in Blood

I

A High Fantasy Novel in an Era of Steam

FOREWORD

This is the first of a two-book finale for the *Emperor's Edge* series. I'd originally intended a one-book finale, but the characters weren't ready to go quietly into the night after a mere 400 pages.

This last story references events from the previous novels and also from some of the *Emperor's Edge* short stories ("The Assassin's Curse," and "The Frozen Water Trade" from the *Ice Cracker II Collection*) and the "Beneath the Surface" novella. Also, in the second part, we'll see characters from *Encrypted/Decrypted* and "Enigma." You shouldn't have to read these extras to enjoy *Forged in Blood I & II*, but if you feel like you've missed some of the details, you can check into those adventures. The short stories are currently only available in ebook form, but, if there's an interest, I'll look into doing a paperback collection.

Thank you for following along with this series. I hope you continue to have fun on the ride.

CHAPTER 1

Wind gusted across the abandoned stadium, rattling chains on flagpoles and stirring the fresh snow coating the rows of stone benches. In the chilly, predawn air, Amaranthe Lokdon stood atop the highest wall, the cold rim of a spyglass pressed to her eye. The empty arena opened to her right, while the cold black lake stretched to the left. A million people dense, the capital of the Turgonian Empire, long ago nicknamed Stumps for its bevy of beheaded statues, spread out in front of her for miles and miles.

One might have expected dormancy at that early hour, but numerous trolleys and steam vehicles navigated the city, and a disturbing number of uniformed people marched along the sidewalks. Some of the soldiers bore flintlock rifles, but many carried the sleek, new weapons Forge had commissioned, weapons that could fire several self-contained cartridges with no need for the separate loading of powder and ball. Out on the lake, all manner of military vessels plied the frosty waters with a number of them forming a blockade across the river to the south.

A locomotive chugged past the stadium, slowing as it approached the city, sooty plumes wafting from the smokestack and blending into the gray sky. It was a black military transport, and Amaranthe had little doubt that it was full of troops, though she didn't know if they were for General Ravido Marblecrest or one of the other potential candidates to the throne. All she knew was that none of those troops were coming to support Sespian; as far as everyone in the city knew, he was dead.

"You are silhouetted against the sky," Sicarius said from behind her shoulder.

Amaranthe hadn't heard him join her on the wall. Not surprising. "It's a little early and cold to worry about snipers gamboling about, don't you think?"

"No."

Of course not. Neither the frosty heart of a glacier nor the molten core of a volcano would have ever kept *him* from his duties when he'd been Emperor Raumesys's assassin. Nor, she reminded herself, had such ever kept him from fulfilling his duties when he'd been working for her. *With* her, she corrected. Though he acknowledged her right to lead the team she'd assembled, he still had a tendency to do things his own way when something truly mattered to him.

"If the people behind those snipers were smart, they'd be more interested in recruiting us than shooting us," Amaranthe said. "We've proven a great aptitude for defeating soldiers through cunning, athleticism, and an uncanny knack for blowing things up at the right time." She admitted it might be more luck than an uncanny knack, but thought her word choice might draw a semi-amused snort from him. As a whole, her men had been grim during the last few days of their overland trek, with the newly amorous Maldynado and Yara being the only exception. They'd been too busy playing swat-and-grope with each other to be bothered by the rain, snow, and hail that had pounded the team as it dodged patrols and skirted checkpoints full of soldiers. She'd struggled to keep her own grimness off her face as well, reflections of the ghastly dreams that stole her nights and sometimes, when she let her mind wander, tried to steal the days as well.

No hint of amusement came from behind her.

"With all this going on—" Amaranthe waved toward the boats, train, and troop-filled streets, "—I doubt anyone will notice us up here." She lowered the spyglass and crunched about on the snow to face him. "Most of the officers leading troops about down there aren't aware that we have tiles in the game, and I doubt Ravido is going to waste time looking for us until he finds out Sespian is here." Maybe not even then if Forge published the news about Sespian's... dubious parentage, and the Company of Lords dismissed his claim to the throne.

As always, Sicarius's face might have been chiseled from granite for all the insight it gave into his thoughts. Though the weeks of travel and battle had wreaked havoc with everyone else's wardrobe—Maldynado was still lamenting the loss of his most recent hat—Sicarius looked the same as always, adorned with copious daggers and throwing knives, and lean and muscular beneath his perennial black shirt and trousers. Somehow he'd even obtained a fresh pair of the soft black boots that allowed him to glide through the shadows without so much as a whisper. Once, in a fit of mischievousness, Amaranthe had absconded with those boots for long enough to try them on and find out if they held any magical silencing properties. Alas, the size difference had only granted her with magical clumsiness, and she'd tripped, rammed her hip against a table, and knocked over a chair. After recovering from the ungainly move, she'd found Sicarius watching her from behind. She'd returned the boots sheepishly, unable to come up with an explanation that he wouldn't find utterly silly.

"Forge knows we are here," he said.

"They're not the types to send snipers though. I don't think they can knock me from the wall with dastardly political or financial machinations."

Without comment, Sicarius hopped down from the wall. The cool glance he sent back over his shoulder meant he expected her to do the same.

Amaranthe sighed and followed him down the stairs and out of the stadium. Since escaping from Pike's torture chamber, she'd teased more conversation, and even some playfulness, out of him, but he wasn't in the mood for it today. Rightfully so, she supposed. It was time to be serious.

"See anything good?" Akstyr asked, when she rejoined the team in the shadows of a tree between the stadium and the train tracks. Actually the team occupied the shadows of a *few* trees. With the addition of Sespian and Yara, her group had grown of late. Eight people, including herself. It seemed like a tremendous number of expectant eyes turned in her direction, though she feared the number would be far too low to make a difference in the city, in deciding who sat upon the throne when the snow melted in the spring.

No, she couldn't think that way. They *could* make a difference. Upon many occasions, small numbers of people had been responsible for great changes in history.

"I saw a good... challenge," Amaranthe said.

Akstyr brushed a few snowflakes out of his spiky ridge of hair—it was green this week. "A challenge? That means a whole lot of injury and death with absolutely no pay, right?"

"There may be *some* pay." Amaranthe watched his face as she spoke, expecting a sullen expression and a threat to leave for the Kyatt Islands, the one place he believed he could study the mental sciences in peace.

Akstyr only said, "Ah," with resignation hunching his shoulders as he dipped his hands into his pockets.

Books lifted his head from an open journal long enough to say, "That's not *precisely* the dictionary definition," before his gaze was inevitably dragged back downward. The book-stuffed rucksack hanging from his shoulders must have weighed close to a hundred pounds. Amaranthe wondered if he'd ever thanked Sicarius for the months of arduous training that allowed him to carry such a load. Probably not.

"Where to first, boss?" Maldynado asked. He and Yara stood a few paces away, not quite touching but standing shoulder-to-shoulder in a pose that said, "Yes, we are a *we* now, thank you very much."

Amaranthe wished she could get Sicarius to stand next to her that way, when there were actual witnesses looking on, but that would probably have to wait until they were finished here and the fate of the empire had been resolved. One way or another. She glanced at Sespian, who'd been in the middle of a sign-language conversation with Basilard when she walked up. They'd stopped and waited attentively.

"Well," Amaranthe replied, meeting everyone's eyes before she continued, "as I've warned a few of you, I have a plan."

"That's why everyone is watching you with looks of concern," Yara said, her voice still gruff and no-nonsense despite whatever cuddliness Maldynado might have drawn out in private.

"And here I thought they were gazes of trust and adoration." Amaranthe supposed Yara was officially one of the team now if she'd joined with the teasing.

Sicarius, who had set himself up a few paces away, where he could see all the roads and paths an enemy might take to approach the group, gave Amaranthe a cool, get-to-business look. So much for gazes of adoration.

"Before I unveil my plan," Amaranthe said, "we need to do some intelligence gathering." A large part of her plan involved infiltrating Forge, and, right now, she had no clue as to where they might be.

Basilard nodded—the gesture might have had a tinge of relief to it. Did they think she'd go barreling into the city, hurling explosives, without finding out exactly what they were facing? Perhaps a couple of her schemes had been a tad extemporaneous of late.

We must learn who controls the majority of the forces, he signed, *and if Forge has regrouped and arrived yet.*

"Agreed," Amaranthe said. "That's why Maldynado and I are going to visit his old journalist friend, Deret Mancrest."

This time Sicarius's look had a baleful undertone.

"With his resources, he ought to know what's going on in the city," Amaranthe said. "Also, given that his newspaper's been prematurely reporting Sespian's death, among other Forge-favoring tidbits, I want to find out if he's in the coalition's pocket, being coerced to write their stories for them, or—"

"Is open to being wooed to our side?" Books suggested.

"Didn't we already woo him once?" Akstyr asked.

Perhaps men only stay wooed so long as the wooing influence is present in the area. Basilard pointed to Amaranthe.

Maldynado raised a finger. "Is anybody else concerned with how many grown men are using the word 'woo' here?"

Amaranthe made a chopping motion to halt the tangent. "While Maldynado and I are looking for Mancrest, I'd like Basilard, Yara, and Akstyr to locate a promising hideout for us. While you three are doing that, you can mill about on the streets, listen in on conversations, and tease out what tidbits you can from the general public. I'm sure I don't have to remind you to keep your hoods up and your faces in the shadows. Many of us are still featured on wanted posters, and Forge may have bounties out on everyone by now."

Yara's lips twisted into a sour expression. She might be lamenting her choice to stay with them. If so, she didn't say anything. Those deadly rockets the team had uncovered on the steamboat ride back upriver seemed to have convinced her that, even if Sespian wasn't the undisputed heir any more, it was worth risking her career to keep Forge from playing puppet master to the new emperor.

"Where are we all going to meet up in the meantime?" Maldynado asked. "Until we find a suitable secret hideout, and, as long as we're on the topic, might I suggest an above-ground hideout without any vermin, scat, urine, or otherwise unsavory leavings in the area? I know the boss is handy with a broom, but she might not have time to clean things up for us for this mission."

Yara took a step away from Maldynado. "*Handy* with a broom? *Clean* for us? Are you telling me that you need Corporal Lokdon to tidy up after you?"

Maldynado avoided her eyes. "Not *me* specifically, but, uhm."

Amaranthe watched the exchange with some amusement. She was certain her fastidious streak had been brought up in front of Yara before, but perhaps her new relationship with Maldynado inspired her to want to... hammer him into the mold, as the marines liked to say of their young recruits.

"I'm positive that Basilard, Akstyr, and Yara will find a suitable hideout," Amaranthe said to keep Maldynado from getting himself into trouble. More trouble.

"Hot water and indoor plumbing would be appreciated," Books said with a weary sigh, one that spoke of being ready for a year's worth of hardship to come to an end.

Amaranthe could understand that; she wouldn't mind easy access to hot baths either.

"I notice you haven't assigned Sespian, Sicarius, or myself to tasks yet," Books went on. "Is that because you know it's important to leave me to my current project?" He tapped the open tome in his hands. "I'm close to having a preliminary constitution fleshed out."

"That's good news, but no," Amaranthe said. "I'd like you to go with Sespian and Sicarius."

Books blinked a few times. Meanwhile, Sespian eyed Sicarius warily out of the corners of his eyes. He'd grown less vocal about his distaste, but he hadn't noticeably warmed up to the idea of having an assassin for a father.

"Go where? And to what end?" Books asked.

"As soon as people from that Forge meeting get up here, if they haven't already, we can expect a newspaper announcement that shares the truth of Sespian's heritage. Maybe they won't bother as long as they believe he's dead, but as soon as we present him as the rightful heir to the throne, they'll seek to discredit him."

"Correctly so," Books said. "If his father is of lowborn origins, his claim to imperial rule comes only through his mother's side."

Sicarius's flat expression turned toward Books. He probably didn't care if he was "lowborn" or not, but Books squirmed and lifted an apologetic hand beneath the stare.

"True, but his mother's line gives him as good a claim as many of the other potential candidates," Amaranthe said, "with the possible exception of Ravido, thanks to the Marblecrests' not-so-distant history with the throne, but what if Sicarius *isn't* of lowborn origins?"

"What do you mean? We don't know who his parents were, do we?" Books pointed at Sicarius.

"No," Amaranthe said, "but we can surmise that Hollowcrest chose based on intelligence and physical prowess, hoping the offspring would receive the traits of the parents. If some notable Crest man were involved, the populace—and the Company of Lords—might find Sespian's pedigree more appealing."

"A Crest?" Maldynado sounded affronted as he regarded Sicarius with new eyes.

"For all we know, Fleet Admiral Starcrest could have been his father," Amaranthe said.

A wistful expression flashed into Sicarius's eyes; it was gone so quickly she doubted anyone else noticed it.

Books scoffed. "Starcrest wasn't blond."

"Not many Turgonian men are," Amaranthe said. "Maybe Hollowcrest picked a Kyattese, Mangdorian, or Kendorian woman to birth him, in hopes that his features would be less classical empire, and that he'd be able to blend in when visiting other countries."

"*Visiting*," Sespian muttered.

Amaranthe ignored the grousing. She couldn't blame him for that one. Visiting was an innocuous word for what Sicarius had *really* been doing when he entered other nations.

"This is baseless speculation," Books said.

"At this point, yes. That's why you're going to research his heritage."

Amaranthe met Sicarius's eyes, wondering how he'd feel about having other team members prying into his past. She could send him alone—his records were probably in the Imperial Barracks somewhere, if they existed at all—but thought Books might have some useful insight into genealogy studies, should Hollowcrest's notes prove difficult to decipher. Sicarius didn't avoid her gaze, but he was being inscrutable, as usual.

"Is it necessary that I go?" Sespian asked, then rushed to add, "Someone should check on Fort Urgot and see what's going on there." It sounded like an excuse.

"Fort Urgot can wait," Amaranthe said. "Aren't you curious who your grandparents might be on your father's side? What if they're still alive?"

Sespian opened his mouth, but shut it again without saying anything. Sicarius's eyebrow twitched ever so slightly. Surely he'd wondered before if his parents were still alive. Or maybe that twitch meant he already knew they weren't.

"Whatever records remain of my training and inception would be in Hollowcrest's office," Sicarius said. "If his office hasn't been disturbed."

"It hasn't been moved," Sespian said, "but Forge owns a number of my... *the* intelligence officers who work in the Barracks. I'm sure it's been searched."

"But Forge didn't have any knowledge of your true heritage until..." Amaranthe winced, reminded that she'd been the one to release the hounds, however inadvertently.

"Hollowcrest was secretive in matters related to my upbringing," Sicarius said. "The documents would have been hidden."

"Good," Amaranthe said. "Maybe they're undisturbed then. If you three can find something favorable to counteract the questionable nature of, ah..." She extended an apologetic hand toward Sicarius. The empire might be full of war-loving soldiers, but it favored those who won battles bravely and openly, not by sticking daggers in people's backs. "It'll be easier to put Sespian forward as the most promising scion if we acknowledge the truth. It'll come out anyway, but maybe we can put a palatable sauce on it."

Sicarius's grunt had a skeptical undertone.

"At the very least," Amaranthe said, "we'll need to know who currently holds the Imperial Barracks."

"The last time I attempted to enter them, they were warded." Sicarius eyed Akstyr.

Without hesitation, Akstyr raised his hand. "I'll go and check them out."

Eager, eh? Amaranthe wondered if it was the chance to study another practitioner's work that interested him or if he was concerned about being seen on the streets. She didn't know how many thugs would be searching for him—his bounty wasn't

as high as hers, and nowhere near Sicarius's, but the gangs had more eyes on the street than the enforcers, so they might represent more of a threat. Things were also more... personal with them. She'd have to do her best to keep Akstyr out of sight until they could deal with the bounty or he could escape the empire. Though he hadn't always been her most earnest worker, he didn't deserve to have his loyalty rewarded with a crossbow bolt in the chest.

"So, this leaves only Yara and Basilard to locate our new hideout?" Maldynado shook his head. "We're going to get something sparse, I know it."

"Are you whining?" Yara asked.

"No, that was observing."

"What's the difference?"

Maldynado snapped his fingers. "Professor Booksie? Would you care to explain?"

"How a grown man can justify constant complaining to his lady?" Books tapped his bulging rucksack. "None of my texts has an answer to that."

"Let's get started," Amaranthe said before Maldynado's sputtered protest could evolve into fighting words. The gray plumes of smoke from the locomotive had faded, and fresh troops were already piling into the city. "We'll meet in the alley behind Curi's Bakery at midnight."

* * *

A faint breeze stirred the darkness in the underground passages, bringing the scents of fresh snow and damp fir needles from the Emperor's Preserve. They'd entered the tunnel system through a hidden and booby-trapped gate in the park a half a mile back, one Sicarius had used often in the past. Hollowcrest hadn't wanted anyone to know an assassin in the emperor's employment came and went in the Imperial Barracks. The mundane booby traps were not a problem. The newly added Science-based ones were a different matter.

Sicarius followed his nose back to the spot where he'd left

the others. The air also carried mold and mildew spores, along with the sharp tang of pine tree resin mixed with bear grease. Akstyr's hair concoction. The smell of ink verified Books's presence. Sespian's scent was more subtle, and Sicarius heard his soft, steady breathing before identifying him in an olfactory manner.

Before speaking and betraying his presence, Sicarius listened, smelled, and touched his fingers to the damp, coarse stone of the tunnel floor, testing for vibrations that would indicate footfalls nearby.

"Maybe he's going to leave us here all night," Akstyr muttered.

"If so, I'll be most put out," Books said.

"Because you didn't bring your work with you?"

"Precisely. He said I couldn't bring my books because they'd slow me down." Books sniffed. He carried only a lightweight satchel with matches and lanterns.

"The man is truly a tyrant," Sespian said, his tone dry.

"No argument there," Akstyr muttered.

Having determined that nobody else approached—despite the distracting babbling of his own colleagues—Sicarius lifted his hand from the stone floor. "I have verified the existence of a ward guarding the Barracks entrance."

Surprised scuffles sounded, along with the thud of flesh bumping against stone. Books cursed beneath his breath. Sespian stirred—uneasily?

Sicarius knew that his soundless approaches startled others, though he did not know why they so often showed signs of discomfort when they realized he'd heard them talking about him. He did not care if they spoke of him during moments of inane chatter, so long as they were not plotting harm toward him.

"I do not believe it has been disturbed since I came this way last summer," Sicarius continued. "Akstyr, come."

Akstyr sighed but did not otherwise object to the command.

Books took a step and banged his knee against the wall.

"If nothing except magic is down here, can we risk a light?" Sespian asked, the material of his sleeve rustling, followed by a pat, suggesting he'd offered Books a hand.

"The *Science*," Akstyr corrected.

Sicarius would have preferred to continue in darkness, but knew the other men's senses were not honed appropriately. "It is unlikely we will encounter another until we enter the basement. Or trigger the ward."

"Good." Akstyr snapped his fingers, and a soft ball of blue light burned into existence.

Sicarius put his back to it to preserve what he could of his night vision and led the way deeper into the tunnel system. Few people knew about the passages. If the curious way Sespian regarded the damp, rough walls was an indication, their existence was new to him too. Raumesys had prepared him poorly. Perhaps because, from what little Sicarius had witnessed of the boy's upbringing, the old emperor had never been impressed with his successor. Even before Sespian had come of age, Hollowcrest had been speaking of arranging a marriage for him so he'd produce an heir early on. So they had an alternative should Sespian one day disappear?

A strident twang plucked at Sicarius's senses, and he slowed down, extending a hand to stop the others. He hadn't heard or smelled anything, nor had he felt the mental sciences being used, but something was amiss.

Behind him, the men halted without saying a word. In his peripheral vision, he spotted hands dropping to swords sheathed on belts.

Ahead, Akstyr's light illuminated a dead end, one that appeared to be of natural origins. It wasn't. There was a stone door, one designed to only allow an exit, not an entrance, but Sicarius knew a way around the locking mechanism. They hadn't reached the secret door yet, though. He'd stopped a dozen meters from it. He'd sensed...

No, that was the problem. He *didn't* sense anything. The ward. It'd been right here. His training had included enough exposure to the mental sciences and practitioner-crafted devices that he knew when he was in their presence. Five minutes earlier, a chunk of the stone wall had been emitting a telltale aura. Now, he felt nothing.

The faintest hint of an odor touched his nostrils. Smoke. Pipe smoke, though the particular tobacco blend wasn't anything imperial men favored. It had a resiny underpinning, one that teased his memory. Nurian *rek rek*. One of his old tutors had smoked it.

He sniffed the air again, trying to verify that identification, but the faint scent proved elusive. Nobody had been smoking in the tunnel, he decided, but someone might have passed through wearing clothing that had been near a smoker.

"Akstyr," Sicarius whispered. "Do you sense anything?"

"No. Should I?"

"There is a ward here." Sicarius pointed to the spot on the wall. Even before, there hadn't been anything tangible to touch or visible to the human eye, but he was certain that it'd been located there. "Now it is gone. Or it has been triggered." He was reluctant to admit that he could have failed to notice another person in the tunnels, but had to inform them of the possibility. "Someone else may be down here."

"I don't sense anything." Akstyr shuffled over to the spot. "Are you sure you didn't imagine it in the first place?"

"I am certain."

"Really? Because you're not a practitioner."

Books sucked in a breath, as if he feared Sicarius would lash out at Akstyr for daring to question. Were Sicarius going to punish the youth for impertinence, he would have done it the day they met. He did let his tone chill when he repeated, "I am certain," thus to discourage further argument.

Akstyr closed his eyes and ducked his head, his upswept ridge of hair bobbing. He placed a hand on the wall.

"If someone triggered the trap, so to speak," Books said, "should we abandon this mission? At least for tonight?"

"Hoping to get back to your work?" Sespian murmured.

"Partially. Partially I'm concerned for our safety if someone was skilled enough to sneak past Sicarius without his noticing. Or any of us noticing," he rushed to add, perhaps feeling he'd offered an insult.

Sicarius ignored the slight. He, too, would find cause for concern if someone had bypassed him without a whisper. Perhaps the person had been there first and had been waiting to deal with the ward until Sicarius left. That idea didn't grate at him any less, for it would have meant he hadn't been paying as much attention to his surroundings as he should have been, but he'd find that more plausible than the notion that someone had sneaked past him in the dark.

"I found it," Akstyr said. "The ward. It wasn't tripped."

"That's a relief," Books said.

Was it? What had happened then? Sicarius waited for a further explanation.

Akstyr tapped the stone wall. "It's been disarmed."

"Disarmed?" Sicarius asked, his tone sharper than he'd intended. Long ago, Hollowcrest and various tutors had drilled into him the importance of maintaining a neutral facade and giving away nothing through expression—or timbre of voice. He wondered, sometimes, if so much time spent amongst men— and women, he added to himself, thinking of Amaranthe—was affecting his ability to distance himself from humanity, from his own frail human side. "Disarmed how?" he asked, making his tone calm and emotionless again.

"It's like… if this were a mine… someone had left the casing and detonator and stuff in place, but removed the charge," Akstyr said. "It's something only a practitioner would know how to do."

"This could be done swiftly?" Sicarius was certain he'd been gone for no more than five minutes.

"If someone had practiced enough, I guess."

"Are you telling me that a wizard sneaked into the Barracks just ahead of us?" Sespian whispered.

"Practitioner," Akstyr corrected.

Ignoring him, Sespian focused on Sicarius. "To what end? Are they trying to beat us to your records? How would they even know we sought them?"

"I doubt this person's presence has anything to do with me,"

Sicarius said.

The others exchanged dubious looks.

Sicarius refused to doubt his statement. Until Amaranthe had voiced her new interest in digging into his past, nobody had been contemplating such matters. Nor had anybody been around spying on their conversation earlier in the day. "It is more likely that another assassin has entered the Barracks."

Such an occupation would explain the person's stealth.

"A wizard assassin?" Sespian asked. "Who's the target?" He didn't point to himself, but he didn't need to. After being a target for so long, he must have learned to worry about his life. Good. Paranoia kept one alive.

"Perhaps Ravido or whomever has taken over the Barracks," Sicarius said.

"Hm, yes." Books stroked his jaw. "If the newspapers speak the truth, the competition is going to be noticeable—and bloody—over the next few weeks. There's an entire empire at stake here."

"We will enter and attempt to avoid the other intruder," Sicarius said, though their errand to Hollowcrest's office would take them to the same floor and hallway that housed the imperial suites. If Ravido had taken the Barracks for his own, he may have decided to set himself up in Raumesys's old rooms, something an assassin clever enough to disarm magical traps would soon deduce.

"What if we're not able to do that?" Books asked quietly. "An assassin with a practitioner's skills sounds formidable."

"We too are formidable." Sicarius headed for the secret door, though a niggling thought followed him, one that suggested someone who had evaded his notice in the tunnel might be *more* than formidable.

CHAPTER 2

SOLDIERS AND ENFORCERS PATROLLED THE COBBLESTONE streets on either side of the canal passing in front of the *Imperial Gazette* building. Amaranthe and Maldynado crouched in the shadows beneath the closest bridge, waiting for night to deepen and for the foot traffic to dwindle. Most of that foot traffic was uniformed. Though numerous eating and drinking houses dotted the waterfront, the sounds coming from within them were muted. Few civilians lingered in the streets. She doubted it had anything to do with the frosty evening air—winter would grow far colder in the coming months, and Turgonians were used to the chill. Those civilians who *did* brave the streets did so using quick, purposeful strides, their coats pulled tight, their eyes watching the troops.

"Those soldiers are taking the joy out of people's evenings," Maldynado said as a squad marched across the bridge above them, the synchronized thuds of their steps echoing from the raised walls on either side of the canal.

Amaranthe eyed the metal support beams overhead. She recalled hearing that soldiers were supposed to break into unsynchronized steps when crossing bridges, thus to keep the vibrations from collapsing the structure, but perhaps that was only for poorly constructed wooden bridges out in the countryside. Still, if the bridge toppled—preferably when she wasn't under it—it'd provide a nice diversion for her and Maldynado to enter the *Gazette* building. She didn't want to light any houseboats on fire this time.

"They're just following orders," Amaranthe said when the

soldiers passed without bridge mishaps. "It's their generals we need to worry about. Have you figured out the armband code yet?" They'd seen soldiers with blue, red, and white sashes tied about their right biceps. Not all the soldiers wore them, and Amaranthe assumed they had to do with identifying allegiance to certain would-be successors. The military fatigues were otherwise identical.

"Aside from the fact that those men have dreadful fashion sense?" Maldynado asked.

"Yes."

"Then... no. Except there seem to be more white armbands than any other color."

"I noticed that too. Ravido's people, you think? With Forge at his back, he should have all the advantages, and he's had more time to gather troops than Lord Heroncrest and Lord General Flintcrest," Amaranthe said, citing two other contenders who'd been named in a newspaper a few days earlier. She had, however, seen men on all sides carrying new rifles and old flintlocks as well. Maybe there was some bartering going on between the armies. Or maybe Forge wanted to confuse outsiders by selling to everyone.

"Ravido *is* thoughtless enough to choose white." Maldynado sniffed. "White, on a soldier. They'll be smudged with dirt and spattered with blood by the end of the week."

"Perhaps so." As of yet, Amaranthe hadn't heard any gunshots or seen signs of fights between the different factions, but she doubted that would last. Right now, the soldiers seemed to be more focused on instilling martial law. Once all the contenders for the throne were ready to make their moves, things would start happening quickly. And violently. "It looks like most of the newspaper employees have gone home for the night." She nodded toward the front of the three-story building across the canal. Several minutes had passed since anyone exited the front door. She hoped to find Mancrest working late, as she had once before.

"I don't suppose, with Sicarius being elsewhere, we could just walk in the front door?" Maldynado suggested.

"With all the soldiers roaming about, I think we should go the same way as last time." Amaranthe waved at the storm grate on the opposite canal wall.

"Are you sure that's necessary? If you're worried we're not being sneaky enough, we could turn sideways and hug the shadows as we go up the front steps."

"Come, come, you don't want me to tell Yara you were whining, do you?" After checking both sides of the canal, Amaranthe left the shadows and jumped, catching one of the iron bars beneath the bridge. The cold metal bit into her hands, but she wouldn't have tried the maneuver with gloves on. She swung her legs for momentum and caught the next handhold, then the next, trusting Maldynado would follow her, despite his complaints. Her short sword hung on her waist, too short to bother her legs as she picked her route. Maldynado's rapier might be more of a distraction, but she trusted he'd be fine.

"We've been comrades for almost a year now." Maldynado grunted as he jumped up and caught the first bar, probably wincing at the icy touch as well. "Shouldn't your allegiance be to me instead of our newest and most untried member?"

"I think she was suitably tried on the riverboat mission." Amaranthe reached the last bar and swung onto the stone walkway, catching herself against the cement wall.

"That is true." Maldynado chuckled.

Somehow Amaranthe doubted he was thinking of the same sort of *trying* as she was. When he dropped down beside her, they headed for the storm grate, passing several tethered houseboats along the way. She looked for the one she'd inadvertently set fire to the summer before, hoping she'd see it repaired and little worse for the experience, but it wasn't there. In fact, none of the houseboats looked familiar. Perhaps the fire had sullied the homeowners' perspectives of the neighborhood. She sighed, longing for a day when her face no longer graced wanted posters, and she could work freely within the bounds of the law again. A day, she thought grimly, that would only come if they succeeded in getting Sespian back on the throne.

"Is it just me," Maldynado asked when they reached the round grate set into the canal wall, "or is that padlock much bigger and sturdier than it was last summer?"

"Possibly." Amaranthe pulled out her lock-picking set, undaunted by the shiny steel.

"Someone must have heard about all the unsavory outlaws roaming the city's sewers, pumping stations, and aqueduct tunnels."

Amaranthe slid a tension wrench and ball pick into the slot and worked on the tumblers. "Did you just call yourself unsavory?"

"Well, I haven't been able to frequent the public baths as much as I like of late."

Voices drifted down from the street above. Just civilians passing by on their way home, Amaranthe hoped.

"Stand watch, please," she murmured, aware of people walking by on the opposite side of the canal as well. This portion of the path wasn't well lit, but she doubted the shadows were thick enough to hide her, should someone peer intently.

"Naturally." Maldynado leaned against the wall.

The lock proved challenging, but Amaranthe thwarted it eventually. She opened the grate, frosty icicles snapping, iron squealing. Someone had supplied a fresh lock, but nobody had thought to oil the hinges? Or perhaps that had been intentional. Thus to alert nearby denizens—or warrior-caste journalists? As soon as Maldynado stepped inside, Amaranthe closed the grate and replaced the padlock on the bars, though she didn't fasten it, in case they needed to exit that way in a hurry.

"You're being paranoid, girl," she muttered to herself.

Even if people on the other side knew her team had returned to the city, they wouldn't know what they were *doing* in the city.

"What did you say?" Maldynado asked, as they strode up the slick tunnel.

"Nothing important."

"Ah. I was hoping you'd been proclaiming that I was in fact quite savory, baths notwithstanding."

"So long as Yara believes that, you'll be fine." Amaranthe

turned into the passage that ran beneath the alley behind the *Gazette* building.

"How could she not?" Maldynado asked, a smile in his voice.

For a while during their travels, Maldynado had seemed glum, due to everyone being suspicious of his motives, but Yara had apparently relieved him of those dark feelings. Amaranthe wasn't sure if that was entirely a good thing. He'd been... bubbly of late.

A scraping sound came from somewhere ahead of them. She halted, flinging her arm out to stop Maldynado as well. At first, she thought the noise had come from the tunnel, but a shadow moved, interrupting the flow of moonlight through drains in the alley above.

"Someone else may be visiting via the back door," Maldynado murmured.

"We'll see." Amaranthe patted her way to a ladder leading to the manhole they'd used the last time they visited. She climbed it and tilted her ear toward the cover.

A rumble sounded above her. A steam vehicle driving down the alley? Amaranthe remembered a loading dock in the rear of the building, but would the *Gazette* be shipping newspapers or receiving supplies at night? She dropped back to the ground.

"Company, eh?" Maldynado asked.

"So it seems." Using the wan light filtering through the drains as a guide, Amaranthe headed farther up the tunnel. Frozen runoff water made the ground slick, and she flailed several times, scraping her knuckles on the wall once and smacking Maldynado in the jaw another time.

"No need to take it out on me," he said with a chuckle.

A minute later, he butt-planted on the ice behind her. After that, there were fewer chuckles.

Treacherous footing notwithstanding, they made it to the next ladder. Amaranthe climbed up, listened at the manhole, and didn't hear anything. They ought to be in the same alley but several buildings down. She unfastened the lid and lifted it a couple of inches.

No less than four army lorries idled in front of the *Gazette's* loading dock. Soldiers idled as well, smoking and talking as they leaned against the vehicles. A few more stood near the doors on the loading dock. The casual stances hinted of boredom rather than alertness, but numerous rifles leaned within easy reach, cartridge-based rifles loaded with multiple rounds. White armbands adorned the men's arms. The drainpipe Amaranthe, Sicarius, and Maldynado had once climbed to gain access to an attic vent snaked up the side of the building in plain view.

She lowered the manhole cover and climbed down again. "I believe it's time to enact Plan Two."

"Go home and snuggle with an exciting and surprisingly randy woman?" Maldynado asked.

"That's *your* Plan Two. Mine is to wait for Deret at his flat."

"So your Plan Two is similar to mine, except it employs a man."

Amaranthe lifted a fingernail to her mouth and nibbled thoughtfully. Going to Mancrest's home was plausible, though, with all the *Gazette*-worthy news occurring in the city, he'd likely be home late. He might even be sleeping in his office here. Also, she wondered what all those soldiers were doing behind the *Gazette* building. Was it possible Ravido was inside, meeting with Mancrest? She hated to think of Deret schmoozing with Forge's chosen figurehead, but Maldynado had said the Mancrests and the Marblecrests had always been close. If such a meeting was happening inside at that moment, a chance to listen in could prove pivotal. Besides, if Deret *was* working for the other side, he'd be less than truthful when she questioned him.

Maldynado cleared his throat. "I notice we're not moving. Won't that be required? To enact *either* of our Plan Twos?"

"The *Gazette* building is a few hundred years old," Amaranthe mused, too far down the trail of her own thoughts to answer his questions. "I wouldn't be surprised if it had a basement. What are the odds that there's access somewhere down here? Or... if it's been retrofitted with indoor plumbing..."

"You're *not* thinking of entering through the sewer, are

you?" Maldynado asked. "That's not whining, by the way. It's righteous indignation."

"Let's take a closer look at the tunnel walls by the building." Amaranthe led the way back past the first ladder. "As I learned in my enforcer days, there are lots of forgotten underground passageways in the city, especially in the older parts of town."

"To facilitate secret trysts with lovers?"

"Not exactly." Once near the *Gazette* portion of the tunnel again, Amaranthe started searching by touch. "The brothels, drinking houses, and hotels used to have deals with the gangs. They'd get their patrons drunk and lure them into the basements where thugs would knock them out, tie them up, and drag them out through the tunnels, all the way to the docks. The victims would wake up chained to an oar bench on some freighter on its way to the Gulf."

"Oh, right, I remember reading about that in school. I think there was a Lady Dourcrest book that used that as a plot device. Of course it was a woman who was kidnapped, and the pirate who owned the ship was roguishly handsome and—"

"Finding anything?" Amaranthe interrupted. She didn't need the plot summary.

"Not yet, no."

She grimaced when she encountered a moist, fuzzy growth too hearty to succumb to the frost. She wiped her hand and contemplated finding a lantern. Of course, if she *saw* the walls she'd feel compelled to scrape off the grimy patches, not simply avoid them. The soldiers might notice the light seeping through the storm drains *and* the sounds of her scouring the tunnel clean of decades of accumulated gunk.

"Didn't most of those old passages get walled up?" Maldynado asked. "On account of... Wasn't some *emperor* kidnapped?"

"Yes, Guffarth the Third. Apparently, he was visiting a brothel to—"

"Get his snake greased?"

"Er, yes. But he went anonymously and without much in the way of security, so his shrewish wife wouldn't find out.

He was kidnapped and nobody believed his claims of imperial greatness. He died from an infection while at sea. It wasn't until a year later that an enforcer investigator put the ore cart on the right rail and figured out what had happened to Guffarth. The freighter involved in the kidnapping was hunted down by the navy, and all the officers were put to death. It was surmised that such a mistake never would have been made if Guffarth's face had been better known amongst the populace. After that, the mint started putting the emperor's head on coins and ranmyas. And, yes, many of the tunnels were walled up, but some of them have been reopened by the gangs in recent decades. Kidnappings still go on, though the enforcers don't look the other way anymore."

Amaranthe's probing fingers encountered a change in the texture of the wall stone. The cement had changed to brick.

"Thank you, Professor," Maldynado said. "That was a story worthy of Books."

"Sh, over here."

When his shoulder bumped into hers, Amaranthe grabbed his hand and put it on the wall. She spent a few seconds following the crease where brick turned to cement. It definitely felt like a doorway—or rather a doorway that had been bricked over.

"There may have been a tunnel here, but it's not accessible now," Maldynado said, echoing her thoughts.

Amaranthe sighed. "We might have to try your idea about sneaking in the front after all."

A number of slams and clangs sounded in the alley above.

"Maybe not," Maldynado said. "Sounds like those blokes are leaving."

That would make getting in easier, but it'd also mean the theoretical meeting she wished to spy on had ended. A few more slams sounded, followed by the heavy rumble of lorries rolling away.

A fresh slash of moonlight flowed into the tunnel. Maldynado had already climbed the ladder and pushed up the manhole. Amaranthe was of a mind to chastise him for being too hasty—they should have jogged back up to the other manhole to check in case anyone remained on the loading dock.

"All clear," Maldynado said before she could phrase an appropriate chastisement. "Someone's still inside too. I saw a bit of light as the back door was closing."

"Coming." Amaranthe climbed up after him.

Maldynado reached the loading dock first and, after eyeing the drainpipe for a moment, put a hand on the doorknob. He paused there, raising his eyebrows hopefully.

"Is it locked?" Amaranthe eyed the street and the dock to make sure they were indeed alone—and to see if the soldiers had left any clues. Only the lingering scent of burning coal remained.

"Nope." Maldynado pressed his ear to the metal door, then turned the knob and peered through the crack.

The sounds of clanking machinery escaped.

"The presses are running early for the morning's paper," Amaranthe said. "It's not even—"

Maldynado shut the door quickly.

"Did someone see you?" Amaranthe crouched, ready to spring off the dock and into the darkness if needed.

"I don't think so."

"We better go in through the attic. There'll be a number of people around to man those presses."

"Not people," Maldynado said, "soldiers."

Another time, Amaranthe might have pointed out that soldiers qualified as people, but not now. Soldiers? Had Ravido or one of the other erstwhile leaders taken over the *Gazette*? "The soldiers are working the presses? Or just in the room?"

"I only saw two men, but it looks that way." Maldynado waved to the drainpipe. "Still want to go in through the attic?"

As Amaranthe knew from her prior trip, the attic would take them to a loft overlooking the journalists' desks. They wouldn't be able to see what was rolling off the presses from that perch. She had a feeling the army wasn't here to simply oversee the production of the next day's newspaper.

"Let's see if we can slip in when nobody's looking." She reached around Maldynado for the doorknob. He frowned, not moving out of the way. She jerked her chin. Maldynado stood, jaw set, as if he intended to insist on going first. She gave him a firm I-appreciate-your-protectiveness-but-I'm-in-charge-so-move-your-round-cheeks look. His lips flattened, but he stepped aside.

Amaranthe eased the door open, pressing her eye to the crack. Sauna-like heat escaped, caressing her face with its warmth. The gas lamps mounted on the walls diminished some of the nighttime gloom of the printing room—a high-ceilinged open space that took up the back half of the building—but the shadows offered hiding spots. The bulky machines, too, provided nooks and obstacles to duck into or behind.

At the moment, she didn't see anyone, so she eased inside, choosing a route between the side wall and a roll of paper on a spindle longer than Maldynado was tall. It supplied a two-story steam-powered press that clanked and thunked loudly enough to drown out voices and everything else that would have warned her people were nearby. She waited for Maldynado to join her, then poked an eye around the end of the roll.

A man in black fatigues was heading their way, and she pulled back. He walked past their spot, but didn't glance behind the press. Instead, he headed toward the back wall where staircases led up and down, and a sign on their floor read WC.

As soon as the man disappeared into the water closet, Amaranthe checked both sides of the long press. Nobody else was in sight.

Stay here, she signed, figuring she'd have an easier time crawling under a machine or slipping into a nook than Maldynado.

He propped his fists on his hips.

Amaranthe slipped out before he could argue. She wanted to see what their roll of paper was being turned into on the other end of the press and didn't know how much time she'd have before the man returned. Automatic cutters rasped on the next machine over, but she found the uncut sheets and, with her back to the wall, stopped to read. Light from a floor lamp illuminated the text, an unfamiliar one-column layout.

"These aren't newspapers," she whispered after she'd read

a few lines. "They're pamphlets." She skimmed further, her gaze sliding over lines like, "...an end to dangerous progressive policies," and "deportation of foreign plunderers." "*Propaganda* pamphlets," she murmured.

Figuring the soldier would return soon, she jogged back toward the rear of the press. She'd like to have one of the pamphlets to take back to Books, but tearing one off from the uncut sheets wouldn't be terribly subtle. Maybe she could sneak around the cutting machine and grab one of the—

Amaranthe halted. Maldynado was gone.

Back out to the loading dock? Or out into the pressroom?

The water closet door opened, and she shifted into the shadows without getting a chance to search. The man returned to the front of the press and resumed his job at the paper cutter.

Amaranthe drummed her fingers on her thigh. Search further into the pressroom or slip back outside? She hadn't felt a cold draft that would have signified the outer door opening. Using the press to hide her advance, she crept farther into the room. A soldier with a box walked past the front end of the machine. She hid in the shadows of the machinery, halting all movement. He said something to the man working the cutter, but the clanking machinery drowned out the words. Someone else called a question from the other side of the room, then a third man walked past with an empty box, heading for the freshly cut pamphlets.

There were too many men around. This hadn't been a good idea. It'd be best to find Mancrest at his tenement building, then, if they couldn't get the truth out of him, return to the *Gazette* at a later hour.

She'd barely finished the thought when she spotted Maldynado. He had indeed gone farther into the room. He'd used a support column to hide his back—most of it—and had climbed up an inactive press to peer over the other side, toward the desk-filled front of the building.

Amaranthe let her head clunk back against the machine behind her. Though he wasn't near any lamps, he wasn't that well hidden. Any of those soldiers strolling about, filling boxes, might spot him when they walked past. Emperor's teeth, *she* wasn't well hidden either. She wanted to get his attention, to sign to him—what was he looking at that was worth risking discovery for?—but his back was to her.

She dropped to hands and knees to get close to him without being seen, and advanced into the room, peering through the legs of the press as she went. The man at the paper cutter had his back to her. The two with the boxes did too, for the moment. She rose to a crouch and slunk toward Maldynado's column.

She almost made it, but the draft she'd been thinking of earlier came, a cold blast from the rear. One soldier held the door open while a second pushed a wheelbarrow full of coal inside. Turning her slink into a sprint so she could escape the influence of the lamps, she darted around the column.

The man with the wheelbarrow had been facing in Maldynado's direction as he entered, and he squinted into the gloom.

Maldynado raised his eyebrows at Amaranthe's appearance and pointed to whatever he was looking at over the press. She was too short to see it, and there was no time to climb up the column. The soldiers at the door had abandoned their wheelbarrow and were walking her way, their hands resting on weapons, one a short sword and the other a pistol.

Maldynado leaped from his spot, sliding out his rapier before he landed, and he charged the pair. Amaranthe didn't know whether he assumed he could handle two trained soldiers on his own, or if he meant to distract them so she could sneak up on them from behind, but as soon as they were focused on him she sprinted from hiding too. She circled wide to stay out of their peripheral vision if possible. The one with the sword had swept his blade out to square off with Maldynado, and the man with the pistol was skittering back, lifting his arm and lining up a shot. Amaranthe didn't want either gunshots or sword clashes ringing out, or the rest of the soldiers in the building would descend on them in heartbeats.

Maldynado feinted a few times, deliberately not touching steel to steel, but maneuvering to put his opponent in his comrade's line of fire. He seemed to know what Amaranthe had in mind.

Yanking out her dagger, she ran up behind the pistol wielder, trusting the noisy machines to bury the sounds of her footfalls. She flipped the weapon and smashed the hilt into the back of his head. Taking advantage of his moment of surprise, she kicked at the inside of his knee, then darted about to wrest the pistol from his grasp. He recovered and spun toward her, tearing a dagger from a belt sheath, but she thrust the firearm into his face.

"Drop it," she mouthed.

He blinked in surprise a few times, taking in that she was a woman, perhaps taking in that her face adorned wanted posters around the capital. The dagger clattered to the floor. He almost threw it—hoping the weapon would make noise and alert his comrades? Thus far, the fight had taken place behind the press, the bulky machine hiding them from the views of the other men, but that luck couldn't hold for long.

Maldynado stood a couple of paces away, near the wall, his rapier sheathed and the newly acquired short sword in his hand. He yawned, standing casually with his elbow on his opponent's shoulder, the blade resting across his neck.

"Who left the slagging door open?" someone called from the other side of the press.

The wheelbarrow stood on the threshold, propping open the door and letting frosty air inside.

"Let's get out of here," Amaranthe mouthed, unable to make hand signs while holding the pistol, and jerked her head toward the exit.

Maldynado tilted his own head toward his prisoner, silently asking what they were going to do with their captives.

"Take them for now."

Amaranthe twirled a finger, indicating her prisoner should spin and start walking for the door. He glowered at her and eyed the pistol, perhaps wondering if a woman would fire, but he decided in favor of acquiescence, at least for now.

Before Amaranthe, Maldynado, and their prisoners had taken more than two steps toward the door, another soldier stomped into view, this one rounding the paper roll by the wall. Amaranthe and Maldynado flattened themselves to the side of the press, yanking their prisoners with them. She kept the pistol pressed to her man's ribs to ensure silence.

The soldier pulled the wheelbarrow inside, then stuck his head outside. "Evik, Rudev, what are you doing out there?"

Amaranthe's man inhaled and tensed, as if to shout and try to escape. She stood on tiptoes to clasp her hand across his mouth as she dug the pistol in deeper. "Nobody will hear the shot over the sound of the presses," she growled in his ear. A lie, of course, but maybe it would give him something to think about for a few seconds. In that time, the fellow at the door stepped outside. He waved to someone, and lights flashed out there before the door closed, blocking the view. Another lorry driving up?

Maldynado looked over his shoulder at her, a question in his eyes. What now? He must have seen the lights too.

There weren't any other doors within sight that they could escape through. Amaranthe eyed the stairs and finally nodded that way. They could go up to the loft, leave these two tied, and escape through that vent in the attic.

Still pressing the pistol into her captive's ribs, Amaranthe guided him toward the stairs. They had to halt twice to duck behind machines. The two men who'd been carrying empty boxes earlier walked toward the door, their boxes full of pamphlets now.

Amaranthe and the others reached the staircase leading down without being seen. She was on the verge of releasing the breath she was holding when the back door opened again, letting more soldiers in. There were shadows around the stairs, but not *that* many shadows. Further, her captive took that moment to test her again. Maybe he'd figured out that she wouldn't shoot after all.

He pretended to trip. She saw the ruse for what it was and adjusted her weight, pulling back to keep him up and on his feet.

"Someone's looking this way," Maldynado blurted and went for the closest set of stairs, the one leading down.

Still struggling to keep her captive on his feet without shooting him, Amaranthe almost tumbled down the stairs after him. If not for Maldynado, pushing his man down at a more measured pace, she would have ended up somersaulting down the hard stone steps, her limbs entangled with those of her prisoner. His broad back acted as a nicely meaty barrier, though, stopping their progress, and she found her balance. Her soldier had a harder time righting himself, and his foot slipped off a step. He lurched to the side, smacking his head on the stone wall. Amaranthe failed to feel sympathetic toward him.

"Anyone coming?" Maldynado whispered at the bottom, all four of them crowding onto the tight, musty landing, hemmed in by looming stone walls and an old but solid oak door.

"Not yet."

The two soldiers were muttering something to each other. Amaranthe, fearing her threats with the pistol weren't proving effective, caught one of his arms with her free hand, digging her thumb into a pressure point in his wrist and twisting the limb behind his back until he sucked in a pained gasp of air. He stopped muttering. One of Sicarius's comments drifted through the back of her mind: the promise of pain is often more effective than the application of pain, for the mind conjures fears greater than reality. Sure, that worked for a scary-looking fellow dressed in black with a reputation darker than an eclipse, but for her? It was ever a struggle to convince men that she'd go through with her threats, hence her preference for avoiding the taking of prisoners. But they could hardly let these men go now. They'd charge right up the stairs, and, judging by the numbers of orders shouted above, there were more soldiers than ever up there. At least nobody had come over to peer down the staircase at them. Yet.

"Why'd you dart over to that press?" Amaranthe asked.

"Sorry about that," Maldynado said. "Seeing Mancrest and that woman surprised me. What are we going to do with these two? They've seen our faces."

Amaranthe was more interested in finding out more about "Mancrest and that woman," but she could ask him for details once they escaped the building. Maldynado's point was pertinent. She didn't want Forge, or anyone else, knowing her team was back in town already.

"If we can get out, we could take them with us," she said. "Tie them up back at our hideout for a few days so they can't blab." Having to guard prisoners would reduce the number of team members she could employ in the field, but maybe, given a little time, she could convince the soldiers to throw in their lot with Sespian. They were young. They might be influenceable.

"We don't *have* a hideout yet," Maldynado pointed out.

"I'm sure we do." Amaranthe trusted the others had found something. "We just don't know where it is yet."

"How is that—"

"Discuss later. Is that door unlocked, by chance?"

Before he could answer, two people walked into view. No, they *stopped* within view. Ugh.

Amaranthe tightened the arm hold on her soldier in case the urge to call out revisited him. He sucked in a pained breath and rose to his tiptoes. Maldynado's prisoner made a similar hiss.

The people who had stopped up above weren't soldiers. It was a man and a woman. The man, a gray-haired fellow in a black and gray suit of immaculate cut, leaned his back against the wrought iron railing at the top of the stairwell. His face wasn't visible, though he seemed to be talking and pointing to his comrade. The woman... she was facing the man, her arm linked with one of his, so Amaranthe could see more of her features. She sucked in a breath almost as sharp as the one her prisoner had made, for she recognized the short, buxom woman with the spectacles perched low on her nose. Ms. Worgavic. Amaranthe's old teacher and one of the Forge founders, Worgavic had been the one to allow—no, *order*—her interrogation.

Anger surged into her chest, a hard tight ball of emotion that dug in behind her breastbone. She forgot about her prisoner. Her hand tightened so hard around the pistol that her fingers

ached. She lifted it, no longer aiming it at her captive but at the woman leaning against the railing above.

Had Maldynado not grabbed her arm, pulling it down, she would have fired. The couple pushed away from the railing, disappearing from sight, and it was too late. The door must have opened again, for a cold draft wafted down the stairs, startling some of the thoughtless fury out of her system when it hit her cheeks.

"What were you *doing*?" Maldynado let go of her arm, but his whisper was harsh. "I thought we weren't letting anyone know we were here. If you'd shot Mancrest, that woman probably would have gotten away. Not to mention everyone left up there would have heard you fire." He jabbed his hand upward.

"Mancrest?" Amaranthe stared at him. What was he talking about? That hadn't been Deret.

Despite her and Maldynado's distraction, the prisoners were being still. Maybe because she was waving her pistol around with a crazed look on her face.

"Lord Colonel Armott Mancrest, retired. Deret's father." Maldynado peered into her eyes. "You didn't recognize him? Why were you going to shoot him then?"

"Not him, *her*. That was one of the Forge founders. The one who—" Amaranthe's voice cracked and she looked away. She was still clenching the pistol like a carpenter bent on smashing an irritating nail into oblivion. Calm down, girl, she told herself. We're past this.

"Tortured you?" Maldynado asked, all the harshness gone from his tone.

Not trusting her voice, Amaranthe nodded. Her prisoner peered back over her shoulder at her.

"Blast it," she said, "let's get these two tied up, so they can't..." What? Hear about this? "Escape," she finished.

Maldynado started removing belts and shirts to obey her order. "I'm sorry. I didn't... Cursed ancestors, I should have helped you shoot the hag."

"Don't worry about it. It probably wouldn't have fixed

anything." Besides, she didn't want to become an assassin herself. That was no way to create a better Turgonia. Instincts, angry vengeful instincts, had been guiding her hand.

Maldynado finished tying up the men and lifted an arm, offering a hug if she needed it.

Amaranthe waved a hand. She appreciated the gesture, but said, "I'm fine."

She was relieved it had been Maldynado here with her instead of Sicarius. That fit of rage... that had been a moment of weakness. She didn't want Sicarius seeing her like that. Not when she was working hard to make him believe she was all right. And she *was* all right. She would be. She just needed to finish with this mess and take a vacation.

And remember how to sleep through the night, the voice in her head added.

A shadow fell across the stairwell above—someone moving past the railing.

"We better get out of here before someone looks down the steps," Amaranthe said.

"Up or in?" Maldynado asked. "And with or without them?"

"Up and out, ideally." Amaranthe didn't want to be trapped in the basement, though there were more sounds of activity than ever coming from above.

"What are all those spirits-licked people doing here after hours?" Maldynado growled.

"Picking up their seditious pamphlets probably. If I'd known the newspaper office would be such a hotbed of activity, I'd have brought Sicarius."

"I'm not manly enough for you?"

"You're fine. I'm just worried that we missed a good chance for spying. I could have sent Sicarius off after those two."

"He probably would have stuck daggers in their backs."

Amaranthe bit her lip to keep from asking what would be wrong with that. It bothered her to think that her experience under Pike's knife had changed her, but she kept thinking that it'd be much easier for their side if they simply ended Forge,

Ravido, and their key allies the most efficient way possible. Was it worth turning oneself into a monster if it made the world a better place for everyone else? Or, once one chose the path to monsterhood, could one still accurately assess what qualified as a "better place" anymore? She feared this last year as an outlaw had already tainted her judgment.

She considered their captives. It'd be hard to escape back up the stairs, forcing them every step. Perhaps it was time to leave them and hope for—

"Can't find Evik and Rudev anywhere," someone called out upstairs. "We may need to search the building, sir."

"Uh oh," Maldynado said.

"About that doorknob…" Amaranthe said.

Lights jittered up above—people entering the room with extra lamps.

"It's unlocked," Maldynado said.

Finally, a bit of luck. Amaranthe stepped past him and eased the door open. Darkness waited inside, so she didn't think they'd have to worry about being jumped by soldiers, but she crept into the basement warily regardless.

A few steps inside, she bumped into something and decided to stop and light a lantern. She was about to tell Maldynado to close the door so their flame wouldn't be seen when someone spoke from the depths of the shadows.

"It's not mealtime," a man said. "I can only surmise you've come to your senses and are here to unlock me."

* * *

"Job's the same, pay's the same, don't really make a difference," one maid said, snapping the sheets in the air before lowering them onto the bed.

"I know," a second maid said, the rasping of a straw broom accompanying her words, "but I liked young Emperor Sespian. He never ordered you around like you were some raw soldier to be broken in. He always said 'please' and 'thank you' when he asked for something."

"Piles of good that did him. He's deader than that roach you stomped on earlier, and I don't think the new regime will appreciate you waxing fondly on the old."

"Marblecrest isn't the new regime, not officially, and I won't call him emperor no matter what he's demanding." Another firm snapping of the sheets accompanied the statement. "Just because him and his troops showed up at the door less than an hour after the papers announced Sespian's death doesn't mean he's the rightful emperor. I don't even figure he's the rightful landlord here. Are you sure about our pay being the same? Because we haven't seen any money yet."

"Bite your tongue, Naniva, or some owl will swoop down and tear it out. Or at least lower your voice. Door's open. Never know who could be about listening."

Outside in the hall, Sicarius twitched an eyebrow. He otherwise remained motionless, braced in a corner above the wall molding, his short hair brushing the ceiling. He couldn't see into the room the maids were tending, but he tracked their movements with his ears, even as he watched other maids and butlers coming and going below him, building fires in stoves for room occupants who would be heading to bed soon. He'd listened to a half dozen servants' conversations so far, enough to verify that Lord General Marblecrest had moved into the Imperial Barracks with hundreds of troops. Marblecrest had tried to wrest control of Fort Urgot out on the northern side of the lake as well, but the commander there, General Ridgecrest, hadn't been cowed by his threats. Ridgecrest had refused to back a new candidate for the throne until the Company of Lords had met with the satrap governors to decide on the official successor.

Sicarius took special note of the information; Ridgecrest and his troops might be available to the right man. The only other pertinent information he'd gathered, more through a lack of mentions or sightings than via positive confirmation, was that the Forge people were not staying in the Barracks.

A maid pushing a squeaky mop bucket passed below Sicarius without looking up. He'd wait for the talkative two to leave,

then return to his comrades. They'd be restless, waiting for him to come back to the furnace room where he'd left them, and he didn't want to be away from Sespian for long regardless, not with some other potential assassin roaming the Barracks, agenda unknown.

The maids closed the guest room door and trundled away with their linens cart. Sicarius waited for silence to descend upon the hall, then dropped to the marble floor without a sound. He unscrewed a vent cover, wriggled into the warm duct inside, affixed the grate again, and improvised with a curved lock pick to refasten the screws from within.

Traveling through the Barracks' hypocaust system was neither quick nor efficient, but it allowed him to bypass halls full of soldiers, guests, and guards without notice. He crawled a few dozen meters, then slipped down a vertical shaft, descending three floors to come out in the furnace room in the basement.

Sespian, Books, and Akstyr were still waiting, though hiding. They stepped out from behind the coal bins when Sicarius popped out of the vent. Someone must have come in to stoke the fires while he'd been gone. It didn't matter, so long as his team hadn't been noticed.

"Did you run into trouble?" Books asked.

"An opportunity to eavesdrop." Sicarius brushed the cobwebs and dust off his black clothing, though he knew he'd return to the ducts again shortly. "Ravido has taken the Barracks."

"Not surprising," Books said. "I'm sure he moved quickly and without asking permission."

Sespian scowled. "Did he wait a week after the announcement of my death to move in? Or was he taking over the imperial suite the very next day?"

"The same day," Sicarius said.

"Lovely," Sespian said.

"That's disgusting," Akstyr said. "He's probably in your bed right now, sheet wrangling with some serving wench."

"Ravido is married," Books said. "Or he was. I wonder if he's learned of Mari's death."

"Do you think being married would matter?" Akstyr asked. "If he's half as horny as Maldynado…"

Sicarius was on the verge of saying something to end the pointless diversion, but Sespian spoke first.

"I doubt Ravido has time for wrangling anyone right now. Regardless, I hadn't moved out of my childhood suite, the last year having been rather fraught and busy." Sespian scowled again, and Sicarius wondered what wringers the Forge people had mashed him through since Hollowcrest's death. He had the impression they'd started applying pressure promptly. He'd like more details, but Sespian still didn't deign to talk to him without Amaranthe in the room, encouraging them to "bond."

Sespian released the scowl and met Sicarius's gaze. "I don't suppose you saw a tan-colored cat with dark brown paws and a mask when you were eavesdropping about, did you?"

"A cat?" Sicarius had been thinking of pains his son had endured in the previous year, and he was worried about… a cat?

Sespian cleared his throat. "Yes, I've been worried… I mean, it's just a pet of course." His wave of dismissal wasn't genuine. "But I'm hoping someone's been feeding him, and that he hasn't met with… trouble with all those extra soldiers stomping about."

"I have not seen such a cat," Sicarius said.

Books patted Sespian on the shoulder, drawing a quick, sad smile.

Sicarius realized that he'd done something wrong—again— in dealing with his son. He should have offered sympathy, or at least the appearance of sympathy. He didn't know if it was within him to honestly dredge up such an emotion, but the trying might matter to Sespian. Yet Sespian would shy away from a hand pat from him, and that would leave him feeling… awkward. That emotion he could somewhat understand. Unfortunately.

"I will watch for it going forward." Sicarius pointed to the vent. "Come. I will lead the way to Hollowcrest's suite."

"Maybe your cat will be in there, pissing on the old general's shoes," Akstyr said.

"It wouldn't be the first time." Sespian chuckled. "He has a feisty streak."

Halfway through the vent opening, Sicarius paused to stare at him. How could Akstyr's crude, ill-considered comment evoke laughter. *Pleasure*?

Sespian caught the stare and shrugged self-consciously. "I may have trained, er, encouraged him to do such things. When I was much younger of course."

"How much younger?" Books asked, his eyes sly.

"Uhm, not as young as you'd think for something like that."

Akstyr smirked. "He was probably eighteen."

Feeling the conversation had grown pointless again, Sicarius headed into the ductwork. The others would follow. And if they didn't... he wasn't positive he wanted people digging into Hollowcrest's old files and snooping into his past. He doubted there was anything aristocratic in his heritage that would change the populace's opinion of Sespian's right, as an assassin's son, to rule. Amaranthe was being idealistic. Or maybe she'd designed this side trip so that Sespian would have a glimpse into the harsh childhood Hollowcrest and Emperor Raumesys had inflicted on Sicarius. No doubt she thought it'd evoke sympathy in the boy. Sicarius did not blame her for trying—he'd come to appreciate that she cared enough to do so—but some things were best left forgotten.

He reached the vertical duct that led to the upper floors and paused, listening for the scuffs and exhalations that would tell him the others followed. Akstyr and Books bumped their elbows and knees against the tile walls numerous times. It pleased him that Sespian moved more quietly, as if he'd had training in the art of stealth. Weaponsmaster Orik's lessons must have been more thorough than Sicarius realized—or Sespian less adept at evading them than he'd heard.

"Make no noise as we climb," Sicarius said when the others, Books and Akstyr in particular, were close enough to hear. "As we continue, the ducts will travel between floors and room walls. People inside will be able to hear noises."

Not surprisingly, the grunts of acquiescence held a sullen undertone. Sicarius found it interesting that Amaranthe always managed to command the men without evoking similar displays of disgruntlement.

Sicarius removed her from his thoughts. He would need his concentration for climbing and remaining silent. It would not do for *him* to make noise.

Hot air swirled about him as they climbed up the shaft. The main arterials of the hypocaust system were made from ceramic tile, and the grouted spots between them offered the only semblances of handholds. He ascended, his palms alternately pressing to either side, feet likewise braced. His mind flashed to a recent instance where he'd been in a similar position, wedged into that smokestack on the steamboat with Amaranthe, her body scant inches from his. It took more effort to push *that* memory out of his thoughts, but he did so ruthlessly, reminded of Hollowcrest's oft-repeated words, "A distracted warrior is a dead warrior."

When he reached the third floor, where the suites of the royal family, commander of the armies, and honored guests awaited, he slipped into the horizontal duct that led to Hollowcrest's old office. He had to wait for the others to catch up and, to keep his mind from straying into distracted territory again, ran through a sensory check—touch, smell, sound, feel—of the dark area. He did such checks automatically, whether he thought of them or not, but the formality of raising it to a conscious level occupied his mind in an acceptable manner.

He turned his nose toward the darkness ahead, detecting... what? He sniffed. It was the Nurian smoke again.

"We're all here," Sespian whispered.

"I know." Despite testing the environment, Sicarius had been aware of the others reaching the horizontal duct and crawling into it. "Come."

He swirled through the maze of ducts he'd memorized long ago, bringing them into the wall between Hollowcrest's rooms and the guest suite to their side. One of the vents opened to the bedchamber and another to the office. Sicarius veered toward the latter. As expected, darkness filled the room beyond the grate. The air smelled stale—nobody had opened a window and freshened the suite in some time. Good. Sicarius had begun to wonder if they would encounter the other intruder, going to the same place as they were, but the ducts had branched a few times since he'd last smelled the smoke odor.

Using one of his more versatile picks—and painstaking patience—he once again unfastened the vent screws from within. Soundlessly, he set the metal grate to the side and slipped out. While the others exited, he prowled about, ensuring his first instinct had been correct and that the rooms were indeed empty. He checked the main door leading into the hall and found it locked, no doubt to discourage casual snooping. He wondered who had the key.

"I pulled the curtain so nobody will see any light," Books was saying when Sicarius returned to the office. "Any thoughts on where we should start searching?"

"Yes."

In the darkness, Sicarius walked to a coal stove in the corner and pushed one of the rear legs with his toe. He didn't hear the secret door open, but its draft stirred his hair. In the narrow, windowless room inside, he had pulled several files out of cabinets by the time Books lit his lantern and found him.

"This is disappointing," Akstyr said when he stepped inside. He ticked a nail against one of the featureless wooden cabinets that lined one wall. Floor-to-ceiling bookcases occupied the others. There was barely room inside to squeeze past the desk and sit in the chair. "You'd expect a secret inner chamber to be more interesting than a little office."

"By interesting, do you mean full of decapitated heads and various other grisly trophies of defeated enemies?" Books asked.

"I don't know. Maybe."

"My fath— the emperor's tastes were more along those lines." Sespian squeezed into the room behind Akstyr.

"Can we visit *his* offices?"

"No," Books said.

Aware of the confined space and the number of people blocking the exit, Sicarius twitched a finger toward Books, then left the files on the desk and returned to the main suite where there'd be room to maneuver in a fight. He would have liked to remove himself further from the conversation, which devolved into further speculation from Akstyr on what the old emperor's vices might have been, but was reluctant to leave Sespian unguarded. Sicarius *should* check on the imperial suite though. It wasn't much farther down the hall, and Amaranthe would want to know what Ravido planned next. He might have left documents secured in his new quarters.

Of course, if Sicarius simply killed Ravido, the general's plans would be moot, and Forge would have to pause to develop a new strategy. Nebulous and elusive, the organization itself would be difficult to decapitate, especially if its members continued to hide behind their technology, but Ravido was a single man, a single target, one who might be on this floor of the Barracks at this very moment.

A throat cleared. "Hear something?"

It was Sespian. He had returned to the larger office and was probably wondering why Sicarius stood motionless, staring at the door.

"No," Sicarius said. In truth, three people had walked by in the hallway while he'd been contemplating assassinations, but none of their footfalls had slowed down, so he judged them inconsequential.

"Do you think...?" Sespian started, then faltered. He plucked at the seam of his trousers.

Sicarius faced him and attempted to look approachable, though facial expressions were not his strength, especially when he was *trying*. Between his weapons, his black attire, and the shadows, he'd probably fail utterly at "approachable" anyway. "Yes?" he asked, settling on an oral prompt.

"If Ravido is in the Barracks," Sespian said, "maybe we should do something about him while we're here."

By now, Sicarius knew that "do something about him," didn't mean kill him, at least not when Sespian or Amaranthe said it. "Such as?"

"I don't know. Kidnap him?"

"To what end?" Sicarius imagined Amaranthe trying to talk Ravido over to their side. He doubted it'd be possible, but watching her attempt to do so might elicit sensations of levity.

"If we could keep him away from Forge and the army while we enact our plan..."

Killing him would be much easier. Sicarius resisted the urge to say it, though the dozens of difficulties inherent in a kidnapping stampeded into his mind. Even if they found Ravido alone, how could they force him to navigate the ducts—or drag his unconscious body through them—without making noise? Sicarius ought to squash the notion, but if nothing came of his backup plan, and Sespian ended up back on the throne, he'd have to take orders from the boy eventually. That had been what he wished once, he recalled, what he'd had in mind when he poisoned Raumesys.

"I will check to see if Ravido is here," Sicarius said. "It's moot otherwise."

"Agreed. And don't... I know what you must be thinking. Please don't take it into your hands to kill him. While I have no reason to love the man and admit there's a certain practicality to the idea, I can't win the throne back that way. I don't deserve it if I have to become the very monsters I wish to displace. Besides, in the people's eyes, if I had him assassinated, I'd be no better than..." Sespian had been looking Sicarius in the eyes as he spoke, but he broke contact now, studying the floor instead. "It wouldn't be a popular choice with the people or the rest of the warrior caste. Given that I'm no longer the automatic blood choice, I'll need a majority vote from the Company of Lords to be reappointed. They'd only approve of me eliminating Ravido if I bested him in a duel or some blood-flinging, eye-gouging, one-on-one grappling competition. Those aren't exactly my fortes."

Though Sespian grimaced as he spoke those last sentences, Sicarius wondered if the thoughts represented an opportunity. "If you feel you're deficient in martial endeavors, I could instruct you."

"Uhhhh," Sespian said, drawing out the syllable in a way that ensured a rejection would follow.

"I have trained the others. They are better fighters for it."

"I don't—"

"I know you prefer cerebral solutions to problems, but, as you said, the people will want a strong warrior to rally behind." Sicarius knew he was "trying too hard," as Amaranthe would say it, and he lifted a hand to signify he was backing away from the argument.

"I'll think about it," Sespian said.

Not an outright objection. Good.

"I'll see if Ravido is here." Sicarius paused, thinking Sespian might volunteer to come along. He'd be more efficient on his own, but found himself hoping for his company nonetheless.

"Thank you," was all Sespian said and headed back into the secret room.

Sicarius bowed his head. So be it.

CHAPTER 3

AMARANTHE TRIED TO PIERCE THE BASEMENT DARKNESS with her eyes, but there wasn't enough light filtering down the stairwell to reveal anything. For all she knew, she might be standing on the edge of a secret bottomless abyss that opened up beneath the newspaper building. However, the amount of dust hanging in the air, tickling her nostrils, suggested a clutter-filled room of manmade origins.

With the grinding and thumping of machinery filtering down from above, she could almost believe she'd imagined the voice, but Maldynado had heard it too.

"That sounded like Deret Mancrest," he said, "but I can't believe a warrior-caste lord would get himself locked in a grimy cell more than once in the same year."

"No, you wouldn't think so." Amaranthe waited for the voice in the darkness to speak again, but all she heard was a soft thump. Such as that of a forehead thudding against a wall? "Watch our friends, will you?"

While Maldynado hauled their prisoners out of the stairwell, Amaranthe shrugged off her knapsack and dug out a lantern. She shut the door before striking a match. The small flame did little more than highlight the scowls of the two captives and Maldynado's perennially amused features. Yara never had a chance. The man even managed to look stop-and-gape handsome with dust blanketing his brown curls, mud on his boots, and a dubious green smudge smeared across one of his well-defined cheekbones.

Leaving him with the soldiers, Amaranthe walked into the

widest of several aisles branching out from the entrance. Old hand-powered printing presses and stacks upon stacks of dusty, faded newspapers filled the basement from faded brick floor to worn wooden ceiling. The box- and press-framed route took her to an open area hemmed in by giant bottles of ink and crates full of machine parts. A six-foot-tall iron cage rested in the center, a single occupant hunched inside. Deret Mancrest.

If his oily hair, limp clothing, and beard stubble were apt indicators, he'd been locked inside for a few days. An empty plate sat outside the door, and a water jug and chamberpot rested inside the cage, so no one had intended him to starve and die, but he certainly didn't look his best. A heavy padlock secured the cell gate. The swordstick he used for a cane, the support necessary due to a war wound that had left him with a limp, leaned against a crate out of his reach. He stared at Amaranthe warily, probably wondering if, in these tumultuous times, she was friend or foe. Or maybe he was simply wondering if she'd mock him for his predicament. After all, she'd once left him in a similar position when he tried to lure her into a trap, intending to turn her over to the army.

Fortunately for him, she was too professional to mock a potential ally.

"Good evening, Lord Mancrest." Amaranthe waved at the cage. "You haven't been pestering me of late, so I'll assume there's some other woman you've irked so greatly that she felt compelled to lock you up." Maybe that wasn't that professional after all.

"I greatly irked my *father*," Deret said.

"Ah." Amaranthe wanted the details, but they could wait until later, when they were somewhere without armed soldiers roaming about on the floor above. "Are you agreeably serving out your paternally-induced prison sentence?" she asked, thinking Mancrest might be grateful enough to share all of the goings on in the city if she freed him from his cell. "Or would you like to be let out?"

"Trust me, nothing about this is agreeable."

"I don't suppose there are keys nearby?" Amaranthe glanced around, though her fingers were already dipping into her knapsack for the lock-picking kit.

"My father has them."

"Too bad. I believe your father just left with Ms. Worgavic." She said it casually, but watched his face through her lashes to see if he knew anything about the affair.

Mancrest straightened, clunking his head on the cage's overhead bars. "You know that woman?" He squinted at her, his listless apathy fading.

"Yes." Amaranthe reserved further explanation for later. If she had information he desired, maybe she could offer a trade. She couldn't count on Mancrest simply telling her all she wanted to know. They hadn't parted enemies last summer, but the last time she'd spoken to him had involved an awkward apology for abandoning him in the middle of their date in the Imperial Gardens. She'd left out the fact that she'd run off to smooch with Sicarius in the hedge maze, but he was bright enough to piece together the puzzle. "Do *you* know her?" she asked.

"Her name, but little else."

"She's one of Ravido's allies, among other things." Amaranthe slipped her picking tools into the padlock.

"Hm," Mancrest said, not giving away much.

"Are you down here because you're not a supporter of Ravido's?" Amaranthe asked, fishing for information, not unlike she was fishing for the tumblers. The padlock, she noticed, was identical to the one that had secured the storm grate. Had the senior Mancrest been responsible for increasing security around the newspaper office? To keep people from learning about the extra publications being printed?

"I'm down here because I refused to be strong-armed into printing lies in the *Gazette*." Mancrest gripped the bars. "Amaranthe, the emperor... is he truly dead?"

"Nah," came Maldynado's voice from behind her. "He's probably out carousing with Akstyr by now, learning about magic, about growing up in the streets, and about how *not* to attract women."

"Aren't you guarding our prisoners?" Amaranthe asked without glancing at him. She kept her focus on the lock.

"I had to come see if you were chatting with who I thought you were chatting with, so I tied them to each other." Maldynado leaned against the cage bars. "So, Deret, how'd you manage to get yourself locked up in your own building?"

"It's my father's building," Mancrest grumbled. "How is it *you're* not locked up somewhere yet? You're the outlaw here, after all."

"Yes, but a dashing outlaw with perfectly proportioned features. One doesn't incarcerate perfect proportions."

"One does if one's earned a decent bounty. I suppose yours doesn't qualify. Your scruffy Akstyr has an impressive one these days though. Were you aware that the gangs want him?" Mancrest had shifted his attention to Amaranthe. Was he making an offering she might find useful in hopes of opening up an exchange of information? If so, they wanted the same things. Good.

"We're aware of it," she said. "He should be safe for the moment. And, yes, Sespian is alive and safe too. He's with—" She caught herself, realizing Mancrest's interest in helping might shrivel up at the mention of Sicarius.

"Your assassin," he guessed, his tone flat.

"Yes." She waited, wondering if he'd heard about the father-son relationship yet. Perhaps not, since he'd referred to Sespian as the emperor. Had Forge not spilled that information yet? If not, why not? If Ms. Worgavic had made her way back to the capital, others in the organization would have too.

Mancrest didn't say anything else. Amaranthe snapped the lock open and let the gate swing wide.

Thumps sounded near the door. At first, she thought they'd been made by the men Maldynado was supposed to be watching, but Mancrest blurted, "The stairs. Someone's coming."

"Maldynado," Amaranthe said, "lock the door, please."

He was already moving. "No lock," he called back, but a heavy scraping sound nearly drowned out the words as he moved a crate in front of the door.

"They'll know something is going on in here as soon as they can't get in." Mancrest hopped out of the cage, winced when his weight came down on his bad leg, and growled as he reached for his swordstick.

Amaranthe didn't point out that they *already* knew something was going on, due to the two missing men.

More thumps sounded, someone pounding at the door.

"What's the plan?" Maldynado asked.

Amaranthe thought of the walled up doorway in the storm water tunnel. "Back door?"

"We're below street level," Mancrest said. "That door and a trapdoor in the ceiling are the only exits we have." He waved toward the sound of Maldynado dragging another heavy crate.

"The only exits you have *now*." Amaranthe winked. She didn't feel as confident as that wink suggested, but she led Mancrest through the shadows of old crates and rusty equipment. Warrior-caste men seemed to appreciate bravado anyway. As she walked, she kept an eye out for anything that might be useful for knocking down brick obstacles.

When they neared the back wall—the one that ought to line up with the storm tunnel—she found boxes stacked to within a foot or two of the ceiling. She grimaced as she lifted her lantern to survey the shadows. They might not have time for her plan.

"What are we looking for?" Mancrest asked.

Amaranthe was about to say nothing, but her light played across the wall above a box of reference books, and it revealed a different shade of brick, more of a dull red instead of the gray that comprised the rest of the basement. A relatively recent addition.

"Help me clear away these boxes." Amaranthe set down her lantern and clambered atop one of the piles.

"Do men always obey your orders?"

"Only when they're curious to see what the result of following those orders will be." Amaranthe heaved a box to the floor. Dust flew into the air, and Mancrest jumped back, coughing. Her fastidious streak cringed at the idea of making a mess, but the thumps on the door convinced her she didn't have time for an orderly rearranging. "There's nothing important in these boxes, is there?" She shoved another one to the floor. "Nothing you'll be upset about losing?"

"If the boxes are buried down here, I guess not." Shaking his head, Mancrest started moving aside the pile of boxes next to hers.

"And this wall? Would you be upset about losing it?"

Mancrest paused. "What?" He stared at the bricks—with some of the boxes out of the way, the outline of the walled-in doorway was coming into view. "Oh." For a moment, he looked like he might object, but then he clenched his jaw and said, "No, curse him. I don't care what happens to this building. Not after he locked me up down here."

"Good." Amaranthe hopped to the floor. "Keep moving those, will you? I need to locate materials for the second half of this plan."

Seemingly forgetting his objection to being ordered around, Mancrest heaved aside the boxes while she hunted for something they could use to blow a hole in the wall. There shouldn't be much structural support behind the brick addition, but it'd take more than a shoulder thump to topple it.

"Maldynado?" Amaranthe called. "How're you doing over there?"

"Between keeping these rowdy prisoners subdued and piling as much junk as possible in front of the door?" came the response.

"Yes."

"Fine, but I heard someone in the stairwell holler to get Lord Mancrest, and I believe the words 'battering ram' also came up."

Amaranthe didn't think a ram would prove effective in that tight stairwell, but if Deret's father came down and started hollering at his son through the door, that might have a scheme-withering effect. If Deret decided they should give in and let the others in, that wouldn't leave Amaranthe and Maldynado in a good place. "If you're done piling up junk, come give me a hand."

"Be there in a minute."

Amaranthe paused beside a rusty press beneath a drop cloth. She eyed the furnace and boiler. It wouldn't be the first boiler she'd caused to explode, but she feared it was too big and too surrounded by other heavy objects for three people to push over to the wall. She kept looking. Perhaps there was a smaller press, or perhaps… Her thoughts took a jog to the left when she spotted the jars of ink again. Nodding to herself, she lugged two of them through the crooked aisles toward the back wall. On the way, she caught sight of Maldynado and his so-called rowdy prisoners. Both were sitting on the ground, their wrists and ankles still tied. She paused, setting down the heavy jars.

"Ten ranmyas says they get caught in the next ten minutes, and these outlaws get shot," one said.

"I'm not taking that bet," the other said. "That's a foregone event. The real question is whether Lord Mancrest will give his son a spanking when he finds him out of his cage."

The two men shared snickers. Maldynado was leaning against one of numerous crates he'd shoved in front of the door, wiping sweat from his brow. "We're not getting caught," he told the prisoners. "But if we did, I'd pay a lot more than ten ranmyas to see Deret spanked."

"Maldynado," Amaranthe said, causing him to start.

"I was taking a break. A quick one. I swear. Look at all I did." He flung his arms wide to highlight the size of the stack he'd piled up.

"You and your prisoners aren't in trouble." Amaranthe smiled at the tied men, figuring it couldn't hurt to start talking to them if she hoped to draw them to her side later. "But I need help." She picked up one of the jars of ink and nodded for Maldynado to grab the other.

"I'd rather see *her* spanked," one of the prisoners said as she moved away.

His cohort guffawed. "I'd pay fifty ranmyas for that."

Maldynado snickered. Amaranthe raised an eyebrow at him.

"Sorry," he said, "I could thump them around so they

couldn't say such things, but you mentioned winning them over. I thought that might be easier if we didn't mash up their faces or perforate any important organs."

"Thoughtful of you." Given that spanking comment, she wouldn't mind some light thumping, but she decided she shouldn't encourage brutality.

When they reached the wall, Deret was still pushing boxes aside. Amaranthe and Maldynado deposited their loads and went to retrieve more jars of ink. By the time they'd made their last trip, Deret had cleared the area. He stopped to mop sweat from his face and eye the semicircle of giant jars.

"You think the storm tunnel is on the other side?" Maldynado waved to the outline on the wall.

Amaranthe pictured the street, the tunnel, and their location within the building in her mind. "I'd guess ten or twelve feet away."

"What if this side stub is bricked in all the way?"

"Let's hope it's not."

A resonating bang came from the stairway. Huh, the soldiers might have gotten a battering ram into the stairwell after all.

"Deret, printing press ink is flammable, right?" Amaranthe had better make sure she had her facts right before she started making fuses.

"Yes. It's made of soot, walnut oil, and turpentine. When we run the presses, we have to be careful not to let the bearings on the rollers overheat or..." Deret's eyes narrowed. "Why do you ask?"

Maldynado laughed. "The more pertinent question, old boy, is which one of us will get blamed when she blows up your father's building?"

Deret looked back and forth from the bottles of ink to the brick wall. "Oh."

Maldynado elbowed Amaranthe. "He's volunteering."

"Really?" Amaranthe asked. "I didn't get that."

"It was inherent in the lack of a strenuous objection. Please note, *I* am objecting. Strenuously."

"We can face the soldiers if you wish, Deret," Amaranthe said, though she fervently hoped he did *not* wish—especially if someone had run off to fetch the elder Lord Mancrest and if Ms. Worgavic was still with him. She was the last person to whom Amaranthe wanted to reveal her presence.

Still eyeing the ink, Deret rubbed his jaw. She shifted from foot to foot, but didn't rush him, though the banging at the door surely made her wish to do so.

"No," Deret finally said. "I meant what I said earlier. I'm done arguing with my father—and those Marblecrest lackeys." He scowled at Maldynado.

"Don't look at me like that." Maldynado prodded his thumb to his chest. "I'm disowned, remember? And when Ravido finds out I was present—though not, I assure you, responsible—for his wife's death, I'll be lucky if I'm not dismembered."

"Mari's dead?" Deret gaped at him, then turned the gape onto Amaranthe.

"I'm not responsible either," Amaranthe said. "I was busy being tortured by Hollowcrest's former master interrogator at the time."

"*What?*" Deret continued to gape, though his gaze shifted back to Maldynado, as if to check if this were a joke. Maldynado shook his head solemnly. Deret swallowed, pity entering his eyes.

Amaranthe hadn't wanted that. She'd just meant to—bloody ancestors, she shouldn't have brought it up at all. They needed to get out of here.

"It seems we have much information we should exchange with each other," Deret said.

Glad he was ready to drop the conversation too, Amaranthe managed a smile. "That's why we came looking for you."

"And here I thought it was because you'd grown weary of the company of that assassin and sought emotionally stimulating conversations." Deret picked up one of the jars of ink.

Amaranthe tried to read whether there was hurt lacing his flippant words—and whether that hurt might be a problem. She *thought* the humor reached his eyes, but she couldn't be sure.

Deret must have understood her uncertain silence, for he patted her arm and said, "I'm teasing. I'm actually seeing a nice girl—or I was until Father detained me." He growled and set the jar down by the wall.

Amaranthe told herself that it was *good* that he'd found someone else, though a silly part of her felt stung that he'd so quickly dismissed her and fallen for another. Come on, girl, she thought, you're not some spell-bindingly alluring maiden from the stories of eld, the kind soldiers pined over for decades while they were away at war. So long as one certain man didn't dismiss her, that was all that mattered.

Deret pushed the other jars toward the wall. "You two stand back a bit. I'll handle this. I've inadvertently started enough fires with the presses that I'm practically an expert."

Maldynado pumped a fist. "*Yes.*"

Amaranthe cocked her head at him.

"He *is* volunteering to take the blame."

Deret snorted and waved for them to back away. "Turpentine is noxious stuff. You don't want to inhale any more than is necessary."

"You be careful, too, then. Especially if there's a new lady worrying about you right now." Amaranthe pushed Maldynado toward the blocked door. "Let's get your rowdy friends."

The two prisoners had been attempting to free each other. One clenched half of a broken pair of scissors in his mouth and was trying to saw the rusty blade across his comrade's wrist bonds. Amaranthe doubted they'd free each other within the hour—or month—that way, but she removed the tool from the man's mouth anyway.

"Sorry, gentlemen, but we're taking a walk." She nodded for Maldynado to hoist the bigger man to his feet. "You'll have to try to escape later."

Amaranthe had no more than helped the second fellow to stand—her pistol nudging his back to encourage alacrity—when an explosion roared through the basement. The ground bucked, and she staggered, catching her balance on a press. Crates and machinery crashed to the floor. The wooden ceiling trembled and groaned. She eyed the old boards through the clouds of dust that arose, choking the little lamplight they had. Maybe setting off an explosion in the basement of a centuries-old building wasn't a good idea after all.

The noise in the stairwell disappeared. The creaks from the presses on the floor above sounded loud in the new quiet, one broken only by soft wheezing coughs and dirt and debris trickling from the ceiling, or perhaps that brick wall.

Still pushing her prisoner, Amaranthe continued in that direction. "Deret? Are you all right?"

The noxious odor he'd promised clogged the air, a charred burnt smell with a piny underpinning. It stung her throat and eyes, bringing on tears. Her prisoner balked, but she prodded him onward. At the same time, she tugged her shirt up over her mouth and nose.

"Did it work?" Maldynado choked out around a cough. "It better have, because it smells worse than an entire battalion's worth of unwashed socks piled up behind a field latrine."

"You've been spending too much time with Akstyr," Amaranthe said.

"Nah, he would have worked donkey droppings into that claim."

The lantern by the brick wall had either gone out of its own accord or Deret had cut it off. Amaranthe lifted her own light high, trying to pierce the cloak of dusty air. The boxes nearest to the explosion had been blown asunder, and bits of old newspapers and books littered the floor. Amaranthe grimaced at this destruction of property—she hoped some university library had copies of the documents somewhere—but forgot her regrets as soon as she spotted the jagged hole leading to a black tunnel.

"Deret?" Amaranthe peered along the wall in both directions.

"In retrospect," came Mancrest's raspy voice, "I should have laid a longer fuse." He staggered out of a nearby hiding spot, leaning heavily on his swordstick. Soot smeared his face and clothing, and his hair stuck out in blackened spicules.

"Neophyte," Maldynado said brightly.

"Are you—" Amaranthe had planned to inquire after Mancrest's health, but the bangs started up at the door again, and she switched to, "—ready to go?"

Mancrest cast a glower in the direction of the cage. "More than ready."

Amaranthe peered into the dark passage behind the wall. "Is there any more ink left? I think we'll have to do that again to reach the storm water tunnel."

Deret rubbed his finger into his eardrum, as if he were having trouble hearing her. "*Again*?"

"Women are never satisfied," Maldynado said. "Not only do you have to impress them once, but you have to keep doing it again and again. You better learn these things if you're going to enter into a relationship with one."

"As if you're such an expert," Deret grumbled.

Already on her way back to grab two more ink jars, Amaranthe missed part of the conversation, but came back to Maldynado explaining his new relationship with Yara.

"She's the tall, muscly one?" Deret asked.

Amaranthe tried to remember if he'd ever met her. She didn't think so, at least not when Yara had been a part of their group, but it wouldn't be surprising if, as a journalist, Deret had been keeping track of the team, including recent acquisitions.

"Oh, yes," Maldynado drawled. "Very athletic."

"Are we preparing for the next explosion?" Amaranthe asked, dumping a jar into Deret's hands. "And watching the prisoners?" She gave Maldynado a pointed look.

"Yes, ma'am," Deret said at the same time as Maldynado proclaimed, "Naturally, boss."

Deret grabbed a lantern and disappeared into the tunnel. Amaranthe intended to follow and help him if he needed it, but a thunderous snap rent the air.

"Was that the door?" she whispered. It'd sounded louder and closer than that.

"Must be," Maldynado said. "What else would it be?" He knocked on a brick. "Hurry up, Deret. I think your old man's about to join us."

"I need some cloth and another jar," Deret called back, his voice echoing in the enclosed tunnel.

Amaranthe eyed Maldynado's shirt. It had... tassels wasn't quite the right word, but the fluffy fringes looked like they could be shorn off for Deret's fuse without leaving flesh exposed. She unsheathed her dagger and lifted a finger, intending to ask.

"Don't even think about it." Maldynado took a large step back. "My wardrobe has suffered dreadfully as a result of knowing you. Do you know that I haven't been able to keep a hat for more than two weeks since we met?"

"Please, you'd find it tedious to wear the same hat for more than two weeks anyway." Amaranthe veered toward the prisoners, lifting an apologetic hand as she sliced into one's jacket.

"True," Maldynado said, "but I prefer to retire a hat to a closet for possible later consideration, not watch it be blown up in a steamboat explosion."

"Fussy, fussy." Amaranthe took the purloined cloth and another jar into the tunnel.

At the far end, Deret was hunched over, assembling his bomb. Amaranthe set down the rest of the supplies, grabbed the lantern, and held it up to improve the light.

Another resounding snap came from out in the basement.

"That's not the door." Maldynado stuck his head into the tunnel. "I think those are the floor beams."

A second noise echoed, this more of a boom than a snap.

"*That* was the door," Maldynado said.

Deret grabbed the second jar. "Going as fast as I can."

"Can I do anything to help?" Amaranthe asked.

"Yes. If my father barges through that door with the soldiers, shoot him."

"Really?" Amaranthe wouldn't have pegged Deret as the type to harm blood relations, even irritating ones.

"Not in the chest. Just blow out a kneecap or two."

"Is he really the one who locked you up down here?"

"Yes."

"Because...?"

"I refused to print Ravido Marblecrest's half-truths. Ravido and his business contacts went to my father behind my back. I wish I could say there'd been blackmail or other coercion, but my father is the sort to believe that warrior-caste families should stick together, and he was never a big supporter of Raumesys or Sespian, so..."

"He was happy to help Ravido?" Amaranthe asked.

"That's the impression I got. When I confronted him... we argued. With fists. He reminded me he owned the paper and sent me home. That was that, or so I hoped he'd think. I brought some of my workers in late that night, intending to change the typeset and print a lengthy story about everything that's been going on in secret, at least that I'm aware of—thanks in part to you. I included that there'd been no evidence whatsoever to verify Sespian's death and that anyone attempting to take the throne was doing so illegally."

"I haven't seen that edition of the paper." Thanks to their travels, Amaranthe hadn't seen a lot of editions, but she doubted *anyone* had seen that one.

"Nor will you. My father guessed my intentions and barged in on me. He was furious. My basement internment was the result." Deret backed away from his improvised ink-based explosive. "Time to light the fuse."

"Are we sure we want to light another one?" Maldynado asked, poking his head inside the tunnel again. "Things don't sound too structurally stable out here." A crash punctuated his last word.

"Do we have a choice?" Amaranthe asked. "Sounds like company is coming."

"Let's get out of here," Deret grumbled and grabbed the lantern.

Since he was leaning on his swordstick, his movements were awkward as he bent toward the fuse. Amaranthe wondered if his earlier near miss, as evinced by his soot-covered face and clothing, had come because he'd misjudged how much time he'd need to give himself to get out of range, thinking of how fast he'd once been able to move instead of how fast he moved today.

"Want me to light it?" she offered.

Deret's glower could have withered daisies on a warm spring day.

"Or... I'll just wait outside," she amended.

"Do that."

Amaranthe scooted out of the tunnel, almost colliding with Maldynado who was loitering at the mouth.

"We need to take cover," she said.

Maldynado started to jog away, but she added, "Them too," and waved at the prisoners.

Maldynado huffed a sigh and grabbed the men, propelling them before him. Amaranthe could understand the sentiment. At least they went along without making trouble. Nobody wanted to get caught in an explosion.

She joined them behind a couple of desks, ducking under one with a solid slab top.

The ceiling creaked ominously above their heads. She hoped the next explosion, which was outside of the building's walls, wouldn't affect the structure or supports.

More bangs sounded—crates being shoved off the pile Maldynado had erected up front. The soldiers must have broken down the door or found a way to remove it from its hinges.

"Deret," a man bellowed. "Are you responsible for this ruckus, boy? I'm going to tie you down range at Fort Urgot for the privates to use for shooting practice."

Deret skidded around the corner of Amaranthe's hiding spot and dropped to the floor. There wasn't room for him to squeeze under the desk beside her, but he pressed himself close and buried his head under his arms.

The thunderous boom that followed wasn't as loud as the first had been, not with the wall blocking some of the noise, but that didn't keep the floor from trembling beneath them. Cracks sounded, this time not in the wood but in the bricks, and more dust flooded the air.

"By great grandmother's funeral pyre, what are you doing, boy?" came the senior Lord Mancrest's voice.

Amaranthe touched Deret's shoulder and climbed out past him. They had better get out of the basement before something important gave way—or the soldiers swarmed inside to capture them. Maldynado had already leaped to his feet, and he reached the opening in the wall first, a lantern in hand.

He stuck the light inside. "It worked."

He'd neglected to grab the prisoners, and they looked like they meant to flee toward Deret's father. Amaranthe was tempted to let them go so they wouldn't have to deal with them any more, but she grabbed their arms. "This way. He won't be happy with you for not capturing us in the first place."

"I don't care any more," one muttered. "So long as we get out of here before—"

Wood snapped above them. A beam bowed down, boards cracking and giving way with each inch it drooped.

Deret grabbed Amaranthe's arm. "Run!"

She needed no further urging and sprinted for the tunnel hole.

"Get back, get back," came a cry from the other entrance.

Just as Amaranthe crossed the threshold, the beam gave away completely. Light fell into the basement as a huge chunk of the floor above collapsed. Steel screeched, then a cacophonous crash filled the space as one of the massive presses tumbled through the opening. Parts flew off, pelting the walls and landing on old machinery, leaving a twisted metal wreck that would never print again.

One of the massive paper rolls was flung across the room toward Amaranthe. She dove, somersaulting down the tunnel to put distance between herself and the machine's attack. Brick crunched as the roller struck the outer wall. A curtain of dust and mortar sprayed the inside of the passage.

Amaranthe climbed to her feet, saw that Maldynado and Deret had both made it inside, and started to release a relieved breath, but a cry of pain came from beyond the entrance. Her first thought was that Deret's father, or some of his men, had been crossing the basement and had been pinned by flying pieces of machinery. Then she remembered the prisoners.

"Maldynado," she whispered, "help me," and headed back.

"Are you crazy?" Deret held the only remaining lantern, and he stood at the far end of the passage, one foot already through the ragged hole leading to the storm tunnel.

"We brought them down here. Maldynado," Amaranthe repeated, knowing she'd need his brawn if someone was pinned.

A hand patted her back. "I'm with you, boss."

Amaranthe stuck her head back into the basement as a metal filing cabinet tumbled through the hole from above, landing on the cage Deret had been confined in before. More wood snapped overhead. Before long, the whole ceiling would drop.

"Help," someone whimpered from a few feet away.

Amaranthe swatted at the dust in the air. Fine particles slipped through her shirt and assailed her nostrils and throat. She stifled a cough. She doubted the soldiers would come streaming into this mess, but she didn't want to let them know where she was. Who knew if they had rifles?

A long arm of machinery had fallen on one of the prisoners. The other man was trying to pull his comrade free, though the wrist ties made it impossible. Amaranthe slid out her dagger and slashed through the bindings, instantly raising her estimation of the soldier for not leaving his colleague. He gave her a quick nod, then bent to grab the end of the beam.

The pinned man groaned, his teeth clenched so hard she could almost hear them grinding above the noise of falling debris. Maldynado grabbed the beam as well. Amaranthe glanced about and found a pole sticking out of the wreckage. She joined the men, thrusting it beneath the beam to use as a lever. Those printing presses must weigh tons, for even this broken section took all three of them to lift.

More pieces of the ceiling cracked and fell as they heaved. The beam inched up.

"Go, Rudev," the pinned man's comrade urged.

As the weight lifted, the prone fellow groaned, his eyes rolling back in his head. For a moment, Amaranthe thought he would pass out, but he stretched his hands across the floor, grabbed the corner of a crate and started clawing his way free.

"There they are!" someone yelled from the other side of the basement.

A shot rang out. Instinctively, Amaranthe ducked, though it was probably the haze that saved her, rather than her reflexes. The pistol ball pounded into the brick wall.

"Go, go," she whispered and risked casting her lever aside. She grabbed the crawling man by the shoulders of his jacket and threw her weight into pulling him.

A pained stream of curses flowed from his mouth, but his legs finally cleared the beam. Maldynado and the other prisoner dropped it, hurling more dust into the air.

A second pistol fired. Amaranthe and the others dropped to the ground and scrambled for the tunnel entrance on hands and knees. This time, the shot hit the ceiling. As if it were the kernel of rice that tipped the merchant's scales, a second ceiling beam snapped, the ear-splitting noise directly above Amaranthe. She lunged into the tunnel, grabbing the others, pulling and urging them along, though nobody needed prompting at that point.

As Maldynado flopped to the ground beside her, the basement ceiling caved in. Dust flooded into the tunnel, and an ominous groan came from the bricks above their heads as well. This time it was Maldynado who grabbed her arm, and her feet barely touched the ground as he raced toward the storm tunnel. She glanced back, ensuring their prisoners were hobbling after—she didn't know what she was going to do with them, but she wasn't going to lose them at that point. In the darkness behind them, it was hard to tell, but she thought the rubble had closed off their escape route.

Maldynado let go of her when they reached the storm tunnel, but she waved toward the bend that led to the river. "Let's get all the way out of here," Amaranthe said. "People were shooting at us at the end."

"Think they figured out who we are?" Maldynado asked.

"Either that, or Deret's pa is very displeased with him right now."

Deret, leading the way toward the river, said nothing to this, though he did give the wall nearest the building a long look. The booms and thuds of equipment falling through the floor continued to emanate from the *Gazette*.

CHAPTER 4

S ICARIUS SLITHERED THROUGH THE WARM DUSTY DUCTS, as soundless as a snake. As he approached the imperial suite, a sprawling complex of rooms large enough to accommodate a family of multiple generations, the resiny scent of Nurian *rek rek* teased his nostrils again. He stopped at the vent leading to the master bedroom. The grate had been removed. The screws had been knocked out from within— warping and destroying them—the culprit obviously not caring if his presence was detected after his deed was done. And the deed was what? An assassination. It had to be. If another had come to assassinate Ravido, perhaps it'd be best to let the man do his work. Sespian might object, but Sicarius refused to rescue Maldynado's rogue relative simply so Sespian could kidnap him.

Unlike Hollowcrest's suite, these rooms had seen recent occupation. Though Sicarius didn't spot anyone at the moment, the lamps burned, a fire crackled in the hearth, and the sheets and furs on the bed had been turned down. In addition to the Nurian smoke, he smelled the leather of bookbindings, the tang of weapons cleaning oil, and the potato-based starch officers employed for pressing their uniforms.

Sicarius remained motionless, waiting for Ravido to come in and listening for the breaths of someone who might already be hiding in the suite. Nothing stirred. The fire in the hearth burned down.

He would need to return to the others soon. It would not prove propitious if they grew restless and started wandering the Barracks on their own.

A series of resounding clangs thundered through the building, echoing through the ducts with the force of a great bell's reverberations. Sicarius recognized the cacophony instantly. The Imperial Barracks alarm.

Doors banged and shouts echoed in the hallway. The team must have been discovered, or perhaps security had stumbled upon evidence of the other intruder's presence. Either scenario would be problematic.

Sicarius backed away from the vent opening, intending to return to Hollowcrest's chambers, but a figure sprinted through the doorway, veering straight for him. He had a glimpse of black clothing, a dark topknot of hair, a dagger clenched in hand, and a silver medallion on a leather thong flapping against the man's chest. Then the figure was diving into the vent, and Sicarius had no more time for observation, no time for thought; he could only react with instincts honed since birth.

His black dagger had already found its way into his hand. Like a viper waiting in a rocky hollow, he waited until his prey was least prepared. The man had thrust himself halfway into the duct and was turning on his side to yank his legs in when Sicarius attacked. Though his target's body blocked all the light, he saw with his other senses, his instincts. The man didn't know he was there until the dagger dipped into his throat. Metal clattered on the porcelain duct tiles—the assassin's own blade dropping.

Throughout the building, the alarm bells continued to clang. Knowing the imperial suite would be searched soon, Sicarius left the dead man's legs dangling out of the duct. Finding the intruder wouldn't delay security for long—they'd assume he had a partner who'd betrayed him and was still in the Barracks—but they'd have to pause to investigate. He hoped that'd give Sespian and the others time to escape without being noticed. Ideally, they weren't waiting for him and had already left.

He backed to the first intersection, using the extra space to turn around, and glided back through the ducts to Hollowcrest's office. The room was dark, though the scent of a recently snuffed wick lingered in the room.

Shouts and heavy footfalls pummeled the hallway outside of Hollowcrest's suite. Inside, it was silent, but Sicarius sensed he was not alone.

Starlight filtered in through a window in the sitting room outside of the office. Still poised by the vent, he picked out a dark figure in the room at the same time as a whiff of Akstyr's hair concoction reached his nose.

"There was an *istapa*," Sicarius said, using the Nurian term for those assassins trained not only to fight but to resist mental attacks from practitioners.

Akstyr twitched. "A wizard hunter? Really?"

"Yes."

"He got away?"

"No."

"Oh." Akstyr sounded disappointed, though less for the loss of the man's life than for the fact that he'd missed meeting a wizard hunter.

"The others have gone ahead?" Sicarius asked.

"Yup, back to the furnace room. I stayed behind to warn you. There's a practitioner, the one who installed the wards, I bet."

"He's here," Sicarius said, guessing the reason for the alarm. If the practitioner lived in the Barracks, he would have sensed that one of his wards was no longer working. The disarming of one might not have alerted him as dramatically as one being tripped, but if he did a nightly check...

"*She*, I think," Akstyr said.

"We'll seek to avoid her then. Come."

Akstyr clambered into the duct after Sicarius. "If she's checking where that one ward was, we'll go right by her."

"There are other ways out. Alert me if you sense a freshly laid trap."

Akstyr grumbled under his breath, but the continuing alarm clamor drowned out the words.

Long ago, Sicarius had trained with a Nurian wizard hunter, one of Hollowcrest's carefully selected tutors. He had never expected to see another one in the Imperial Barracks. Was his original theory correct? That the man had been an assassin sent to kill Ravido? And if so, why? If Nurians were here, did they simply want to create chaos, more than there already was, or did they have a different candidate they intended to back, another puppet, this one loyal to Nuria instead of Forge?

Either way, Amaranthe would want this information. It would add further complications to her plans, plans she'd not fully revealed to him yet, a fact that concerned him. She'd used him often as a confidant in the last year, and the only reason he could see her withholding information was because she knew he wouldn't approve of what she had in mind.

"Hst," Akstyr said, the sound somewhere between a grunt and a warning.

Sicarius halted. They'd dropped down to the subterranean level, and the intervening tons of rock were muting the alarm clangs. "Problem?"

"I'm not sure. I thought I felt... I don't know. Something like power being unleashed. It's gone now."

"Understood."

Sicarius hastened forward, winding through the wider ducts of this level, and heading toward the furnace room from whence they originated. A string of pain-filled curses came from somewhere ahead. Books?

Sicarius turned the last corner. Hot air blown from the furnace pushed against him. Light flowed through an access panel in the ductwork, one they'd removed earlier. *Earlier*, the furnace room hadn't been illuminated. Now, orange and yellow firelight flickered beyond the open panel.

Though Books clearly sounded distressed, Sicarius didn't rush his approach. He wanted to assess the situation before bursting into it. He listened as he continued forward at his same steady pace. Metal clacked twice—a dagger hitting a wall, then dropping to the floor. Boots stomped about, more than one set.

Sicarius drew his own dagger, using his ears to pinpoint the likely location of the nearest attacker.

"Look out!" Sespian barked as Sicarius flowed out of the duct.

The warning almost made him pause, for he thought it was meant for him, but he went with his instincts, hurling his dagger before visually taking in the scene. He trusted his senses.

His black blade whistled through the air and smashed into the chest of a black-haired woman. Instead of piercing flesh and organs, it ricocheted off with a twang and landed on the floor.

"She's a wizard!" Books blurted from where he hid behind the furnace, flapping his jacket to put out flames crawling up his sleeve.

Sicarius was too busy racing across the room to respond to the obvious comment. He took in the winking light of a square box hanging from the woman's belt. It must indicate an armor tool similar to the ones he'd encountered earlier in the year, amongst the practitioners in the underwater laboratory. This woman appeared Turgonian, though. Odd.

The thoughts in his head did not slow the pace of his legs. The woman saw him coming and spread an arm toward him, fingers stretched outward. A hint of concern widened her eyes, but he wouldn't bet on it being enough to disrupt her conjuring. Anticipating an attack—similarly to a warrior about to strike a blow, wizards tended to tighten their diaphragms, exhaling as they released their mental energy—Sicarius threw himself into a roll.

Yellow flames burst from the woman's fingers, the intense light blasting the shadows from the room. Heat seared the air above Sicarius's back, but the fire didn't touch him as he somersaulted along the floor. He came up by the woman's side, his elbow glancing off the invisible shield encompassing her. It sent a cold numbing tingle up his arm, but he ignored it, instead lashing toward her eyes with his dagger. The shield would protect her, he knew it, but her instincts might instruct her to retreat.

It worked. She backpedaled three steps, crossing the threshold and stumbling into the whitewashed stone corridor outside. In the ideal situation, she would have bumped the artifact off her belt—he couldn't physically harm her so long as her shield remained in place—but she didn't lose that much composure. Indeed, she recovered quickly, righting herself against the wall and glowering at Sicarius.

He shut the door in her face. It didn't have a lock. He grabbed a half-empty coal bin and dragged it over, the squeal of metal scraping across stone deafening.

"That's *not* going to stop a practitioner." Akstyr stabbed a finger at the blocked door.

Sicarius gave him a flat look as he picked up his black dagger. *Akstyr* wasn't doing anything better, and Books and Sespian had taken refuge from the flame-flinging woman by hiding behind the furnace door.

"A delay will be sufficient." He jerked his head toward the open duct panel. "We'll find another way out."

A thunderous boom came from the hallway, and the door rattled on its hinges.

"Good idea," Akstyr blurted and raced for the duct.

Sicarius, his dagger in hand, cut off a large clump of Akstyr's hair as he passed. His blade-work was swift enough that the boy didn't notice, though Sespian gawked in disbelief.

"Follow him," Sicarius told Books and Sespian. He'd explain later if they insisted.

Books gave his jacket a final flap, stirring smoke but not more flames, and hustled after Akstyr. The fistful of hair in hand, Sicarius strode toward the furnace.

"You should go next," Sespian told him. "They don't know where they're going."

"I'll follow and direct from behind." Sicarius grabbed a shovel, flung open the furnace door, and used the tool to close the flue. "Go with them."

Shouts filled the hallway outside, male and female voices raised in an argument. Sicarius sensed the Science being used again and glanced back. The door hinges glowed cherry red; they'd expand and snap soon.

Sicarius tossed the clump of hair onto the flames.

"What are you doing?" Sespian asked.

"Creating a malodorant."

With the flue closed, smoke flowed out of the firebox and into the room. Sicarius pushed Sespian toward the duct as the stench of burning hair oozed out with the smoke. Sespian coughed and sprinted the last few paces for the opening. Finding the sulfuric scent equally unpleasant, Sicarius dove in behind him.

Sespian smothered a cough. "Well, that would keep *me* out of the room anyway."

"The scent is not dissimilar to burning coal gas," Sicarius said, watching over his shoulder as they crawled through the passage, making sure nobody was following them. "The gas table for the lighting for the Barracks is two rooms down. If we are fortunate, they may believe there's a rupture somewhere."

"Ah, a rupture that would take priority over intruders, due to the flammable nature of the gas."

Sicarius tried to decide if Sespian's words carried a hint of approval. It had been years since someone's approval meant anything to him—Raumesys and Hollowcrest's had stopped mattering long before the emperor's death—and he suspected it a sign of vulnerability on his part. Still, he acknowledged that he wanted Sespian's approval nonetheless. Odd. Weren't sons supposed to seek the approval of their fathers, and not the other way around?

Footfalls hammered the floor somewhere above the duct. Sicarius let his fingers brush Sespian's boots, encouraging greater speed. Possible gas leak or not, with so many people searching the building, it would be best to escape quickly, especially given that they'd have to get past another ward due to their change in route. *This* one wouldn't be deactivated. If Akstyr couldn't equal the wizard hunter's skill, and accomplish the same feat with the ward, they'd be in for a long night.

"I think I'm stuck," came Akstyr's voice from ahead, barely distinguishable from the still-clanging alarm bell.

"I told you not to go that way," Books said.

"No, you told me to wait. I thought it'd be smart to wait out of the way."

"Not if it involved getting your elephantine head stuck."

"It's not my head that's stuck. It's—ow."

"Continue forward," Sicarius said, "choosing the passage that angles to the right at approximately thirty degrees from the intersection."

"Thirty what?" Akstyr asked.

"Degrees, you dolt," Books said. "A degree is a unit of measurement for angles on a plane, each representing one three-sixtieth of a full rotation."

"What does that have to do with ducts?"

"How can you *possibly* be our expert on the Science?" Books asked. "Or anything?"

Sicarius tapped Sespian's boot again. They needed to keep moving. He decided not to voice his agreement on Books's assessment of Akstyr's brightness. Akstyr could prove his intellect on the ward. Or not.

Sespian moved forward, passing Books and Akstyr who'd squeezed into ducts on either side of the five-way intersection.

"Angles weren't real important on the streets," Akstyr muttered, continuing the argument as Sicarius and Sespian passed.

"Without *angles*, a proper understanding of geometry if you will, the buildings on those streets would have collapsed," Books said.

"That happened sometimes."

"Follow," Sicarius said, letting an icy tone creep into his voice. He wondered if Amaranthe knew how much of his respect for her came from her ability to harness these lunkheads to a cart and get them all moving in the same direction. Basilard was the only one who might have lasted more than three days as a recruit in the army.

"I can't go any farther," Sespian said after a few moments of crawling. "The duct curves upward and stops at a vent in the floor. If my nose isn't failing me—and it was somewhat damaged by that hair stunt—we're near the kitchens. We don't want to come up in such a busy area, do we?"

"No." Sicarius pulled out his dagger again.

If he remembered his map of the Imperial Barracks correctly—and Hollowcrest had once insisted he be able to draw it from memory—the old dungeons lay below them, a section that had not been modified or modernized. Though he did not expect anyone to be down there, Sicarius pressed an ear to the warm tiles anyway. Books and Akstyr caught up, their breaths stirring the hot, dry air behind him.

Satisfied nobody awaited below, Sicarius chiseled into the bottom of the duct. The black dagger made quick work of the tile mortar and also that of the bricks below. Stale, cool air wafted up. As soon as he'd removed enough bricks, he dropped through, landing in a crouch fifteen feet below, his fingers touching down beside his foot, resting upon the porous stone floor. That floor had been carved from rock long before the original barracks building had been built. Darkness filled the space, but he could tell they were alone. The cool draft brushing his cheeks carried the scent of earth, rock, and mildew, nothing of people or other creatures.

"It's safe," Sicarius said. "Come."

Clothing rubbed and a soft thump sounded as the first person dropped down—Sespian. The second came with an, "Ooophf."

"Can't see a thing," Books muttered from above. "Probably fall on my—" He dropped, landing softly beside the others and making less noise than Akstyr.

"This way." Sicarius led them out of the stone room, following the draft into a passage.

"Can we risk a light?" Sespian asked.

"Once they realize the intruders are attempting to escape down instead of up and out, they'll start searching in here," Sicarius said.

"Was that a no?" Sespian asked, his tone light.

"We'll be faster if we aren't groping our way along the walls in the dark," Books said. "Besides, we have a head start, right? You're taking us directly to a secret passage, aren't you? We'll be out of here soon."

"Not quite." Sicarius rounded a bend and stopped. "Akstyr."

"I feel it." Akstyr came up beside him.

"What?" Books asked.

A faint whisper of power brushed Sicarius's senses, senses that had nothing to do with sight or sound or smell, and the hairs on the back of his neck wavered. Several paces ahead of him, a soft red light appeared, emanating from a fist-sized octagonal spot on the chiseled stone floor. It was strong enough to illuminate old shackle holders on the walls and rusty torture tools leaning in nooks.

"That's the ward," Akstyr said, his voice full of concentration. "I lit it up so we can see. I'm going to have to figure out..." His nose wrinkled, then he grunted and took a step back. "Yup, I'm going to have to figure out something."

Prepared to wait, Sicarius put his back to the wall so he could see in either direction down the passage. The cacophony of noise continued in the building above—it wouldn't be long before someone thought to check the dungeons.

"What happens if we walk past it?" Sespian asked. "Does it warn that wizard? Or... more?"

"More," Sicarius said.

He'd attempted to infiltrate the Barracks the summer before, when Sespian had first sent a note to the team asking to be kidnapped. He'd tried three different approaches, including an above-ground climb over the walls. Humans he could evade, but he hadn't been able to get past the wards.

In the face of Sespian's curious look, Sicarius tossed a pebble into the air above the glowing octagon. A sheet of red sprang into existence, blocking the route and hurling heat down the passage. Prepared for it, Sicarius merely turned his cheek. Sespian and Books stumbled backward, lifting their arms to protect their faces. Akstyr grimaced, but seemed too focused on his task to bother moving.

"So, we get incinerated if Akstyr can't disarm it?" Sespian asked.

"Or we go back and face the practitioner," Sicarius said.

"I bet she's in an amiable mood after you slammed the door in her face."

Sicarius said nothing. Best to be quiet and let Akstyr concentrate. This night had proved pointless thus far, unless Books had found something useful in Hollowcrest's archives. It mattered little to him. Any curiosity Sicarius might have had as to his parents' identities had been lost long ago. As a boy, he'd occasionally wondered about such things, especially insofar as they might involve escaping his rigorous training and living a different life, but at this juncture, the die was cast.

Books must have felt his gaze, for he looked at Sicarius. Sicarius waited for him to say something—if there was something to say. Dust and cobwebs clung to Books's scruffy brown hair and wariness edged his eyes, but that wariness was always there when he regarded Sicarius. A new emotion seemed to lurk there as well. Sicarius didn't read such things as intuitively as Amaranthe did, but, given the context, knowing what those files had contained, he could guess. Pity. Sicarius stared back, willing Books to look away, to forget such ridiculous feelings. He wanted pity from no man. Not even Sespian. From Sespian all he hoped for was... understanding, for it would be useful in establishing a relationship.

While he considered these thoughts, Sicarius's subconscious mind remained alert, detecting a faint scuff and placing the source. He spun, flinging a throwing knife down the tunnel before his conscious mind fully registered the danger. His blade thudded into the neck of someone who'd been leaning around the bend. A man in a black uniform made a choked, gurgling sound and toppled. A pistol dropped from his fingers, clattering onto the hard stone floor.

Sicarius sprinted toward the bend, assuming there'd be others. Before he reached the spot, footsteps started up— *running* footsteps—and he picked out three distinct patterns. Two men on the right side of the tunnel, one on the left, all fleeing. In case anyone might be waiting, unmoving, Sicarius feinted, dipping his shoulder around the corner to draw fire if it came, then pulling back. No one attacked. Sicarius risked enough of his body to pump his arm three times, hurling three more throwing knives down the hall. The blades thudded into the backs of the men he'd been picturing in his mind. Before they finished toppling, he was crouching, scouring the tunnel for threats with his eyes and listening for any sign that more enemies were on their way. A whimper and gurgle came from one of the fallen men, but nothing else moved.

Sicarius chastised himself for missing his mark by half an inch—the death should have been instant. When he was certain there weren't any other immediate dangers, he rose and collected his knives. He swiped a blade across the throat of the dying man to ensure he'd pose no further threat. As he cleaned his weapons, he noted the silence in the hallway, though the alarm gongs continued in the building above.

For a moment, Amaranthe intruded upon his thoughts— would she have objected to the killing of these men? They could not have been permitted to run back for reinforcements, and attempting to subdue them would not have allowed him to bring them down as efficiently. It was possible one might have escaped to warn others. Yet the dead men wore the uniforms of Imperial Barracks security and were quite possibly the same guards who'd once worked for Sespian. Simply people doing their jobs, being caught in the middle, Amaranthe would have said.

Sicarius pushed the thoughts aside and rose, sensing Books had come up behind him. He was staring at the dead men. Sicarius walked past him without a word.

Sespian remained with Akstyr. His face was grim, but otherwise difficult to interpret. Good. A man should not be as readable as a book.

"This licks street," Akstyr grumbled after a time, making a crude gesture at the ward.

"That would be an impressive feat," Books said, having rejoined them, "given its lack of a discernible tongue."

Akstyr gave him a withering glare. "I can't concentrate with all that noise going on." He made another crude gesture, this one involving the forearm as well as the fingers, aiming it at the ceiling this time.

"He has quite the non-verbal repertoire," Sespian noted.

It seemed to be a comment aimed at the group, rather than anyone specific, but he glanced at Sicarius. Checking for a reaction? Did he expect disapproval? Or maybe it had been an invitation to comment. And join in the... did this qualify as banter?

"Yes," Sicarius said, but his thoughts scattered after that, and he couldn't think of an appropriate addition to the conversation. "It is unfortunate he does not apply his finger dexterity more assiduously to his blade training."

The three men stared at him in unison, then exchanged those looks with each other that implied his ore cart was, as the imperial saying went, missing a wheel.

"Just what this group needs," Sespian muttered, "another expert knife thrower." He gave the bend, beyond which the dead men lay, a significant look.

For Sicarius, trained so long to hide his emotions, the sigh was inward. "I will stand watch." Before he headed for the bend, he told Akstyr, "If you cannot deactivate it, see if you can move it out of the way."

Sicarius retreated—he reluctantly admitted that *retreat* was indeed the correct word—around the bend and stood with his back against the wall, out of sight of the others. He wondered if he'd ever be able to talk to his son without a sense of awkward discomfort cloaking them. Perhaps he shouldn't try when Amaranthe wasn't around. There was still discomfort when she was part of the conversation, but she didn't seem to mind filling it with the sort of ambling chatter that put Sespian and the others at ease. He admitted it put him at ease as well. He couldn't remember when that had started happening. When they'd first met, he'd merely thought her overly gregarious.

"I think... Did that work?" Akstyr's voice floated down the tunnel.

"I don't know," Books said. "We can't see it any more."

"Oh. Here."

A renewed red glow filled the hallway. Sicarius returned to

the group. Instead of floating in the middle of the tunnel, the ward was now wedged into a crevice near the ceiling.

"It looks like it was protecting a flat area, rather than a whole chunk of the tunnel." Akstyr pinched the air with his fingers, then spread his arms to demonstrate.

"A plane," Books said, perhaps intending to sneak in another geometry lesson.

"What?"

"A flat area is—never mind."

"I turned it, so the plane thing is along that wall now," Akstyr said. "We should be able to walk by if we stay by this wall."

"Should?" Books asked.

"We *can*. I'm sure of it."

Books and Sespian looked to Sicarius. For advice, an order, or because they wanted him to go first and be the one incinerated if it came to that? Whatever the reason, it made Akstyr scowl and stick his fists on his hips.

Sicarius closed his eyes for a moment, sensing the ward instead of seeing it. Yes, Akstyr had succeeded in moving it. Thinking of the bodies in the tunnel behind them, he realized he should have made that suggestion earlier.

"It is safe." Sicarius led the others through the tunnel and toward another secret doorway that would let them out into the night. They'd gone perhaps half of the distance, when a startled wail came from behind him.

"Blood-thirsty butchering ancestors, what *happened* to my *hair*?"

* * *

Sicarius wondered at Amaranthe's choice of a meeting place. The alley behind Curi's Bakery? The establishment was frequented by enforcers with no less than three different patrol routes crossing through the intersection out front. Normally, it wouldn't matter this late at night, but these weren't normal times. With the university only a few blocks away, this was a likely area for dissent to arise, and pairs of uniformed men

trod the streets, enforcing the curfew. In addition, squads of soldiers marched through from time to time, ensuring civilians were inside where they should be, and subdued.

To avoid the patrols, Sicarius led Akstyr, Books, and Sespian across the rooftops for the last half mile. Though the gangs weren't traditionally active in that part of the city, Akstyr stuck close and kept his complaints to himself when they were shimmying up drainpipes and ducking under clotheslines. Despite the unique route, they startled a few thieves and other miscreants seeking refuge from the enforcers. Most were young, but youths could send messages to bosses as easily as adults. Sicarius suspected it would soon be common knowledge that Amaranthe's team was back in the city.

They reached Curi's Bakery, hopping across a four-foot gap between it and the next building, to land on the flat roof. Sicarius jogged to the back corner so he could check the alley for the others. The delays in the Imperial Barracks had caused him to miss the midnight meeting point by twenty minutes.

Nothing stirred in the narrow back passages. He would have expected Amaranthe to wait, but perhaps she'd left a message somewhere with directions to the new hideout. He was on the verge of checking when two figures turned off the street and into the alley. Though darkness hid their features, he recognized them by height, build, and gait, Basilard with the stocky form and short steps—along with occasional glances at weeds growing from crevices—and Sergeant Yara with longer legs and steps influenced by broader hips.

"I can barely understand your signs in the daylight," Yara whispered, "but if you're wondering where everyone is, I'm with you."

Basilard's response was indiscernible from the rooftop.

Sicarius was of a mind to wait a moment before revealing himself, and make sure nobody followed the pair into the alley, but Sespian had joined him at the edge of the rooftop and he waved and whispered, "We're up here. Some of us anyway."

Keeping a hand on the gutter, Sespian swung down from

the two-story building, landing softly on a large square trash bin, then hopping into the street. Not for the first time, Sicarius noted the boy's natural agility. He could become a talented fighter if he ever pursued the training with any enthusiasm.

Books and Akstyr joined Sicarius at the edge of the roof.

"No sign of Amaranthe?" Books asked.

"I will check the area to see if they were here or left a message," Sicarius said.

Books and Akstyr dropped down to the street, taking the same route as Sespian. They also made it look effortless. Neither had natural athletic aptitude, but they'd grown far more capable at physical feats in the last year. Sicarius noted his own satisfaction in regard to how the men's training had come along. The feeling surprised him, and he decided it must have to do with his own growth as an instructor or perhaps the mere achievement of creating a more capable team to help with Sespian and Amaranthe's goals.

Sicarius headed off to scout the streets and alleys around the bakery. At first, he was merely looking to see if Amaranthe and the others were on their way, but then he dropped to ground level, sniffing the air for the familiar scent of her shampoo, and searching the streets for signs that she'd been there. Her training had come a long way, as well, and he doubted she would have inadvertently stumbled into a squad of enforcers or soldiers, but Forge represented a unique threat, with its access to superior technology, and now they must worry about Nurians as well.

Snippets of the rest of the team's conversation floated to Sicarius's ears as he searched.

"...slagging cut my hair off. With that ugly black knife of his." Akstyr's petulant grousing rose above all the others.

"It'll grow back," Yara said. "Maybe you should cut off the rest of it for a disguise. Aren't the gangs hunting you?"

"Oh, huh. I hadn't thought of that."

"If we could discuss a more important matter," Books said, "did you locate a suitable hideout?"

"Yes," Yara said. "There's a molasses factory near the

waterfront that's for sale. It doesn't look like anybody's been around for a month or two. Basilard said there's some winter weather coming in, so we figure there won't be a lot of people browsing around for new business endeavors."

"Molasses?" Sespian asked. "Sounds... sticky."

"I understand this team wields brooms as well as swords," Yara said.

"Only because Amaranthe has a knack for talking people into doing things," Books said.

Still searching, Sicarius drifted out of ear range at that point. He hadn't seen anyone walking around, aside from a pair of yawning enforcers, but he hadn't seen sign of Amaranthe and the others either. It didn't seem that they'd been ensnared upon arriving; they'd simply never shown up. That implied trouble at the *Gazette*, or perhaps they'd gone to Deret Mancrest's residence. If the man had attempted to trap Amaranthe again, Sicarius vowed to deal with him in, as she would say, an assassinly way. On this point, he didn't care if she approved or not.

On his way back to tell the others of his suspicions, Sicarius's route took him past the front of the bakery. The trays behind the large windows were empty, though etchings in the glass illustrated a wide variety of sweets available during the day. A sign beside the door, the writing visible thanks to the corner gas lamp, suggested patrons inquire about bulk orders as well as day-old pastries. Knowing of Amaranthe's fondness for such things, Sicarius wondered if she might have led the others inside to wait—and perhaps sample some of those "day-old" sweets? Sicarius slipped out his toolkit and went around to a side door where his back wouldn't be to the street as he worked on the lock. The others were still discussing the merits and demerits of a molasses factory as a hideout.

The streetlight's influence didn't reach the alley, so Sicarius had to find the door lock by feel. Scratches marred the metal around the hole, suggesting others had attempted to pick it before. Perhaps Amaranthe *had* gone inside. Or perhaps hungry university students had attempted infiltrations in the past.

Either way, it wouldn't take long to check. The lock proved simple by his standards, and he entered through the side door a couple of minutes later. He tested the air with his nose again, searching for the team members' familiar scents, but the heady smells of cinnamon, cloves, and maple overpowered lesser odors.

The light from the corner streetlamp provided enough illumination for Sicarius to glide through the interior, skirting counters and tables up front and cupboards and baking racks in the back, without making a sound. There wasn't anybody else in the building. A pointless diversion.

Sicarius headed for the door again, though a raised glass-covered tray next to a cash register caught his eyes. It contained a tidy arrangement of pastries, including a couple he thought might be of the "Emperor's Buns" variety. Though he could not condone the eating of sweets, he knew Amaranthe liked them. She'd risked exposing herself on that riverboat to acquire pastries from the kitchens—and gone to great lengths to try to hide those pastries from him. With good cause. Such food was hardly appropriate to one seeking to regain mental and physical stability. Sicarius took a step toward the door but paused again. Such treats *did* bring inexplicable pleasure to Amaranthe.

Hoping he wasn't setting a precedent, he selected a pair of tongs, opened the lid, chose a pastry that looked like it might survive time spent in a pocket, and deposited it in one of the paper bags next to the register. Though he could only guess at prices, he left a couple of ranmya coins on the counter.

Before he reached the door leading to the alley, a faint noise drifted to his ears. Footsteps. Not from inside, but from the sidewalk in front of the building. Suspecting a pair of enforcers on patrol, he crouched behind the counter. A single slender figure in black came into view. Wraps covered the person's hair and face, leaving only eyes visible, but he had the impression of a woman beneath the clothing. She looked both ways down the street, then pressed her face against the window, peering into the bakery.

Sicarius had long ago learned how many shadows it took

to hide him—and his short blond hair, which he usually left uncovered—so he didn't bother lowering his head. He knew she couldn't see him. After taking a long look, the woman left the window and headed for the alley where the side door was located.

She *would* see him if she strode through the entrance that was two feet from his side. He'd locked the door after entering—one didn't leave sign of trespass, even if one was still inside the building—but if this person had a key, she could be in momentarily.

He'd already committed the layout to memory, so he took a few steps into the half of the open room dedicated to baking and scaled a sturdy rack mounted to a wall. He climbed into the rafters, finding a spot between two parallel beams. Scratches sounded at the doorknob. Lock picks. Interesting. Feet and hands pressed against opposing beams, the shadows cloaking his body, Sicarius found a position that he could hold for hours—though he hoped she proved a more adept lock picker than that.

A few minutes passed with nothing except the soft scrapes of metal tools probing within the doorknob. He couldn't hear the rest of the team from inside, but while he waited motionless in the rafters, he thought of Amaranthe. It had to be an hour after midnight by now. It was time to find her.

He was of a mind to hop down, open the door, and confront—or perhaps stalk past and ignore—the other intruder. That was when the lock thunked. The door eased open, and the woman's head poked inside. Sicarius had left himself a clean line of sight to the entrance, and he could have hurled a throwing knife, even from the precarious position in the rafters, but the woman hadn't done anything to prove herself an enemy yet.

Once she believed the building was empty, she hustled inside, heading straight for an office in the rear. She didn't bump any of the racks or counters in the dark, so Sicarius surmised she'd been there before, perhaps at night. He remembered the scratches around the lock.

The office door was open. The woman stepped inside only

for a moment, then slipped out again, weaving back through the kitchen and toward the exit. Having no reason to suspect her errand had anything to do with him, Sicarius let her go. The lock thunked again, and she was gone.

After waiting a few moments, he dropped to the floor. On the chance it was relevant, he headed for the office to see what the woman had done. Though shuttered, the wall window let in an iota of light, enough for him to see an envelope on the desk. It might have been there all along, but the woman hadn't been inside long enough to do more than grab something or drop something off, and she hadn't left with anything noticeable.

After taking note of its exact position on the desk, so he could return it to the appropriate spot, Sicarius picked it up and explored it with his fingers. A wax seal secured the flap, so he couldn't break it without revealing that the contents had been read. He probed the pattern with his fingers. The elegant calligraphy style of the single letter gave him trouble at first, but he eventually identified it by touch. An F. His mind went straight to Forge. Was the owner of the bakery a member of the organization?

He thought about breaking the seal to see what was inside, but there wasn't enough light to read by anyway. He held the envelope to his nose. The scent of the wax, freshly pressed, was the most prominent odor, but something else underlay it, something very old and distantly familiar, a unique mix of staleness and antiseptic cleanliness and—

Sicarius lowered his hand, almost dropping the letter. It was the smell of those strange alien tunnels he'd been sent to almost twenty years prior. He'd been little more than a boy, but the week he'd spent up there in the Northern Frontier was indelibly imprinted on his mind. He doubted this letter had come from there, but that aircraft Amaranthe had been in had the same scent. The smell of it had been in her hair, along with the dirt and blood, when he'd retrieved her.

He eyed the letter. This meant the craft was no longer in the wetlands, hundreds of miles to the south. It was here.

Curi, Sicarius decided, wasn't going to get her mail. He tucked the envelope into his pocket. He'd wait to read it until he could share it with Amaranthe.

Reminded of her missing state, he jogged out of the bakery. Once outside again, with the door relocked behind him, he strode toward the others. It was time to check the *Gazette*.

A few steps before he reached the group, the sound of low voices drifted to his ears. Enforcers? Or the rest of the team? The voices were coming from the street on the other side of the bakery, a block away. Sicarius glided past Yara, Books, and the others without them noticing and eased around the corner.

Amaranthe led the approaching group; he'd recognize her gait at any distance. Thanks to the feminine curves that the military fatigues and weapon-laden belt didn't quite hide, there was a touch of hip sway to her determined stride. Further bundled in a parka with the fur-lined hood pulled around her face, she spoke with the man beside her as they walked. Even without the swordstick and the confident but lopsided gait, Sicarius would have known it to be Mancrest. He refused to acknowledge any residual jealousy that stirred at seeing them together; he'd made his interests clear to Amaranthe and offered himself as a mate. When she decided she wished such a thing—not, he reluctantly admitted, guaranteed to be soon, thanks to Pike—he trusted she'd choose him.

Maldynado strolled behind them, a pistol pointed at a pair of men in army fatigues. One of the prisoners walked with a pronounced limp and had his arm slung over the other.

After the group passed the streetlight, Sicarius stepped out of the shadows, falling into place at Amaranthe's side. Deret flinched, fumbling his grip on his swordstick. It clattered to the street, and the group paused while he muttering curses and retrieved it. Normally Sicarius thought little of it when his appearance startled people, other than that they should be more aware of their surroundings, but he admitted a modicum of satisfaction at the aristocrat's stumble.

Amaranthe merely arched an eyebrow at him, as if she

knew exactly what he was thinking. Perhaps she did. That often seemed to be the case.

The group had not entirely moved out of the streetlamp's influence, and Sicarius made a point of examining her soot-stained clothing, dirty hands, and the numerous strands of hair that had escaped her usually perfect bun. When compared to Mancrest, whose ripped garments were coated in blood as well as soot, she appeared only moderately disheveled, but the group had clearly seen action.

Sicarius heard the soft footsteps and rustling clothing of Books and the others a couple of seconds before Amaranthe's gaze shifted in that direction. At first, she simply nodded toward them as they approached, but her eyes widened when Akstyr came into the light, revealing the freshly hacked locks atop his head.

This time, the eyebrow she arched at Sicarius rose even higher. "Trouble?"

"No." The mild altercation at the Barracks hardly qualified as thus. Sicarius brushed some of the soot off the pale fur trim of her hood. "You?"

Amaranthe smiled. "No."

Books looked back and forth between them, shook his head, and walked back into the alley, muttering, "Crazy. Both of them."

Deeming the alley a more suitable place to catch up, Sicarius also strode in that direction.

"No, no," Maldynado said, "I can keep taking care of these blokes. No need for anyone to offer to help."

"Has he been complaining again?" Yara asked Amaranthe.

"No more than usual."

"*That* much?"

"I'm not as enamored with this group now that there are two women," Maldynado announced to no one in particular. "Too much girl talk."

"*Girl* talk?" Books asked. "You're the only one who blathers on about hair, hats, and fashion. The last chat I overheard between Amaranthe and Sergeant Yara involved plans for acquiring troops and munitions."

"I fail to see your point," Maldynado said blandly.

They'd reached the alley, and Amaranthe cleared her throat and waved toward the shadows, shadows she probably saw as potentially threatening, though, of course Sicarius had checked the entire area and continued to listen for the approach of others. "Perhaps," she said, "we can head to our new hideout for further discussion."

"I didn't know outlaws discussed hair, hats, and fashion in their hideouts," Mancrest said. "I'd always been under the impression that more nefarious topics were covered."

Sicarius didn't miss the smile Amaranthe gave him. It wasn't flirtatious, but it was a reminder that both she and Sespian appreciated humor, something that he had a poor grasp on.

"This group talks about a wide variety of subjects, from what I've seen," Sespian said from the wall he leaned against. He'd remained in the alley instead of going out with the group, and Mancrest noticed him for the first time.

"I... is that...?" Mancrest squinted. The darkness masked Sespian's features, and the two had probably never met in person. "Sire?"

"Just Sespian. If you haven't heard, I'm not—"

Amaranthe had taken a couple of nonchalant steps toward Sespian, and she interrupted his words with an elbow nudge to the ribs. Sicarius nodded at her. If Forge hadn't come forth about the paternity information yet, there was no reason for them to announce it of their own accord. They could worry about being honest with the populace after Sespian had regained the Barracks and the throne—if that was what he and Amaranthe wished to do. Sicarius would prefer to see another with the responsibility and Sespian free to live a life of his choosing.

Sespian got the message, for he switched to, "Let's just say someone else is sleeping in my bed at the moment."

"Though it seems not everybody is happy about that," Books said. "We stumbled across an assassin who was apparently in the Imperial Barracks to cut Ravido's throat."

"I hope you left him alone then," Amaranthe said.

The two prisoners were gawking at Sespian. Sicarius wondered why Amaranthe had brought them and was speaking so openly in front of them. Had Books truly overheard her discussing the acquisition of troops? Did she intend to start with this random pair? More likely, she'd had to choose between killing them or bringing them along to keep them from tattling about the team's presence in the city. Now they were stuck with them.

"Not exactly." Books looked at Sicarius.

Sespian, Basilard, Yara, and Mancrest all frowned at Sicarius. Amaranthe didn't frown, but there was a sad acceptance to her gaze. Sicarius was tempted to explain what had happened, letting her know he'd been forced to kill the other assassin, but she was right: this wasn't an appropriate place for storytelling. Besides, he refused to get into an argument, defending his actions, with this many people looking on.

"The molasses factory on Fourth and Waterfront, is that your suggested hideout?" Sicarius asked.

"Yes," Yara said.

"We should ascertain its acceptability and share information there instead of dawdling here." He strode off without waiting to see if anyone followed, in part to avoid seeing further disappointment from Amaranthe and, in larger and more practical part, he told himself, to arrive ahead of them and fully scout the proposed hideout for trouble.

CHAPTER 5

AMARANTHE WALKED PAST TWO HUGE CYLINDRICAL tanks, wondering if they still held liquid, and led the team toward the back door of Svargot's Molasses Distillery. Sicarius was presumably already there, scouting the place. On the walk over there, he'd returned to the group twice to warn them of enforcers along their route. Wanting to avoid more confrontations that night, she had veered out of the way to slip past the patrols unnoticed. She'd been walking alongside Sespian and their two prisoners, Corporal Evik, a rangy man with black hair that did its best to curl despite the short soldier's cut, and Private Rudev, the fellow who'd been pinned beneath the beam. With every limping step, he gritted his teeth. Most of them anyway; a couple of front ones were missing. He was the one who'd made the spanking comment in the basement, and Amaranthe had caught a few other sarcastic mutterings from him, so she wasn't surprised his face had met a few fists in its day. He'd grown respectful, or at least quiet, in Sespian's presence though, and she sensed there might be hope in winning them over.

Basilard trotted ahead of the group to open the back door while Yara dug in her rucksack to produce a lantern.

"Thank you," Amaranthe said.

Though she believed Sicarius was around, she stepped to the side as soon as she entered, putting her back to the wall, so she wouldn't be outlined in the doorway. She trusted that Yara and Basilard had scouted the building during the day, but the temperature had dropped below freezing, and they weren't far from a populous part of the city. Vagrants might also find the quarters amenable for the night. Or bounty hunters.

The air smelled of charred wood, a different scent from the pervasive coal smog that permeated the city in the winter. Someone had made a campfire recently.

The rest of the group entered, with Yara and Books carrying lanterns. Their lights did little to brighten the massive facility, and all except the area around the door remained in shadows. Pipes snaked up and through nearby walls, running out to the tanks in the yard. Catwalks crossed the open space overhead, and, in the distance, Amaranthe detected the dark outlines of furnaces and huge vats with equally huge ladles. The place reminded her of the smelter where she and Sicarius had first clashed with Forge.

Yara sniffed at the smoke smell. "There were a couple of homeless people camped in the back when we came in, but Basilard convinced them to leave."

"Basilard did?" Amaranthe cocked her head at him. Despite his briar patch of knife scars, which his jacket and gray wool cap didn't entirely hide, he was a peaceful warrior, rarely one to lose his temper or impose his will on strangers.

At her consideration, his expression turned wry. He lifted his fingers and explained, *I walked up to them and attempted to sign a greeting.*

Yara smirked. "They thought he was a crazy Kendorian shaman casting a spell."

Basilard sniffed. *Kendorian. Really.*

"That's what you get for looking so inimical, my friend." Maldynado thumped him on the back and considered what they could see of the facility. "So, the place is ours?"

"Let's keep to back areas and upper levels if possible." Amaranthe nodded to the catwalk. "In case any prospective buyers come to tour the facilities while we're..."

"Plotting crimes?" Deret suggested.

"Of course not," Amaranthe said. "We have a former emperor with us, and Books is penning some sort of constitution. That means we're no longer outlaws, we're revolutionaries."

Books snorted at this redefinition.

"Whatever we are, I'm tired." Maldynado yawned. "I think sleep is in order. Say, Yara, you didn't happen to find any *private* rooms while you were scouting around, did you?"

"There are three offices." There was nothing suggestive or inviting about Yara's tone, but Maldynado found the comment grin inspiring regardless. Amaranthe wondered if Yara would allow him to call her by first name someday.

"With doors that can be locked?" Maldynado asked.

"As if anyone wants to walk in on you two playing blanket hornpipe," Akstyr grumbled.

A yawn tugged at Amaranthe's lips, too, but she'd come to dread sleeping since escaping Pike's torture table. That first night after escaping, with thoughts of Sicarius's promises in her head, had been the only nightmare-free one. Ever since, she rarely went to bed before exhaustion forced it upon her. She was glad to have an excuse to keep people up with her this night. "I believe Lord Mancrest and I have some information to exchange before anybody plays with anything."

Deret rubbed his face, then grimaced at the soot on his fingers. "I wouldn't mind cleaning up first."

"We'll settle into the facilities then," Amaranthe said, "and throw dice for watch duties. Sire, do you mind staying for a moment? We should have a chat with our new friends."

Sespian blinked a couple of times at the Sire address—nobody had called him that since the news about his true father had come out—but he glanced at the two prisoners and nodded.

I will stay and guard them while you talk, Basilard signed, apparently deciding the soldiers, despite injuries, were dangerous enough to keep an eye on.

Amaranthe didn't think they'd threaten Sespian, but waved for Basilard to follow when she went in search of a place where they could all sit down. They found a cafeteria in the back and made use of a table. Basilard leaned against the wall beside the door, his meaty forearms folded over his chest.

"Private Rudev, Corporal Evik," Amaranthe said, meeting

their eyes in turn, "we didn't intend to take prisoners tonight, or cause so much trouble at the *Gazette* building—" Basilard gave her a curious look, no doubt wondering if he'd get the story, "—so please allow me to apologize for manhandling you and for your injuries."

"Whatever." Rudev shrugged. Ah, another Akstyr. Wonderful.

"Listen, lady," Evik said, "I don't know who you are, but..." He gave Sespian a long look. "If that's really the emperor, uhm, well we need to know what's going on. Where has he—where have you *been*, Sire?" This time the corporal's expression was plaintive, almost betrayed, when he regarded Sespian.

Sespian winced and pushed a hand through his soft brown hair, hair in need of a cutting. They'd have to spruce him up if they planned to start showing him off to potential troops.

"My departure from the city was not of my own doing." Sespian glanced at Amaranthe, asking perhaps how much he should share.

She spread her hand, palm up. Young though he may be, if he wanted the throne back, he'd have to take charge and make many of the decisions. She trusted him not to share anything too secret here.

Sespian sat at the table across from the two soldiers where he could look into their eyes—good choice, Amaranthe thought—then launched into an explanation of who Forge was and how long they'd been in the Imperial Barracks, trying to wrest control of the empire from him.

"We knew," Evik said, "or we'd heard... General Marblecrest has support of the business people in the city."

"Support?" Amaranthe snorted. "He's Forge's figurehead in this."

The soldiers watched Sespian for his reaction. Good. They seemed to believe they were dealing with the real emperor here. After hearing from her men how the enforcers had attacked the steamboat heading downriver, believing Sespian was a lookalike impostor, she'd feared they would have to deal with more of the same in Stumps.

Sespian nodded in response to their unspoken question and explained how Forge had gotten him out of the capital, forcing him to tour the forts of the empire on a three-month-long inspection, and then tried to kill him upon his return. He was honest in regard to the events and what he perceived as his failings—more so than Amaranthe would have been—though he did leave out all the details about the ancient alien aircraft, saying only that Forge commanded great resources and it would take a lot to bring them down.

"But I have a plan for that," Amaranthe said from the end of the table. During Sespian's speech, she'd found a rag and started dusting and scraping away leftovers crusted into the wood. "I believe my team can nullify the Forge threat."

Sespian didn't dispute her statement, but he did give her a did-you-forget-to-drop-that-memo-on-my-desk eyebrow arch when the soldiers weren't looking. She smiled back at him. She was still working out the details herself, but she'd had an idea sauntering around in the back of her head since meeting Retta, the woman who'd studied the ancient language and learned to pilot that gargantuan aircraft—and who'd weaseled Sicarius's secrets from Amaranthe's head. Through that mind link, Amaranthe had learned that Retta's sister was a Forge founder, one that few people had seen due to her years working for the organization in foreign lands. She intended to use that information.

"If we can handle Forge," Amaranthe said, "all the emperor will have to do is deal with Ravido Marblecrest and the other upstarts who have taken premature liberty in regard to the throne." She made a note to remind everyone else to start calling Sespian, "Sire" and "the emperor" again. If they meant to raise a force that could confront those of the other would-be successors, these two soldiers were going to have to be the first of many to join the team.

Private Rudev's nose scrunched up. "I don't understand. Can't you just go to... somebody, the newspapers or some public venue, and let everybody know that you're back?"

"Only a naive turnip would think it'd be that easy," Evik

said, giving his private a thump on the shoulder. "But, if people knew you were in the city, Sire, you'd be sure to get support. I know our sergeant is only backing General Marblecrest because his superiors told him to and because you're, er, everyone thought you were dead."

"I'd prefer to quietly gather forces before making my presence known," Sespian said. "People have tried to assassinate me before. If I go forward with nothing but this small group to protect me, I'd be an easy target."

Amaranthe barely kept herself from dropping the rag, propping a fist on her hip, and issuing an indignant response. She wouldn't be surprised if Sicarius was lurking nearby even now, ready to lift a dagger in defense of Sespian, should anyone raise a hand in his direction. But they could hardly utter the truth, that Forge would print the facts about Sespian's unfavorable heritage as soon as he stepped forward and tried to reclaim the throne.

Instead, she slid into the seat beside Sespian, so that she too could face the soldiers. "However unintentional it was, you two have been given the greatest opportunity of your lives."

"We have?" Rudev asked.

Evik didn't look so surprised. No, his narrowed eyes held wariness. He knew where this was going.

"We don't want to hold you prisoner here indefinitely." Amaranthe pointed to the private's white armband. "We want you to forget Ravido Marblecrest, be the first to join Emperor Sespian's forces, and stay with us of your own accord."

"We have to, don't we?" Rudev asked. "I mean, he's the rightful emperor."

Evik licked his lips. "It's true we owe our allegiance to the rightful emperor, but if we walk away from our unit... I mean, 'course we hope you win, Sire, but if you've only got ten people right now, and a bunch of them are women... we could get hanged for desertion if it ends up Marblecrest takes the throne. It's a real tough spot for us." Indeed, he glanced toward the door, as if he wanted nothing more than to flee back to his company and pretend he'd never seen Sespian. What he saw gave him a start, and he nearly fell out of his chair.

Sicarius leaned against the doorjamb, hands clasped behind his back, the closest to casual as he ever became, but the ever-present knife collection and the black attire always made him appear menacing even when relaxed, at least to those who didn't know him. And to most of those who did too. Amaranthe didn't know how long he'd been there, but Basilard didn't appear surprised by his presence. She'd been yawning every other second while Sespian spoke and hoped Sicarius hadn't seen. She didn't want him to know about the nightmares or her lack of sleep these past couple of weeks—he might see her as less than fit for leading the team, and, for what she planned, she needed everyone to trust her. More than ever.

His gaze was too knowing as it came to rest on her.

Seeking to distract him, she signed, *Making guests feel comfortable as always, I see.*

His fingers twitched. *Yes.*

Scrapes and clunks sounded as the soldiers attempted to arrange their chairs so they could still face Sespian but so they could also see Sicarius. Nobody wanted that many knives at his back.

I guess they recognize you, Amaranthe signed.

Sicarius didn't bother responding. The thought gave Amaranthe an idea though.

"We can understand your uncertainty," she said, addressing the soldiers again, "but, as you can see, we have powerful allies too."

"Didn't think the emperor would employ an assassin," Private Rudev muttered.

Sespian winced. Maybe that hadn't been the right tactic after all.

"If you two were the first to sign on to help the rightful emperor..." Amaranthe tried not to feel dishonest in calling Sespian that. After all, she'd yet to hear the news about the research excursion in the Barracks. "I'm certain he'd be grateful.

As I said before, you have an opportunity. If Marblecrest wins, and you do your jobs, then that's fine, no change to the status quo. But if Emperor Sespian comes out on top, and you were among the first to support him, well, I should think he'd remember your names."

"This is so," Sespian said.

"Were you to prove yourself exemplary soldiers and invaluable members of the team, I imagine there'd be promotions." Hadn't the promise of a promotion enticed Amaranthe to partake in Hollowcrest's questionable assassination mission once? Even if she hadn't gone through with it in the end, it'd been an appealing reward to have dangled before her eyes.

Indeed, Evik stroked his chin, suddenly thoughtful. "Like I could be a sergeant?"

"You'd have to prove yourself skilled and dedicated enough for the rank, but that doesn't sound unreasonable," Sespian said.

Amaranthe liked that he didn't over-promise. He could have offered warrior-caste status and who knew what else, but they didn't know yet if these two were worth such rewards. After all, one was injured—he wouldn't be marching on the Barracks any time soon—and even before then, they'd been easy enough for her and Maldynado to capture. They were young, though, and wore mechanic's patches, not the crossed swords of infantry.

"Could I be a sergeant, too?" Rudev asked.

"You've only been in the army six months, you dolt," Evik said. "You barely know which end of your sword goes into the other bloke."

"We'll see," Sespian said.

"Do we stay prisoners if we *don't* agree to sign on?" Evik asked.

"Unfortunately, since I'm not ready to announce my return," Sespian said, "you would be for a short time, yes. You're free to go after everyone knows I'm in the city though."

"As long as you're here," Amaranthe asked the soldiers, "why not agree to stay and try it out first? We're going to be bringing more men in, and you'll be able to see that we're contenders. You'd have seniority amongst any new recruits, not to mention you can pick your lodgings. There might still be private rooms available."

"Lodgings here?"

"Until we take over the Imperial Barracks," Amaranthe said.

"You don't lack for ambition, do you?" Sespian murmured.

"Probably easier to claim the throne if you're already there, sitting on it. It might be more feasible to get Fort Urgot now, though, if Ravido is in the Barracks." She'd need to send someone to scout Fort Urgot and see who was in charge over there. Though these two enlisted men were useful as an early test, it'd make far more sense to take Sespian out and try to win over brigade commanders.

"Sire, who *is* this woman?" Evik asked.

Private Rudev nodded vigorously, reminding Amaranthe that, though she'd talked her group of men into going along with her crazy plans, women simply weren't a part of the military or the political arena in Turgonia. These two probably hadn't taken orders from one since they were prepubescent boys running around their mothers' houses.

"Ah, she's my..." Sespian's fingers groped in the air as he sought an appropriate explanation.

Still leaning in the doorway, Sicarius lifted a single brow, also curious as to the status she'd be granted. Basilard cocked his head with interest. Amaranthe didn't think Sespian would be naive enough to give her military rank—none of the soldiers, these two included, would accept that—but she *would* need some kind of authority in the eyes of those who signed on with him. She was about to suggest "personal assistant" when Sespian spoke.

"High Minister in charge of Domestic and Foreign Relations," he said.

"Huh?" Rudev asked.

Evik cleaned out his ear with his finger. "Is that a...?"

"It's a Kyattese position," Sicarius said.

To anyone else his tone would have sounded deadpan, but

after a year around him, Amaranthe had no trouble picking up the underlying amusement—or was that bemusement, as in what *are* you doing, son? A hint of the feeling touched her as well. Sespian's choice sounded like a fancy title to mean someone who has to do a lot of paperwork.

"It's a diplomat," Sespian explained to the scrunched up faces in the room—and Amaranthe as well. She smoothed her own face, fearing her nose might have been scrunched as well. "With a little power. Once I have the throne back—" he was either warming to the idea or getting more into the role now, "—I'll need to make a few changes to the government to ensure there's less of a rift between the old aristocracy and the new, self-made entrepreneurial class."

"So, uh," Corporal Evik said, no interest in bureaucratic changes evident on his face, "what do we call her?"

"You can call her ma'am," Sespian said.

"Guess that means spanking is out," Rudev muttered.

Evik elbowed him. Sicarius's formerly bland gaze grew icy, though the two soldiers seemed too occupied by these new circumstances to remember he was there.

"I guess it makes sense for us to go along with you, Sire," Evik said.

Rudev shrugged and nodded. "Sure. Sire."

Not exactly a heartfelt head-pressed-to-the-floor-in-genuflection promise, but Amaranthe sensed the men were being truthful, not simply telling Sespian what he wanted to hear. Of course, she'd keep a guard on them for a while nonetheless.

"Excellent." Sespian stood and thumped his fist to his chest. "It's good to have you here."

The soldiers stood and returned the salute, bowing deeply as they did so.

Amaranthe took the moment to sign to Basilard, *Will you find them a place to sleep and assign one of the men to keep an eye on them?*

I can do it, Basilard signed.

I have another task in mind for you. Amaranthe smiled and

nodded toward Sicarius. *I'll explain shortly.* Noticing the private was watching her, she switched to speaking aloud. "Basilard there will help you two find racks."

As soon as Basilard and the soldiers left, Amaranthe lifted a hand, intending to wave Sicarius inside, but he was looking at something outside of the room, his face flat and unfriendly.

"Lord Mancrest must be coming," she murmured to Sespian.

A second later, Deret appeared in the doorway. For a moment, Sicarius looked like he wouldn't move, forcing Deret to find a way around him, but he stepped inside, taking up the spot Basilard had vacated.

"Good guess," Sespian said.

Amaranthe decided not to explain that it hadn't been a guess, that Sicarius reserved his ultra icy glare for those who threatened him, those who spoke disrespectfully about his son, and those who dared invite Amaranthe to picnic dinners in the park. "Lord Mancrest," she said, "please join us. Do you by chance have any information you'd like to share? Such as the recent goings on in the city? We've been out of town for a few weeks."

Pointedly putting his back to Sicarius, Deret slid into one of the seats opposite Amaranthe and Sespian. "So long as you're willing to share information with me as well. For instance, I'm aching to know where the emperor has been of late and why he's allowed himself to be reported dead. No disrespect intended, Sire."

"Perhaps I should have waited and told this story to everyone at once," Sespian said.

"I expect lots of people will be wondering," Amaranthe said, "and if we're planning to recruit piles of soldiers, you'll have to tell it numerous times. Maybe Books could put together an explanatory brochure to hand out."

Sespian snorted. "Now there's a thought."

"*Piles* of soldiers?" Deret asked. "Not only am I wondering where you're going to get piles of soldiers, but, as a former officer, I feel I should inform you that they prefer to be called squads, platoons, companies, or brigades. Piles sound rather less flattering."

"I'll keep that in mind," Amaranthe said. "Now, since we've done you a favor tonight by freeing you, won't you consider sharing your information first?"

"I've already told you why my father locked me in the basement. What else would you like to know?"

Sicarius eyed the spot between Deret's shoulder blades and signed to Amaranthe, *He was locked up? Why did you free him? You could have questioned him then. It's easy to get answers from men who are already in vulnerable positions.*

Amaranthe wasn't going to sign an explanation, not with Deret watching her, so she merely flicked her fingers in response. Besides, Sicarius couldn't seriously believe she would have interrogated a potential ally by force.

"In case you're curious," Deret added, glancing back at Sicarius, "I've decided to be pleased rather than affronted that your explosions resulted in the floor collapsing, destroying hundreds of thousands of ranmyas worth of machinery along with our archives. I wonder if the *Gazette* will even get out tomorrow. If nothing else, it should be some time before more late-night printings of propaganda pamphlets occur."

"Explosions?" Sicarius asked.

"They weren't mine, exactly." Amaranthe pointed a finger at Deret's chest. "He turned the ink jars into bombs and lit them after all."

"After *you* said you wanted explosives. Maldynado told me not to let others believe that I was to blame for all that."

Huh, she'd have to have words with Maldynado. He was supposed to be on her side. "I was merely looking for a way to free you that didn't involve bloodshed."

Deret's fingers drifted to a fresh scab on his temple.

Sicarius was watching Amaranthe, his expression hard to read. Sespian was shaking his head, as if he'd already come to expect such tactics from her. Or maybe he was thinking of revoking her new title.

"Let's get back to the important part." She twined her fingers together and rested them on the table. "When did you first see

Ms. Worgavic with your father?" In other words, how long had the Forge leaders been in town?

"Maybe five, six days ago. Before the old man locked me in the basement. Though I gathered he had known her for longer than that."

"Worgavic?" Sespian asked. "This is the woman who was behind Pike's... ministrations? How'd she get back to the city so much faster than us?"

How indeed? Amaranthe met Sicarius's eyes. "I guess that answers my question as to whether Retta is still alive."

Sicarius nodded once. "The aircraft is located nearby."

"The what?" Deret asked.

"Retta? Who's that?" Sespian asked.

"A Forge recruit who studied in Kyatt and learned how to operate the ancient technology."

"The what?" Deret repeated, then noticed Sespian nodding, and asked, "Am I the only one who doesn't know what we're talking about?"

"I'll explain later," Amaranthe said. "In the meantime, I don't suppose you've heard of any massive dome-shaped flying monstrosities drifting through the skies around the capital? About the size of a small city?"

"Uh. No."

"It can't be far away if Worgavic is here," Amaranthe said, "but they couldn't have landed it within fifty miles of the capital without someone seeing it." Unless Forge no longer cared if someone saw it. Dear ancestors, what if they planned to use it to ensure their man came out on top? Entire armies would seem puny next to all that power. They could take the city for their own—or raze it.

"The lake," Sicarius said. "It hasn't frozen over yet."

Amaranthe sank back in her chair. Yes, assuming that thing was waterproof—and there seemed to be few limits to what the technology could do—it could be hidden on the bottom of the lake.

"I did hear a couple of reports that the water level in the

lake mysteriously rose last week," Deret said. "By over a foot. It caused some damage at the marinas."

The *Behemoth* was big enough to displace a lot water, no doubt about that. "Maldynado won't be happy if we have to find dive suits again," Amaranthe said.

"I do not believe we would find gaining entrance possible that way," Sicarius said.

"Well, this doesn't change my plan much. It just means..." Amaranthe tapped a beat on the table with her fingers. "I'm more certain than ever I have to go."

"*Go?*" Sespian asked.

"Explain," Sicarius said, his tone making it clear it was a command, not a suggestion.

"Just a moment." Amaranthe help up a finger. "Deret, do you by chance know where Ms. Worgavic is staying?"

"At the yacht club, I think. Are you planning to visit?"

A waterfront locale. That made sense.

"Not until I've gone costume shopping," Amaranthe said, "and even then... I should seek to avoid Ms. Worgavic. She knows my face." And, as one of the original founders, she knew Retta's sister's face too.

"Costume shopping?" Sespian asked. "I find myself in rare synchronization with Sicarius—I too wish you to explain your plan."

"Why, I'm going to infiltrate Forge, of course." Amaranthe smiled and waited for a response. It seemed she hadn't lost her knack for stunning groups of men when announcing her schemes.

"How?" Sicarius said flatly.

"I have an image in my head of what Retta's sister, Suan looks like. She's been roaming the globe, managing Forge's foreign affairs for the last ten years, and few in the organization know her by face."

"How do you have an image of her if nobody else does?" Sespian asked.

"Her sister knows her well, and she's the one who gave me... I don't know what you'd call it. A vision? While she was rooting around in my head telepathically, I saw some of her memories." Amaranthe hitched a shoulder. "This Suan went to my school, so Ms. Worgavic will know what she looks like, and other founders, too, but if I could avoid them and talk to lesser ranking officers... All I need is an invitation into their hideout." No, a random hideout wouldn't do, not if that monster craft was here. "Into the *Behemoth*," she amended. "With a small team of elite men at my side, we can figure out a way to destroy the aircraft, thus stealing Forge's greatest weapon, one they haven't deployed yet in this bid for the throne, but one that I believe they will, if things don't go their way. If we *can't* figure out a way to destroy it, we can at least kidnap Retta and anyone else they've got who knows how to fly the thing. I doubt it's many people. That place was...." She shuddered at the memory of the labyrinthine tunnels and what she'd experienced within them. "Utterly alien."

"Who's on this small elite team of yours?" Sespian asked. "Him, I suppose—" he waved at Sicarius, "—but do I qualify?"

"You have work to do here, Sire." Did he actually want to go along? Surely, he must know he had a more important duty in the city. As far as that went.... "Sicarius isn't invited either." Though Sicarius's eyes bore into her with the intensity of artillery fire, Amaranthe continued to speak to Sespian. "You're going to need him at your back when you go recruiting. If you come up against men loyal to Ravido or the others seeking the throne, men who won't turn... It'll be dangerous for you."

"It'll be dangerous flinging oneself into the middle of the Forge hornets' nest too," Sicarius said.

"I don't disagree with that," Amaranthe said, "and I will take some of the men to back me up, Akstyr and Books probably." She expected Sespian to face armies and wanted to leave the best fighters to him. She suspected it'd be technical knowledge she'd need down there, anyway, not brute force. "Maybe Yara, too, if I can pry her away from Maldynado's..." The first two words that came to mind were on the lewd side, so she left them unspoken.

"Promises of amorous congress?" Sespian suggested.

Deret snorted.

"They're more than promises, I understand." Amaranthe waved a hand to dismiss the side trip. "In the end, Sespian, you're our priority here. I'm just the... ah, what was it again?"

"High Minister in charge of Domestic and Foreign Relations," Sespian said.

"Right. While I'd hesitate to call the person who holds such a lofty—and currently illusionary—office expendable, she's no emperor."

Sicarius's eyes hadn't softened since she'd started talking of going off on her own, and his jaw tightened at the word expendable. She'd have to talk to him alone later. She had no intention of sacrificing herself, but she knew he'd never forgive himself if he was off with her and Sespian got killed. He might not forgive *her* either. Even if he would, she didn't want to have that stain on her soul. There were already far too many deaths darkening it.

"About that..." Sespian eyed Mancrest. "Amaranthe, could we talk alone for a few minutes?"

Amaranthe could guess at the reason—they must not have found anything useful in Sicarius's files, and he was wondering how long he could pretend to be the rightful heir before the truth got out. "All right. Deret, do you know who's in charge of Fort Urgot, right now?"

"The fort commander is still General Ridgecrest, and I understand he refused to promise his men to General Marblecrest. That may be what prompted Ravido to take over the Barracks. I understand that all of his highest ranking men have been moved in there, as well as a good deal of ordnance."

"Excellent information." Amaranthe gripped Deret's forearm. Explosions notwithstanding, she'd known it would be worth detouring to the *Gazette* to find him. "Thank you."

Sicarius's gaze was following that grip, and Amaranthe released it.

"That's enough debriefing for now, I think," she said.

"Deret, why don't you get some rest, and we'll continue to trade information tomorrow?"

Deret met Sespian's eyes. "Is it just me, Sire, or did she get a lot more information out of our meeting than I did?"

"Well, he didn't make me his new High Minister of..." Cursed ancestors, she was tired. What was it again?

"Domestic and Foreign Relations," Sespian said drily.

"Yes." Amaranthe smiled. "He didn't make me that without reason."

Muttering to himself, Deret pushed away from the table, grabbed his swordstick, and headed for the door. He did his best to hide his limp as he passed Sicarius.

"What did you want to discuss, Sespian?"

"It's private." His gaze flicked toward Sicarius.

"Of course it is," she murmured. "Sicarius? Why don't you get some rest? When you're ready, I'd like you to take Basilard and scout Fort Urgot. Let's get some fresh intelligence on what's going on over there. In particular, I'd like to know if this General Ridgecrest might be amenable to giving his loyalty, and his troops, to someone else." She tilted her head toward Sespian.

"I have news too," Sicarius said.

"Er, what?"

Sicarius pushed away from the wall and stood, hands clasped behind his back again, his dark eyes pinning her, trying to relay some message it seemed.

"What is it?" Amaranthe asked.

"It is also private."

Amaranthe closed her eyes and exhaled slowly. Why couldn't these two simply share a drink, thump each other on the back a few times, and decide to stop having secrets from one another? What was it? Three hours past midnight? She wanted to curl up under the table and sleep—preferably without any pesky nightmares that jolted her awake ten minutes after she nodded off.

"Can it wait until later?" Amaranthe tilted her head toward

Sespian. If Sicarius said no, she'd go chat with him first, but did he truly want to preempt the son he was trying to win over?

"Yes." Sicarius lifted his chin and strode out of the room. It was doubtlessly only in her mind that she imagined a sullenness to that chin lift.

Amaranthe rubbed her face. "Go ahead, Sespian."

He walked around the table and shut the door before sitting down again, this time facing Amaranthe.

"As soon as Ravido knows I'm here and a threat, they'll print the details of my... flawed heritage in the newspaper."

Amaranthe grimaced, wanting to call Sicarius anything but flawed, but she knew what Sespian meant.

"An easy task," he continued, "since the Forge leaders are in bed—literally—with the owner of the Gazette."

"Just one leader, I'm guessing, unless Deret's father is as much of a bedroom warrior as Maldynado."

Sespian didn't smile at this attempted joke. "Nobody will follow me once they learn the truth, and those we've gathered in the meantime will feel betrayed."

"I assume this means you didn't find anything useful in Sicarius's files?"

Sespian studied his fingernails. "Books read the records more closely, and I'm sure he could give you further details, but Hollowcrest and my fath—Raumesys picked a common-born male because they weren't sure if they were going to let the parents live after the... experiment. They wouldn't consider killing a warrior-caste man, I suppose. They happened to find an extremely gifted athlete and warrior in a marine sergeant named Paloic who came to their attention because he served with a young Captain Starcrest. He was something of an unsung hero, standing in the shadow of his superior officer, but the way he fought and led his marines was impressive enough that Starcrest sent a letter to the Admiralty, suggesting him for officer training. Instead, he got turned into brood stock."

"Hm, not warrior-caste, but the sort of hero imperial citizens like. I don't suppose he's still alive somewhere?" Amaranthe imagined dragging Sicarius off on a hunt to find his parents when this was all over. *He* might not be enthused, but she'd be tickled to meet them.

"No," Sespian said with a grimness that implied there was more to the story. "He committed suicide shortly after his summons to the capital."

Definitely more to the story.

"Go on," Amaranthe said.

"It seems Hollowcrest had a notion of creating a mixed blood assassin, one who could pass as a Turgonian but one who could also blend in should he be sent on missions across borders."

Yes, that was something that Sicarius *had* done, with chilling success.

"They kidnapped a Kyattese ambassador in the capital, a bright woman with numerous degrees who'd come to work on establishing better trade and tariff policies with Turgonia."

"Oh?" Amaranthe asked, though she had an inkling of where the story was going. Maybe she didn't want the details.

"Paloic was instructed to inseminate her. Given the results, he must have done it, but one can surmise that it was a forced mating, something that, given his subsequent suicide, didn't sit well with him."

Amaranthe dropped her chin into her hand. Hollowcrest had certainly had a knack for taking upright young soldiers—and enforcers—and using their indoctrinated loyalty to the empire to force them to do as he wished.

"After a suitable male child was delivered, the mother was killed," Sespian said. "Not only is the story of how my grandfather raped my grandmother to produce my father not one I want to see in the newspapers, it's not going to improve my claim on the throne. If anything I'm in a worse spot now, because I'm one quarter Kyattese instead of being full-blooded Turgonian."

"That... shouldn't be that important. All Turgonians have mixed blood if you go back far enough, but, yes... I don't think that story would stir the hearts of the people."

"Sicarius's heritage should remain a secret, as far as I'm concerned."

"Well, let's not give up. If I can discombobulate Forge enough before you make your main push, maybe they'll be too distracted to get their article into the newspaper." Or maybe they could lock up the senior Lord Mancrest and put Deret back in charge of the *Gazette*. The backs of Amaranthe's eyes throbbed. Her project list was getting longer and longer.

"Maybe." Sespian didn't sound convinced. He stood up, putting a hand on her shoulder before leaving. "I do appreciate what you're trying to do for me. Thank you."

Amaranthe could only sigh as he headed for the door.

Sespian paused with his hand on the knob. "If it means anything to you, I saw some of the details of his childhood and how they raised him. I... can't imagine ever wanting to spend time with him, but I... get why he is what he is."

You've seen him fight for us, for *you*, Amaranthe wanted to say. Wasn't that enough? She clenched her teeth to keep from speaking aloud and tried to tell herself this represented progress. At least Sespian didn't hate him any more. But, bloody dead ancestors, she wanted so much more for them, for Sicarius.

Out in the factory, someone had covered all the windows and lit a few lanterns, so one might find one's way to a room—or the water closet—without falling off a catwalk and into a vat along the way. She offered a silent thank you to Books or whoever had taken the initiative.

A yawn so huge it evoked tears took over her mouth. She supposed she should find a place to sleep—were any of those offices left at this point?—but she remembered Sicarius's request for a private audience. She should see what he wanted. *He* would have found a private room or nook somewhere for himself. She wondered what he'd say if she asked to share it with him. Maybe having the indomitable Sicarius's arms around her would let her mind rest enough for a peaceful night of sleep. Of course, if past moments of closeness were anything to go by, she'd be too distracted to think about sleeping.

Clangs sounded on the nearest set of catwalk stairs. Akstyr shambled toward her, his hair in disarray, even more disarray than earlier in the night.

"We've got a problem," he announced.

"Oh?" Amaranthe asked.

"I better show you." With nothing more helpful than that, he climbed back up the stairs.

Amaranthe followed him, not simply up to a catwalk but up a ladder as well. It led to a trapdoor that opened onto the roof. She climbed out after him and pulled her jacket tighter. Cold wind gusted in from the lake, which was just visible from the three-story perch. She wondered if their guess was correct, and the *Behemoth* lay on the bottom. Given how many inimical things her team had found lurking underwater, she was beginning to think the capital should have been settled in the mountains, with nothing except a small stream nearby.

Clouds hid the stars and moon, and Amaranthe almost missed the dark figure stepping away from the chimney. She tensed, hand dropping to her waist, but she hadn't been carrying her weapons around the factory.

"Oh, good," came Yara's voice. "I was thinking about getting someone. I thought I heard... I'm not sure what it is. Something heavy pacing about down there."

"You're standing guard?" Amaranthe peered about. "Alone?"

"I drew the black tile, and, yes, alone because someone with a tendency to whine got cold when I pointed out that snuggling to share body warmth would be distracting and inappropriate during guard duty."

"Nobody wants to hear about that stuff," Akstyr said. "Over here, Am'ranthe. We might be able to see—"

A cringe-inspiring canine howl drifted out of the night, the eerie tone raising gooseflesh on Amaranthe's arms. It made her want to run inside and hide behind Sicarius.

Trying for a modicum of bravado, she finished Akstyr's sentence with, "—something we don't particularly want to see?"

"*What* was that?" Yara demanded.

Instead of saying what she wished, such as, "Why don't we go inside, lock the doors, and *not* find out?" Amaranthe walked toward the edge of the roof on the lake side of the building. She thought the noise had come from that direction, but the way the wail had coursed through the streets all around them made it hard to tell. Wondering if she should have gone back inside for weapons, she peered over the side. Somehow she doubted weapons would help. If Akstyr had been the one to come and get her, it had to be something—

Another yowl erupted from the shadows. Even expecting it this time, Amaranthe flinched. At least she drew a better bead on its location—perhaps a half a block away and in one of the alleys between the other buildings, but she still couldn't tell what had made the cry. No wild animal, she feared. Snow dusted the ground and, in the light of a streetlamp down the block, she spotted prints, large prints made by something heavy.

Akstyr shuffled up beside her. "I think it's another soul construct."

Amaranthe groaned, remembering the night she and Sicarius had spent hiding in a storage cubby in the icehouse. Even he'd feared to face that beast. In the end, they'd defeated it by tricking it into hurling itself into a pit and burying it beneath bricks and cement, topped off with a steam lorry.

"I don't suppose there are any handy pits in the factory," Amaranthe murmured.

"What do you mean?" Yara had joined them also.

"Nothing. Let's hope it's not looking for us." Amaranthe thought of the assassin Sicarius had mentioned. "Maybe it's here hunting Ravido." She supposed it was uncharitable to be cheered by that thought.

"Why would it be *here* then?" Akstyr waved toward the snow-dusted waterfront, which was, at this time of night, devoid of people. Except for her team.

"Let's just... make sure our guard stays near the door," Amaranthe said, "and keep everyone else inside until dawn."

"What about Sicarius and Basilard?" Yara asked.

Uneasiness settled into the pit of Amaranthe's stomach. "What about them?"

"They left a little while ago."

Amaranthe slumped. "I didn't mean for them to go scouting tonight. I told Sicarius to get some rest."

"I don't think Sicarius sleeps," Akstyr said. "He's not very human."

Amaranthe barely heard him. She was staring toward the black lake, a fingernail lifted to her teeth. Now she *knew* she wouldn't sleep that night.

CHAPTER 6

AN OTHERWORLDLY SOUL-PIERCING HOWL DRIFTED across the lake. Sicarius prodded Basilard's arm, then jogged into the trees lining the frost-slick jogging path. He stopped beneath a stout cedar with branches that didn't start until they were twenty feet up and put his back to the trunk. By unnoticed reflex, his dagger found its way into his hand. As he listened for further howls, he scanned the dark path in front of them, the patchy snow on the hills, and the mud-turned-to-ice training fields of Fort Urgot. A few early-rising soldiers on those fields stopped and turned toward the lake.

Basilard joined Sicarius in the shadow of the tree, a dagger in his hand as well. It was too dark to read hand signs, if he was making them, but the outline of the weapon stood out against the white ground beneath it.

"A soul construct." Sicarius couldn't be positive yet, but no natural animal had issued that keen. "If we cross its path, our weapons will be useless against it." His black dagger *might* hurt it, but he wouldn't bet on it.

Basilard pointed up the tree. *That* gesture Sicarius had no trouble seeing and interpreting in the darkness.

The howl came again, eerie and undulating as it wafted across the hills. It was vaguely wolf-like, but deeper, with a more resonating timbre, as if issued from a great barrel chest.

"Tree climbing may be premature," Sicarius said. "I'd guess its origins at two miles away. Do you concur?" He rarely asked anyone for second opinions, but Basilard was a skilled woodsman with hunting skills as great as his own, perhaps greater when it came to tracking prey outside of an urban environment.

Basilard nodded, but also pointed at the Stumps waterfront, its lights visible across the lake. Yes, the source of the howls was prowling about in the direction they were traveling.

"If it is a soul construct, it may return to whence it came at dawn," Sicarius said, though he and Basilard would cover those last two miles well before the winter sun crept over the horizon. They'd completed their scouting mission at Fort Urgot, so there was little reason to dawdle. "Come."

Basilard gripped his arm and held up a palm. He stepped out of the shadows and exaggerated his hand signs so Sicarius could read them.

If we have no way to fight it, we should make sure we won't cross its path. We could go back into the fields and circle into the city from the north. It would add a few miles, but— Basilard shrugged, *—we travel greater distances in training each day.*

Sicarius considered this piece of wisdom. Basilard was correct. A year ago, he would have nodded in agreement; no, he would have come to the same conclusion without being prompted. What had changed?

"Amaranthe and Sespian will want information about this new Nurian player." For the first time, Sicarius noticed that he wasn't calling her by last name any more when speaking to the others. He supposed there was little point in continuing to pretend he was keeping her at arm's distance. "Whoever sent the wizard hunter may control the soul construct as well."

A moment passed before Basilard signed, *You want us to risk our lives to get a look at it?*

"I'd prefer not to risk anything, but it might be possible to find its trail and follow it back to its master." It occurred to Sicarius that he was using Amaranthe-like logic on Basilard, albeit without the smile or any of the charisma. She truly was having an effect on him. Why should he talk Basilard into risking his life? He'd been useful enough for splitting up the large task of scouting the entire fort, but this was different. "I will go the direct way back to the factory." Sicarius pointed in the direction of the creature's howl. "Go the safer way if you wish."

He returned to the trail, taking up the soundless, tireless jog that he could maintain all night. A moment later, Basilard appeared at his side.

Huh. Sicarius truly hadn't meant to talk Basilard into joining him. It seemed strange that he would stay out of loyalty or some notion of comradeship.

As if guessing his thoughts, or feeling the need to justify his presence, Basilard signed, *Someone will need to tell Amaranthe what happened to you when your body is found mauled and half-eaten on the dock.*

"Of course," Sicarius said.

They continued their jog and, by unspoken agreement, stayed close to the trees. Images of past dealings with soul constructs came to Sicarius's mind, most recently the blocky panther-like one that had chased him all over Larocka Myll's mansion and the surrounding grounds. He'd barely stayed ahead of the preternatural predator, and if Amaranthe hadn't come up with that scheme to bury it in cement, he would have died that night. There had been another instance where he'd dealt with a Nurian soul construct. A giant viper-like creature ritually raised from the sacrifices of a dozen villagers had been sent to chase him, to avenge the death of a great chief Raumesys had ordered assassinated. He hadn't killed that soul construct, only evaded it long enough to catch a ship back to Turgonia. To this day, he wondered if it still prowled the Nurian continent, waiting for him should he ever step foot on the mainland again.

This one, Sicarius told himself, pushing aside the memories to focus on the present, probably wasn't here for him. His senses nudged him, and he slowed down. They were nearing the north end of the docks, not far from that yacht club where the Forge woman was supposed to be staying. Coincidence?

Before they reached the first private docks, a faint crunch reached his ears. This time he stopped, easing to the side of the path, hugging the shadows provided by a snow-dusted evergreen bush.

Basilard stepped off the trail with him. *You saw something.*

The sky had lightened enough in the east that Sicarius could make out the hand signs more easily. He touched his ear in response. It had been a few minutes since they'd heard a howl, but that crunch—

He lifted his head. There it was again.

He pointed.

A creature four or five times the size of a lion hound—it must weight over six hundred pounds—padded out of an alley. Though there were no nearby lamps to illuminate it, Sicarius made out massive muscular limbs and the huge barrel chest he'd imagined when he first heard the howl. Like the panther-like construct they'd faced the year before, it lacked fur, having instead the bare, lumpy features of something sculpted from clay, if by a fat-fingered artisan. The fangs ringing the inside of its stout maw were too long to allow its jaw to close fully, but it probably didn't matter; it could tear off a man's limbs—or rip his heart from his chest—without closing its mouth. It didn't need to eat meat, subsisting, if the stories were true, on less tangible fare. Human souls.

The creature was padding across the waterfront street, toward the lake, but it paused in the middle. Its broad head swung to the right, crimson eyes directed at Sicarius and Basilard. They'd gotten too close. So much for the tracking plan.

A hound-like nose lifted, and snuffling sounds whispered across the intervening quarter mile as it tested the air. A long, thin tail stuck out straight behind it like a flagpole.

Basilard touched Sicarius's arm and pointed at the closest trees. Sicarius had already taken note of the surrounding options, choosing a sturdy hemlock as a likely candidate. If that creature, with those thick muscled haunches, sprinted toward them, it'd cross the quarter mile in heartbeats, but he believed he could reach that tree and scale it to twenty feet in the same amount of time. What he didn't know was whether wood would be strong enough to deter the creature. It didn't *look* like something built for climbing, but it might have the power to tear a tree's roots from the ground.

The sniffs halted, the tail grew even more rigid, and its front paw lifted. Like a pointer targeting grouse in a thicket, the creature aimed at Sicarius.

"Go," he whispered.

Basilard was already in motion. So was the creature.

Sicarius sprinted for his chosen tree. Basilard had picked the same one. Fortunately, the trunk was wide enough for both of them to scramble up on opposite sides. In the quiet morning surroundings, the beast's exhales were audible, as was the churning of claws on snow as it covered the ground in twenty-foot bounds.

Halfway up to the first branch, Sicarius paused to hurl his throwing knife. The mundane blade would not hurt the otherworldly creation, but maybe it would pause.

Without waiting to see if the blade struck the construct's eye, Sicarius returned to climbing, his practiced fingers finding holds in the rough bark. He reached for the first branch, his hand brushing the cold wood, but the creature slammed into the tree. The force knocked his hand to the side—he was lucky it didn't knock him out of the hemlock entirely.

Wood snapped somewhere above, and green needles rained onto the creature. It merely backed up to charge again.

Sicarius picked out a second tree for a backup perch, though it was too far away to reach without returning to the ground first. Crossing the distance would take an eternity during which they'd be vulnerable to attack.

Basilard lowered his hand, offering help. Sicarius climbed into the lower branches without it, giving Basilard a flat look. He'd merely been considering other options, not pausing because he needed assistance.

Basilard looked… amused. At least until the creature slammed into the tree again. More needles fell to the snow below, and a groan emanated from the trunk. Their perch wouldn't survive the battering indefinitely. Sicarius decided he'd made a mistake in not taking Basilard's earlier advice. The admission would gain him little now.

Basilard wrapped an arm around the trunk, freeing his fingers so he could sign. *This isn't the first time I've been stuck in an awkward position with you, due to your interest in seeking information for Amaranthe.*

"It was your choice to come."

Sicarius considered his knives and the contents of his pockets, wondering if he had anything that could harm the soul construct, or at least deter it from further molesting their tree. His black dagger might scrape its flesh, but he doubted even a pierced eye would stop it. He considered the cloud-filled eastern horizon and thought about sawing through a few branches and dropping them on its head, if only to buy them time. The last soul construct had possessed a built-in sense to stay hidden, meaning it had disappeared at dawn or when great numbers of people were approaching. He hoped this one had a similar instinct, or they would be in trouble.

If I returned and you didn't, Amaranthe would have been upset with me.

Gnawing sounds arose from below—the canine construct had changed tactics. Instead of ramming the tree with its shoulder, it was tearing huge chunks from the base. The scent of freshly cut hemlock drifted up.

"She would have forgiven you," Sicarius said.

At least we have clothing this time.

"Nudity would have been impractical given the season," Sicarius said before realizing Basilard had been joking. Determined to improve his skills in that area, he added, "Also given our need for pockets." He pulled out a foldaway serrated knife from one of his own pockets.

Basilard grinned. If only Sicarius could get that response from Sespian.

Since the creature was staying in one place—though gnawing off shards of wood at an alarming rate—Sicarius decided to try the branch idea. He shifted positions so he could get to one over its head.

Basilard waved at the base of the tree—the trunk must have

been six or eight feet in diameter, but the construct had already gnawed a third of the way through. *Where to when it fells this tree?*

Still sawing, Sicarius considered the tall brick buildings across from the docks. If they had a suitable distraction, they might be able to reach the first of them, climb up, and hop from rooftop to rooftop. Otherwise, their best bet was to run up another tree.

Before the serrated blade cut all the way through, the weight of the branch took it down. It plummeted, and his aim proved true. The branch smashed into the top of the creature's head. It staggered back, startled for a moment, but it didn't let out a yelp or whine or anything to indicate it had been damaged. Instead it glared up at Sicarius, crimson eyes full of threat.

Basilard signed, *Is it my imagination or does it seem to be glaring at you specifically?*

The massive hound returned to tearing chunks out of the base of the tree.

Sicarius eyed the waterfront street. With the approach of dawn, men and women were about, heading for work. Several blocks away, a trolley pulled around a corner, its bell dinging as people hopped off.

"There *is* easier prey around if all it wants is a meal," Sicarius said.

A shudder coursed through the tree. Wood cracked, and creaks and snaps sounded from within the trunk. Sicarius braced himself, preparing to leap free.

Basilard signed, *The next closest tree?*

"You go that way. I'll run for the buildings."

Are you being noble and sacrificing yourself so I can get away, or do you believe it'll chase me, giving you time to reach the rooftops?

The trunk shuddered again. The soul construct backed up, preparing itself for one last ramming.

"Amaranthe would be displeased if I deliberately sacrificed you," Sicarius said, on the balls of his feet, ready to spring free.

*It's not escaping me that you didn't answer my question.
You've displeased Amaranthe before.*

Sicarius didn't answer. He doubted the soul construct would
follow Basilard; for whatever reason, it was intent on him.

The creature raced full speed at the tree and leaped, hurling
all of its weight at the trunk. A final snap announced the
hemlock's demise. The tree pitched several feet to the side, and
Sicarius was on the verge of leaping, but the trunk halted, not
quite ready to plummet all the way down.

"Wait," Sicarius said, for the construct had paused, an ear
cocked toward the lake.

Basilard had been in the middle of springing away, and he
tried to catch himself, lunging for a branch, but another shudder
coursed through the tree, and he missed the grasp. He dropped
to the ground not ten feet from the creature, his feet slipping on
the ice.

Sicarius jumped down, hurling the serrated knife to draw
the beast's attention, then raced toward the buildings. He knew
as he ran that he wouldn't have enough time—he'd gauged
the speed at which the construct covered ground and run the
calculations in his head—but maybe if he got close enough to
the dockworkers, it'd decide that it couldn't reveal itself, then
turn away.

When he didn't hear paws hammering the ground behind
him, Sicarius glanced back. The creature wasn't following him.
A feeling of concern—one he wouldn't have expected in regard
to anyone except Amaranthe or Sespian—came over him. He
slowed down, searching the snow for Basilard. He wasn't
anywhere to be seen. But there wasn't any blood nor other signs
of a fight either. Only the wool cap he'd been wearing lay in the
snow. Maybe he'd simply run up the next tree. The construct
remained in the same spot, its head cocked toward the lake.
Like a dog that had heard its owner's whistle to come home?

That big, blunt head rotated slowly, its red-eyed gaze
landing on Sicarius again. Maybe not a command to come after
all. Maybe one to kill. The creature turned so it faced him, and

Sicarius prepared to race away. He had a head start this time. He'd reach the buildings. He'd—

The creature sprang. Not, as he expected, toward him, but toward the lake. It ran to the shoreline, leaped into the air, and was paddling its legs before it hit the water.

Still crouching, ready to run, Sicarius watched for a long moment before he relaxed. Remembering the bounty on his head and that human dangers existed in the city as well, he took a quick survey of his surroundings—in the poor lighting, nobody seemed close enough to have seen the incident, though a couple of men on a dock were pointing in the direction of the destroyed tree. Sicarius jogged back to see if Basilard was indeed safe.

As Sicarius approached, Basilard shimmied down the trunk of the nearest standing tree. He appeared unharmed, though he offered a sheepish shrug and retrieved his cap. *That was lucky.*

"Indeed." Sicarius watched the creature as it continued to swim. It wasn't heading to the yacht club after all. Recalling the theory about the ancient aircraft hiding on the lake bottom, he wondered if the construct would disappear beneath the waves, swimming down to join an underwater master. But would Forge be working with Nurians? Their plans were to support Ravido, not assassinate him.

Where's it going?

The size of its head kept it in view for several moments, and Sicarius guessed it had swum a couple of miles before it finally faded from sight. In that time, it didn't dip below the surface. Perhaps it had nothing to do with the Forge people. He considered the direction it had been swimming. Southwest. He'd run around the entire lake enough times to know the geography by heart. "In the winter, there's an ice harvesting camp over there," he said, remembering a mission he and Amaranthe had shared there once. "It's too early in the season for that though." He nodded toward the few inches of frozen crust at the edge of the lake.

I know the settlement of which you speak, Basilard signed. *There are permanent log dwellings. Perhaps someone has moved in. Such as a Nurian wizard.*

Sicarius thought about jogging out to investigate, but it would take a few hours, roundtrip, and he still needed to talk to Amaranthe and share that letter with her. And the pastry. He admitted it irked him slightly that she'd been too busy to talk privately to him, but he wouldn't want to push Sespian aside for something that might be insignificant.

Mancrest may know if someone is over there, Basilard added.

Sicarius didn't let any reaction onto his face at the mention of the name, but Basilard gave him a sidelong look anyway.

He is a handsome man. Do you fear he will...

Basilard's hands faltered, hanging in midair as Sicarius gave him his most quelling glare. He did not wish to discuss the possibility of a relationship between Deret and Amaranthe. That would *not* happen.

Basilard diffidently finished with, *...print news of your relationship to Sespian if he learns the truth?*

"He is not the one most likely to do that," Sicarius said.

Have you seen Books's documents? What he proposes in this new government?

"No." Sicarius didn't know what Basilard's topic shift implied, but, after one last look toward the lake, he headed toward the city.

Basilard walked beside him. *Among other things, he suggests an elected official take the role of emperor. Rulers that go in and out of office every few years. Though the Turgonian empire has problems as it is, at least in the eyes of the rest of the world, I know that if Sespian returns as emperor, I have a chance at having an advocate for my people's concerns. An unknown has no reason to help me. I do not know if I'd wish to fight for this.*

So, Basilard was thinking of leaving the team if they couldn't get Sespian onto the throne. Why divulge this to him? Maybe he thought Sicarius had some insight into Sespian's thoughts. Or maybe Basilard simply thought they had bonded in the tree and should now be divulging secrets. Right.

"Understood," Sicarius said, because Basilard's continuing glances meant he expected an answer. The answer seemed to satisfy him.

* * *

Though daylight had come, it had not yet permeated the darkness in the factory. On his way in, Sicarius had spotted Maldynado taking a turn at watch on the rooftop, but everyone inside seemed to be sleeping. Basilard had gone straight to his bedroll. A few occupied blankets lay on the cement floor near a back wall covered with pipes. Stacks of books edged a couple of them—Books and Akstyr's areas. Sicarius recalled a mention of private offices upstairs, so he glided past the snorers without rousing anyone, heading for the nearest set of metal steps.

On the wall near the base of the staircase, a recently used mop hung from a peg, a bucket upturned to dry beneath it. He wished Amaranthe had been sleeping instead of cleaning, but the damp implements didn't surprise him.

The stairs led to a wide landing and catwalks allowing access to giant vats and two- and three-story-high machinery. On the left, there were three offices with windows and closed doors. In a less olfactory-dense environment, he might have been able to identify which room belonged to which team member before entering, but the pungent odor of syrupy molasses, mingled with hints of sugar beets and alcohol, dominated the air, even weeks after the factory had closed for work. Fortunately, the last office offered another clue: a clean window. Trusting it marked the spot Amaranthe had claimed, he strode toward it.

Sicarius entered soundlessly—if she'd managed to achieve sleep, he did not wish to disturb it. Her blanket was stretched on the floor behind an old metal desk. She wasn't lying on the blanket; rather she was hunched in a ball on one end, leaning against a rickety filing cabinet. Though her eyes were closed, distressed mumbles came from her lips. Her hands twitched, clasping and unclasping the blanket.

Sicarius closed the door and considered whether to wake her or simply leave the letter and the pastry on the desk. Had her sleep appeared restful, he would have done the latter, but perhaps she'd appreciate an escape from whatever nightmare haunted her.

On the journey to Stumps, after they'd been forced to abandon the steamboat, the team had camped in the woods each night, many people shivering under shared blankets to stave off the late autumn cold. Amaranthe had refused to sleep with the group, not wanting to disturb anyone with her rough nights—or perhaps not wanting anyone to know she *had* rough nights. As if that were possible with everyone living in close quarters— she and Yara had been roommates on that boat before it sank. Sicarius, of course, had known. Requiring little sleep himself, he was often up at night anyway. He'd thought of going to her, offering a shoulder to lean on or whatever else she might wish, but whenever she'd seen him watching her, she'd been quick to proclaim herself fine. Fit to fight. Perhaps he'd focused too much on training in the last year, for she seemed to think that was all he ever had on his mind. He'd done little to show her otherwise, he admitted. He didn't know how.

Sicarius set the items on the desk, intending to leave, but Amaranthe's twitches and mutters grew more agitated, more pronounced. She gasped, blurting a clear, "Don't! Please, not again. I—I can't tell. I won't."

He padded to her corner. He doubted it was in his capacity to help her, but he would try.

"Amaranthe," he murmured, touching her shoulder.

She cringed inward, tucking into a tighter ball, burying her head in her arms.

Though he knew she wasn't experiencing the here and now, and the gesture didn't signify fear of *him*, it stung anyway, having her shy away from him. Once it wouldn't have mattered. Once he'd expected that response from everyone and had not cared whether he received it or not.

Sicarius sat down beside her, his shoulder to her back. Face to her knees, she only muttered, "No, no," over and over.

"I suppose telling you it's dawn and time to train would only evoke a similar response," he said.

He didn't expect the comment to pierce her dreams and was mulling over ways to wake her without distressing her further, but her head jerked up, eyelids springing open, her hand clutching her chest. Sitting with his arm against her back, he could feel her heart slamming against her ribcage.

"Train?" Amaranthe blinked, confusion crinkling her brow. Her eyes focused on him, and she gulped, lowering her hand.

"Not now," Sicarius said. "Everyone is sleeping after the late night. You should go back to sleep too. A more restful version."

Amaranthe winced. "Sorry, did you hear me?" She glanced at the door, as if fearing her outcries had been audible throughout the factory.

"Not until I came in."

"Oh." She drew away from his arm, eyeing his position on the edge of her blankets.

There was a time, Sicarius thought, sighing inwardly, when she would have been pleased to see him sitting so close with blankets spread out beneath them. She would have made self-deprecating jokes, or perhaps teased him playfully, all the while looking up at with him with hopeful eyes, wondering if perhaps he'd be interested in doing more than simply talking.

It was your choice never to act on those opportunities, Sicarius reminded himself. Now, she merely looked uncertain. And self-conscious.

Amaranthe scraped her hair away from her face, pushing locks behind her ears. The windows weren't the only things she'd washed before bed—her face and hands were clean of the grime from the *Gazette* explosions. The scent of her almond bark and cherry blossom shampoo teased his nostrils. After the restless sleep, her garments were in disarray. Though few would categorize long underwear as sexy, his gaze snagged on the skin exposed between waistband and shirt. That was clean, too—he removed his gaze and kept his attention from deeper contemplations of that skin and surrounding... skin.

"You had news, right?" Amaranthe rubbed her eyes.

"Yes."

She waited expectantly.

"I will deliver it in three hours."

"What's happening in three hours?" Amaranthe asked.

"I will deliver my news."

She snorted. "I mean, what's happening now and for the next three hours that will delay this delivery?"

"You're going back to sleep."

"Erg, I think I've had enough of that."

"You require more than two hours to function optimally as team leader." Yes, he told himself, keep saying things like that. That's what'll teach her to relax in your presence. "I will stand guard to ensure your sleep is restful." There, maybe that was a little better?

"Oh, really?"

Good. She looked intrigued, despite his tactless way of letting her know he was concerned for her and wished her to find peaceful rest. There'd been so few times in his life when he'd attempted to appear inviting that he didn't know how to manage it, but he lifted an arm, hoping it would be enough.

"Hm." Amaranthe rearranged the blankets, shifted her body so they faced the same direction, and slid in under his arm. After a tentative glance at his face, she slipped her arms around his torso. Mostly. The dagger collection gave her trouble as she tried to avoid being poked by hilts. "Do you always climb into women's beds with all your weapons bristling?"

A few Maldynado-esque comments floated into his mind, but Sicarius squashed them. He'd been spending far too much time in close proximity to that man this last year. He thought about explaining the soul construct and his trip to Fort Urgot, but he wanted her to sleep. Any talk of work would convince her it was time to start the day. "It would be amateurish of me to stand guard without them."

"Of course. What was I thinking? I'll just... make do."

He took satisfaction in the upturning of her lips as she wriggled closer and let her eyelids droop closed. For once, it seemed she was too tired to worry about appearances. Or perhaps, all along, he should have been offering to stand guard from her bedside instead of outside her door.

Sicarius closed his own eyes, though he pursued meditation instead of sleep, the quiet, thought-free state of mind he'd learned to achieve from the same Nurian tutor who'd taught him defenses against the mental sciences. It allowed the body to regenerate as efficiently as a night's sleep and in less time. During the meditation, he could also focus on healing wounds more quickly than nature would have accomplished on its own. It was the calming effect it brought to the mind that he appreciated most. The skill had allowed him to deal with his own nightmares in the aftermath of Pike's... lessons.

Sicarius's eyes popped open. Perhaps he could teach the practice to Amaranthe. With the way her mind raced about at all times, scheming up some plot even when she was in the midst of a training session, she would find it difficult to free it of thoughts and find tranquility, but if she could master even a modicum of the ability to meditate, she might be able to push the nightmares from her mind.

Later, he decided. She had nodded off, her head on his chest, her breathing gentle and even. He closed his eyes again, his mind empty, his senses focused inward, though he remained distantly aware of his surroundings. Something metal batted against the roof as the wind picked up. Someone walked across the catwalk, heading to the water closet. Men snored on the floor downstairs. Maldynado returned from his watch shift and, a short time later, engaged in coitus with Yara, an activity that continued for a tediously long time and made it difficult for Sicarius to remain in a meditative state. He was relieved when, near the end of the three hours, Amaranthe roused of her own accord. It was time to get the team to work—and share his news.

She smiled up at him, not yet lifting her head from his chest. "Thank you. You should come stand guard for me more often."

"If you found it valuable," Sicarius said, his chin drooped, his eyes half-lidded as he gazed at her. Strange how much it pleased him that she'd slept quietly in his arms. He'd distanced himself from so much of the human experience over the years that he hadn't realized he *could* be pleased by anything. He'd been denied pleasures in his youth and, after that, it'd seemed practical to abstain—a man with so many hunting him shouldn't allow himself any predictable vices.

Thumps and groans reached his ears from the office next door—Maldynado and Yara, embarrassing rabbits all over the empire with their superior breeding instincts. Amaranthe blushed, apparently having no trouble identifying what the sounds indicated. Not for the first time that morning, Sicarius thought of the kiss they'd stolen in the smokestack of that steamboat. It'd been unprofessional, ill timed, and inappropriate. He wanted to do it again.

Amaranthe cleared her throat and sat up, drawing away from him. "I believe you mentioned news."

"Yes." Sicarius rose and plucked her gifts off the desk. He handed her the bag and held up the envelope. "This was delivered to a desk in a back office at Curi's Bakery last night while I was waiting for your party to rendezvous with ours."

Amaranthe started to reach for the letter, but something about the rumpled bag distracted her, and she opened it first. When she peered inside, her mouth fell open. "For *me*? You stole a pastry for *me*?"

"I *paid* for a pastry for you." Albeit he didn't know if he'd paid the right amount. He held the envelope out, offering her the chance to break the seal.

Amaranthe was busy staring into the bag. Her mouth continued to hang open, though it stretched into a wide grin. "*Thank* you." She flung her arms around him, this time not worrying about whether knife hilts poked her in the ribs, then she pulled the pastry out of its bag.

Sicarius was still holding out the envelope, now somewhat crinkled after her embrace. Since she seemed unfathomably distracted, he slid out a dagger and broke the seal himself.

Ms. W. –

As requested, I am securing passage and will be returning

to the empire within the next two weeks. While my sister is more than apt in handling the ancient language, I have been in contact with the Kendorians and the Nurians and can advise you more closely in person. The Kendorians are open to working with our bankers and your imperial figurehead, but the Nurians are enacting some plan of their own. I've traveled extensively in their country and may be able to negotiate with whatever spy they've sent to observe the action. It will be good to see you and the others again and finally bring our plans to fruition. Where shall we meet?

~ S.

Sicarius would have expected Amaranthe to be at his shoulder, reading as he read, but she was near the window, holding the pastry to the light and squinting suspiciously at it.

"Is there a problem?" he asked.

"No. I just thought there might be fish eyes or cut up bits of liver hiding under the frosting. You're always trying to feed me healthy food. And you always have derogatory comments for anything sweet. Even fruit, which I'm sure has never looked at you in a threatening manner." She lowered the pastry and studied his face. "This is... I want to adore you, but I fear a trap. Will I have to run twenty miles after eating this?"

Earlier, Sicarius had been dwelling upon how much she thought about everything. Clearly receiving a treat was no exception. He couldn't blame her—he'd never brought her such a thing before. "If you fear it's a trap, you needn't eat it. I would approve of such a refusal, as it would indicate you're finally coming to accept that superior foods must be consumed to ensure superior physical performance."

Amusement touched Sicarius as Amaranthe's slit-eyed gaze went back and forth from him to the pastry. Finally she took a chomp, and, after a few test chews, grinned broadly with frosting smeared across her nose.

"Oh, fantastic," she purred. "The pastries on the steamboat were tasty, but nothing is as perfect as a Curi's bun."

"I trust your taste buds detected no hidden liver morsels." Sicarius joined her by the window, intending to show her the letter, though his gaze did snag on that smear of frosting. She must not know it was there. Perhaps he should clean it off... somehow.

The catwalk creaked beyond the window, and a few seconds later, Akstyr shambled into view, heading for the water closet with his book stuffed under one arm. Sicarius straightened, adopting a professional distance between himself and Amaranthe, and held out the letter for her perusal.

"No liver." Her cheeks were flushed, and she was quick to lower her face to read the note—perhaps she too had been thinking about frosting cleaning?

Often, she'd teased him about dragging him off somewhere private once they'd accomplished all of their goals. Since reuniting with Sespian and retrieving her from the alien vessel, he'd been experiencing similar thoughts. Often.

"You found this on Curi's desk?" Amaranthe asked, anguish in her tone. She stared at the half-eaten pastry, an expression of betrayal on her face. "She's part of *Forge*? She's... she's... seventy years old and matronly and plump and *nice*. She *can't* be colluding with the villains."

Sicarius refrained from mentioning that many people in the capital would consider Amaranthe and her men villains, and that few *wouldn't* consider him one. "She may simply be allowing them to use her premises for message delivery purposes."

"That's still colluding."

"They could be blackmailing her."

"Oh." Amaranthe brightened. "True. I'll reserve judgment of the baker until I know more." She took another chomp out of her pastry. "Thank you for bringing the letter. If they're expecting Suan to show up, that'll be perfect for my plan. Hm, mostly. It does mean I'll need to get started more quickly than I'd had in mind."

"This is your Forge infiltration plan?" Sicarius did not approve of her new scheme, since it thrust her into danger all over again. A part of him wished he hadn't shown Amaranthe the letter.

"Exactly so. Would you mind using your artistic skills to make a copy of this letter? Only change the first line to say 'S' will be arriving in the next day or two. This is fantastic luck. Or is it too much luck? Is there any way they could have anticipated we'd visit Curi's and see the letter being delivered? No, that doesn't seem likely. Does it?"

"It is likely a chance occurrence," Sicarius agreed.

"Great. I'll grab Maldynado and go costume shopping today. Our world-traversing Forge founder is a blonde." She touched her brown locks, which she hadn't tied up in her customary bun yet this morning. "Maldynado probably knows how to dye hair nicely. Or he'll know someone who does."

"You should reconsider taking me with you."

"To shop for clothes?" Amaranthe touched his sleeve. "Did you want to try on some outfits too? Something more daring and vivacious than your customary black? Gray perhaps?"

Sicarius let his eyes close to slits. He knew when she was feigning misunderstanding and attempting to redirect someone's displeasure elsewhere. It was not an uncommon tactic for her. "You'll need someone good at your back if you're trapped on the bottom of the lake in that craft and your true identity is discovered." He thought it unlikely that Amaranthe could pass for long, if at all, as a woman who shared a long history with her colleagues, however little visual contact they'd had. "I could also... wear a costume."

"That'd be interesting to see, but I could be stuck down there for days. Do you want to leave Sespian for that long? He's going to need someone good at his back as much as I do, if not more."

Sicarius was going to retort that Sespian would be fine for a few days, but an image of the soul construct flashed into his mind.

"I know." Amaranthe gripped her arm. "You wish you could be in both places at once. And I wish you could be with me."

Sincerity warmed her eyes as she spoke. "But your place is with Sespian."

Sicarius exhaled slowly. He wouldn't object to standing at Sespian's back if she weren't determined to fling herself into a smoldering volcano. "You should not go. Not into their lair. We could find Worgavic and kidnap her as an alternative. Question her or hold her hostage. Get the information we need that way."

"But it's not just information. It's the *Behemoth*. You told me what it did to that swamp, to your dirigible. Am I wrong in believing it's very likely the most powerful weapon in the world?"

"No," he admitted.

"It has to be nullified somehow. Otherwise... as long as they have it, they could kill us all. If things don't go as planned for them, maybe they can simply wipe out the entire city and start from scratch."

Sicarius understood the power of the technology perfectly. It was why Starcrest had worked against him all those years ago, to keep Emperor Raumesys from acquiring it; the admiral had known it'd give one man the tools needed to rule the world. What was harder to understand was why it had to be *their* fight. Sespian wasn't the rightful emperor, so what obligation did he have to the people now? And Amaranthe. Would this clear her name? Probably not. It was possible nothing would at this point. They ought to walk away from Stumps, all of them, and leave this battle for others. He was on the verge of voicing his thoughts when Amaranthe spoke again.

She gripped his arm and gazed into his eyes, her own eyes liquid brown and imploring. "Someone has to stop them, Sicarius, or they'll own the world before long, a world that we might not like living in very much, one that our *children* won't like living in."

It was as if she'd thrown a wrench into the workings of his mind. His mental machinery ground to a halt, locking onto that single word. Children. She'd never mentioned wanting any. Was she now implying she did? With him? Or had it been figurative?

Now who's thinking too much, he asked himself with a silent snort.

"Nobody else knows that thing is out there in the lake," Amaranthe went on. "Nobody else is in a position to stop them."

But was she? Amaranthe was capable of much, he knew that, but this sounded like *too* much. Yet he wasn't going to be able to talk her out of it; he could see that.

"At least take Maldynado and Basilard, not Books and Akstyr," Sicarius said. "You'll need fighters at your back."

"I... think I'll need brains at my back to navigate around in there. It's a confusing warren. Even the doors don't look like doors. I'm hoping one of them can figure things out."

"Take all four of them then."

"I'll be lucky if I can get *myself* invited down," Amaranthe pointed out. "I'm sure Suan doesn't travel around with an army of mercenaries."

The doorknob rattled.

She let her hand fall away from Sicarius's arm. Akstyr poked his head inside, his lopsided hair sticking out all over like a topiary shrub abandoned in the aftermath of a war.

Amaranthe's fingers twitched and pointed. "Do you want me to... cut that today? Trim it up so it's even?"

"I guess."

"That," Amaranthe said, eyeing Sicarius, "is the response you're supposed to give when a woman offers to cut your hair. An enthusiastic 'yes' is also acceptable."

Sicarius did not respond, though he knew what she referred to—she'd been offering to cut *his* hair all year, as if such things mattered beyond social conventions. All he required was for it to be short so it couldn't be grabbed in a fight and didn't fall into his eyes when he worked.

"Is there any food in this place?" Akstyr asked.

"No," Amaranthe said, "but I'll take Maldynado shopping later."

"I thought he might have gone this morning. I'm starving. And tired. Some idiot has been up here moving furniture around

for hours. Who could sleep through that?" Akstyr glowered around the room, as if Amaranthe might have been responsible for the disturbance.

"Moving... furniture," she said. "I believe that was Maldynado. Perhaps you can ask him to do it more quietly next time."

"He's going to do it *again*?"

Sicarius listened to the exchange impassively, though Amaranthe seemed amused. Given Akstyr's forays into the Pirates' Plunder and other brothels, he was more naive than expected in this regard.

"Oh, I think that's a given." Amaranthe pointed toward the roof. "Was there any sign of the—"

"Nah, I checked right off," Akstyr said. "The soul construct left before dawn."

"Good," Amaranthe said.

"You knew about the soul construct?" Sicarius asked her.

"Last night after you left, it visited our factory, doing a good long stalking-about."

The statement chilled him. Sicarius remembered the creature's focus on him that morning, but what if the Nurians had found out Sespian was alive, and they'd sent it for *him*? They'd have no more use for Sespian than they would for Ravido Marblecrest, not if they had some other candidate in mind for the throne. It might have been Sespian and Sicarius's shared blood that confused the soul construct, making it veer from its path to chase Sicarius up a tree. Had it mistaken him for Sespian? If it *was* after him...

Amaranthe had been right; Sicarius couldn't leave Sespian, not now.

CHAPTER 7

A SQUAD OF SOLDIERS MARCHED DOWN THE STREET, white armbands taut about their biceps, their sleek repeating rifles held diagonally in front of them. Amaranthe eased deeper between two clothes racks, ensuring the hat stand blocked her from the view of anyone looking in the window. Though she wore a costume—and, yes, she found it ironic that she was wearing a costume to go costume shopping—she didn't trust the cap, ruffle-laden dress, and artistically arranged ringlets of hair to withstand close scrutiny. A lamppost at the entrance to Millinery Square had shown off her and Sicarius's wanted posters.

"Oh, there you are, Ruffles," Maldynado drawled, strolling into view.

He'd been calling her that all afternoon, since she found and donned the frumpy dress, one of a handful of garments in the boss's closet in the molasses factory. She hadn't thought anyone over twelve wore such clothing and wondered if the manager's fashion taste had anything to do with the business's failure to thrive. Maldynado had made matters worse—he'd called it "flowing with the natural ripples of the ensemble"—by curling her hair into tight ringlets that bounced around her face like trampoline springs.

"Here's the first and most important item." Maldynado held up some sort of garment comprised mostly of string. "A foundation piece, if you will."

"A foundation for *what*?"

A broad smirk stretched across his face, and Amaranthe

started to get the idea. She imagined Maldynado making bets with the men as to whether he could convince her to don such an item or not.

"Underwear?" she asked. "It had better be for you."

Maldynado extended his arm, the strings dangling on his fingers. "Would you like to try it on?"

Amaranthe blushed at the idea of wearing nothing except that beneath her clothing. Especially during winter. It wasn't practical at all. "Maldynado, nobody's going to be checking out my underwear. I need to look like a world-traveling woman from a well-to-do family, preferably with lots of exotic clothing to suggest recent trips to Kendor, Nuria, and the like. What's underneath that clothing is irrelevant."

"Of course it's not." Maldynado twirled the skimpy garment around his index finger. "What if you find out this woman you're impersonating has a boyfriend? Or a girlfriend? And you're expected to get amorous?"

"That's not going to happen. She's been out of the empire for ten years."

"I've reconnected with all sorts of former bedmates after years apart," Maldynado said.

Yara stepped out of a nearby aisle. "Is that a fact?"

After proclaiming all the garments in the office closet too small, Yara wore her usual trousers and sweater, her only concession to a costume being a hat with a broad brim that hid her face. Her homespun clothing had caused a few eyebrows to rise as the three of them walked through the upscale neighborhood—her response had been to either ignore or glower at the pretentious eyebrow-raiser.

The underwear stopped twirling and wilted limply about Maldynado's finger. He cleared his throat, but by the time he'd turned to face Yara, he'd reclaimed a calm smirk. "Of course, but I have no need to seek out such personages any longer. I've found true love." He beamed a smile at her.

Yara scowled and stabbed a finger at the string undergarment. "You expect her to wear that? It's ludicrous."

"I was suggesting *he* wear it," Amaranthe said.

"That'd be even *more* ludicrous," Yara said.

"Oh, I don't know." Maldynado stretched the strings and considered the tiny triangle of emerald green material in the center. "It'd be too small to hold anything of mine in, but it's a lovely hue. Perhaps this could lie beside my... appurtenances. Like a flag meant to highlight a particularly fine specimen in a garden."

Amaranthe shook her head and met Yara's eyes, half-expecting her to slap him on the back of the head. "When he started associating with you, I thought he might be encouraged to say less... well, *less*."

"You mean you thought I'd beat such nonsense out of him? I'm working on it." Yara waved a fist under Maldynado's nose.

He winked. "Alas, I'm an obstreperous student."

"Just find her some suitable clothing, so we can get out of here, you clod." Yara thrust a hand toward the window where another squad of men was marching past. "There are soldiers crawling all over this neighborhood."

"Yes, you'd think Millinery Square was on the way to a particularly boisterous drinking house," Maldynado said.

"We're less than a mile from the Imperial Barracks." Amaranthe squeezed a little deeper between the clothing racks. "I'm sure Ravido is keeping these neighborhoods heavily patrolled so he'll get an early warning if anyone marches on his new home."

"A good reason to finish up and get out of here." Yara handed Amaranthe two dark brown glass bottles. "Here's the bleach and the dye."

"Let me see those." Maldynado intercepted the exchange and held the bottles to the light, examining the labels. "You don't want the cheap stuff. Your hair will turn orange. Or white. Then you'll look old."

Amaranthe stuck a fist on her hip. "I will not look *old*."

"Add it to those bags under your eyes, and you will. Don't you sleep?"

Yara smacked him.

"More than you," Amaranthe blurted. It was the first thing that came to mind. Cursed ancestors, could everybody tell she wasn't sleeping? "Akstyr was complaining this morning about all the furniture moving that was going on in the room you two claimed for your own." When the truth struck too close to the target, and a suitable comeback wasn't available, divert the topic of conversation.

"Furniture moving?" Maldynado blinked a few times before a fresh smile sprawled across his face. "Ah, yes. *Furniture* moving." He winked at Yara, eliciting a deep blush from her. "It is invigorating. And you sleep like a turtle basking on a log afterward. You should try it, boss. For health purposes." He tapped his jaw thoughtfully. "Though I'd recommend you try it with somebody *fun*. For maximum effect."

Not Sicarius, Amaranthe assumed that meant. This new shift in conversation wasn't any better than the last. "Still lobbying for Mancrest?" she asked.

"Nah, he's a grump of late too. Maybe I can find you a sexy young wrestler at the gymnasium."

"Let's... focus on acquiring this costume and getting out of here. Finishing this mission will be the best thing for my health." Amaranthe grabbed the dubious underwear from his grip. If it would move them onto the next round of this dueling bout, she'd take it.

Yara's mouth drooped open at the garment exchange, but her cheeks were still red, and she didn't comment.

"Oh, sure," Maldynado said. "Let's hurry up and get you onto a ship full of old matrons. Just where a young woman in need of a furniture mover should go." He lifted his eyes skyward and strolled into the bowels of the shop.

"Don't stop yourself from punching him on my behalf," Amaranthe told Yara. "He could use a little—" A flash of light outside of the window caught her eye.

Another squad of soldiers was marching past, identical to the others except for the leader. The man walking at the head

of the column had salt-and-pepper hair beneath his cap and a row of medals hanging on his jacket. The sunlight glinting off them—or perhaps off the large four-sword brass rank pins on his lapels—must have been what had drawn her eye.

"A general," Yara whispered, slipping behind the garment rack with Amaranthe.

"Not just *a* general." Amaranthe hadn't seen Ravido in person before, but he possessed Maldynado's chiseled jaw and high cheekbones. If all the Marblecrests looked like that, she'd never misidentify one.

"Let's hide," Yara said at the same time as Amaranthe said, "Let's see where he's going."

Yara snorted. As soon as the last soldier's back was to the clothier, Amaranthe slipped out from between the racks and jogged to the window. She leaned close to the glass, only to jerk her head back. The entire squad of soldiers had halted at the shop next door.

A commanding bark of, "At ease," passed through the window. The soldiers broke ranks, no longer all facing the same direction. More than a few eyed the surrounding stores.

Amaranthe scurried sideways, ducking behind a thick, velvety curtain. She peeled back an inch so she could see out the window without—she hoped—anyone seeing her. Someone leaned an irreverent elbow onto a weathered headless statue perched between the clothier and the building next to it—a military uniform shop, she recalled. Was Ravido shopping for new belts? She pressed her nose against the glass. Gray mingled with the brown in the hair of the man leaning on the statue, and she realized it was Ravido himself. What was he doing? Waiting for someone?

A sergeant barked a few orders to the squadron, but Ravido said nothing. His head did move, though, and Amaranthe stood on her tiptoes, trying to follow his gaze. A second officer, this one with slate-gray hair and a colonel's rank pins, strode down the street, also with a squad of soldiers trailing him.

In the back of her head, Amaranthe acknowledged that this

probably wasn't a good place for her to loiter, but she couldn't pass up the opportunity to spy on the opposition. Even if it was some sort of military shopping trip, she might be able to glean a—

A throat cleared behind her.

Amaranthe jumped, letting the curtain fall as she spun about. The store proprietor stood not three feet away, both hands on her hips, her lips pursed as she stared through her spectacles and down a long nose at Amaranthe. When she noticed the nose print on the window, those lips went from pursing to puckering. She couldn't have made a sourer face if she'd been sucking a lemon.

Yara stepped away from the other curtain, a defiant lift to her chin. Feeling like a kid caught stealing pies from windowsills, Amaranthe couldn't manage the expression.

"Are you ready to make your purchase?" the proprietor asked.

"My what?"

The woman pointed to Amaranthe's hands. Erg, she hadn't realized she was still carrying the skimpy underwear around. At some point, she'd draped it over one wrist. "I, ah, yes, but my designated shopper will be making the purchases. I believe he's—we're—getting quite a few things." She held out the underwear, stealing a glance toward the window as she did so. Ravido no longer leaned on the statue, and the other officer had disappeared as well. "Would you mind putting this with his—our—other purchases?"

"Your designated shopper? Is that the dandy wandering around with a peacock-feather hat on his head?"

Maldynado hadn't come *in* wearing a hat, but Amaranthe said, "That sounds like him. He'll handle the rest. We need to meet a friend. Can we use your back door?"

The proprietor checked outside the window, no doubt noticing all the soldiers. "Your friend awaits in the... alley?"

"He doesn't like crowds." Amaranthe gave a cheery wave and hustled away before the woman could interrogate her further. She hoped her actions hadn't already made her suspicious enough to report.

On the way to the back door, she passed Maldynado, who was indeed trying on hats, decidedly masculine hats designed to fit *his* head, not hers. Numerous feminine garments—not so feminine as the string underwear, thank his ancestors—were draped over his arm, so Amaranthe didn't chastise him for wandering off task.

She stopped long enough to whisper, "Keep the proprietor busy, will you? She may have decided Yara and I are... suspicious."

"You're aware," Maldynado said, "that it takes a special kind of female to get in trouble while clothes shopping, right? Women are supposed to be naturals at this."

"Sorry." Even as she apologized, Amaranthe hastened toward the door. They might not get another chance to spy upon Ravido. She didn't intend to miss it.

Belatedly, when she was already in the alley, it occurred to her that she should have warned Maldynado his brother was next door, or at least told him that she meant to poke her nose into a pregnant badger's den. Well, if gunshots fired and chaos broke out in the street, he'd know she'd found trouble.

Surprisingly, Yara followed her into the alley.

Amaranthe asked, "Are you coming because you're curious, too, or because you think I'll need someone to keep me out of trouble?"

"Yes."

"I see you've been training with Sicarius."

Amaranthe climbed three steps to the back door of the neighboring shop and tugged on the latch, relieved to find it unlocked. She slipped into a dark cubby cluttered with officers' dress uniforms and fatigues in various stages of customization. Baskets of pincushions and spools of thread littered a workbench. Brown curtains sectioned the work area off from the rest of the shop. As soon as Yara closed the door behind her, cutting off the outside light, Amaranthe crept forward and parted the curtains an inch. She pressed her eye into the gap while listening for familiar voices.

It would have been convenient if Ravido and his chum had

been chatting in front of her peephole. Alas, they were near the front of the shop, some thirty feet away. Racks and shelves filled the space between, along with several soldiers shopping for themselves. Not five feet from the curtains, a bald man in a vest adorned with as many needles as the pincushions, tutted to himself as he worked on the trousers of an officer standing before a mirror. Up front, Ravido was talking, but Amaranthe couldn't make out a word.

She let the curtain fall shut, then leaned close to Yara's ear to whisper, "I'm going to get closer."

"How?"

Amaranthe mimicked Basilard's hand gesture for a snake moving through the grass.

Yara peeped through the curtain, no doubt considering the likelihood of using the intermittent cover to remain hidden from all the shoppers. There weren't any other women in the establishment.

"I'll stay here," Yara whispered. "I wouldn't make a convincing snake."

"Never had to slither across a field to sneak up on criminals, eh?"

"In my experience, it's usually the *criminals* who partake in such actions."

Amaranthe waved a hand in agreement, then dropped into a crouch at the side of the curtain, as far away from the tailor as possible. Working with Sicarius had given her copious practice in sneaking about. Now to see if she could employ the lessons in a clothes shop instead of in woods or alleys.

The tailor bent to examine a trouser cuff. The officer was admiring his form in the mirror. Amaranthe slipped out, forgoing the instinct to rush in favor of a less urgent move to the nearest case of shelves. Rapid movement would be more likely to draw the eye.

When no startled shouts arose, she considered herself past the first obstacle. It took another five minutes to slip around and wriggle under sweater cubbies and jacket racks, all the while making sure nobody was turned in her direction. She feared Ravido would be done talking about important things by the time she reached him and would be discussing reputable eating and drinking houses.

That's ridiculous, she told herself. Chances were he'd never been talking about "important things" to start with, not in the middle of a busy store. Still, she held out hope that she'd overhear something worthwhile.

As she belly-crawled the last ten feet, Ravido's voice finally grew distinguishable, though she struggled to hear all the words. He and his confidant were keeping their voices low, and the racks full of clothing muffled their words further. How irritating when the villains didn't enunciate clearly when discussing dastardly plans. Didn't they want everyone in the store to be impressed by the cleverness of their schemes?

With trouser cuffs swiping the top of her head, Amaranthe inched closer. Her movements stirred strands of thread and clumps of dust on the floor. The fine particles tickled her nostrils, and she crinkled her nose to keep from sneezing. It'd be hard to explain herself if someone hauled her out from beneath the garment racks.

She inched closer. The light from the storefront window highlighted two pairs of brown leather military boots, recently shined and rarely scuffed military boots.

"...Company of Lords," Ravido said, his low baritone drifting down to her. "They're being pests about the boy because there was no body. If I'd been running that train attack, I would have grabbed a random charred corpse and brought it back for a public funeral pyre. Cursed women."

"You're the one working with them." The other officer had a gravelly voice, like someone might have tried to garrote him once.

His boots turned toward Amaranthe, and a squeak sounded as he pushed hangers across a metal bar. She scooted back, nearly cracking her head against the rack stand. More voices sounded as other customers entered through the front door. Wasn't this a workday? Shouldn't these officers be out ordering their soldiers to do important military things?

Conscious of someone walking by behind the rack, Amaranthe tucked her legs to her chest to make sure nothing was sticking out on the other side. Her movements stirred dust, and she pinched her nostrils shut to stave off a sneeze. What kind of self-respecting rebel leader sneezed on the usurper's boots?

"Sorry about your wife," the second officer added once the new shoppers had moved into another aisle.

Amaranthe grimaced. She hadn't heard all the details when it came to Maldynado's sister-in-law's death, but suspected her team would get blamed for it. She pulled out a kerchief and swept up some of the dust balls.

"Yes, thank you, Horat," Ravido said. "It's hard to find a woman of the proper lines who's horny and unfaithful."

His comrade, Horat, grunted. "You'll miss her. You're just as horny and unfaithful. You had a good arrangement."

"I'm more concerned about *arranging* things with the Company of Lords right now. Unless I'm willing to replace every dissenter in the chamber, it won't matter how many troops I control or how much of the city I take over. If they don't make my claim for emperor official it isn't."

The hangers squeaked and the men's boots shifted again as they grunted greetings toward someone passing, then turned their backs toward the room. A couple of salutes might have been exchanged, but it was hard to tell from under the trousers.

"You *can* replace people," Horat said. "It's been done in the past."

"I know, but killing a bunch of warrior-caste men would set a bad precedent for a new ruler. Your father's on the Company. Talk to him, will you?"

"What's in it for me?"

"I've already promised you the Commander of the Armies position," Ravido said. "What more do you want?"

"You could send a few of the younger, more buxom women in that business organization to warm my toes at night." Horat chuckled. "No, I jest. I'll talk to Father. But you better figure out if the boy is really back in the city. With your family connections, you could *have* most of the votes from the Company if you could prove he's dead, but if he's not..."

Amaranthe's kerchief stilled. The *boy*. Sespian.

"If he was dumb enough to come back here, he won't be alive for long. If my men don't get him, there are others who will. Besides, my contacts said he's not even the legitimate heir."

Horat let out a low whistle. "Truly?"

"I'm surprised the papers haven't run the story yet. They—"

"Lords General?" came a solicitous call from a few racks away. "I have those uniform designs ready for you to look at now."

"Good," Ravido said.

As the two men walked away, the last thing Amaranthe heard was Horat saying, "You better find something you like this time. Those gutter-swinging gang brats can do better than sashes tied around their arms."

"One can't rush fashion decisions, old boy," Ravido said, for a moment sounding exactly like Maldynado. "An impeccably dressed army is full of pride—it makes your men fight better."

If Horat had a response, Amaranthe didn't hear it. A pair of alligator-skin boots with lizard-riding spurs clanked into view behind her. She vaguely remembered Maldynado mentioning the Kendorian attire was growing popular in the capital. It hardly mattered. She took the foot traffic as a sign that it was time to scoot out of the shop before someone spotted her. She turned about, preparing to scurry to the next rack as soon as the man passed, but a silver ranmya coin clunked onto the wooden floor and bounced under the rack with her.

She stifled a groan. If he noticed and stopped to hunt for it...

The alligator boots halted, and the man turned around. A knee came into view, then a hand touched down, patting the floor not inches from Amaranthe's legs. For lack of a better idea, she picked up the coin and rolled it back out into the aisle. Maybe he'd think it had bumped against the rack stand and was coming back of its own accord—his lucky day.

The hand jerked back as the prize rolled out. The blunt, stubby fingers made a grasp, but missed, only bumping the coin and causing it to spin out of sight beneath the trouser rack on the opposite side of the aisle.

A head wearing an outlandish ostrich feather hat dropped into Amaranthe's view. If she hadn't known Maldynado was in the building next door—and wearing different clothes—she might have thought it was he. It certainly seemed his style of clothing. But, no, *he* had better reflexes. He would have caught the coin.

While the man patted around beneath the opposite rack, Amaranthe eased backward, thinking she'd risk slipping out that way, even if it wasn't far from the front window. She could take a side aisle toward the rear of the store. But a fresh pair of boots came into view over there. It had to be lunch hour or something. Or this was *the* trendiest military clothier in the capital. Given that Maldynado had chosen the shopping district, it might very well be true.

She scrunched up into a tiny ball, hoping the shadows would hide her if Alligator Boots looked her way. He was fishing all over for that cursed coin. Couldn't someone who could afford to shop in Millinery Square afford to lose a coin?

Finally, he knelt back with the ranmya in his hand. He glanced under Amaranthe's rack. She froze, holding her breath. There *were* shadows. Were there enough? Now and then, Ravido's voice drifted up from the back of the store—it wasn't safe to be spotted yet.

The man squinted into her gloom. What was he doing? Hoping there were more lost coins down there?

He must have seen her, for he parted the trousers, letting light beneath the rack.

With no other options, Amaranthe scrambled out. She stayed on her knees, so nobody in the back of the shop—or standing in the street beyond the window—would see her and waved her kerchief up at the man.

"Those are fine ones," she said. "I'll only charge you five ranmyas if you're interested?"

The man rose to his feet, the ostrich-feather hat shadowing his features, but not quite hiding his blinks of confusion. "For... what?"

"Your boots, of course." Amaranthe waved the kerchief again, hoping the dust smearing it made it look authentic. Of course, boot polish would be better, but she hadn't come that prepared. "A shine. It won't take long."

"You work here?"

Right, her ruffled dress didn't exactly say shoeshine girl. "During my lunch break," Amaranthe said, though she couldn't imagine what sort of daytime job she might claim while wearing the childish dress. "A girl's got to make a ranmya when she can. For a handsome gentleman such as yourself, I'll do your boots for four ranmyas." She beamed a smile up at him and gazed into his eyes—hadn't Sicarius said something about her eyes being warm and innocent once?

The ostrich-hat turned toward the back of the shop. "Murkos, do you know there's a shoeshine girl trying to home in on your customers?"

In the seconds his head was turned, Amaranthe slithered under another rack and into the aisle along the wall. Staying low, she darted for the curtain in the rear.

"A what?" came the return question. "No, there shouldn't be. Grab her, will you?"

Not likely. Amaranthe reached the back curtain, belly-crawled under it so she wouldn't disturb the fabric, and popped up. Yara was still there, though she stood by the back exit, the door ajar as she peered into the alley.

"We need to go," Amaranthe whispered.

"My oaf is outside chatting with a squad of soldiers," Yara said.

"Chatting?"

Yara closed the door. "Chatting at gunpoint."

"Their gunpoints, I presume." As much as Amaranthe appreciated the idea of Maldynado surrounding a squad of soldiers by himself, she doubted it was the case.

"Yes, and they're right in front of the door. Any chance we can go out the front?"

"No, Ravido is still out there."

"Where'd she go?" a familiar voice demanded from somewhere in the middle of the store—the miserly ostrich-hat man who couldn't let a coin go.

"Also, it's possible I'd attract attention going that way." Amaranthe slipped past Yara. She wanted her own peek outside.

Unfortunately, her peek didn't reveal anything more appealing than Yara's. Eight burly soldiers surrounded Maldynado, four on each side of him, trapping him in the narrow alley. Though he was amiably talking and gesturing as they searched his shopping bags, there were no less than six guns pointed at his chest. The men's white armbands proclaimed the squad belonged to Ravido, detached from the group out front most likely.

Amaranthe closed the door. Yara was right; there was no way they could walk outside without being seen. If they caught the soldiers by surprise, she, Yara, and Maldynado might get the best of eight men in a fight, but with twenty more waiting out front, she didn't like the odds overall.

"I don't suppose telling them that their general is in here buying them new uniforms would excite them to the point of forgetting about us," Amaranthe muttered.

Yara's only response was a withering look. Probably a no.

Amaranthe peered about the back room, searching for inspiration. The recently tailored uniforms hanging on the wall and the cloth swatches on the worktable might be flammable, but she couldn't picture creating anything spectacularly explosive using them. Aside from scissors and needles, there wasn't much else to note. A couple of featureless ceramic busts held wigs, while others supported fur caps in the middle of receiving embroidered designs that signified prominent battles the owner had served in. Amaranthe touched one of the wigs. Explosions might not be the *only* way to escape.

She considered the uniforms again. On some of them, the rank pins hadn't been removed. She selected one that might do for someone around six feet tall and handed it to Yara with a smile.

"Congratulations on your promotion to—" she glanced at the brass swords on the collar, "—captain."

"Are you *insane*?" Yara whispered. "Nobody's going to believe we're officers. Or *men*." She waved toward Amaranthe's chest.

"It's cold outside. We can bundle up. We only need to pass scrutiny for a minute. I'll think of something to distract them."

"Why don't I find that comforting?" Yara growled, but she snatched the uniform.

"I'm certain I don't know." Amaranthe gave a cheery wink and grabbed the shortest uniform on the wall.

"They'd be more likely to be distracted if we ran out naked," Yara muttered, fiddling with buttons.

"We want to distract the *soldiers*, not Maldynado."

"...look around, don't you think?" someone asked from the front. "...was a shifty looking girl... stealing from you."

Stealing? Shifty? Hmmph. Amaranthe tore off her distasteful dress, hid it in a waste bin, and pulled on the uniform trousers. She donned a white shirt, not bothering to button or tuck it in before throwing on the jacket. There wasn't time to dally over the subtleties of the costume. All she could do was make sure the rank pins on the collars matched those on the hats she grabbed. She'd be the lieutenant to Yara's captain. She hoped the men outside didn't stop to wonder why an LT was doing all the talking, or to look too closely at the ill-fitting uniforms. Too bad it wasn't dark out. That would have hidden a lot of discrepancies.

"What about boots?" Yara whispered.

Amaranthe didn't see any lying around. The military cobbler's shop was probably next door. "Just wear your own."

"We're going to be the most disheveled officers in the army."

In the midst of pulling up a pair of suspenders, Amaranthe froze. The "something to distract them" she'd been trying to think up had popped into her mind. "Yes," she said, smiling.

"Yes, we will."

Yara shook her head in an I-don't-want-to-know manner and pointed at Amaranthe's face. "You look too much like a girl."

Yes, between Yara's height, more angular features and her short hair, she'd have an easier time passing for a man at a glance, but Amaranthe...

She grabbed a pair of scissors and cut off a swath of hair on one of the wigs. She dug into a brown glass jar labeled *wig glue* and cobbled together the worst fake mustache anyone had ever seen.

"That is *not* going to fool anyone," Yara said.

"Sure it will," Amaranthe whispered as she glued hair to her upper lip, "because I'll be standing behind you and staggering."

"Staggering?"

"I'll check in the back," someone said from the other side of the curtain.

Their time was up. Amaranthe grabbed Yara's elbow and propelled her toward the door. "We've just been mauled in a surprise attack, and we're injured. Stagger!"

Yara growled again, but she shoved open the door and staggered appropriately. Amaranthe clutched her abdomen, hunched over, and tumbled outside and down the steps after her. She bumped into Yara's back, adding realism—she *hoped* that was the right word for it—to the staggering.

"What—" one of the soldier's near the stairs asked.

Fortunately, none of the guns swung toward Amaranthe and Yara, not yet anyway. Maldynado, still surrounded by soldiers, his shopping bags on the ground with their contents strewn about, stared at Amaranthe, but didn't say anything.

"They've got General Marblecrest," Amaranthe blurted, making her voice as deep as she could. "General Flintcrest's men." She flung her arm toward the door, even as she tumbled to her knees. "Hurry, the others are knocked out. Some slagging magic."

Before she'd finished speaking, soldiers were charging for the stairs. Only a sergeant and private with their guns trained on Maldynado hesitated.

"But, sir, we've got a prisoner. It's Lord Marblecrest's little brother. He might be in on it!"

"I'll watch him," Yara said gruffly, doing her own male-voice impression as she reached for the soldier's pistol.

The private started to hand it to her, but the sergeant was peering at Yara's face. "Wait. Who are—"

With the sergeant's attention on her, Maldynado launched a fist at his jaw. It connected with enough force to spin him about. Maldynado rammed his shoulder into the man's back, sending him face-first into the side of the stone building. Before the private could react, Yara grabbed his pistol with one hand and slammed her heel into his nose with the other. He reeled back, and she thrust him into the other wall.

Confident her comrades could handle those two, Amaranthe sprinted past them, scooped the fallen clothing into the bag, and grabbed the handles. "We need to get out of here. If Ravido's still inside, it's only going to take them a second to—"

The back door of the uniform shop slammed open.

"Go, go," Amaranthe barked.

Yara took off promptly, though Maldynado paused to snatch a bag that Amaranthe had missed. "Can't forget this one."

"There they are!" someone shouted from the doorway.

Amaranthe shoved Maldynado toward the nearest intersection and took off at a sprint. Yara reached the corner first and raced around it. A pistol fired, a ball blasted into the brick building, inches above her head. Shards of red dust flew everywhere.

Amaranthe took the corner so quickly she almost smashed into the far wall.

"Careful," Maldynado warned from right behind her. "Those bags have already been—" another weapon boomed, though he'd already ducked around the corner, escaping the line of fire, "—manhandled enough by ill-mannered louts with no fashion sense."

Amaranthe had no idea how he could spout all that while sprinting. She followed Yara, who was weaving into alleys at random in the maze between thoroughfares, content to let her lead until a sturdy drainpipe came into view ahead. Conscious of the shouts and boots pounding the cobblestones behind them, she surged forward, tapped Yara's elbow, and mouthed, "Up."

"Up?" Yara slowed, neck craned as she considered the flat roof four stories above them.

"Up," Amaranthe confirmed, darting past her and shimmying up the drainpipe. The climb would take a moment, so there was no time to spare.

Maldynado leaped and caught the pipe several feet up, scurrying up as nimbly as a cat scaling a tree. "Like this, my lady."

Yara hadn't experienced Sicarius's urban obstacle courses yet, but it didn't seem she'd let Maldynado show her up. She clawed her way up after him.

Amaranthe reached the rooftop and pulled herself over, dropping into a low crouch to scan the area. Though she didn't expect anyone to be up there waiting, Sicarius had, more times than she could count, drilled her to always be aware of her surroundings. Nobody was up there. She could, however, hear the soldiers racing down the alley perpendicular to the one she'd just left. If they rounded the corner before Yara and Maldynado reached the roof...

Maldynado popped over the side, spun about, flattened to his belly, and caught Yara's hand as soon as it was close enough. He hauled her up and over the edge as the soldiers rounded the corner.

"This way," Amaranthe whispered, then led them in the opposite direction from their pursuit.

She'd been across the rooftops in that section of the city before, often in the dark, and she chose a route where the jumps between buildings weren't too far apart and the vertical rises and falls weren't too challenging. More than once, Yara cursed, arms flailing as she struggled to keep up without losing her balance, but she stuck with them.

The sounds of pursuit faded, but Amaranthe stayed on the roofs as long as possible, suspecting more soldiers would be

scouting below. Even if *she* hadn't been identified, word would get out quickly about Maldynado's presence in the area.

The clang of a trolley bell floated above the din of the city. Amaranthe veered in that direction, reaching Third Street in time to spot the two-car vehicle ambling up the track toward their corner. The wooden sign dangling above the cab promised the trolley was on its way to the waterfront.

Amaranthe pointed. "That'll work."

"You *are* insane," Yara said, no longer asking but making statements. Breathing heavily, she added, "It's coming down the... middle of the street. That's at least a... ten foot jump."

"Ah, but we're higher. It'll be easy. Just get a running start and soften your knees when you land."

With the trolley approaching, there was no more time to debate it. If Yara didn't want to jump, Amaranthe trusted she'd find another way down and back to the waterfront. For her and Maldynado... this would keep them from being seen. There were pedestrians on the street, but nobody in uniform—at the moment. It wouldn't take long for those soldiers to set up a search net though.

"Ready, boss." Maldynado hefted his shopping bags and jumped first.

He sailed through the air, landing lightly behind the smokestack without dropping a bag. Amaranthe leaped after him, dropping into a low crouch, trying to keep her touchdown soft so people in the trolley wouldn't hear a heavy thump. Fortunately, there weren't many passengers aboard in the middle of the workday.

She looked up in time to see Yara run off the edge of the roof, arms flailing, an expression of anger on her face. She was angling toward the second car, but Amaranthe feared she'd thrown too much power into her leap. If she overshot, that'd be a painful landing.

Amaranthe ran across the roof of her own car and leaped onto the second. Yara was already landing. She'd spun in the air, obviously realizing she'd over jumped, and caught the lip of

the car. Her torso hit, and a painful-sounding *oomph* shot from her lungs. Amaranthe dropped to her knees and grabbed her hands. With Yara's legs dangling in front of the windows, there was zero chance she wouldn't be noticed, but Amaranthe pulled her up as fast as she could.

Yara flopped onto her back, that expression of anger still riding her face as she glared up at Amaranthe. It shifted over her shoulder.

"Where were *you*?" Yara demanded as Maldynado plopped down beside them.

"Sorry." Maldynado tucked a dangling garment back into one of his bags. "The boss's new scarf got caught on a screw."

"I'm going to start sleeping with *her* if you can't be bothered to save me when I fall," Yara growled.

Amaranthe blinked in surprise at this threat. Maldynado only grinned. "I get to watch, right?"

"You people are insane." Yara must have decided that would be her word of the day.

"You're just now noticing?" Amaranthe forgot sometimes how much Sicarius's training had inured her to daunting feats of athleticism. A year ago, she also would have found it nerve-rattling to fling herself from rooftop to rooftop. Somewhere along the way, such exercises had become commonplace.

"Soldiers ahead." Maldynado flattened himself to his belly.

Ravido's men—Amaranthe recognized a few of the faces from the uniform shop—spewed out of an alley, halting on the sidewalk to look in both directions. She and Yara also dropped flat. The height of the trolley ought to keep anyone on the street from noticing them, but if some of the men farther back in the alley had a better angle to see up there...

A scrape sounded beneath the trolley roof. A handsome fellow wearing a fur cap stuck his head out of the window and peered at the collection of people who'd landed above his seat.

With her ear flattened to the roof, Amaranthe was looking right at him. She had no idea if he'd raise an alarm or simply gape at them for their audacity, so she groped for something to say that would distract him, at least until the trolley moved away from the soldiers.

"Can you believe how much the fares have gone up this year?" She vaguely remembering reading that they had in a newspaper article that fall.

The man blinked a few times. "You're a woman."

Oh, right. Amaranthe had forgotten about her officer costume. She touched her upper lip and was surprised to find the hastily constructed mustache still adorned it, if crookedly. "Yes. Yes, I am."

"Are you *all* women?" the man asked.

"Yes," Yara said, as Maldynado issued an emphatic, "*No*."

The man's chin tilted upward, toward the roofs drifting past on the side of the street. "That was *amazing*. Are you burglars or outlaws? Wait, I've seen your face before. You *are* an outlaw. That female one who runs with Sicarius."

"Uhm." Amaranthe lifted her head to check on the soldiers. They were a few blocks behind the trolley now, and she relaxed a bit. "Possibly. I'd appreciate it if you didn't mention you saw us."

"Hm." The man's head dropped out of view.

"Was that a hm of assent or a hm, I wonder if there are any enforcers on board?" Amaranthe wondered.

"I think he liked you," Maldynado said. "Even with the mustache."

The man's head reappeared. This time he held a pen and a piece of paper. "Will you sign this, please?" He thrust the page into her hand before she could respond.

Amaranthe found herself looking at her own face. Tack holes dotted the corners of the familiar wanted poster—dear ancestors, were they hanging her likeness in trolleys now? The man waved the pen, a wide grin across his face.

Well, at least he wasn't threatening to turn them in. She took the pen and signed her name at the bottom. What could it hurt? By this point, any of her enemies who were paying attention knew her team was back in town.

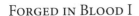
"Thank you!" the man said when she returned the pen and paper.

Maldynado propped himself up on an elbow and touched his hand to his chest. "Do you want *my* signature?"

The man considered him for a moment, then said, "No, thank you," and dropped out of view again.

Maldynado sniffed. "How disappointing."

"Sorry," Amaranthe said.

Yara rolled her eyes.

The trolley rounded another corner and the lake came into view, frost edging the banks and the pilings on the docks. Their abandoned molasses factory was only a few blocks away.

"Time to get back to work," Amaranthe said.

"Yes, but in the meantime you—" Maldynado was farther ahead on the rooftop and had to use his toe to nudge Amaranthe, "—should remember that you have *options*. Just wait until we get Sespian back on the throne and it comes out that you were instrumental in saving his life and putting him there. You'll have men lined up, hoping for a lot more than signatures. No need to stick with a humorless, glowering assassin."

"Shall I let him know you said that?" Amaranthe asked.

"Ah, no. That's not necessary."

"You *are* an oaf," Yara told him.

CHAPTER 8

AFTERNOON SUNLIGHT FILTERED THROUGH THE DUSTY windows of the molasses factory, gleaming on the brass rails of the catwalks and brightening the cement floor below. Sicarius was perched in the rafters, waiting for Amaranthe to return and observing a knife-fighting practice session led by Basilard. The two new recruits were his students, though one was too injured to do much. When Sespian had walked through a few minutes earlier, he'd joined in. His face set with concentration, he seemed far more determined to learn the skills than he had as a youth. Perhaps he'd decided that he wished the throne back after all, no matter who his father was and how slanted the odds were against them.

One of the side doors squeaked open, and three figures walked inside. Maldynado came last, identifiable, as always, by his swagger, though the emerald-green hat, its band glittering with tiny gems, and armful of shopping bags would have marked him as well. After a second, Sicarius recognized Amaranthe and Yara, too. They were wearing military uniforms, so his first thought had been that Maldynado had been captured and was leading officers to the hideout.

"...supposed to know there was a squad of soldiers standing in the alley?" Maldynado was asking. "*You* two had gone out that way."

He, Yara, and Amaranthe headed for the stairs leading to the second-story offices. When Basilard paused and signed a question, Amaranthe waved for him to continue with the training.

"Why didn't you check before bursting out of the shop?"

Yara asked. "The fact that we'd been gone so long should have told you to be wary."

Sicarius glided along the narrow support beam, heading for the catwalk so he could intercept Amaranthe. He'd been keeping an eye on Curi's Bakery, and their forged letter had been picked up by a young woman in business attire who'd also collected a box of pastries. Sicarius had followed her to the yacht club. She'd disappeared into a building at the end of one of the docks and hadn't come out again.

"You weren't gone that long," Maldynado said.

"Lokdon was under those racks for eons," Yara said as the trio climbed the stairs. "I think she forgot she was spying on Ravido and started dusting."

Sicarius, almost to the landing, paused. How had they chanced across Ravido when they'd gone costume shopping?

"I did *not* forget that I was spying." Amaranthe stepped onto the landing and headed for the door of the office she'd claimed.

"You'll note she's not denying the dusting," Maldynado said.

"How can I? It was filthy down there. If I hadn't cleaned away a few dust balls, I would have sneezed all over your brother's boots."

"You say that as if it'd be inappropriate," Maldynado said.

Sicarius hopped off the beam and landed in front of Amaranthe's door. Yara jerked in surprise. Maldynado dropped a shopping bag on his foot and cursed. Amaranthe gave him a you-can't-be-bothered-to-use-the-stairs-eh eyebrow quirk.

"I have news." Sicarius flicked his gaze at the others. "Private news." In truth, the news about the letter pickup wasn't anything that couldn't be shared, but he wanted to speak to Amaranthe about the meditation training and assumed she would not want to discuss her sleep issues in front of Maldynado and Yara.

"Let me drop off the boss's bags, if it won't disturb you terribly." Maldynado took as wide a route around Sicarius as the confines of the landing would allow.

"Thank you, Maldynado," Amaranthe said. "Yara, why don't you grab some lunch, then see if you can find Books and

Akstyr? We'll all need to try on our costumes and discuss our infiltration plans."

"I don't see why you're not planning to take me." Maldynado gazed soulfully at Yara, as if it'd eat at him like an *iraki* fungus if he had to be parted from her for a few days.

Yara folded her arms over her chest and returned his soulful gaze with a deadpan stare.

"I told you," Amaranthe said, "Sespian is going to need our best fighters. Where I'm going... well, if we start playing fisticuffs with Forge, it'll likely mean we've already failed the mission."

"Guess I'll take a nice nap until someone needs me then," Maldynado said, heading for the stairs.

"Actually..." Amaranthe met Sicarius's eyes. "Are you planning to take Sespian to see General Ridgecrest tonight?"

"Yes." Sicarius had an inkling of what her next words would be and made his tone forbidding.

"Why don't you take Maldynado with you?" Amaranthe asked, undeterred by his tone. "If Ridgecrest hasn't picked a side, Maldynado ought to be able to come up with family gossip to completely discourage the general from falling in with Ravido."

"You want me to go off alone with him?" Maldynado pointed at Sicarius. "At night?"

"Sespian will be there too," Amaranthe said. "It'll be fun. Like a boys' night out."

"The proper place for a boys' night out is a brothel, gambling hall, or drinking house," Maldynado said. "Not a dark forest with a soul-devouring monster roaming about."

Sicarius had no interest in taking Maldynado either. Even if his self-aggrandizing babble weren't grating, Sicarius had been looking forward to an outing alone with Sespian. Without others around to talk to, Sespian should be more likely to talk to *him*.

"He is disowned," Sicarius said. "It is unlikely General Ridgecrest will listen to him."

"Or," Amaranthe said, lifting a finger, "Maldynado will

irritate him so thoroughly that Ridgecrest will be doubly certain that no Marblecrest blood should make it onto the throne. Either way would work."

Maldynado's wry smile wasn't triumphant. He'd doubtlessly rather spend the night engaged in coitus with Sergeant Yara.

"Of course, it'll be up to you to convince Ridgecrest that Sespian is the candidate he wants to side with," Amaranthe said.

"Me," Sicarius stated at the same time as Maldynado asked, "*Him*?"

"You three. As a group."

"That'll be a unique conversation," Yara said.

"I'm confident they can do it," Amaranthe said.

"All right, all right, I'll go." Maldynado sighed dramatically and slouched to the door. "Women," he muttered. "Might as well put one of them on the throne. They're the ones running the shop anyway."

Yara's hand twitched as she followed him out, as if she wasn't sure whether she should smack him on the back of the head or pat him on the shoulder for accepting the truth.

Sicarius closed the door. Amaranthe tilted her head, waiting expectantly. Thus far, he'd said nothing about the women's costumes, but he found his humor piqued by the overlong trousers slumped about her ankles, the sleeves draped to her knuckles, the ill-aligned buttons on the lieutenant's jacket, and the crooked mustache drooping from her upper lip. Whatever scheme had precipitated the need for what must have been a hasty clothing change, he doubted it had worked as planned.

"I was going to offer to stand guard for you again tonight," Sicarius said, "but if that's what you're wearing, I might be less motivated."

Amaranthe blinked a few times. Though she was the one encouraging him to develop a playful side, she always seemed surprised when he attempted to make jokes. He could conclude little except that he was inept at it. Practice was required. As with knife throwing and any other skill, he supposed.

"Stand guard?" Amaranthe leaned against the desk, the

corners of her lips twitching as she regained her equilibrium. "If that's what you're planning to do, then, yes, I'm wearing this. Now, if you wanted to come inside my room and pursue a more active endeavor, I might be persuaded to wear less…" Another woman might have wriggled her hips, touched her chest, or made some otherwise suggestive motion, but Amaranthe looked like she'd gone farther down the road than she'd planned and didn't know how to finish the journey. Or wasn't sure if she was ready to.

"Facial hair?" Sicarius suggested.

"*Yes*." The relief was evident in her tone, when he responded with a joke rather than… naked interest. She surprised him by crossing the room and wrapping her arms around him.

It was, he sensed, a thank-you-for-understanding hug. He returned it, though he once again wondered how things might be between them now if he hadn't pushed her away for so long. Pike's torture would have been devastating regardless of the physicality of their relationship, but perhaps he would have a better idea of how to help. That reminded him of his idea—the meditation.

Sicarius stepped back so he could look into her eyes. "I wish to teach you a Nurian meditation technique. It is useful in finding peace and rest in times when the mind would otherwise be busy." And filled with memories of old pain and fear of new pain, he added to himself, remembering his own days with Pike. He'd endured pains enough as an adult too. He'd not been caught often during his missions, but there had been a few instances when all his rigorous childhood training had been required to survive, escape, and regain equanimity in the days and months after. As he held Amaranthe's gaze, he trusted she knew what he meant, even if he left the words unsaid.

Indeed, Amaranthe's face grew speculative. "This meditation, can it replace sleep?"

"It lessens the need for sleep. I have often found it more restorative than unconscious slumber."

"And you think I could master it?"

"You may find solace in the study and pursuit," Sicarius said.

"That's... a no, right?"

Sicarius responded with the bland stare the question deserved.

"If you're willing to teach me, I'll give it a try. Regardless, I..." She bit her lip, her gaze dropping to his chest.

He knew she didn't intend the lip bite to be alluring, certainly not when she was wearing that lopsided mustache, but he found himself watching it intently. Distractedly.

"I would appreciate it if you stayed with me," Amaranthe finished. "I know I'm not much... fun right now. Well, maybe a little during the day." She smiled at some memory. "But at night, uhm, I guess you saw." She swallowed, not meeting his eyes. "I keep telling myself to forget about it, that it's over now, and he's dead, so it's never going to happen again. But... myself won't listen. In my mind, I keep reliving... things."

"I know." It seemed an inadequate thing to say, but words would do nothing to help her, and it wasn't in him to utter inanities.

"I know you do."

Maldynado's voice, as obnoxious as ever, sounded from downstairs, a lewd comment about the nature of all-male knife-training sessions.

Amaranthe stepped back, returning to the desk. She tugged off the mustache, wincing at the glue's bite. "This plan of mine, I figure it'll either be therapeutic—returning to the *Behemoth* and facing the source of my nightmares—or it'll destroy me, and I'll end up curled up in a tight ball under a table, crying out for my father." She spoke the words nonchalantly, removing the military jacket as she did so, but Sicarius didn't miss the concern, the naked truth, within them. She truly didn't know if she'd mentally survive walking those alien corridors again.

He simmered with irritation at the situation. He should go with her, so he could stand at her back if she needed him. But, as she'd said, he couldn't walk away from Sespian, not with a soul construct stalking the streets. Maybe they could figure out a way to destroy it before Amaranthe left. They'd killed,

or at least incapacitated, one before. If they had time to set a trap, they ought to be able to do it again. After that, if they could secure Ridgecrest and, through him, Fort Urgot's support, Sespian would be in a strong enough position that Sicarius could risk leaving him for a few days. Except what of the letters at the bakery? Worgavic would be expecting this Suan's arrival soon.

"You're not saying anything," Amaranthe noted. "Does that mean you think the worst of those two scenarios is likely?"

"No." Hoping he wouldn't regret it, Sicarius added, "Your letter was picked up at the bakery."

"Ah, good. Then they'll be expecting Suan Curlev to visit soon. Thank you for the report." Amaranthe lowered her voice and said, "Let's hope this isn't the rope with which I hang myself."

After he'd been considering similar possibilities, her words slammed into him like arrows striking a bullseye. Emotion was something he'd long ago learned to lock away, knowing it had no place in his work, but he couldn't deny the surge of concern that welled in his chest.

"You will *not* hang yourself," Sicarius said, the words coming out harsher than he wished.

Amaranthe drew back, her brown eyes distressed as she searched his face. "No, I... that's not the goal certainly. I'll be careful."

Sicarius closed his eyes. What was he doing? He needed to batten down his emotions again, but some uncharacteristically impulsive thought stalked into the forefront of his mind: *give her a reason to return.* He would have shoved the words away, reminding himself that he'd promised to wait for her to initiate physical relations, but she'd responded with interest to the experimental kiss he'd offered on that steamboat. More than interest, he thought, remembering her enthusiasm. If not for those enforcers and their mission...

Sicarius opened his eyes and stepped toward Amaranthe, resting a hand on her waist. Scant inches separated their chests. He lifted his other hand to her face, brushing her cheek, drawing

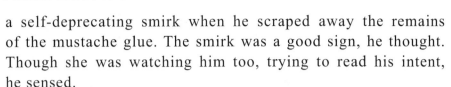

a self-deprecating smirk when he scraped away the remains of the mustache glue. The smirk was a good sign, he thought. Though she was watching him too, trying to read his intent, he sensed.

As his fingers roamed, he tried to soften his face and gentle his eyes. He had so little experience with it that it took conscious effort. He'd so rarely cared if anyone thought of him as anything except a monster trained to kill. He'd certainly never thought the opinion of a woman would matter. For him, sex had always been a physical release, nothing more. A biological need to be taken care of, nothing bound up in emotions. The need to consider another's feelings left him less certain than usual, more likely to hesitate, especially now, in the aftermath of Amaranthe's time with Pike. If in his haste, or even in innocence, he hurt her further, he would not forgive himself. He'd never quite understood why she felt loyal to him, but that loyalty had never wavered, even when it should have, when his methods veered onto different tracks than her morality rode down. So often he'd been on watch, or otherwise observing from the shadows, when she'd spoken on his behalf to the others and, more recently, to Sespian. He'd listened to every word outside that boathouse on Marblecrest Island, and her conviction that he wasn't a rapist when she had no way of knowing the truth, that Marathi had chosen him... It filled him with—he didn't know what to call it. Gratitude, he supposed, and an equally deep sense of loyalty toward her. Not even Hollowcrest, for all he'd attempted to indoctrinate loyalty in him, had inspired such devotion from him. The difference between a relationship founded on fear and one based on mutual respect. And love, Amaranthe would say.

"Sicarius?" Her voice broke into a squeak in the middle of his name.

This time his face softened of its own accord, and his lips stretched in a faint smile at the satisfaction her reaction gave him. After her earlier uncertainty, he'd not known if a kiss would be welcome, but he'd been letting his fingers wander as he considered his thoughts, his—yes, he admitted to himself—

feelings, and how to approach her. His upper hand had drifted to the back of her neck, and he was massaging the taut muscles, easing the tension bunched there. She'd let her chin droop and was leaning against him. Though their layers of winter clothing stole most of the sensation of having her soft breasts pressed against his chest, he'd seen her naked often enough to have little trouble imagining how they would feel, his flesh against hers. His lower hand had slipped beneath her jacket and his fingers were tracing warm bare skin. Less of a massage and more of a promise in line with his "give her a reason to come back" thought. The ministrations of *that* hand, he suspected, were responsible for the hitch in her voice.

"Yes?" Sicarius asked calmly, keeping any hint of expectation out of his voice.

He'd had to learn such rigid control over his body during his years of training that he had little trouble suppressing sexual urges, though if she decided she wanted more, he'd have no problem obliging. Her question in the smokestack as to whether he was capable of enjoying intercourse... If he remembered how to laugh, that would have been the time for it. She had no idea how many nights he'd thought of little *but* intercourse. Especially of late. Since he'd spent those hundreds of miles chasing after that ship, since she'd admitted what she'd endured to withhold his secrets...

He lowered his head, brushing his cheek against hers, inhaling the scent of her shampoo and the salty warmth of her skin. She'd been running not long ago—sweating. He'd have to get the details of that shopping mission. Later.

Amaranthe cleared her throat. "I, uhm... Tonight? When you come to... stand guard?"

"Yes?" he murmured, his lips against her skin now, touching, tasting their way down her neck.

He ought to pull away, to let her finish her question, especially if it was going where he wished it would go, but the pleasure of letting his hands roam, brushing along soft, taut flesh that shivered in response to his touch, and the taste of that skin

beneath his lips, his tongue... He enjoyed the feel of her quick breaths whispering past his ear, stirring his hair. More, it pleased him that he affected her so. When her arms slipped around his back and the remaining space between them disappeared...

"You should," Amaranthe said—gulped, "do it... from my blankets."

"Like last night?" He lifted his head, intending to accept her offer with a kiss, but he paused at her earlobe, giving it a nibble.

She gasped, and her arms tightened about him. This close, she'd have no trouble discerning his own interest in... standing guard.

"Not exactly," she breathed, pressing her hips into him.

He responded with an unintentional growl, capturing her against the edge of the desk, locking her to him. His lips found hers, a different taste, a different texture, even more arousing. Why wait until night? With her invitation on his mind, he'd be distracted during the trip to Fort Urgot. Besides, he was tired of suppressing himself, over and over...

Footsteps sounded on the stairs below the office. He didn't care. If anyone opened the door to interrupt them, he'd—

Amaranthe broke the kiss, her gaze darting toward the window. "Yara, I told her to come back after lunch."

"Unfortunate," Sicarius said, mostly because he was thinking of hurling a knife at the door if Yara came in. Not to kill... but a blade quivering in the jamb inches from her ear would convince her to leave them alone.

Amaranthe squirmed out of his grip, though, rushing to straighten her clothes like a thirteen-year-old girl in danger of being caught necking by parents who'd arrived home. "I know," she said as the footsteps reached the landing. "You should have told me you wanted to deliver more than news. I'd have told her to wait until after dinner." Her cheeks were flushed and she sounded as though she'd just finished a hard run. She flashed a grin at him. "Or maybe breakfast?"

Breakfast indeed, he thought, his eyes arrested by her lips. If the door hadn't opened, Sicarius would have pulled her back,

and slag Yara or anyone else who wandered upstairs. He had a lot of knives he could throw to ensure privacy.

"Are you two done?" Yara asked from the threshold.

Absolutely not, Sicarius thought.

Amaranthe cleared her throat. "Yes."

"Books and Akstyr are coming," Yara said. "Maldynado was explaining his costume choices. You may find some resistance."

"Ah. Yes, he did mention something about a robe and... tassels, didn't he?"

"I don't know, but they better not be for me."

Yara came in and more footfalls sounded outside. Amaranthe upended the shopping bags onto the desk. Sicarius found a corner, lamenting this swift return to business, though it didn't surprise him. Before Amaranthe, he never would have considered engaging in carnal activities, or even permitting himself such distracting thoughts, during the course of a mission. Somewhere along the way, though, this had become more than just a mission. It was... life, he supposed. A way of existing that was more interesting than simply accepting orders and obeying them.

Amaranthe held up a shiny silver chain with a medallion formed by a pair of slitted eyes. "Uhm. Whose costume is this a part of?"

"In Kendor, the gia gia lizard features in many legends," Sicarius said, "always wise and often all-knowing. Those eyes are its typical representation. They're popular in jewelry worn amongst those with status. Or who wish to appear to have status."

"I think he just said that's yours," Yara said.

"Unfortunately, that's the message I got too." Amaranthe pulled out a matching silver chain, or perhaps a woman might wear it as a belt. It, too, featured the eye motif. "Hm."

Yara plucked a small emerald green piece of material from the pile of clothing. "Did he truly buy these? What a rock head."

Amaranthe grabbed the garment, strings twitching in the air, and stuffed it in a bag. She glanced at Sicarius, cheeks flushing anew. Undergarments, he guessed, and decided he didn't care for

the idea of Maldynado picking such things out for her. Though his mind did snag for a moment, imagining a modeling show.

Books and Akstyr strolled in, each with a fat tome held under one arm, and Sicarius was glad the undergarment had been hidden. An uneven gait and the clack of a swordstick announced Deret Mancrest's approach. The office was growing too crowded for his taste.

After Mancrest entered, Sicarius slid toward the door. The warrior-caste man sidestepped, putting his back against the wall, as if he worried Sicarius had been attempting to get behind him. Sicarius ignored him. The movement by the door had drawn Amaranthe's eyes, but she looked at Sicarius, not Mancrest. She lifted her eyebrows and mouthed, "Tonight?"

He held her gaze for a long moment and nodded once before stepping outside.

CHAPTER 9

THERE WEREN'T MANY TROOPS PATROLLING THE STREETS in the upscale neighborhood that housed the Mildawn Business School for Women. A good thing, since it wasn't as late an hour as it should be for sneaking into a locked building. Wanting to a meet a lover for a midnight tryst probably wasn't a valid reason for a rebel leader to rush her breaking-and-entering plans, so Amaranthe decided it was the need to acquire information with enough time to study it that motivated the evening infiltration. Anyway, it was dark and late enough that the students and faculty should be gone for the day.

"Let me know if anyone comes." She slipped out her lock-pick set.

"Of course," Yara said, a hint of indignation in the tone. Yes, she hadn't needed to be told. She already had her back to the wall beside the kitchen door, and was watching the alley.

"You didn't answer my question on the trolley," Amaranthe said after a few minutes of prodding in the lock. Down on one knee, the cold from the concrete stoop seeping through her trouser leg, she figured this would take a while. The school could afford high quality locks.

"That's because we had to jump off between stops to flee enforcers who were squinting suspiciously at you," Yara said.

"We didn't flee anyone. We were simply disembarking preemptively to ensure the enforcers didn't have time to confirm those suspicions."

"Disembarking preemptively. I see."

Amaranthe supposed Yara would be offended if she pointed

out that she, with her brusque, sometimes humorless manner, reminded one of Sicarius at times.

"Yes," Yara said, finally answering the question, "things are going well with Maldynado."

She started pacing the alley, checking the streets on either end. Meanwhile, Amaranthe finished with the lock. She pulled matches and lantern out of her pack, and stepped into the kitchen. By the time Yara joined her, shutting the door at their backs, the light from the flame played over polished wood cabinets, countertops, and flooring.

"Are there likely to be squatters?" Yara asked.

"At Mildawn School for Women? I should think not." Amaranthe issued her best haughty sniff. "But we'll keep an eye out regardless. It's early enough that a night janitor might be around."

Amaranthe led the way past large coal stoves and racks of hanging pots. They slipped into the wide empty hallway that ran the length of the building. The last time she'd been here had been with Sicarius—nicknamed, to his disgruntlement, Hansor at the time—and she smiled to think how far they'd come in the last year. And how far they might go later that night. She flushed at the memory of the afternoon's... promise. If she'd known talking about hurling herself into danger could bestir *that* response in him, she would have done it more often. Usually she hurled herself into danger without warning him beforehand.

Of course, she was nervous at the prospect of "later that night" too. What if she were overcome with some intense memory of being sprawled on Pike's table? What if, in the middle of things, she grew scared and decided she couldn't go through with it? What if she were so cursed tired that she passed out and drooled all over Sicarius before they got started? Sure, girl, she thought with a snort, that'll happen. He could rouse the unconscious with those roaming fingers. All this time, she'd been certain he wouldn't be all that practiced with women, at least not in the art of teasing... physical responses from them. Princess Marathi must have given her teenage paramour some lessons.

Amaranthe couldn't imagine anyone else in the intervening years who might have had the gumption to dare instruct him.

"Are we going in or will the records magically appear under the threshold?" Yara asked.

Amaranthe blushed. They'd climbed the stairs to the third floor and were standing in front of the headmistress's office. Judging by the comment, they'd been standing there for a while. "In." She tried the knob and found it locked. "Shortly." She set down the lantern and withdrew her tools.

Yara sighed and leaned against the wall again. "Are you sure you'll need me for this underwater adventure of yours? Someone should take a portion of Sespian's funds and try to acquire some of the Forge prototype rifles. For our new troops."

"All two of them?"

"You'll get more. I've heard your spiel," Yara said with a pointed sidelong look. Yes, she'd received the recruiting speech herself. "Besides, Sespian is out trying to get more men right now, isn't he? We should be prepared."

"Would you prefer a weapons-acquisition assignment for yourself? Instead of going to the Forge lair with me?" Amaranthe hadn't been certain about bringing Yara anyway. She could imagine getting two "assistants" past the Forge ladies, but, as she had told Sicarius, it was unlikely the real Suan traveled with an army.

"I wouldn't mind," Yara said. "I could take the new men, make them feel useful and part of your team. They'd be less likely to cross us that way."

Amaranthe appreciated her initiative. Yara's enforcer promotion hadn't come simply because she was a woman, and Sespian wanted a few female sergeants on the force, Amaranthe was certain of that. She couldn't resist the urge to tease Yara though. "Are you sure you aren't simply looking for a way to get out of wearing the costume Maldynado picked out for you?" Surprisingly, the velvety blue fabric was quite attractive, but if one didn't like dresses, one didn't like dresses.

"It's the ridiculous footwear that always comes with those

sorts of clothes," Yara said. "My feet are already big enough that I don't need snowshoes in the winter. Those dumb... *girl* shoes just draw attention."

Hm, she must harbor secret longings to experience life as a modestly proportioned waif of a woman. Amaranthe wondered how many waifs out there saw Yara's height, athletic form, and easy power and wished they could experience *her* life. The veins were always richer in someone else's mine.

"Your feet are perfectly proportionate," Amaranthe said. "Maldynado certainly doesn't seem to mind them."

Yara snorted.

Amaranthe replaced her picking tools and pushed the door open. They entered a tidy office overlooking the street, with a floral seat cushion on the desk chair and light airy curtains framing the window the only feminine touches. She moved the lantern to a bookcase and tried the door beside it, one of two that led to the records area. The other door was in the scholarship office—a room she and Sicarius had visited. She sighed when she found it locked. "They're dedicated to security around here."

Fortunately, this last lock could have been picked with a rusty hairpin, so she made short work of it. They walked into the long aisles of the records room. Long, *dusty* aisles. Amaranthe crinkled her nose and resisted the urge to whip out a kerchief.

"Maldynado is too busy being impressed, so he says, by my other attributes," Yara said, surprising Amaranthe by continuing the conversation. "And attitude. And willingness to do... Well, I like a challenge. I think he expected me to be shy. I'm not."

No, Amaranthe imagined Yara would have no problem telling a man exactly what she wanted. And what *he* wanted too. "He's probably not used to that. Not all of us are that..." Brave was the word that came to mind, but she didn't want to confess to being cowardly. "Unshrinking," she finished lamely.

She waved away the sentence and focused on the rows of student records, hunting for less recent ones. Suan Curlev would have graduated in—

"If it makes you feel better," Yara said, "I'd be intimidated by your assassin too. His list of kills, his reputation, his sheer deadliness. If someone like that ever got mad at you... I don't know that I could—I mean, what could anyone do? Woman or not?"

"Oh, I've seen his temper. It takes a lot to disturb his rigid control, but I've... pushed him. He didn't take it out on me, though a cabinet door did suffer ignobly. I trust him not to hurt me. He hasn't even... there are times when he could have said cruel things—I've deserved them—but he didn't. Even when he lost his temper, he was more irritated with himself than me." Amaranthe chewed on her lip. Why was she sharing all this? "Anyway," she said by way of closing off the conversation, "I've learned that reputation is a truth others concoct to serve their own needs. Genuine truth is revealed in one's actions, actions performed under duress without the time to calculate how they'll make one appear in the world's eyes."

Yara digested that for a moment, then responded lightly, "Are we still talking about bed play?"

"I don't know," Amaranthe said, relieved her comrade had chosen light over serious. With Sicarius being so private, she almost felt like discussing their personal moments was an act of betrayal. "Is duress often involved in your bed play?"

"Often."

This time, Amaranthe snorted. She wouldn't be surprised. Maldynado probably had handcuffs, rope, and ancestors knew what else rolled up in his blanket.

She tapped her fingers on the shelves. "It looks like the records are only kept for ten years. Suan graduated before then. I guess this trip was wasted, and we should have gone shopping for ammunition after all."

"Is it possible older records are stored in a basement or some secondary archive system?" Yara asked.

"I don't remember hearing about anything like that, though let's check the library. If this Suan was so brilliant and so beloved by her teachers, maybe some of her papers were kept for posterity."

They locked the doors and returned to the hallway. Amaranthe led the way back down to the first floor, though she paused as soon as she stepped out of the stairwell. A mop and bucket rested near the wall.

"That wasn't there on our way in, was it?" she murmured.

"No," Yara said.

Amaranthe shuttered her lantern and skirted the bucket. With luck they could slip into the library without chancing across the janitor. She didn't want to leave a trail of bound-and-gagged people stuffed into closets, not on this excursion. If Forge learned she'd been at the school, they might make some guesses as to *why* she'd been at the school.

She slowed as they neared the double-door entry to the library. One of those doors stood ajar, faint light seeping out from within. She stopped on the threshold and risked peering inside. If the janitor were down on his hands and knees scrubbing floors, maybe they could sneak in behind him without being noticed.

Whatever he was doing, it wasn't visible from the doorway. The light from a single lantern brightened the end of an aisle several meters into the library. If the furnishings hadn't been rearranged in the last ten years, tables and desks lay down that wide book-filled corridor. Maybe the janitor was dusting. Amaranthe wanted to look in an alcove on the other side of the room, one that held copies of periodicals and newspapers featuring articles from former students, as well as a handful of economics books written by faculty.

She'd taken no more than a step when a chair creaked, followed by a sigh. Keys jangled on the person's belt. He might be rising to his feet, or simply shifting his weight.

Amaranthe ducked back into the hallway. She waited, but nobody walked out of that aisle.

Before she stepped into the library again, Yara tapped her on the back and signed, *Smart do this? You don't know if anything good inside, right?*

Yara hadn't yet learned all of Basilard's hand signs, but

she knew enough to be understood. Amaranthe shrugged and stepped back into the library again. This time, she padded to her destination as quickly as she could. Yara waited in the hallway.

The illumination from the janitor's lantern didn't reach the alcove. With no other choice, Amaranthe risked unveiling a sliver of her own light. The periodicals and newspapers were organized by date rather than author contribution, so she checked the books first. She doubted Suan had taken the time to write a three-hundred-page epic on economics before heading off on her adventures, but one never knew. And the books were alphabetized.

Curlev, read a name on the spine of a narrow tome.

Surprised but pleased, Amaranthe slid it out. It wasn't something published via the academic presses, but a hand-written treatise in a leather-bound journal. The title, inked on the front, read, *The Distribution of Wealth in Modern Day Turgonia*.

It must be nice to be so brilliant that one's final-year report was set aside in a special spot in the library. Amaranthe could understand why Retta had been jealous of her older sister.

She tucked the journal under her arm and shuttered her lantern again. About to step out of the alcove, she halted when the light flickered ahead. The wooden floorboards creaked. This time the janitor was definitely moving.

Hidden by the shadows, she remained stationary, though she glanced at the door. Out in the hallway, there weren't many places for Yara to hide, unless she ran all the way back to the stairwell.

The janitor walked into view and... wasn't a janitor at all. Dressed in black army fatigues with lieutenant's tabs on his collars, the man headed for the door. The jangling she'd heard hadn't been keys at all, but ammo pouches and other military appurtenances hanging from his belt, including a dagger and a pistol. He didn't wear a colored armband to link him to any of the current factions.

So what was he doing here? And where was the janitor?

The lieutenant strode into the hallway, and Amaranthe held

her breath, hoping he wouldn't spot Yara. His footsteps faded into the distance down the hall without any pauses to investigate something breaking their even rhythm.

Amaranthe started for the door, but curiosity steered her feet toward the aisle the lieutenant had vacated. He'd taken his lantern with him, so she risked opening hers a sliver again. All save one of the tables were empty. The closest one held a single book, left open to an index. Careful not to lose the page, she lifted it to check the title.

The title blurred into insignificance before she read it. It was the *author* that commanded her attention. Worgavic. Neeth Worgavic.

So. Someone had figured out the name of at least one of the Forge founders and had come to do research. At that point, Amaranthe didn't know whether this was good or bad for her. If it meant someone else was angling to take out Forge, that might be good. If it meant another of the factions wanted to ally with Forge for a chance at some of those weapons, that might be less good.

"Hsst," came a soft voice from the end of the aisle.

Amaranthe replaced the book on the table.

"He's gone to the WC," Yara said. "He'll be back in a second."

"Right, let's get out of here then."

They didn't make it out of the library before the lieutenant returned, but hid in the alcove until he'd gone back to his reading. A part of Amaranthe wanted to question him, but a bigger part wanted to make sure nobody saw her at the school, not until she'd completed her infiltration of Forge and no longer needed to be able to pass as Suan Curlev.

She and Yara eased out of the building unnoticed. They jogged into the city, taking a circuitous route back to the factory to make sure they weren't followed.

* * *

Sicarius led Sespian, Maldynado, and Basilard across the dark field toward the towering walls of Fort Urgot. After their training

session, Sespian had asked Basilard to join them. Sicarius did not know if they'd struck up some affinity with each other, or if Sespian had merely wanted more people around to lessen the chances of ending up isolated with a father he felt awkward around. Logically, Sicarius could not expect any other reaction, given their history and his life's work, but the thoughts roused disappointment nonetheless.

The sun had set a couple of hours earlier, but there were no culverts or hallows to hug on the flat, cleared parade fields that extended for a half mile in each direction from the fort. The cloudy sky promised snow, but none had fallen yet, a fortunate circumstance. Sneaking up to the walls on bright white ground would have been close to impossible. They'd have a challenge even without snow. Though he and the others wore black, with their knapsacks and climbing ropes also made from dark material, alert guards in the towers perched along the walls might pick out movement on the stark field. Mortars and rapid-fire cannons were mounted along the parapet in between the towers, and soldiers strode back and forth up there, more men than usual for the fort, which, this deep into imperial territory, had rarely seen action in the last couple of centuries.

Lanterns burned in some of the towers, and Sicarius picked an illuminated one for their approach. The night vision of whoever stood watch inside should be dulled by the nearby flames. Staying low, he and his team closed on the base of the wall.

In the darkness, hand signs were useless, but he'd already told the others he'd go up first, take care of the nearest guards, then signal for them to follow. He wasn't expecting anyone to attempt communication, with soldiers roaming about a mere twenty feet above their heads, but, after he'd unslung his rope and grappling hook, someone gripped his arm. Sespian.

He leaned close to whisper in Sicarius's ear, "You *can't* kill anyone, if we're to have any chance with Ridgecrest."

An obvious statement—these were the very men Sespian hoped to make his own, after all. Sicarius didn't allow himself

to feel irked at this unnecessary reminder. He simply returned the grip, not wishing to speak with men so close above, then drew away to give himself room to toss the grappling hook.

He tilted an ear toward the parapet, listening for footsteps and the clanks of weapon-laden utility belts. Fortunately, his own men remained still and silent, and did not issue any competing noises. Muted voices drifted on the wind, coming from the guard tower to the north, the lighted one. Not a sound came from the one to the south, a dark one. Once he topped the wall, he'd check that one first. With two men stationed in each tower, it was unlikely anyone was asleep on duty. No, those two were probably the more attentive. Though he understood why killing wasn't an option here, the practical part of his mind lamented it, for it was much faster than subduing. He'd have to move quickly to gag and tie the men before others spotted him. Amaranthe, he knew, would have had Maldynado and Basilard go up at the same time he did, trusting their stealthiness and capabilities, but Sicarius trusted his own abilities more.

The footsteps he was waiting for grew audible. Two sets. These were the roving guards for this, the north wall. When he and Basilard had scouted the fort the night before, Sicarius had counted how long it took the men to complete each pass. He'd have approximately ninety-five seconds before they walked this way again.

After the footsteps faded from hearing, he waited five more seconds, then swung the grappling hook, releasing it at the apex. For a moment, its prongs were outlined against the cloudy sky above, then it disappeared over the parapet. Thanks to padded tips, the clank as it landed on stone was muted. Not completely silent, though, and Sicarius's ears had no trouble picking it up.

He gave one quick tug to test the line, then skimmed up the rope, reaching the top in a couple of seconds. Though his ears promised him no one waited above, he paused for a quick glance in either direction, and also toward the brick buildings and walkways inside the fort. In a grassy square lined with streetlamps and bare trees, several whitewashed wooden houses stood—the homes of the high-ranking officers stationed here. General Ridgecrest's family should live in one of them.

As he took in these details, Sicarius released the grappling hook for the others to catch—he'd leave no telltale sign of his arrival on the wall. Then he skimmed down the walkway toward the dark tower.

The stout wooden door stood closed, but there wasn't any glass in the windows overlooking the fields. Sicarius leaped onto the wall, fingers finding grips in the mortar between the stones, and, like a spider, he crawled around to the closest opening. As he'd guessed, two soldiers waited inside. Nobody was sleeping. They were standing with their backs to him, one pointing toward the ground outside the other window, one lifting a rifle.

Sicarius's gut clenched. They were aiming at the spot where he'd left the others. Sespian.

He launched himself into the room, his black dagger finding its way into his hand. Instincts told him to ram the blade into the man's back, to the left of the spine, between the ribs, to find his heart. At the last instant, he flipped the weapon in his hand and shifted targets. He slammed the hilt into the soldier's head, then grabbed him by the back of the neck and thrust his face into the stone wall. When flesh met unyielding granite, the man crumpled. Sicarius tore the rifle out of his hands before it could clatter against anything.

The second man spun in his direction, but he moved too slowly. Sicarius slammed his elbow into his solar plexus. He gasped and bent, staggering backward. The soldier tried to yank out the pistol at his belt. His hand never reached the weapon. Sicarius swung the butt of the rifle upward, clunking him beneath the chin. The man jerked backward and toppled to the ground. Clothing rasped against the stone floor—the first man trying to grab a knife at his waist. Sicarius stepped on his windpipe to discourage further struggles and pulled out his gags and ties. While keeping an eye on the second man—he'd gone down hard and wasn't moving—Sicarius bound the first.

Aware of the heartbeats passing—and the footfalls as the roving guards approached—he tied the knots as swiftly as possible, again reminded why his instructors had simply instilled in him the instinct to kill. He could have nullified every guard on the wall in the time it was taking him to subdue two.

As he moved onto tying the second person, the footfalls stopped outside the door. The roving guards didn't usually check inside the towers. They must have seen or heard something. A soft clank sounded, the latch releasing.

Sicarius tied the last knot and leaped for the window. The door swung open. He scurried around the outside of the building, using the bulk of the open door to hide his return to the parapet.

"What?" one of the guards blurted.

It was all he got out before Sicarius landed behind them, bringing the hilt of his dagger down onto the speaker's head as he dropped. The blunt end struck the coronal structure hard enough to cause the soldier to stagger forward, gasping in pain and confusion, but not hard enough to kill him. Before his comrade could whirl about, Sicarius pinched his fingers together into an arrow shape and dug them into the pressure point near the man's kidney. Trusting the pain to be intense, he snaked his free hand around the soldier's head, flattening it against the mouth. With those hard fingers jabbed into his back, the man staggered into the tower on his tiptoes. His back arched as he tried to squirm out of the iron grip. Using his boot, Sicarius tugged the door shut behind him. He bound and gagged the standing soldier, then attended to the second.

With four men now subdued in the guard tower, he returned to the rest of his team and signaled for them to climb up. While they did so, Sicarius took down the soldiers in the lit tower using similar methods. When he returned, Sespian, Basilard, and Maldynado waited in low crouches, hugging the shadows between the towers. They'd wound up the rope and grapple and were ready to move on.

"If nobody escapes," Sicarius whispered, "and nobody checks the towers before the shift change, we'll have two hours before anyone notices security has been compromised."

"What happens if they *do* escape?" Sespian asked.

Sicarius admitted that was a possibility. For all that he'd tied the knots tightly, the men would have nothing else to do but work on freeing themselves. "We'll have less time."

Maldynado grunted at this statement of the obvious. "We just have to get to Ridgecrest and convince him to have a chat with us. If we're having cider in his office with him, nobody's going to start shooting at us. He's got a wife and a couple of teenage daughters, too, if we need them."

"Are you suggesting we use *hostages* to arrange our escape from the fort?" Sespian asked, his tone oozing disapproval. For once, it wasn't aimed at Sicarius.

"Uhm, no?" Maldynado said. It sounded like a lie, but then he smiled and added, "I figure they'll fall in love with me after I've been flirting with them for a while, and they'll help us escape of their own volition."

"If we stop talking, we can get in and out without anyone but Ridgecrest knowing we're here." To announce the conversation at an end, Sicarius left them, trotting for a stone staircase leading into the streets below.

He kept an eye out as they traversed the fort, sticking to unlit alleys as he picked a path toward the officers' houses. It was past bedtime, but not so late that nobody would be about, and he paused, waiting for more than one person to pass. During peacetime, many officers and senior enlisted soldiers, especially those who were married, stayed in the city, bicycling or jogging to work each morning. But now, with the capital poised for battle, those who were stationed here were sleeping on base, and lights burned behind many of the barracks windows. The armory and several supply and office buildings were lit as well with people working late. Every bicycle rack was occupied and military-style steam carriages and lorries were parked before the senior officers' houses.

They reached the grassy square, and Sicarius headed for the largest house. The first snowflakes drifted down from the sky.

Sespian jogged a few steps and caught up with Sicarius, matching pace, perhaps wanting to be the first person General Ridgecrest saw. Without knowing where Ridgecrest stood—just because he wasn't eager to jump into bed with Ravido didn't mean he'd be delighted to see the emperor he'd thought dead— Sicarius had no intention of letting him walk in first, nor would he knock on the door as if they were coming for a friendly chat. It was possible that force or manipulation would be required to win the general's hand—and his agreement to turn over Fort Urgot to Sespian. This was a man they should catch off-guard.

"We must conclude our business swiftly," Sicarius said. It wasn't in his nature to start conversations that had little purpose, but he felt the need to try with Sespian. As Amaranthe had pointed out, if he never said anything, how was his son to get to know him? "The snow will make it hard to stay hidden at night."

"Swift sounds good to me," Maldynado said. "It's getting cold out here. My brother should have waited until summer to try and take over the empire."

Sicarius leveled a cool stare over his shoulder. He hadn't intended his words to be an invitation for *Maldynado* to participate in a conversation with him. Maldynado didn't notice the stare. He was sniggering over some response Basilard had signed.

A hint of laughter drifted to Sicarius's ears, and he lifted a hand to alert the team. He led them into the shadows between two trees. Engaging Sespian in conversation would have to wait until later.

They'd drawn near the largest house. A gas lamp burned on the porch, lighting a sign that read *Lord General Ridgecrest*.

They'd reached the right place, but two figures were turning off the street and heading up the walkway to the house. One wore an officer's pressed black fatigues, but the other sashayed along in an ankle-length dress and woman's parka. One of Ridgecrest's daughters?

The two advanced to the porch, talking and giggling, their

heads bent toward each other. Sicarius settled on his haunches to wait, expecting the young man to drop his lady off, then leave. But they went from talking and giggling to kissing and giggling. Bundled up for the weather, they didn't seem to notice the cold.

"If I'd known we were going to get a show," Maldynado whispered, "I would have brought candied pecans and a flask of cider."

Basilard elbowed him.

Sespian was averting his eyes from the display. "Maybe we can go in the back?"

"Yes." Sicarius had been eyeing the towers on the wall, thinking of their limited time. "Maldynado and Basilard, stay here." He slipped out his lock-picking kit. "Warn us if someone comes or..." He waved at the kissing couple, meaning he wanted an alert if they entered the house.

Maldynado chose to misconstrue the unfinished sentence. "The show gets better?"

Sicarius gave him a hard look, but a brief one. They had work to do. "Sespian, come."

The darkness cloaked Sespian's expression, but there was a stiff set to his shoulders as he followed. He must not be accustomed to being ordered around. For Sicarius, he either issued commands or followed the orders of others, those rare few who had earned his respect. He didn't know how to relate to people outside of that realm. He'd called Sespian "Sire" when it had applied, but it had been difficult giving that reverence to a youth, and he found it hard to do so now.

They reached the back deck and Sicarius tried the door, found it locked, and knelt to work. This side of the house lay in shadows, just as he preferred. Sespian shuffled to the side to watch the street behind the square. The snow had picked up and a layer dusted his shoulders.

"Do you know how to pick a lock?" Sicarius murmured.

"My how-to-be-an-emperor lessons didn't cover it."

The answer didn't invite further questions, but Sicarius tried anyway. "Do you wish to learn?"

Sespian didn't answer. He might have been mulling over the question or ignoring it.

Sicarius's inclination would have been to work in silence, but he launched into instructions, softly explaining what he was doing as he maneuvered a pick and tension tool. He probably could have found an unlocked second-story window, but on the chance Sespian might appreciate learning a new skill, he pressed on.

"Hunting and fishing," Sespian said at the end of the explanation.

"What?" Sicarius finished with the lock and stood.

"I have no personal experience, but from the stories I've read, fathers and sons are supposed to go hunting and fishing together. There were never any mentions of picking locks and breaking into houses."

Sicarius suspected this was some sort of joke, but he couldn't guess at what the correct response should be. "You wish me to take you fishing?"

"No. I meant... Never mind."

Sicarius pushed open the door, paused to listen, then, upon hearing nothing, slipped into the house. The lingering smells of a kitchen greeted him. The scents of cinnamon and cloves from a baked apple dessert nearly overpowered the lesser odors of elk stew with carrots and parsnips that must have comprised the main meal. A hint of lye soap hung in the air as well.

When Sespian entered, Sicarius headed for stairs, the outline visible at the end of a hallway leading away from the kitchen. There were no lamps lit in the house, though that might change when the daughter entered. He glided up the wooden staircase, pausing only when a creak sounded on a step below him.

"Sorry," Sespian whispered when he glanced back.

"Wood is challenging," Sicarius breathed, hardly believing he was talking when they were sneaking into someone's house, but they'd have to wake Ridgecrest soon regardless, and Sespian might appreciate the instruction. "Step near the edge of the treads for less risk of creaks, and walk near the walls when we reach the hallway."

"All right."

Sicarius continued into the hallway above, opening doors to check for slumbering occupants as he went. They passed two children's rooms, an office, and a library. At the end of the hall, double doors opened to a room with a wide bed in the center. Two people lay in it. The air smelled of sweat and sex, but whatever had happened earlier, the man and woman were both breathing rhythmically in sleep now.

Sespian hesitated in the hallway. "Should we... maybe we should have knocked on the door."

Except that the porch was occupied. Besides, the houses were close enough together that a shout from the general would wake the neighbors. Sicarius didn't want any shouting tonight.

"Wait in the office," he whispered. "Light a lamp."

"What are you going to...?"

"Wake him and bring him to you." And dress him, Sicarius thought.

"Don't... irk him."

Sicarius gave Sespian a gentle push toward the office. Seeing Sespian would surprise Ridgecrest enough that he'd forget any feelings of ire this waking would bring.

After checking to see if the general kept knives or firearms within reach, Sicarius stepped up to his side of the bed. He checked a dark piece of cloth near the nightstand, but realized it was an eyepatch, not any sort of weapon holder. Yes, that was right. He'd seen the general before. Ridgecrest had lost an eye during some past battle.

Sicarius pulled the general upright, clasping a hand to his mouth. He woke with a start, reflexively trying to grab his attacker. Expecting it, Sicarius caught the arms. He locked them behind Ridgecrest's back and tugged him from the bed without jostling the mattress. The woman slept on.

Chest heaving, muscles bunching, the general tried to pull his arms free. From behind him, Sicarius had all the leverage. He propelled the general to a chair, where a pair of trousers hung over the back.

"Dress," Sicarius said in his ear.

Ridgecrest tried to ask a question, but couldn't with the hand clasped across his mouth.

"Answers shortly." Sicarius jostled Ridgecrest again to reinforce his "dress" suggestion.

A stiffness set into the general's spine. He wasn't going to comply. His state of undress mattered nothing to Sicarius—he'd simply assumed the general would prefer to be clothed to face visitors—so he turned his prisoner about, pushing him toward the hallway. The older man dug his heels into the floorboards. He was taller and heavier, but Sicarius lifted the arm lock a couple of inches, and Ridgecrest lurched up onto his toes. Sicarius shoved him down the hall toward the office. The wife never stirred.

The glow of lamplight escaped beneath the office door. Sespian must have heard something for he opened it as they arrived. Sicarius pushed the general inside and toward an oversized brown chair. Seating him required Sicarius to release the arm lock, but he kept his grip on Ridgecrest's mouth and moved around behind him. He withdrew his dagger and rested it on the general's collarbone. Sicarius hadn't interacted with the man, having only seen him in passing a handful of times, but it was possible he would recognize the black blade. Indeed, Ridgecrest's single eye went wide as he glimpsed the tip below his chin. That eye grew wider still when Sespian brought over the lamp and sat in the chair opposite from him.

"Release him, please," Sespian told Sicarius.

If they meant to continue the ruse of Sespian as legitimate heir, Sicarius should follow his orders. Sicarius lifted his hand from Ridgecrest's mouth—he could quickly muffle it again if needed. He let the dagger remain, resting on that collarbone. Ridgecrest didn't squirm, but he looked like he wanted to. With the cold alien alloy against his flesh, perhaps he regretted passing up his chance to put on clothes.

As befitting a sixty-year-old officer, he recovered and found his equanimity. His arms lowered to the chair rests, and his chin rose. "Sespian. You are looking well. I am pleased to see you are not, as the newspapers have been reporting, dead."

Sespian. Not, Sire. Someone must have told him the truth.

Sespian met Sicarius's eyes over Ridgecrest's head. Yes, he'd made note of the address too.

"I apologize for rousing you from bed in this unseemly fashion." Sespian's spread fingers encompassed the general's nudity. "I'd like to talk with you for a few minutes. If you'll agree to listen without raising an alarm, I'm sure I can allow you to get more comfortable. More clothes, fewer daggers at your throat, that sort of thing." He tried a smile.

"I do not need comfort." Ridgecrest propped an ankle over his opposite knee, hiding nothing of his nudity. If anything, he looked pleased at the idea that his state might make Sespian uncomfortable. "Say what you came to say."

The general had assumed an unthreatening pose, but Sicarius kept an eye on him. Though gray hair ringed his bald spot, he was still muscular with broad shoulders that filled the big chair. He carried many a scar from old wounds, including the deep gash that had stolen his eye. His nose had been broken on more than once occasion too. He had survived numerous battles.

"It's quite simple," Sespian said. "I intend to retake the throne. Whatever you've heard, I believe my policies are superior to those of the others who want the position for themselves, with Ravido Marblecrest, in particular, being ready to act as a figurehead while businesswomen run the empire behind his back. I am open to working with the warrior-caste and ensuring they have a say in the government going forward, even as we strive for a more progressive stance when it comes to dealing with our subjects and people from other nations as well."

Ridgecrest watched Sespian as he spoke, but his face never changed, and he didn't say a word.

"I have powerful allies already." Sespian nodded toward Sicarius, though there was nothing smug about it—Sicarius had the sense that Sespian didn't truly want to claim him as an ally and was only doing so because it might help. "I need troops,

however, to march into the city, to retake the Imperial Barracks, and to oust Ravido."

"Why not simply have your powerful ally assassinate Marblecrest?"

"I have never sought to rule through such means, and I'll not descend to those depths now," Sespian said.

"Couldn't get to him, eh?" Ridgecrest studied his blunt fingernails. "I understand someone's employed a wizard to keep the riffraff out of the Barracks." He didn't look at Sicarius when he made the comment, but the insult hung in the air regardless.

"Actually, we've been inside," Sespian said. "Recently. We ran into a Nurian assassin there. I'm not the only one who doesn't approve of Ravido as a successor it seems." Sespian watched Ridgecrest intently. Wondering if he had something to do with the assassin?

Sicarius doubted he did. Ridgecrest didn't have the proper bloodlines to make a claim of his own, and it'd be dangerous for him to risk picking the wrong side. That was why he was trying to remain neutral—and why it'd be difficult for Sespian to get him to commit.

"Interesting," was all Ridgecrest said.

Something tinked against one of the office's glass windows. Trusting he could still stop Ridgecrest if he tried something, Sicarius slipped around a desk and bookcase to check outside.

Though the office faced the unlit yard behind the house, a dusting of snow helped him locate a familiar black wool cap. Basilard moved closer to the light from the window. Even with the movements exaggerated, his hand signs were hard to read, but Sicarius caught the gist.

They're coming inside.

Even as Basilard signed, the faint *snick* of a door being shut drifted up from below. The front door, not the back, Sicarius decided. Footsteps followed, two sets.

Sicarius signed, *The suitor is coming in with the daughter?* That might cause some drama if the father was unaware of the relationship—or aware of it and disapproved. Ridgecrest,

intent on Sespian, didn't seem to have noticed the sounds from downstairs yet.

Not exactly, Basilard signed. *Maldynado went in with her.*

What?

Basilard lifted his shoulders and, though it was hard to tell in the dark, that might have been an eye roll. *He said Amaranthe said he was supposed to come in and help sway the general.*

Somehow Sicarius doubted that had been Maldynado's motivation in approaching the girl. *Remain on guard*, he signed.

Basilard lifted a hand in acknowledgment.

"I think it's admirable—or ambitious—that you want to reclaim the throne," Ridgecrest said, "especially given that Ravido's business allies have a few cannons aimed in your direction. But from what I've heard, you no longer have a stronger claim than any of the others descending on the capital."

"If Ravido is your source, he can hardly be trusted," Sespian said. "He'd say anything to legitimize his attempt at usurping my position."

"Are you saying the assassin lurking at my window is *not* your father?"

Sicarius returned to *lurk* behind Ridgecrest again. Soft murmurs drifted to his ears via the hallway. Maldynado must have stopped to chat with the girl in the kitchen. Sicarius was tempted to check on him and ensure all he was doing was *chatting*. Sicarius didn't care with whom Maldynado engaged in coitus, but doing it with the daughter of the general they were trying to win to their side would prove problematic.

"That *he* thinks he may be my father does not make it the truth," Sespian said. "My mother was sleeping with Raumesys at the same time."

Sicarius wondered if Sespian believed his own words.

Ridgecrest rotated in his chair, his single eye squinting up at Sicarius. "Enh." He turned back to Sespian. "You look more like him than Raumesys."

"You look more like a knife fighter off the streets than a general." Sespian waved to the older man's battered face. "But I'm not going to hold it against you."

Ridgecrest chuckled at that. When Amaranthe was negotiating, Sicarius usually found it to be a good sign when the enemies started laughing, but Sespian didn't have her charm, and Sicarius didn't know if he'd won anything yet.

"No matter who ends up on the throne," Ridgecrest said, leaning back in his chair, "many men will be killed in the fighting, men who signed on to defend the empire against foreign invaders, not to battle each other. No matter who wins in this, Turgonia loses. If you were the ancestors-decreed proper emperor, I'd be obligated to back you, but if your claim is no better than several others..." Ridgecrest hitched a shoulder. "I'm not going to commit Fort Urgot, especially when you, pocket assassin or not, have so few forces at your command. Do you have *any* forces, yet?"

"I do."

Good, Sespian didn't state numbers. A handful of outlaws, and the two soldiers Amaranthe had schmoozed into joining their side, wouldn't impress a general.

"Why didn't you join Ravido?" Sespian asked. "He seems to have the most forces on hand, along with his wealthy female allies. If you seek to stave off bloodshed, wouldn't you find it propitious to ally with him? And have the deed, as it were, done the quickest?"

"I haven't said no to him," Ridgecrest said.

"Oh." Apparently that wasn't the answer Sespian had hoped for.

"I'm waiting to hear from the Company of Lords," Ridgecrest said. "And... an old colleague."

"Is there anything I can do that will change your mind and convince you to join me?"

"No."

This time Sespian didn't say the, "Oh," but it was on his lips. He met Sicarius's eyes. Sicarius tried to read the thoughts behind the gaze. Did he want suggestions for other arguments to use on Ridgecrest? Or did he want Sicarius to apply force?

"What old colleague?" Sicarius asked, wondering if anything had come of the letter he'd posted weeks earlier.

The hallway stairs creaked.

Ridgecrest rose from his chair. "Friend of yours?" he asked Sespian.

"I don't..." Sespian looked at Sicarius.

"Maldynado and the girl."

"The *girl*?" Ridgecrest strode to the door.

"Sir, uhm, you're naked," Sespian reminded him.

Ridgecrest had already flung open the door. The young woman from the porch stood there, her wavy black hair framing a face dominated by puffy red eyes and pouting lips. The expression changed to one of surprise at the sight of her father standing in the doorway.

Maldynado ambled into view, holding a lantern. "Oh, hullo, Lord Ridgecrest. Haven't seen you for some time. Doing well?"

"What's going on?" Ridgecrest growled.

"Daddy, you're *naked*," the daughter said, raising a hand to shield her eyes.

She was younger than Sicarius had first guessed. Fifteen, perhaps. Sespian frowned fiercely at Maldynado, though Maldynado probably didn't see it. Ridgecrest filled the doorway.

"Where have you been with my daughter?" Ridgecrest's hand dropped to his waist, as if to grab a pistol. The only thing down there within reach wasn't going to be much use against Maldynado.

"In the kitchen. Consoling her," Maldynado said. "Platonically, I assure you. I'm involved now, you know. But that fellow who brought her home wanted to send his snake into her garden, if you catch my meaning, and she wasn't ready for all that. Apparently he tried to pressure her and stormed away when she refused to give in to his charms. Charms probably not being the right word. What're they teaching in officer training school these days anyway?"

Maldynado's babble was doing nothing to placate Ridgecrest; the general's fingers had curled into fists, and the veins on his arms stood out. Since Sespian wasn't the target of his ire, Sicarius simply folded his arms across his chest and waited.

Maldynado could handle himself if the conversation devolved into pugilism.

"*Snake?*" Ridgecrest's voice had increased in volume. "*Garden!*"

Doors creaked open in the hallway. "Daddy?" came an uncertain inquiry from another young female.

"Joth?" an older woman—the wife—asked. "What's going on?"

"Bloody beheaded ancestors, I don't know." Ridgecrest lifted a fist and shook it at Maldynado, though he didn't cock it back for a punch. "How did all you miscreants get into my fort to start with?"

"Over the wall, naturally," Maldynado said.

Had Amaranthe truly sent him along to *help*? Maybe she simply hadn't wanted to take him on *her* team.

"Daddy, you need to demote Lieutenant Mosscrest tomorrow. He is *not* a gentleman."

Sicarius headed to the window to check on Basilard. He doubted Sespian was going to get anything more out of Ridgecrest, and it seemed like a good time to leave. Surprisingly, he caught amusement on Sespian's face.

At his look, Sespian shrugged and signed, *It must be quite the experience to be the only man in a house full of women.*

"Ouch," Maldynado blurted from the hallway. "Why—*I* didn't do anything."

This is irrelevant to our mission, Sicarius signed back. *We should go.*

The amusement on Sespian's face disappeared. He seemed stung by the brusque dismissal, and Sicarius regretted it. He should have tried to respond lightly in kind. But this blowup could bring soldiers to check on the house. He and the others needed to leave before—

A flash of orange brightened the horizon. A boom echoed in its aftermath, and a tremor ran through the house, rattling windows and a glass chandelier downstairs.

The shouts halted.

"What now?" Ridgecrest stomped to the window.

"Artillery fire," Sicarius said.

"I know that, but whose?"

Sicarius didn't have the answer to that. It had come from beyond the walls of Fort Urgot.

A chorus of deep bongs arose from outside, someone sounding the alarm. Booming knocks reverberated from the general's front door.

Ridgecrest strode for the stairs.

"Clothes, dear," his wife said from the other direction.

Ridgecrest bellowed a, "Coming," to whoever was pounding at the front door and stomped back up the hall toward his forgotten trousers. "Stay in your rooms," he told his daughters.

Maldynado took the opportunity to sidle into the office. "Time for us to go?"

Sicarius was inclined to say yes, but Sespian shook his head. "Let's see what's going on. Maybe we can help Ridgecrest in a way that would endear me to him."

Maldynado shrugged and followed Sespian into the hallway. Sicarius wondered when his son had started thinking like Amaranthe.

Taking the stairs two at a time, Sespian looked like he meant to stride out the front door. That'd be a good way to get shot, especially since the general hadn't answered it yet.

"Out the back," Sicarius said, diverting him into the kitchen.

He passed the other two and reached the door first. Basilard was waiting on the steps.

Trouble, he signed.

"We gathered that," Maldynado said.

Squads of armed soldiers, their gear clattering with each step, were jogging toward the various sets of stairs leading to the parapet on the wall. All of the guard towers were lit now, and lamps were coming on in buildings all over the fort. Shouted orders echoed through the streets, with the words "attack" and "siege" repeated over and over, amidst commands for soldiers to join their units and find their battle posts.

"We're not going to get near those walls without someone seeing us," Sespian said. "I'm joining Ridgecrest."

"Sespian." Sicarius gripped his arm.

"You heard him. He hasn't committed to anything yet. Regardless, nobody here is going to shoot *me*. I agree that *you* may want to stay in hiding, but I'm going to see what's happening."

Sespian pulled away. Sicarius could have kept him from going—indeed, he wasn't entirely sure soldiers *wouldn't* shoot Sespian if word was getting out about his true parentage—but he'd probably be safe tonight. The soldiers would have other things to worry about. They might put aside their other concerns if they saw *Sicarius*, though, so he searched the buildings in the fort for a less populated place that would afford him a view. A clock tower rose from the square near the front gate. That would have to do.

"Want me to go with him?" Maldynado asked. "I think Ridgecrest is past wanting to hit me. Much."

"No," Sicarius reluctantly said. "Our team is too notorious. The soldiers would capture—" or kill, "—us if they got the chance. Among them, Sespian should be safer without us." Though Sicarius resolved to acquire a rifle on the way to the clock tower in case anyone standing near his son *did* make a hostile move. He ought to be able to hit most targets from that vantage point.

Basilard signed, *Where to?*

"Follow me," Sicarius said.

He jogged through the alleys, taking to the rooftops to avoid troops jogging for the walls. At one point, running along the gutters of a barracks building, he spotted a straggler coming out of the front door. The soldier paused, leaning his rifle against the wall to tug on his helmet and fasten a chinstrap. By the time he turned around to retrieve his weapon, it was gone.

With the rifle and an ammo pouch in hand, Sicarius skimmed behind evergreen hedges fronting the building until he reached the corner. From the alley, he climbed a downspout, regaining the roof again before the private asked, "Did anyone see my gun?"

Maldynado was waiting with Basilard, sharing hand signs and snickers. More booms reverberated through the night, and something slammed into one of the fort walls. Their faces sobered. Sicarius sped past them, across two more rooftops, and down into the square with the clock tower in the center.

By this time, most of the troops had reached the walls and were lining the parapets, several teams manning weapons. In front of the massive double doors leading out of the fort, two infantry companies formed precise squads, rifles in hand, swords hanging from their belts. Nobody had opened those doors, but if someone gave the order, the soldiers would storm out.

With their faces forward, none of the men saw Sicarius, Maldynado, and Basilard running through the shadows behind them. The clock tower was unguarded, so they slipped through the door and jogged up the spiral staircase unopposed. Chains and gears filled the empty air to their right, but Sicarius's only interest was in the view from above. He outpaced the others and reached the wooden platform several stories above the square. After ensuring no enemies occupied the space, he ran to a window facing west, the direction from which that first round had been fired.

The snow had picked up, but it didn't hide the sea of lanterns burning a half mile from the walls. Not just to the west, but to the east and north as well. The cold, dark lake lay to the south, making it difficult to move companies of men into position in front of the fort's double doors, but lanterns meandered through the trees along the jogging path there as well. There were thousands of soldiers out there, maybe tens of thousands. And they'd brought weapons. The lights revealed the hulking shapes of steam trampers, armored lorries, and all manner of mobile projectile launchers. It was Turgonian technology, not that there'd been much doubt. There was no way a foreign invasion force of this size could have come up the river, along the roads, or over the mountains without being spotted. This was another warrior-caste competitor for the throne, someone doing a much better job of rounding up troops than Sespian.

"Oh, that can*not* be good," Maldynado said, coming up beside Sicarius.

We're surrounded, Basilard signed. *We can't even go back to the city.*

"Not easily," Sicarius agreed.

He suspected he could make it—he thought of his promise to return to Amaranthe and "stand guard"—but he wouldn't go without Sespian, and Sespian... Sicarius pulled out his spyglass and searched along the wall until he found General Ridgecrest, gesticulating and barking orders. Yes, there was Sespian at his side, his hood pulled up to hide his face as he gazed thoughtfully out at the massed troops. He didn't look like a man thinking of fleeing; he looked like an opportunist seeking an opportunity.

A faint howl floated across the fields. It was distant, originating somewhere beyond the sea of troops, and someone unfamiliar with it might have mistaken it for a wolf. Sicarius did not.

Basilard didn't either. *The soul construct?*

"Is it with *them*?" Maldynado pointed toward the besieging army. "Because they don't look like they need magic and monsters in addition to all those people and artillery."

"Unknown," Sicarius said. What he did know was that he wouldn't be returning to the city that night, perhaps not for some time.

CHAPTER 10

"**H**ALT, AND IDENTIFY YOURSELF," CAME A VOICE from a nook beside the back door to the molasses factory. At first, Amaranthe didn't recognize it, but then she remembered. It was one of her new "recruits." Private Rudev. Not only had the two soldiers not wandered off, but they were standing watch. Huh.

The sun had long since set, and she supposed he couldn't identify them in the darkness. "Amaranthe and Sergeant Yara," she said.

"You may enter, Sergeant and, er, ma'am."

"Thank you."

Amaranthe shifted the book she was carrying under one arm and opened the heavy metal door. Inside, a single lantern burned beside the entrance. The only other light came from the offices on the landing. The dusty machinery and empty vats lay dormant and dark. Amaranthe lamented that she hadn't had time to tidy the place up much yet.

"I'm going to find something to eat," Yara said and headed for the cafeteria.

Amaranthe waved. "I may join you later." Her stomach protested at the delay of food, but she wanted to check on the others and examine her pillaged book.

Coldness hugged the inside of the factory, so she hustled for the steps. Snow had started falling outside. If the temperature dropped much more, they'd have to start one of the furnaces to heat the building. Or start sharing bedrolls. Her lips twitched into a private smile.

The light was coming from the office next to hers. Inside, Books and Akstyr sat on opposite sides of a desk. Stacks of papers and tomes in foreign languages, along with a pile of gnawed pork ribs, covered the surface, no plates in sight. The scent of a honey-apple glaze lingered in the air. Amaranthe's stomach issued a pitiful whine.

"You missed dinner," Akstyr said. "Basilard made some tasty sauce."

Her stomach's whines grew more plaintive.

"You've been gone a long time." Books sat at the desk, his hands folded over a stack of papers, a bright and alert expression on his face. He'd combed his hair and shaven, something he hadn't bothered with the last few weeks. "Were you at your old business school the whole time? Did you run into trouble?"

"No. A delay or two, but we got past them." Amaranthe chose not to go into the details of how easily she was gaining access to locked buildings these days—Books always pursed his lips in disapproval at the development of her thief-appropriate skill set. "I didn't find the records I sought, but this was written by Suan, so it may prove enlightening." She tapped the leather-bound book. "I was hoping someone would save me dinner."

Akstyr picked up a rib with most of the meat gnawed off. "There's a little left on some of these bones. If you don't mind Books's slobber."

Books's lips flattened. "Are you ever going to start acting like an adult?"

"What do you mean? I was real mature about a certain assassin hacking off all of my hair and burning it like some funeral pyre offering." This time Akstyr's lips flattened, the expression oddly similar to Books's. "I could have spent the day plotting revenge, but I've been studying instead."

"You only came up here a couple of hours ago," Books said.

"All right, I've been studying *part* of the day. I didn't let go of the revenge plotting until after lunch."

"You're not going to try and convince some bounty hunter to go after him again, are you?" Amaranthe pulled a crate up to the desk and sat down between them.

"No, he'd kill me over that. I was thinking of a revenge that he couldn't pin on me. Like using my Science skills to light his socks on fire."

"While he's wearing them?" Amaranthe eased a few papers to the side, looking for a place where she could set the book.

"Preferably while he's tormenting us during some training session." Akstyr grinned. "But he'd probably know it was me who did it then, 'cause I'd be falling down laughing."

"If you used magic, he'd know it was you anyway," Books said.

"Not necessarily. Fire's natural. And things catch on fire sometimes. The Science wouldn't be the only possible explanation."

Books stared at him. "Name one possible non-magical explanation that could account for socks randomly taking flame."

"Well... there's that one thing. When stuff blows up of its own accord."

"Spontaneous combustion?" Books asked.

Akstyr snapped his fingers. "That's it."

"That generally applies to piles of hay and compost, not undergarments."

Amaranthe shook her head and opened to the first page. She'd get more read with fewer distractions if she went into the other office, but she didn't want to be alone. Especially—a yawn stretched her jaw so wide that it popped—at night. Books and Akstyr would help her stay awake until a certain night watchman returned.

Before she could delve into the text, Books cleared his throat.

"I asked you about your evening," he said.

"Yes..." Amaranthe said.

"Aren't you going to ask me about mine?"

"I wasn't planning to, no." She smiled, but Books's expression grew consternated, so she relented. "How was your evening?"

"Most excellent. I finished my treatise, my Constitution for the Turgonian Republic, outlining specific government responsibilities and powers along with declaring fundamental

rights for its citizens. *Citizens*, mind you, not subjects. It is, of course, a preliminary draft. I'd like feedback from my peers, but, ah—" Books gazed out the window at the factory's innards, "—due to my limited access to colleagues learned in manners of history and politics, I'd like you to read over it."

"*Me?*" Even if she hadn't had an infiltration to plan, Amaranthe wouldn't have thought herself knowledgeable enough to weigh in on such a document.

"Sespian, too, of course. Despite his youth, he'll naturally be well versed in the matter of ruling a nation. Sicarius's opinions might be useful as well, if he'll deign to read it."

Yes, and what exactly would Sespian think when he found out Books's new ideas revolved around a government that *elected* its leaders? In such a scenario, what odds would a nineteen-year-old boy have of claiming the throne? Would it even be called a *throne* if Books's future came to pass?

"It's not that bad." For once, Akstyr was paying attention, noticing her hesitation. "I've read part of it."

"*You've* read part of it?" Amaranthe didn't know whether it surprised her more that Books had shared it with him or that he'd actually looked the documents over, especially given the encyclopedia-sized stack of pages beneath Books's folded hands. Weren't constitutions supposed to be short and concise?

"Not exactly, but we've been sharing lanterns at night, and he mutters a lot when he writes." Akstyr shrugged. "I liked the part where it says citizens are freely allowed to pursue the careers of their choices and study whatever subjects they wish."

"Page eighty-three," Books said. "Paragraph three."

"Ah, would you stay in the empire if you were allowed to use the mental sciences?" Amaranthe doubted a government document would change the imperial beliefs about magic, nor how fast people were to punish others who used it, but she latched onto the topic, hoping to distract Books from the idea that she should read his opus that night. After she returned from her mission, she could peruse it. Or—she eyed the thickness of the stack again—ask someone for an abbreviated version.

"Maybe," Akstyr said. "Though those Kyatt Islands sound real nice. And warm." He pulled his jacket tighter about him. "Besides, I've got that other problem."

Yes, Amaranthe needed to send the team out to find Akstyr's mother or blackmail whomever it would take to get the bounty removed from his head. Unfair of things to pile up on one's to-do list while one was off being tortured. There was a particular cosmic cruelty to that.

"You can take it with you to your room," Books said, "so long as you promise to be careful. It's the only copy I have so far, and it's already been dreadfully difficult to keep the pages together. Oh, when you get to the singed ones in the middle, the new writing is on the back. I must have copies made. I wonder if either of those two soldiers you picked up is literate enough for the task. Probably not. I'll have to hire a scribe."

"I could wait to read it until after you have more copies." Amaranthe tapped the book she'd brought. "I need to study up on the woman I intend to impersonate first, and I wouldn't want to lose any of your pages."

"Yes, but if you finish with that... you'll have something nearby for when you can't sleep."

Erg, did *every*one know she wasn't sleeping? "I intend to sleep well tonight." She chomped down on her lip to keep from grinning and adding that it'd be after some vigorous exercise.

"Oh." Books's gaze drooped with disappointment.

"But why don't I take the first few pages, just in case?" Amaranthe found herself saying. She had a feeling she wasn't going to get out of reading the thing.

Books brightened. "Yes, good. Here." He handed her a third of the stack, far more than a few pages. "I'll see about having the rest copied."

Clomps sounded on the metal stairs leading to the offices. Amaranthe lifted her head. Sicarius? He wouldn't make any noise climbing the steps, but maybe Maldynado and the others were with him.

It was Deret Mancrest who walked into view however,

yawning and leaning heavily on his swordstick. Amaranthe hadn't spoken to him since the night before, nor had she thought overmuch of him, she admitted with a guilty twinge. If nothing else, she should be keeping track of him and the new recruits, to ensure everyone remained suborned to her side.

Deret noticed Amaranthe watching him through the window and straightened, making it seem as if the swordstick were a decorative prop, not a necessary tool. He lifted a hand to knock, but Amaranthe waved and said, "Come in, Lord Mancrest." She gave him a warm please-don't-get-bored-lingering-in-our-hide-out-and-go-back-to-your-father smile, hoping it would make up for her neglect.

Deret entered, looked around for a chair, and settled for perching on the edge of a low bookcase. "I need to talk to you, Amaranthe, but I have news also."

"Oh?"

"I've been communicating with a few of my contacts, those I can be reasonably sure my father doesn't own—" his lip twisted in a sneer, "—and there are a couple of tidbits I believe will interest you."

Amaranthe leaned toward him, elbow on the edge of the desk. She waited for him to continue, but he merely met her gaze frankly.

"Are we trading information again?" she asked.

"I'm still waiting for the information you promised me yesterday."

Another task she didn't have time to complete. "Books has recently completed his project. I believe he's available to brief you."

Books had indeed been watching the exchange—Akstyr had his nose pressed into the pages of some tome on Kendorian magic and probably didn't know Mancrest was in the room—though his eyebrows twitched at this new assignment. "You've certainly learned how to delegate in this last year as a leader, haven't you?"

"It's part of my important new job. Didn't you hear? Sespian

named me as..." Hm, what was that title again? Oh, yes. "High Minister in charge of Domestic and Foreign Relations."

Books's eyebrows went from subtle twitching to outright acrobatics on his creased brow. "Are we then throwing our weight behind Sespian as emperor? Rather than establishing a new more modern and progressive regime?"

"Such as a republic?" Amaranthe asked.

"Such as."

"I don't think we'll get the backing we need if we attempt to open with that gambit. However, if we can get Sespian onto the throne, he'd be amenable to giving up absolute power in favor of gradually instituting some of your suggestions. He's often spoken of how he wants to turn the empire in another direction. He might be willing to carry your documents to the Company of Lords himself."

"I was imagining this as a revolution, one that would render the Company of Lords obsolete," Books said.

"Nonetheless, I think we'll have less opposition if we try to make these changes gradually."

"*I* think that a revolution must be swift, thus to catch the power players by surprise, or it'll never take place at all. This is the time. Forget trying to win the favor of lords or even soldiers. It's the common man to whom we must appeal. With no obvious choice to put forward as an imperial candidate, this is the ideal time for upheaval. If we wait... those currently in power are perfectly capable of burying my ideas in a quagmire of bureaucracy."

"Quagmire of bureaucracy?" Deret asked.

"If your question is, 'Does he always talk like that?' the answer is yes," Akstyr said.

"No, I'm curious about these ideas and..." Deret leaned forward, eyeing the stack of papers on the desk. "What is that? Have you drafted up a proposition for a new government?"

Deret oozed interest, and Books latched onto it like a tick on a dog. "Indeed I have. Would you like to see what I have so far?"

Before Deret could do more than nod his head, Amaranthe gripped his arm. "You had other news, I believe?"

Deret tore his attention from Books's opus. "Yes. You've heard that the ships coming up the Goldar River are being detained, right? They're being searched by the military to make sure no unauthorized troops or weapons are ferried into the city."

"Yes, we had to come in on foot to avoid being discovered that way ourselves," Amaranthe said.

"That's not the *only* reason we came on foot," Books murmured.

Deret's eyebrows arched.

"We sank the steamboat we were taking upriver," Akstyr said.

"For good reason," Amaranthe said when Deret's curious gaze swung in her direction. "Books will explain it to you when you two chat."

"That should prove interesting," Deret said. "The reason I bring it up is that there's a ship being detained now that's out of Kendor. The *Dancing Salamander*. One of my contacts got the roster, thinking there might be something newsworthy— warrior-caste families returning home who might have a sway in the succession struggle, that sort of thing."

"And?" Amaranthe prompted, though she had an idea as to why Deret was bringing this up.

He dug a slip of paper out of his pocket and handed it to her. Amaranthe skimmed through the names, and her shoulders slumped at the familiar one two thirds of the way down the page. *Suan Curlev.*

"Bloody ancestors, I knew she was coming, but I thought I had a couple of weeks."

"What is it?" Books leaned across the table to read the list.

"The lady I want to impersonate may be arriving at the same time as me."

"The boats have been delayed up to twenty-four hours at the mouth of the lake," Deret said.

"I don't think that's going to be enough time, even if I go tomorrow. Unless..." Amaranthe tapped her chin. "Yara isn't that enthused about going with us. Maybe she can stay here, while I take only my mental sciences adviser and the scribe who handles my business books." She waved to Akstyr and Books, naming the roles she'd made up for them. "Deret, I don't suppose you and Sergeant Yara would like to go on your own mission together?" Yara could hunt for weapons on the side.

"I don't know. I had a mission of my own planned. Besides, I can't imagine what I'd talk about with a woman who finds Maldynado fascinating enough to sleep with."

"I'm not sure it's his *fascination* that draws her," Amaranthe said.

Books snorted.

"What mission did you have in mind?" Deret asked.

"Nothing particularly challenging. Just kidnapping an intelligent globe-traveling woman and holding her here until I get back."

Books lifted a finger. "Perhaps I should volunteer for that one."

This time Amaranthe snorted. From the description, this Suan did sound like the type of woman for him. But... "I need you down there, Books. You and Akstyr, both. If Retta isn't there, or if we can't find her, we're going to need to figure out how to destroy the *Behemoth*, or at least nullify it so Forge can't use it. Succession squabbles aside, Forge could take over the city with the power of that craft alone."

"I know," Books said. "I understand."

Deret stroked his chin. "If I help you do this, will you help me take my newspaper back?"

Amaranthe almost blurted a 'yes' right away—she'd much rather have an ally in charge of the city's most influential paper than an enemy or indifferent party manning the presses—but she didn't have many people left to send with him. "How quickly do you need it done?"

"The sooner the better. Right now, the *Gazette* will be somewhat... disheveled. An ideal time to attack."

"I'll help as soon as I'm able," Amaranthe said. "You could take Yara now and... the two soldiers down there on guard.

Maybe Akstyr can heal the injured one—" she almost choked on the idea of introducing a superstitious imperial man to magic that way, "—and you can take them on the kidnapping too." Better to have them off on some mission than here alone where they might decide to wander back to their own unit and, oh, report the location of Lokdon, Sicarius, and their heinous band of outlaws while they were at it.

"For my team, a woman and two soldiers inept enough to be caught by the likes of Maldynado, eh?" Deret asked.

"Yara's an enforcer sergeant and extremely capable."

"And the two soldiers?"

"I don't know them that well yet," Amaranthe said. "They stand guard nicely."

"What an accolade," Books said.

Amaranthe spread her hand. "If Sicarius and the others return tonight with good news, I may have more men that I can assign to your task. Retaking the *Gazette* would benefit us as well, so I'd be pleased to help you with that."

Deret grimaced. At first she thought it was because Sicarius was the last person with whom he'd want to work, but he said, "That's my second piece of news."

A heavy feeling of dread settled in Amaranthe's stomach. "What is?"

"Your other men... They went to Fort Urgot tonight, didn't they?"

"Yes..."

"Fort Urgot has been surrounded by twenty thousand troops."

Amaranthe gaped at him and mouthed, "What?"

"I don't know if you've kept up with the papers, but Satrap Governor Lord General Heroncrest captured one of the railroads a couple of weeks ago, and he's been ferrying soldiers into the area. He has enough of the right blood in his veins to make a bid for the throne. It seems he's ready to make his first move."

Amaranthe dropped her head onto the desk. If her men had been caught inside, she might not see them for days. Or weeks. And Sicarius certainly wouldn't be standing guard for her that night.

* * *

Inches of snow blanketed the walls around Fort Urgot as well as the window ledges in the clock tower overlooking the square. Thick flakes wafted down from the dark sky, and, even with a spyglass, Sicarius could barely see the knot of uniformed men huddled on a white field to the west. Four of General Ridgecrest's officers were out there along with a small contingent from the invading army. Whatever they were discussing, they'd been at the conversation for some time.

He shifted the focus of the spyglass to Ridgecrest and Sespian again. Along with several other officers, they stood on the west wall, overlooking the group of men on the field. Sespian was keeping his hood pulled close to his face. If anyone except Ridgecrest knew who he was, it wasn't apparent.

Hours had passed since the thousands of soldiers had amassed around the fort, and they were setting up tents and digging trenches out there, but no weapons had been fired since the opening rounds from the invaders, more of a warning to cooperate than a true attack. The auto cannons mounted on the walls remained quiescent, though they'd been loaded, ready in case the invaders drew close enough for an assault on the fort.

Sespian's head turned, and he scanned the rooftops inside the compound. Looking for someone? His father? He must wonder where Sicarius and the others had gone, if they'd stayed inside or left him to fend for himself.

Though it went against his nature—the last thing he wanted to do was draw a soldier's attention to his position—Sicarius waved a hand when the searching gaze drifted in his direction. Sespian's eyes lifted, then halted. They looked at each other for a moment, then Sespian turned back and responded to some comment Ridgecrest had made. It occurred to Sicarius that all Sespian would have to do was say a few words, and squads of soldiers could be sent to the clock tower with orders to kill him. Sespian didn't have the heart of a murderer, but was it truly murder to give an order to have a notorious assassin slain? Or,

in his eyes, was it justice? Perhaps he'd find that more amenable than having to deal with his father's attempts at establishing a relationship with him.

Stop being melodramatic, Sicarius told himself. Sespian might have once loathed him, but surely familiarity had resulted in a modicum of... tolerance. Hadn't Amaranthe often said that people had a hard time killing those they knew? Of course, she had a knack for getting people to like her, not simply know her. Either way, he'd already picked a couple of likely escape routes if he had to flee the clock tower. Even if the exit below were blocked, he had rope in his pack and could toss a line to the wall or a rooftop. Besides, the soldiers were intent on those *outside* the walls at the moment.

"Is there an army order against pissing in a corner of a clock tower?" Maldynado asked.

With his back to the men, Sicarius didn't see Basilard's signed response.

"Are you sure?" Maldynado asked. "You're not even Turgonian. How would you know?"

Sicarius ignored the conversation and shifted the spyglass back to the field. The knot of men was breaking up with the four from the fort heading back to the gate.

"Fine." Maldynado walked up to the window beside Sicarius. "Then is there a rule about pissing *outside* of a clock tower? We've been cooped up in here for hours, and I haven't unleashed the snake since we left the warehouse."

Without lowering the spyglass, Sicarius turned his coldest stare onto Maldynado. "You will *not* urinate out the window." Soldiers previously occupied by the invaders might develop an interest in the clock tower should suspiciously yellow snow catch someone's eye.

I told you, Basilard signed.

"Where then?" Maldynado propped his hands on his hips. "The way things are going, we'll be here for days. Even *you* can't hold it that long."

A creak drifted up from the double doors marking the fort

entrance. The four officers jogged through the sally port and headed for General Ridgecrest's portion of the wall. Their route took them near the clock tower, so Sicarius drew back into the shadows, glancing at Maldynado to ensure his "snake" wasn't anywhere near the window. Intent on their mission, the officers did not look up. They ran up the stairs, stopping before Ridgecrest, and a long dialogue ensued. At the end, Ridgecrest drew Sespian to the side.

Sicarius lifted the spyglass again, trying to read lips. Ridgecrest's back was to him, though, and he couldn't decipher much of the conversation. After a few minutes, Sespian nodded, pointed toward the field, then walked down the stairs. Ridgecrest also descended, though he strode in another direction, toward the headquarters building in the center of a complex of offices.

Sespian's route zigzagged, first down one street, then up an alley, and Sicarius realized he must be coming to see him, choosing a route that someone watching from the wall wouldn't be able to follow. Judging by the gesticulations and curses being flung in the direction of the army outside, few people were paying attention to him. Sicarius didn't think anyone noticed him come out of an alley and jog across the square to the base of the clock tower.

A soft thump drifted up from below, the sound of the door closing.

"What was that?" Maldynado blurted, in the middle of... Sicarius stared at him. He had chosen a dim corner in which to relieve himself.

I told you, Basilard signed again, this time adding, *They're coming for you.*

"What? Who?"

The military police.

"Very funny."

The wooden stairs leading to the top of the tower creaked. Cursing under his breath, Maldynado hastened to button himself in.

A second step creaked, and this time it was Sespian who

cursed under his breath. "Just so you know," he called up softly, "I *was* stepping on the edges. These stairs are hundreds of years old. And creakier than a granny's rocker."

Sicarius grunted softly and almost responded that it took time to master the art of stealth, but Maldynado and Basilard's presence squelched his thoughts of speaking.

Sespian climbed out of the shadows and went straight to Sicarius at the window. "I have a message for you."

Sicarius waited.

"The confabulation out there wasn't useful. General Ridgecrest hasn't learned anything except that the army is being led by Satrap Governor Lord General Heroncrest—his are the soldiers who've been wearing the blue armbands around town— and that he has a lot more men in the area than anyone expected. He's got one of the railroads, which everyone has known about, but the last stop before Stumps has been monitored, and *that* many people—" he waved toward the encamped army, "—never disembarked. We're surmising that his men have been coming in day and night, but getting off at the previous stop and forming up in the mountains."

"This message is for me?" Sicarius asked.

"No, but I thought you'd want to know the background information. What Ridgecrest is interested in from you is... he wants more intelligence, for someone to spy on that camp and report back to him."

Sicarius stared.

"You can't be surprised," Sespian said. "Everyone's heard of you. As his X.O. said, you're legendary."

"He used that word?"

"It was close to that word," Sespian said. "His actual choice might have been infamous."

"I see."

"But Ridgecrest nodded."

"They thought of me for this intelligence-gathering endeavor? Of their own accord?" Sicarius deemed it unlikely. To the army, he was nothing more than a loathed criminal

who'd killed dozens, if not hundreds, of soldiers over the years. Besides, the general would have his own trained spies.

"I... may have volunteered you," Sespian said.

"Oh, this should prove interesting," Maldynado chimed in.

Basilard gave him a shushing swat.

Sicarius said nothing, merely waiting for a further explanation. He understood that Sespian wanted to ingratiate himself to Ridgecrest, but found it hard to believe the general would have accepted this offering.

Sespian lifted a hand. "Now, before you get huffy..." He glanced at Maldynado and Basilard and whispered, "Does he ever get huffy?"

Not in a manner that would cause most people to notice it, Basilard signed at the same time as Maldynado said, "Yes."

Sicarius stared at them briefly—this caused defensive shrugging, then squirming from Maldynado—before returning his attention to Sespian.

"I've volunteered myself for the mission too," he said.

Maldynado gaped at Sespian. "You did what?"

Though also surprised, Sicarius kept his face neutral. "You wish to go on a dangerous mission with me?"

Sespian grimaced. "I'm not sure *wish* is the word, but I sense that this might improve General Ridgecrest's opinion of me. He hasn't been rude, but from a few comments... I had the impression he doesn't have a lot of respect for... what did you call me?" He glanced at Maldynado. "Bookish?"

"Bookly."

Basilard signed, *Is that a word?*

Maldynado pointed a finger at him. "Don't you start. I get hounded about words enough from Books."

"Bookly, yes," Sespian said. "I don't think Ridgecrest respects bookly types as much as warriors."

"That's not exactly true," Maldynado said, dropping his goofy expression in favor of a more serious mien. "He came by the house some when I was a boy. He'd served a few years on the west coast and was a contemporary of Lord Admiral Starcrest.

He had all sorts of respect for him, and by all accounts Starcrest was on the bookly side. But he used his smarts to succeed in war, and the stories say he was the type to lead men into battle, a cutlass in one hand and a pistol in the other."

Sicarius had wondered if Ridgecrest had ever met Starcrest. If the two had a past bond, it could prove useful if—

"Perhaps I should have been asking you for cutlass- and pistol-wielding lessons these last weeks," Sespian told Sicarius with a sigh.

Sicarius refrained from pointing out that he'd been available and that if someone hadn't been sulking someone could have had as many lessons as he wanted. "We can begin anytime you wish."

"Can we gather intelligence for Ridgecrest first?" Sespian asked. "Everything Maldynado said makes me believe my impression was correct, and that Ridgecrest might respect me more—no, be more willing to *ally* with me—if he saw that I'm capable of the sorts of physical feats that Turgonian emperors have always demonstrated. He needs to know that I'm a man who's not afraid to walk into danger; I won't simply hide in the Imperial Barracks and send others out to die for me."

Normally, Sicarius would approve of this line of reasoning, but the earlier howl of the soul construct concerned him. If the creature was, as he suspected, after Sespian, he'd be safer inside these walls and surrounded by thousands of people. Heroncrest might be the man who'd allied with the Nurians. If Sespian walked into their camp and was captured... Heroncrest would get rid of him in a second to make his own route to the throne simpler.

Sespian cleared his throat, breaking the silence that had fallen upon the clock tower. "I know I'll slow you down, but I thought... maybe you could show me a few things out there—the things you do so well. Less the throat-cutting ideally. Amaranthe said... I mean, it seems like you want to. Show me things, that is." He gave a self-deprecating eye roll at the awkwardness of his words. This must mean much to him—perhaps he saw Ridgecrest as his only chance.

Basilard and Maldynado's heads swung toward Sicarius. He sensed that they were enjoying the chance to see a side of him that was more than the assassin. Sicarius, however, didn't care to share that side with anyone except Sespian. And Amaranthe. He did his best to ignore them.

"I thought you were more interested in fishing," he said.

Sespian managed a wan smile. "Wrong time of year for that, I fear."

"Are we coming too?" Maldynado asked.

"As I recall, you're here to spread rumors about Ravido," Sicarius said.

"Preferably not through Ridgecrest's daughters," Sespian added.

"They're absolutely no fun, either of them," Maldynado muttered to Basilard.

Basilard ignored him, signing toward Sicarius, *And me?*

Sicarius considered the question. He'd prefer to take no one and gather intelligence on his own—or simply eliminate this Heroncrest—but if he had to take someone, he'd rather have the more proven Basilard than Sespian. Practically speaking. But if he went with his heart, something Amaranthe would doubtlessly encourage, he'd take Sespian and Sespian alone. How could he refuse to do so when Sespian had finally asked for it? He'd made no mention of taking Maldynado or Basilard.

Hoping this decision of the "heart" wouldn't get his son killed, Sicarius said, "Keep watch from in here, Basilard. If an alarm is raised or if we're captured—" or killed, he added silently, thinking of the soul construct, "—let Amaranthe know what's happened."

Understood, Basilard signed.

"A word," Sicarius said, waving for Sespian to join him to one side.

"Yes?"

"I'd be remiss if I didn't point out the logic of assassinating your rival instead of spying on him," Sicarius said.

Sespian sighed. "I knew you'd bring that up. We're not killing anyone."

"It's unlikely we'll make it in and out without casualties."

"I thought you were better than that—in and out without anyone knowing you're there. Or are you worried I'll be the one to snap a twig and alert someone of our presence?"

Yes, Sicarius thought, but he didn't say it.

He didn't need to. Sespian sighed again. "If that happens, just knock the person out or otherwise subdue him. I know you can do that. We don't need to kill anyone."

"You're being optimistic."

"Better than pessimistic." Sespian set his jaw.

Sicarius flicked away the argument—the guards were inconsequential anyway—but he wasn't ready to concede on the enemy commander. "If we're going through the effort of sneaking past the perimeter, which won't be easy because they'll be expecting spies, it's logical to kill Heroncrest while we're there. If these two armies clash, he'll be a target in the battle anyway. You or Ridgecrest will be standing on the wall, directing artillerymen to shoot rounds at him. He's someone who is plotting to take the throne. With you still alive, that's treason, punishable by death. Getting rid of him in the beginning could save lives later. Further, there'll be a headless army out there without a candidate to back. If you show your face, you'll be their logical leader. You could have thousands of men, at which point Ridgecrest might be more likely to back you as well. The combined forces would rival those Ravido can claim."

Sespian shook his head and walked to the window. He gripped the sill, hands tight on the cold snow and stone. Sicarius didn't know if that was an utter rejection or not—Amaranthe was always more vociferous about her rejections. He went to stand beside Sespian, curious if he'd be pushed away.

"I understand your logic, and I won't try to pretend that it's false," Sespian said, "but you can't always use logic when it comes to human beings. There are methods that are honorable and others that aren't. I won't win Ridgecrest's respect by sending in an assassin to kill my competition in his sleep. And I won't... respect myself either. I refuse to believe that a man has

to give up his self-respect, his sense of honor, to rule a nation."

Sicarius doubted many leaders of nations, especially ones not born into the position, had reached such lofty heights without trading their honor for gains somewhere along the way. For good or ill, Hollowcrest and his tutors had chosen to instill practicality into him, not honor. If he saw an opportunity to assassinate Heroncrest, he'd take it. Sespian's honor need not be besmirched if he wasn't a part of it.

Out loud, Sicarius said, "Very well. I will not mention it again."

"Thank you," Sespian said. "Do we go tonight?"

Sicarius gazed out the window, back toward the city. As much as he'd like to return to the factory—to Amaranthe—he doubted it would happen soon. "The night is already half-spent, and many will be alert still. We'll go tomorrow night."

"I'll be ready."

"As will I," Sicarius said and pulled out the sharpening kit for his knives.

CHAPTER 11

E VENING APPROACHED AS AMARANTHE STRODE DOWN THE nicest part of Waterfront Street with Books and Akstyr at her side, though, thanks to the gray sky and snow, it had never truly felt like daylight. She'd spent the afternoon studying Suan Curlev's book and watching the windows, hoping Sicarius and Sespian would walk into the factory. With the news of Fort Urgot being surrounded, she wasn't surprised they hadn't returned, but she'd hoped anyway, wanting to see Sicarius again before her mission. If things didn't go well...

No thinking like that, she told herself. Things *would* go well.

With her shoulders back and her head lifted, Amaranthe was trying to appear confident as they walked, or at least like someone who believed her plan had a chance to work. But every time one of her newly blonde locks flopped into her line of sight, it gave her a start—and reminded her that she wore a costume, a costume that was nothing better than a guess at what a woman returning from Kendor might look like. A tintype in the back of Suan's book had shown her wearing half-frame reading glasses, often pushed up into her shoulder-length hair, but the rest of the outfit was a guess.

The brown and tan pattern of the dress swirling about Amaranthe's ankles had a desert feel, though the leggings and fur boots beneath were purely Turgonian and designed for winter weather. Maldynado had picked out a pair of suede wedge sandals, complete with skin-tickling tassels, to complement the dress, but she did not wish to invite frostbite to visit her toes. Nor could she imagine fighting in footgear that hoisted

her heels three inches into the air and threatened to tip her nose-first onto the ground every time she took a step. Much to Sergeant Yara's amusement, Amaranthe *was* wearing the string lingerie, if only because there'd been no time to shop for more practical underwear. Her regular cold-weather undergarments would have shown through the low-cut dress. *Not* the sexy look of an exotic globe-exploring woman, Maldynado had informed her. He refused to accept the idea that someone who explored the world could do so without being sexy. The final piece of the costume lay beneath a mink jacket, the slit-eyed medallion dangling on its silver chain.

Books was lecturing on Kendorian economics as they walked, and Amaranthe turned her attention back to his words, knowing she might need the information. Since Suan had last been traveling there, and the Forge people all had business interests, it might come up in an early conversation.

"...relatively meager gross domestic product in comparison with the empire," Books was saying. "It's not surprising given how much of the population is nomadic. Kendor is, however, known for a few niche industries, such as wool, copper, and sartorial crafts with their lizard-skin products being recognized all over the world. Some of the tribes also lease land to foreigners for ranching and mining, though Turgonians are not allowed, so an interested imperial entity must find a creative workaround, typically by engaging a third-party representative, to tread upon Kendorian soil."

Books continued to speak, needing amazingly few breaths or breaks to rest his lips. He ignored Akstyr's pronounced yawns and muttered asides. Only when Akstyr raised his voice and said, "Enforcers," did Books pause.

A pair of patrollers had walked out of one of the steep side streets and rounded the corner onto the waterfront.

"Up the alley?" Akstyr asked.

"No." Amaranthe touched her prosthetic nose, one that added length and a slight hawkish aspect to her face, to assure herself it was still attached; the rest of her makeup was cosmetic, and

she didn't worry so much about it, but if the nose happened to fall off at an inopportune time... She dropped her hand. It was fine and would, no doubt, be more likely to stay so if she stopped prodding it. "Let's see how well our costumes work."

"Looking for trouble before we reach the yacht club?" Books asked.

"If we can't pass as non-outlaws in front of a couple of rookies, there's no point in attending this meeting."

"Very well."

Books and Akstyr also wore costumes designed to make them appear traveled. Books's long legs were clothed in sedate brown corduroy trousers, but the apricot and yellow silk "scholar's robe" definitely bespoke Nurian origins. The lizard-skin satchel slung over his shoulder was out of Kendor, but, according to Maldynado, catching on in the capital, much like the boots she'd had so much time to study from beneath the clothes rack.

Akstyr had painted shamanic tattoos on the backs of his hands, one of which covered up his gang brand. For clothing, he wore a white shepherd's robe, a winter-thick version of the ones the southern Kendorian nomads favored for tending bighorn desert sheep. Predictably, none of the Stumps clothiers had carried shamanic robes, but it would have been dangerous to put him in them anyway. Akstyr's only comment had been to say that robes were stupid and his "pickaxe and diamonds" were freezing.

The enforcers traveled down the street toward Amaranthe and the others, using the same sidewalk. Once, she would have lifted a hand in a comradely wave. Lately, her instincts were to flee down alleys. This time... she kept her chin up and strode straight toward them. Books and Akstyr eased in behind her, ostensibly to make room for the enforcers to pass, but they didn't wear any face-altering makeup or prosthetics, so they wouldn't want to test their costumes quite as rigorously. They'd altered their hairstyles—poor Akstyr had had little choice—allowing her to clip their formerly longish locks closer to their heads. They didn't look much like their bounty posters, but

she couldn't blame them for not wanting to test the enforcers' observation skills. Few in Forge should be that familiar with her team's visages, especially for the lesser known members.

Engrossed in their own conversation, the enforcers walked past without giving them more than a glance.

Amaranthe exhaled slowly and said, "A good beginning," when Books came up to her side again.

"All you've proven is that you don't look like a notorious outlaw any more."

"That's not a bad place to start."

"Do you truly believe you can pass as this Suan?" Books asked. "Someone you've never met?"

"We went to the same school, and I've read her book. Also, I *have* met her, sort of, through the mind link I shared with her sister."

"Isn't the girl supposed to be a genius though?"

Amaranthe stepped closer to a building to avoid a delivery boy slipping and skidding down the sidewalk on a bicycle laden with boxes. "What are you implying, Books? That I'm too dim for the position?"

He brushed dirty snow from his trousers, courtesy of the bicycle's wheels and the surrounding slush. "What are the chief industries that comprise the Kendorian economy?"

"Leased land, wool, copper, and sexy lizard-skin purses, boots, and lingerie," Amaranthe said, relieved he'd asked a question about the part of the lecture she'd actually been listening to.

"Hm."

Maybe she should have quoted him directly instead of adding flair in regard to the lizard-skin items. Still, he'd have to know she'd been listening and passed his test. "Hm? That's it? I get more enthusiastic praise from Sicarius."

Books missed a step. "Truly?"

Amaranthe smiled. "No."

Akstyr snorted.

"I can do this. I'm sure of it." Amaranthe didn't know how to

express the richness of the vision she'd gotten through Retta's link. She had a vivid impression of this sister, specifically how others viewed her. Instead of trying to explain that, she smiled again and said, "How hard can it be? Nobody's seen Suan in ten years except her sister, and I'm hoping the sister will ally with us and help out." *If she's still alive,* Amaranthe added silently. She believed the arrival of the *Behemoth* meant she had to be— she was the pilot after all. Of course, Retta could be alive, but not in good standing with the outfit.

"What if you didn't bond with this sister as much as you think, and she turns you in?" Books asked.

"Then they'll take us prisoner, and we'll get a ride to their ship regardless."

"Or they'll shoot us," Akstyr said.

Amaranthe patted him on the shoulder. "If they seem so inclined, I hope you'll magic something up to prevent that."

"Magic." Akstyr scoffed at the inappropriate word. "I don't know if I'll be able to concentrate when my apples are freezing."

"It's not *that* cold out," Amaranthe said, though she would have preferred her long wool underwear to Maldynado's string garment.

"It is when you aren't wearing anything under your robe."

Books frowned at him. "*Why* aren't you wearing anything? I showed you how to make appropriate Kendorian smallclothes."

"You showed me how to wrap a sheet between my legs. I could barely walk."

"The Kendorians manage to walk, run, and make war without trouble while wearing the *daikka*."

Amaranthe pointed at a teak sign with golden letters that read *Summer Point Yacht Club and Sailing Association Headquarters*. From the impressive gleam, the embossed letters might have been crafted using actual gold flakes. She led the men left, down a broad, well-maintained dock—not so much as a splinter was gouged from any of the boards, which had been swept free of snow. The mildew invasion stampeding across the docks at the southern end of the waterfront wouldn't dream of

inserting a colony here. Most of the boats had been removed in anticipation of the lake freezing over, but a few craft remained, their skeletal masts stretching toward the gray skies.

"Maldynado spotted me trying to put it on and said no woman would sleep with me if she saw me wearing a big sheet diaper," Akstyr said.

"Amaranthe," Books said, "at what point when you were explaining this mission did you mention that Akstyr would be required to lift his robes for women?"

"I don't remember mentioning it." She glanced down a branch in the sprawling dock system, toward a two-story building with tall glass windows overlooking the lake. Clinks of pots and dishes drifted from it, so she assumed it was an eating house, not a likely place for Forge to store its secret underwater pod, or whatever they were using to reach the bottom of the lake.

"It could happen," Akstyr said. "These Forge people are mostly women, right? Some of them might think I'm cute and get antsier to rip off my robes than a smoke-head tearing into a *caymay* wrapper."

"Ancestors save us," Books muttered.

"You know," Amaranthe told him, "I'd prefer it if you not goad him in such ways that he shares his lurid fantasies with us."

"Yes, I'll remember that in the future."

"Whatever," Akstyr said, and repeated, "it could happen. Especially if I get to share about how… skilled I am." He wriggled his fingers.

"Let's wait until we get a read on our hosts before making announcements about that." Amaranthe did intend to introduce him in a manner that suggested he had such skills—she hadn't been able to imagine any other capacity in which Suan might employ a teenage boy in her entourage—but most of the Forge people were Turgonian. Despite their eager adoption of the ancient technology, they might share the national prejudice against practitioners.

"That may be the spot." Books subtly turned his chin down another branch in the dock system.

Two men in green wool uniforms with silver piping stood guard in front of the entrance to a one-story building built on piers. Amaranthe didn't recognize the attire and guessed they belonged to a private security outfit. Short swords and batons—given the girth of the wood weapons, *clubs* might be a better term—hung from their belts, and they glared down the docks, their meaty forearms crossed over their broad chests.

Amaranthe strolled toward them as if she had every right to be there. Remembering how Maldynado dismissed or looked *through* servants, she angled for the door as if the men weren't looming on either side of it. Suan wasn't warrior-caste, but she'd grown up amongst the affluent.

"Pardon, my lady," one of the guards said, "are you a member? I don't recognize you." He'd guessed she was warrior-caste; that was good. He'd also stepped sideways to block the door; that was less good. The second guard glowered at Books and Akstyr.

"Oh, no, I prefer to let others handle the organization of my water-based transport," Amaranthe said, "but I have an invitation to meet with one of the yacht club regulars. They should be expecting me. Suan Curlev." She hoped Ms. Worgavic wasn't the one waiting inside. She'd deliberately waited until nightfall for this approach, thinking she might be greeted by a more junior Forge member during off hours.

"I wasn't told about any visitors, my lady."

Er, what if this wasn't the right place? A plaque on the door read *Sailing Association Headquarters and Ballroom.* Sicarius hadn't mentioned a specific building when he'd reported trailing the messenger back here, but the presence of security personal made her assume there was something to hide inside. The eating house hadn't been bedecked with big beefy guards.

"Can you check, please?" Amaranthe asked. "I can wait."

Books and Akstyr shuffled from foot to foot behind her as the speaker eyed her thoughtfully. Suspiciously?

"Very well," the guard said. "Wait here, please."

At least he was being polite, though that would change if

he figured out she wasn't warrior-caste, amply moneyed, or otherwise elite and special. When he unlocked the door and stepped inside, Amaranthe tried to get a glimpse of the interior. Despite dusk growing deeper, nobody had lit any lanterns, at least not within view of the door. She had a sense of a high-ceilinged open room devoid of furnishings, but that was it. The guard disappeared down a hallway.

The remaining man cleared his throat, the multi-syllabic rumble aptly conveying that she shouldn't be peering so intently inside. Amaranthe smiled and clasped her hands behind her back. She was debating whether she should try to engage him in conversation or merely gaze blandly out at the lake when movement in the water caught her eye.

Three young men and a boy of twelve or thirteen were rowing a weathered dinghy through the area. They were all dressed in mismatched and ill-fitting clothing, with the oldest, a gangly fellow in his early twenties, wrapped in a gold silk cloak decorated with knife holes and faded bloodstains. Two youths rowed while two dragged weighted nets. A pile of waterlogged boots, soggy clothing, tin cans, and other dubious treasures was heaped in the bow.

"Street eaters," Akstyr growled and shifted to stand behind Books. He glanced at his hand, making sure his Black Arrows gang brand was still hidden.

The young men in the boat had branded hands as well, theirs also displaying arrows. One of them muttered something to his colleagues and pointed toward the trio on the docks. Amaranthe didn't know if they'd picked out Akstyr specifically—they could be commenting on the value of her jewelry—but given the shared Black Arrows background, they easily could have recognized him.

"Maybe *you* should have been the one to dye your hair blond," Books whispered to him.

"Isn't it enough that Si—someone hacked it all off?" Akstyr whispered back.

"Apparently not."

"I don't suppose we can wait inside?" Amaranthe asked the guard amiably, as if the answer didn't matter one way or another. "It's getting colder out here."

The guard was glowering at the dinghy and didn't respond. He strode three paces to the end of the dock, puffed out his chest, and rested a hand on his sword. This new view of the man revealed a throwing knife holder on the back of his belt, three flat steel hilts protruding from the compact sheaths. "You sewer mutts get out of here. This is private property."

"You can't own the lake." Gold Cloak sneered, flinging up a hand in an old gesture once used as a command for castrating irresponsible servants. "We'll go wherever we want."

"Ignorant thugs, you can too own water rights. These docks, those beaches, and the lake out to those buoys belong to the yacht club."

"Come make us leave, why don't you?"

Almost fast enough to impress Sicarius, the guard pulled out a throwing knife and hurled it. The path of the blade was hard to track in the dim lighting, but Amaranthe heard the thunk of it landing and the cry of pain that followed. The knife had sunk into one of the wooden benches, pinning the gold cloak—and the hand that made the rude gesture.

The display of accuracy didn't surprise Amaranthe—after all, wouldn't Forge hire the best in private security?—but it did make her decide not to irk the guards. She didn't want to pick a fight with them.

Much cursing arose as the gang members hastily rowed beneath the docks and out of the guard's line of sight—and blade hurling.

"Thanks for the knife, Fatty!" the youngest called when they'd rowed far enough away that they thought they were safe.

Obnoxious laughter followed, even from the injured man. The street-raised youths probably would think such a fine blade a worthwhile trade for a little pain.

"Sorry you lost your knife," Amaranthe told the guard.

He shrugged and returned to his station at the door, his

glower no different than it had been before. "My employers will compensate me."

Akstyr wasn't paying any attention to the conversation; his gaze remained to the south, the direction the gang members had been heading when they rowed beneath the docks. They hadn't reappeared. They might have continued south, using the docks for cover, but they could be plotting nearby too. The value of that knife was minuscule compared to the bounty the gangs had placed on Akstyr's head.

"So, no waiting inside?" Amaranthe tried again. The guard had been distracted before.

"Sorry, no."

On the waterfront street, at the head of the dock, couples started arriving in steam carriages. Dressed in furs, jewelry, and displaying the latest fashions—Amaranthe smirked when she spotted a lizard-skin purse—they strolled toward the eating house. A woman in city worker's overalls walked onto the dock with a lantern and tools for lighting the lamps along the way. She must have veered too close to some of the wealthy diners for their tastes, for someone in a group of well-dressed women snapped at her. The worker scurried away, chin ducked to her chest.

Amaranthe couldn't know for certain if the diners were warrior-caste or part of the successful business class, but the fact that she couldn't tell the difference said much. Forge simply wanted to replace the aristocracy with another group of power-caressing snobs. In the end, nothing would change. Forge spoke of merit-based wealth, but all of their scheming and blackmailing proclaimed they wanted special privileges to ensure they were at the top of this merit-based system. Sespian was still the best bet for a better world. If Books were one of his advisers, they could work together to implement a more egalitarian system.

The door swung inward, and the first guard reappeared. "Need you for a minute, Lors."

"What about us?" Amaranthe asked at the same time as the second guard asked, "What about them?"

"We've got to do that special... procedure. It'll just take a minute." The first guard lifted a hand toward Amaranthe. "My lady, the people who can verify the validity of your claim will be here shortly. Please continue to wait outside."

"Very well," Amaranthe said, letting a hint of haughty exasperation into her voice.

The guards disappeared inside, and a solid thunk sounded as the lock turned.

"It sounds like their underwater conveyance is docking," Books murmured. "It must come up under the building. If those hooligans are still down there somewhere, they might get an interesting show."

"They're not still down there." Akstyr's eyes had that faraway look that meant he was practicing his Science.

"Where are they?" Amaranthe asked.

He waved toward the dock behind the headquarters building. "Get ready for a fight."

"A fight?" Books whispered. "I'm not properly geared for a fight. I was told to look academic and interestingly exotic. All I have with me is a dagger."

"I know. We have the same weapons." Amaranthe carried a satchel with some of Sicarius's dried meat bars and a few other supplies, but she hadn't known if it would be searched, so she hadn't dared bring a pile of weapons. There hadn't been any thoughts of Suan participating in dueling or wrestling classes in Retta's memories.

Though he must have heard the lock turning, too, Books tried the door. The knob didn't turn.

The hinges and wood had a sturdy mien, not that Amaranthe was ready to try breaking down the door. "Sicarius would be disappointed in us if we couldn't handle ourselves against four untrained street youths."

"Eight," Akstyr said, eyes half-lidded. "They have friends."

Wonderful.

"I'd like to sear them into lumps of charcoal," Akstyr growled. "That one boy with the droopy eye, that's Edge. We

used to run together until he turned on me. He was one of the ugly sock stuffers who attacked me and handed me over to the enforcers right before you came along last year."

"Sock stuffers?" Books murmured.

"Don't ask," Amaranthe said. "Please."

Books grunted in agreement. "Shall we look for a more amenable place to make a stand? We're at a dead end here, and I don't fancy taking a swim if we're forced back. Also, if they're bright, however unlikely that is, they may think to come at us from water as well as land. Er, dock."

"Not a bad idea, but we'd have to run back to the street before we'd find such a spot, and I'd hate to miss our appointment." It'd be handy if the door opened then, and they were invited in before they had to fight anyone.

"They're climbing up the back of the building," Akstyr said. "Bet they're going up on the roof to try and jump on us."

"All the more reason to move." Books stepped toward the intersection of docks.

Amaranthe caught his arm. "Wait. Akstyr, how would you like a chance to deal with them in your way?"

His ears perked up. "By searing them into charcoal lumps with my mind?"

"No," Books said, then, with concern in his voice, added, "You can't actually do that, can you?"

Akstyr shrugged. "Maybe. Partially."

Erg, that would be an unappealing way to die. And an unappealing way to watch someone die.

"Perhaps you can use a more imaginative method and simply scare them away," Amaranthe said. "The yacht club is in an upscale neighborhood after all. Finding charcoal-lump corpses on the docks might alarm the clientele."

"I should hope so," Books said.

"I guess I could try something else." Akstyr grinned. "It'd be ball-licking righteous if I could get them back." He leaned around the corner of the building. "I bet those sludge suckers don't even know they'll be in full view of the eating house if they get up on the roof."

"Is it my imagination," Books murmured, "or has his vernacular grown more colorful since those hoodlums approached?"

"I could embarrass them good." Akstyr nodded to himself.

"Yes, you could." Amaranthe squeezed Akstyr's shoulder. "Books and I will protect you so you can concentrate."

"Really? Like my bodyguards?"

Books arched his eyebrows.

"Yes," Amaranthe said firmly. She didn't have a problem with all three of them standing back-to-back and fighting off the youths if that was required, but this was, at its heart, Akstyr's problem, and she thought it'd be good for his growth—or at least his ego—if he handled it himself.

"Very well." Books drew his dagger, sighed at it, and placed himself to Akstyr's right side.

Amaranthe stood to his left. The water lay behind them and the building to the front, the door still shut. The windows next to it were shuttered, though wide ones farther down the wall and overlooking the water provided an open view. Unless someone was standing inside with a nose pressed to the glass, the dock shouldn't be visible though.

A scrape sounded on the roof. Amaranthe thought about telling Akstyr that sooner would be better than later for whatever action he wished to take, but she kept her mouth shut. She'd made it clear that he was in charge of this battle; she had to trust him now to handle it.

Beside her, Akstyr's eyes were fully closed—not something he usually dared during a fight—his face scrunched in concentration. A sign that he fully trusted her? If so, they'd come a long way in the last year.

Prepare yourself, Books signed.

More scuffles sounded on the roof, closer this time. Amaranthe bent her knees and shook out her arms to relax the muscles. She was glad she'd chosen boots instead of those sandals; otherwise she'd be kicking them off and fighting barefoot. Not an amenable practice with snowflakes dusting one's shoulders.

A dark bottle sailed over the edge of the roof, a fuse dangling from the top, a flame dancing along its length.

"Watch it," Books barked.

Knowing the gang members meant the bottle to hit the dock and drench them with burning kerosene, Amaranthe jumped up and forward, catching it in the air, careful to soften her grip so it didn't break in her hand. Before her feet hit the dock, she'd tossed the incendiary. It splashed into the water behind them, the flame snuffed out as the bottle sank.

Two figures, Gold Cloak and a new man, leaped over the edge, clubs raised high in both arms. Surprise twisted their faces, and one blurted, "It didn't work!" as he fell.

Assuming Books would take the man closest to him, Amaranthe targeted Gold Cloak. She lunged under the eave to evade his dropping form, then stepped in as he landed, launching a side kick. Her heel thudded into his kidney like a battering ram. He dropped the club and staggered forward. He tried to spin toward her, but Amaranthe had a second kick waiting. This time, she took him in the hip, and he pitched sideways, following the bottle into the water. A second big splash went up beside him, Books hurling his opponent off the dock.

Nobody else was leaping off the roof, so Amaranthe risked a glance at Akstyr, wondering if he was doing anything yet. Though she couldn't feel the Science being used, not the way Sicarius could, his face held a familiar expression of utter concentration, and his arm was outstretched, his fingers splayed.

Grunts and heavy footfalls came from the roof, but nobody else leaped into sight. Were they regrouping? They sounded... discombobulated.

Amaranthe grabbed the fallen club with her free hand and turned sideways so she could watch the roof as well as the water, in case the first two thugs tried to throw something or crawl up behind Akstyr. The golden cloak floated on the surface, but its owner had disappeared. Back under the docks to recover perhaps.

On the roof, a new thug came into sight and Amaranthe

readied herself, expecting more to jump down. This one was stumbling as he approached the edge, though. In one hand, he grasped a rust-pitted short sword, but the other was busy holding up... his pants? That's what it looked like.

Before she could decide if it was Akstyr's doing, the boy from the dinghy rolled off the roof and landed on his side on the dock. Something popped, and he cried out, but he didn't remove his hands from his waistline. "Get it out, get it out!" he yelled and kept trying to yank off his trousers.

Two more men leaped from the roof, forgoing the dock and angling toward the water. Black smoke streamed from their rear ends. Amaranthe thought to shove the writhing boy into the lake, too, but he glimpsed her when she approached, the club in hand, and jumped to his feet of his own accord. He took off running for the street, still clawing at his waistband. The ragged trousers *did* appear to be pulled uncomfortably high.

Amaranthe quirked a brow at Akstyr. He was still concentrating with his eyes closed, but a smirk had found its way onto his lips.

"Curse you!" the man who remained in sight on the roof shouted. He'd lost the battle with his trousers, and they were tangled about his ankles, revealing knobby knees and hairy legs. Rage twisted his face, and he lifted his arm to hurl something.

In the poor lighting, Amaranthe couldn't tell what he held, but she guessed the target. As the thug released the weapon, she grabbed Akstyr's arm and yanked him out of the way. His eyes flew open, his concentration broken, but she didn't have time to apologize. The throwing knife the guard had used earlier lodged into the piling behind Akstyr. Amaranthe jumped up, her dagger in hand, intending to return the throw—without missing. But the hairy-legged fellow was already pitching off the roof to the dock in front of her. Cries of pain escaped his lips, as he clutched at his thigh. Books's dagger protruded from the muscle.

At that moment, the door opened and the two guards stepped into view.

"Problem?" one asked mildly.

Splashes sounded as the men in the water swam out of sight beneath the dock. Amaranthe pinned the whimpering man's shoulder with her boot, so Books could retrieve his knife. His lips flattened with disapproval of this necessary causing of further pain, but he knew the blade would have to come out eventually, one way or another. He pulled it free as quickly as possible, and Amaranthe let the man up. He didn't bother glancing about to check on his comrades; he ran away as well as he could, half dragging the injured leg as he clutched at the wound to halt the bleeding.

"No problem," Amaranthe told the guards, wondering what they'd think of her and Books's display of pugilistic competence. She hoped their task inside had kept them too busy to wonder about the thumps on the roof and the shouts outside. If they'd been watching at the window and had seen proof of Akstyr's unique talents, that'd prove nettlesome at best. She strove to keep the concern off her face, instead turning her back to them to retrieve the throwing knife from the piling. "No problem at all," she repeated as she returned it to its original owner.

Books sheathed his dagger and straightened his colorful robe. "Have we been vouched for?"

The guards exchanged looks with each other, but only said, "Your lady has been invited inside, yes."

Amaranthe wondered if that invitation included her men. Better to act than ask permission and be denied. She waved for them to accompany her. The guards led the way inside without comment.

As soon as their backs were turned, Akstyr's fingers twitched in a flurry of signs. *Was that all right? Should I have killed them? It seemed funny when I thought it up, but now... I messed it all up, didn't I? They'll run back and tell everyone where I am, and there will be a thousand Arrows and bounty hunters and ancestors know who else waiting for us to leave the docks.*

His jaw firm, Books signed, *You should never feel you 'messed up' when you chose a path that spared lives instead of taking them. If there are consequences, we will deal with them.*

The guards were leading them across the ballroom toward a door at the back, so there wasn't much time for a lengthy conversation, but Amaranthe gripped Akstyr's shoulder and signed, *Books is right. You should also never regret that you took advantage of an opportunity to light someone's underwear on fire.*

That brightened Akstyr's consternated expression.

You've been spending too much time with Maldynado, Books signed to Amaranthe.

Have I? She smiled innocently.

They'd reached the door, and, when one of the guards opened it for her, she rearranged her face into what she hoped passed for the bland indifference of a world-wise businesswoman who'd never doubted her right to join her colleagues here. One guard in front, one behind, they were ushered down a hallway. The walls were painted with murals of yachts, their sails full of wind. Though Amaranthe had never followed the art world, even she recognized the name of famous muralist Ansil Inkwatercrest painted in the corner, under the title "Regatta."

While she was noting the artwork, she also noted a trail of wet footprints leading out from a shut door on that sidewall. She itched to open it, suspecting their submersible craft was docked somewhere behind it, but the guard trailing behind Akstyr and Books didn't spread his arms in an invitation for them to explore. Rather his brisk pace assured they wouldn't dally.

At the forward guard's gesture, Amaranthe stepped into a parlor with tall windows on three sides. Three women in ankle-length felt skirts and blouses with jackets sat at one of several round tables in the room. A tidy white tablecloth cascaded to the floor, and silver tea and cider pots steamed on the surface while the women sipped from the smallest, daintiest cups Amaranthe had ever seen. A platter in the center of the table held cookies shaped into boats with a familiar stylized C stamped in the centers. Curi's. The idea that the baker supplied cookies to Forge filled her with a sense of betrayal. That had been her favorite place to buy sweets for *years*.

She didn't think she'd seen the women before, though one was somewhat familiar, someone who'd been in that big Forge meeting, perhaps. She felt the blessing of her ancestors that Ms. Wargovic hadn't shown up, but the cool eyes that narrowed at her approach stole her sense of relief. Did they know what Suan looked like? And that Amaranthe wasn't she?

To avoid their hard gazes, Amaranthe pretended to admire the views through the windows. On one side, the two-story eating house rose, along with a view of some of the yachts. On the far side one could see the rest of the waterfront. The lake-side windows... She hoped their little skirmish hadn't been visible outside them. As she'd noted earlier, the dock wasn't in view, but the two men who'd sailed off the roof with smoke streaming from their underwear... She forced herself not to grimace as she acknowledged that unique sight might have been in view.

"Suan?" one of the women asked.

"Yes." Amaranthe faced them again and walked up to a chair. "Forgive me, please, but I've been out of the capital for so long. I haven't missed the *sak lee* winters, but there is a beauty about the lake in winter." She wasn't trying to adopt any sort of accent—after all, Suan had been born in Stumps—but Books had made her memorize a few Kendorian, Kyattese, and Nurian words to toss into regular conversations. "It'll ice over soon, don't you think?"

The three women were exchanging glances with each other. Amaranthe might have to prove herself before they invited her down to their secret lair. Well, she was ready. This was why she'd been studying.

"Yes," the first woman who'd spoken said. "Those who fancy themselves prognosticators suggest this snow will keep falling all week and bring in colder weather. Were the winters chilly down there in... where were you last? I've forgotten."

Amaranthe doubted it. This was Test Number One. "Ibyria," she said, "on the Gulf Coast. They don't see snow down there. The orange and lemon trees wouldn't care for it. Before that, I was securing trade deals in many of the desert city-states.

Camel, Tiger, Red Cactus—" she paused when Books, standing at her back, nudged her, "—but you probably don't want all the names." He was right—if she spewed too much background information, they'd wonder what she was trying to prove. "The cacti also do not tolerate freezing temperatures, I understand. The Torrel ones that the shamans use for making their healing syrups are particularly valuable, so you'll see them running about, tossing blankets over the thorny things if a frost is incipient." Amaranthe waited for Books to nudge her again, but he didn't. Of course, if his own tactics were something to go by, he approved of pedantic asides.

"I see." The speaker was in her late thirties or early forties with a few lines creasing her brow. The other two were in their twenties—too young to be Forge founders probably. But then, Suan was one, and she was only thirty.

When nobody else spoke, Amaranthe gestured to Books and Akstyr. "You're probably wondering who my comrades are and whether you can speak freely in front of them." And in front of me, she added to herself. "This is Erav, my scribe." She lifted a hand toward Books. "And this is Rist, my... adviser in things of an otherworldly nature."

All three women's eyebrows flew upward. It was true they were Turgonian, and Amaranthe wouldn't normally speak of the Science to imperial subjects, but these people were flying around in an ultra advanced alien aircraft. Surely the notion of magic couldn't alarm them at this point.

"He's young for that, isn't he?" One of the younger women eyed Akstyr from head to toe.

Maldynado would have assumed a pose that accented his features, insomuch as a heavy cotton robe could accent anything; Akstyr crossed his arms and issued his surliest I-am-*not*-young sneer. The haircut may have improved his looks, but with his attitude, his dream of antsy women tearing off his clothing wasn't likely to happen.

"He is the apprentice of a shaman I worked with," Amaranthe said, "and is accomplished in many areas. Also... I couldn't

be as choosy as I might have otherwise wished. Convincing shamans to take a trip into the empire isn't easily done, but Rist was born here and only fled south to learn his art."

Akstyr's surly expression grew wistful. Yes, he'd like to be somewhere south—or south and west if one were thinking of Kyatt—studying his art now.

"I thought his skills, being unique here in the empire, could prove useful for us as we go forward," Amaranthe said. "Though perhaps I underestimated your need for assistance. I understand Ravido Marblecrest has already taken the Imperial Barracks, is that right?"

The women shared glances again.

"We're waiting for a couple of others to join us before we speak of business matters," the middle-aged woman said.

Uh oh. Amaranthe did her best not to lift a fingernail for nibbling or otherwise exude nervousness. "Who else would be joining us? I long to see familiar faces."

"Then you'll enjoy seeing those who are coming."

Another "uh oh" pranced through Amaranthe's mind. If someone familiar was coming, someone who knew Suan and what she looked like...

Books bumped Amaranthe's elbow, directing her to a newcomer entering the parlor. Her heart leaped to attention, but it didn't know whether to dance or flee.

Retta strode toward the table, pinning Amaranthe with a one-eyed stare. Yes, *one* eyed. The other lay behind a brown velvet patch. Correction, it probably *didn't* lay behind that patch, Amaranthe thought, shock filling her. Pike. When had he had time to do it? When she'd escaped, he'd collected his men and charged out of the *Behemoth* on her heels. Maybe he'd left instructions for the punishment to be carried out. Or maybe the Forge women had done it themselves. She couldn't imagine Ms. Worgavic wielding a blade or hot iron, but her old teacher had demanded *she* be tortured, so who knew?

Retta wore Kyattese single-strap bamboo sandals and a brown velvet dress to match the eyepatch—clothing that

suggested she'd come from a warm, controlled climate, not the snowy outdoors—and looked as put together as one might expect from a young Forge acolyte, but pain lines edged her face, lines that hadn't been there a few weeks before, and her jaw was tight. Angry.

"Retta!" Amaranthe exclaimed, stepping toward her with arms outstretched, half because it seemed like something sisters should do and half because she had to keep Retta from blurting out that this intruder was *not* her sister. "What happened to you? Your eye... is it...?"

"How did you heal so quickly?" Retta demanded.

Er. Amaranthe clasped both of her arms and pulled her close for a hug, all the while wondering if Retta would leap away or punch her. "I'm your sister," she whispered in Retta's ear. "Go with it, please. I'll get you out of here this time."

Retta backed away from the hug. On the outside, Amaranthe remained calm, but inside... she was cursing and cringing. This wouldn't work. Retta wouldn't go along with it. It was already obvious Amaranthe wasn't Suan. Indeed, the three women were watching the exchange intently, trying to figure out what was going on. Retta was... staring at the medallion dangling on Amaranthe's chest.

She cleared her throat. "I mean, you look so well. Your last letter said you'd come down with that desert flu and would be delayed in your return."

Letter? Such as one sister might send to another? "Yes, I thought I'd be delayed, but it turns out that Rist here knows a few things about herbs."

Akstyr's eyes widened at this claim; Amaranthe hoped her statement didn't make trouble for him later. If some Forge lady approached him, hoping he could make an apothecary's tincture for wrinkle removal... She didn't think Akstyr could even pick out the common herbs Basilard used in his culinary preparations.

Retta's lips pursed as she studied Amaranthe. Her expression wasn't welcoming. No, she looked irked that Amaranthe had survived Pike's ministrations less scarred than she had.

Understandable. Hearing about Amaranthe's bad dreams probably wouldn't mollify a woman with a missing eye.

"I also have a comrade who knows all the best foods to eat to hasten healing," Amaranthe added. She wondered if Retta would be more sympathetic, or at least less irritated, if she knew how many meals of fish eyes and organ surprises Sicarius had foisted upon her. "But what happened to you, sister?" she deliberately used the word instead of a name, hoping Retta would vouch for her. "Your eye. Is it injured or...?"

"Cut out," Retta said icily. "A psychopathic madman decided to punish me for dropping a branch across his path." And causing him to trip, the rest of the saying went. She'd done more than that. Retta must know Pike was dead. Did she care? It wasn't as if his death could bring back her eye.

"Do Mother and Father know?" Amaranthe demanded. The indignation in her tone wasn't feigned—it frustrated her to know that helping her had caused Retta to be punished. At the time, she would have done just about anything to free herself, but she wished there'd been a way to keep anyone from knowing Retta had a hand in that escape. "Surely they can hire someone to exact revenge."

The three women were sipping from their cups, watching with interest, though it seemed academic. As if they didn't truly care one way or another about the outcome. Given the size of the organization, Suan's return was probably of little consequence.

Amaranthe widened her eyes slightly, trying to get Retta to proclaim their kinship. Her team had to get onto the *Behemoth*, and she doubted they'd be offered a ride down without credentials.

"From what I've heard, the perpetrator has been killed," Retta said. There was no gratitude, no "Thank you for hurling your assassin at that bastard" in her expression.

"A deserving end," Amaranthe said. "What coward would cut out a woman's eye?" And then she stopped talking. Nobody was listening to her. They were all staring at Retta, waiting for the word. She'd halfway helped Amaranthe, mentioning some letter, but everyone was waiting for something more solid.

But Retta seemed reluctant to give it. And why shouldn't she be? What might it cost her to help Amaranthe again? To be *caught* helping?

"A cast-out from the warrior-caste." Retta sighed. "Come, Suan. I'll tell you about it on the way down."

"Down?" Amaranthe asked, guessing that no one had explained the *Behemoth* in written communications with Suan.

"You'll need to wait," the middle-aged woman told Retta. "Neeth needs to go back down too. She's on her way."

Amaranthe swallowed. She recognized that first name. Neeth. Neeth Worgavic.

CHAPTER 12

ICARIUS CROUCHED ON THE FIELD, A PACK FULL OF GEAR and a harpoon launcher strapped to his back, as he waited for Sespian to catch up with him. An owl hooted from the trees near the lake, but the dense coin-sized snowflakes dropping from the black night sky made it impossible to see more than a few feet in any direction. Somewhere behind him, the walls of the fort rose. Ahead, thousands of soldiers waited, some snoring in their tents, but many on the night shift, awake and prepared to fight off intruders. Heroncrest would know Ridgecrest would want an intelligence report.

Several inches of fresh powder blanketed the field, meaning footprints would be problematic. If Sicarius and Sespian walked straight into the camp, the roving perimeter guards would see the evidence of the incursion.

Soft crunches and squeaks of boots on snow arose behind and to the right, preceding the appearance of a dark figure in army fatigues. Sespian. Not certain his son saw him, Sicarius took a few steps in that direction. Sespian twitched in surprise, then sank into a low crouch.

"I knew you were there," he whispered. "It just startles me seeing you in army fatigues. Given how many soldiers you've... It's disturbing."

Sicarius did not respond, though an image of Amaranthe flashed into his mind. She always seemed to like the idea of him in a uniform, lamenting that the role of assassin had been chosen for him and that he'd never had a choice in the matter. Sespian knew his past now, some of it anyway—Hollowcrest

hadn't recorded everything—but he seemed less inclined to make allowances for it. Not that Sicarius wanted any allowances. He was too old to blame his youth for the man he'd become.

Sespian plucked at his own borrowed uniform. "I suppose it doesn't really fit me either."

Thanks to the snow, the night was bright enough that the dark army fatigues stood out on the white field. Sicarius had debated over the appropriate attire for the infiltration, almost choosing whites and grays, but once they slipped into the camp they'd be less noticeable if they blended in with everyone else. Like Heroncrest's soldiers, they'd tied blue bands around their arms.

"This way." Sicarius rose slightly, staying low as he picked a path through the curtain of falling flakes.

"I can't see anything," Sespian whispered as wind stirred, slanting the snow sideways, the icy kisses cold against their cheeks. "How do you know we're going in the right direction?"

Sicarius would have preferred to use Basilard's hand signs to speak, but, though the white blanket made the night brighter than usual, there wasn't enough light to pick out gestures. They weren't close to the enemy perimeter, so he responded—the snow would muffle their voices to some extent.

"My sense of direction is well-honed," Sicarius murmured.

"If I said something cocky like that, I'd end up leading us into the lake."

Sicarius did not think the statement cocky, merely an utterance of fact. "We approach the water tower," he said, hoping Sespian would remain silent without needing to be told. As they'd already discussed, there might be soldiers guarding the tower. Normally Fort Urgot men would be out there, but they'd retreated inside at the approach of the invasion force. There was a well within the walls, so the tower was a matter of convenience rather than necessity—water that could be diverted for indoor plumbing, rather than the fort's only source. It may, however, have been claimed by Heroncrest's men, so they needed to approach with care.

Sespian did indeed fall silent, though when the first crumbled stone ruin came into sight, a remain of the original brick water tower, he grunted a soft, "Huh," at this proof of Sicarius's honed sense of direction.

Sicarius held up a hand, silently instructing him to wait in the shadow of the half wall, then skirted the ruins, seeking signs of soldiers. Or other entities. Memories of climbing the tower with Amaranthe to escape the first soul construct came to mind. He hadn't heard any howls yet that evening and hoped the new creature had simply been passing through the night before. It was possible it had nothing to do with Heroncrest's army.

With the snowfall making visibility so poor, Sicarius lifted his nose at times, testing the wind like a hound. It'd be easy for a couple of soldiers to be stationed in a niche in the ruins, hidden by the shadows. He sensed nothing, though, except for the rumble of ambulatory vehicles patrolling the enemy's perimeter and the occasional plops of snow growing too heavy for its perch and falling to the ground in clumps. The water tower had been abandoned, neither side willing to risk the lives of a team to guard it.

"We're the only ones on the hill," Sicarius whispered to Sespian when he returned, his words causing another twitch of surprise since he'd approached from behind. He recalled Sespian's interest in learning from him in regard to stealth. Presumably that included defending against being caught unaware. "Keep your back to a wall when you're waiting, so you can't be approached from behind. Also, when visibility is low, it's imperative to focus more on one's other senses. Hearing is obvious, but you might also smell another's approach."

Sicarius pointed toward the water tower. It was time to see if his plan worked.

"Smell?" Sespian followed him to the metal beams supporting the steel tank above.

"Many people have distinctive scents. With soldiers, you can often detect a hint of black powder or weapons cleaning oil." Sicarius stopped in the shadow of the tank, placing a hand on one of the icy support posts. He had not yet donned gloves, not

deeming the night that cold. Besides, he'd need finger dexterity for the next few moments. "Can you climb up without a rope?"

"I think so." Sespian tightened the straps on his pack. "I've never noticed anyone's scent unless they're wearing perfume or haven't bathed in a while. Is there some trick for more fully developing one's sense of smell?" He sounded genuinely interested.

"It can be trained, much like skills relying on muscle and agility can be improved, by practicing identifying scents. Punishment for failures cements the lesson in the mind more firmly." Sicarius hesitated, realizing Sespian wouldn't likely place himself in a situation where someone stood behind him with a whip, prepared to administer a correction should he fail to identify a tree species when blindfolded. "Rewards would work, too, likely."

Sespian opened his mouth, as if he might say something, but decided against it. He pointed at the I-shaped support beam, its rivets the only things offering handholds. "Do you want me to go first, so you can catch me if I fall?"

"You may go first."

"No promise of catching me, eh?"

"I will strive not to allow you to become damaged tonight," Sicarius said.

"An interesting way to put it."

Sespian wrapped his fingers around the post up high, then jumped, his feet slipping several times before he figured out a way to grip it with his legs. Lifting one hand at a time, he picked his way up, his speed increasing as he grew more familiar with the climb. Clumps of snow fell from above as he reached the top and slid out onto the narrow ledge. Sicarius touched his harpoon launcher, ensuring it was firmly secured, then climbed to the top in a couple of seconds. A ladder led up the side of the tank, and he skimmed up that as well. Wind, more pronounced so high above the ground, swirled the snow about and threatened to tear his fur cap from his head. He stopped at an edge overlooking the white expanse below that led, he remembered in his mind's eye,

to evergreen trees edging the parade field. He couldn't see them through the snow, but he'd observed the area with a spyglass during the day, so he knew they were there and that there were tents in front of them. The trees rose a few meters behind the front edge of the camp. The roving guards would be marching past on snowshoes perhaps twenty meters out into the field.

Sicarius prepared the harpoon for flight by attaching the thin, strong cable to it. Before they'd left, he'd wrapped it carefully so it would unspool without a hitch.

"Uhm," Sespian said, "I can't see anything to shoot at over there. Are you going to tell me your eyes were enhanced by training as well?"

"I *have* had vision training," Sicarius said, "but I also cannot see the trees or the camp right now."

"Are you waiting for the snow to clear to shoot then?"

"No. Our approach depends on the heavy snow to mask us."

Sespian waved at the harpoon launcher. "How're you going to hit your target then? Even with a clear sky, it'd be almost impossible. Those trees are what, a hundred meters away?"

"Slightly more."

"You'll be lucky if the harpoon even reaches that far. I hope you don't hit anyone. This isn't how you're planning to get rid of Heroncrest, is it?"

"It's unlikely he'll be near the perimeter."

"That was a joke."

Sicarius tied the end of his cable to an eyelet and lifted the harpoon launcher to his shoulder. He closed his eyes, seeing the topography in his mind, conjuring up a picture of the tower, the field, and the trees. He'd been past the area often enough to be able to do so. Of late, his mind had been occasionally wandering on missions—a worrying sign of the distractions caused by this new fostering of interpersonal relationships—but he'd once been trained to notice everything, to analyze distance, patterns in nature, lifeforms, species of foliage, and every detail of the world around him as a way to remain focused and aware of his surroundings. Hollowcrest had often demanded he verbally

relate those details or draw accurate to-scale representations of them.

From his mental image of the trees, he selected an old, thick pine on the edge of the field. The softer wood would allow the harpoon to sink in deeply. The strong but fine cable he'd chosen didn't weigh much, but he and Sespian were another matter.

When he was certain of his aim, Sicarius pulled the trigger. The harpoon sped away, the cable trailing behind it. Though he'd shown only confidence to Sespian, he waited, doubting, in the long seconds that followed. The heavy snowfall continued to hide the trees, and it was only the fact that the cable stopped speeding past that he knew the harpoon had struck something. Judging by the few meters of tail left, it had struck at the right distance. The angle suggested an elevated height too. In truth, he wouldn't know if he'd pegged his chosen pine until he reached the harpoon.

Sicarius tested the strength of the anchor, then retied the cable, pulling it taut. He fastened a couple of screw pin shackles he'd dug out of one of the mechanics' shops inside the fort. Lastly, he attached short ropes for handholds. He'd been listening as he worked and hadn't heard any shouts drift across the snow to suggest someone had noticed the harpoon thunking into camp—or the cable stretching overhead. The falling flakes must be providing adequate camouflage, for the moment.

"Give me a minute to get down there and, if necessary, subdue nearby guards." Sicarius pushed one of the screws toward the end of the cable and nodded for Sespian to grip it. "There's no way to brake with your hands, so we'll use our boots. Don't let yourself get going too fast, or it'll be difficult to slow down in time. Remember there's a tree at the other end."

Sespian snorted. "If it's the pine tree you claim it is, I'll eat my boot."

Sicarius gazed blandly at him.

"Perhaps just the tongue."

"One minute," Sicarius said. "I'll be waiting on the ground."

Grabbing the rope grips with either hand, Sicarius pushed

away from the tower. He mentally prepared himself to land in the snow on the slope of the hill if the anchor failed and the cable wilted, but it held fast, and he sped into the night. Mindful of Sespian watching, he swung his legs up, using the sole of one boot and the side of the other to cup the cable and apply friction to slow his descent. As he swept downward, closing on the camp, a steam tramper on patrol clanked past below. He sped over its mechanical back without the pilot ever seeing him. Campfires came into view next, and he made out a few silhouettes of tents, though the trees coming up dominated his attention. He braked further, the scent of scorched leather reaching his nose—he'd need new boots after this.

The familiar outline of a pine, its needles longer than those of the firs beside it, formed out of the snow. He alighted on a branch forty feet in the air. Though tempted to wait and see if Sespian needed help, Sicarius descended instead. If anyone had witnessed his approach—or heard the harpoon thunking into the tree—there could be armed soldiers poised at the bottom.

Dagger in his mouth, he half climbed and half slid the last twenty feet. When he landed, the weapon was in his hand.

But nobody waited in the snow-free hollow at the base of the pine. He peered up at the gray sky, searching for evidence of his cable. Even knowing its location, he couldn't spot it. Good. There was no way to cut it down without the risk of someone seeing it fall, so they had to leave it intact.

Lanterns burned along paths winding between tents and past clearings filled with parked vehicles. Heroncrest's men had settled in, prepared for the possibility of a long siege. The smoke of coal stoves hung densely around the camp, filling Sicarius's nostrils. He'd have a hard time impressing Sespian with his olfactory skills with that pall blotting out lesser odors. Snores came from a few tents, but the susurrus of dozens of conversations filled the camp.

It would have been safer to come later, when more people were sleeping, but this way there was a chance they'd overhear plans being formulated. The boughs of the evergreens blocked

some of the snowfall, and Sicarius picked out a large tent a couple dozen meters away with lanterns on either side of the door flap. Numerous people were talking inside. It was unlikely that he and Sespian would stumble upon the command tent so easily, but it was worth checking.

Pine needles fluttered down, dusting Sicarius's shoulders. He took that to mean Sespian had arrived. He hadn't heard a telltale thump—or grunt of pain that would suggest a clumsy landing. Good.

A few seconds later, Sespian dropped to the ground beside him. He, too, had pulled out a knife. A lantern burning outside the closest tent provided just enough light for Sicarius to see the huge grin of exhilaration splitting his son's face. He must have enjoyed the airborne ride. The grin pleased Sicarius, an unusual feeling for him. Perhaps it had something to do with why Amaranthe was always trying to get him to smile.

After glancing about, Sespian pointed to the large tent and signed, *That way?*

Sicarius nodded and, fur cap pulled down to hide his blond hair, led the way. Instead of skulking amongst the shadows, he strode across the snow-dusted forest floor, as if he were a soldier sent scurrying off on some mission from a superior. It'd take forever to search the camp if they stuck to stealth, and with the uniforms for disguises, he deemed the tradeoff for speed worth the risk of being stopped. If necessary, they could tie up anyone who confronted them.

Sespian followed suit, and they soon arrived at the large tent. It was only a chow hall. From the sounds of the conversations within, the soldiers had long since finished their meals and were using the tent as a common area for games of Tiles and Bones.

Scrapes and clanks came from an attached kitchen on the backside where a few lowly privates scrubbed at pots. Sicarius paused and grabbed a couple of empty water jugs, gesturing for Sespian to do the same. They'd be less likely to be stopped by a sergeant or officer if they appeared to be on some mission already.

So laden, they continued on, ostensibly in search of a lorry

hauling the potable water tank, but Sicarius took in every detail of the camp as they walked. Other soldiers were about, but most had their heads down as they hustled from one tent to the next, in no mood to linger outside as the temperature dropped. Still, he was careful to avoid getting too close. As one would expect this close to an enemy outpost, everyone carried his rifle and ammo belt. It didn't matter that "the enemy" was a part of the same army. The weapons were standard army issue—muzzle-loading rifles that required reloading after each shot—rather than the more advanced Forge firearms.

A large clearing held a pair of mechanics' tents and numerous lorries, rough-terrain trampers and armored steamers. Sicarius halted, his back to a tree, to eye a large conical shape on the back of a flatbed.

"Any idea where the command tent is?" Sespian whispered, stopping beside him. He was glancing all around, but hadn't noticed the object of Sicarius's interest yet. "We've passed three water tanks. If anybody's watching us... What are you looking at?"

"Unless I am mistaken, that's a replacement drill head for a tunnel-boring machine."

Sespian took a longer look at the vehicle yard. "I guess they're not going to be content to wait for us to run out of food and water, eh?" He brushed snow out of his eyelashes and squinted at the huge drill head in consideration. "If they're down there tunneling, that'd be a lot of effort to get into Fort Urgot, wouldn't it? There's nothing that strategic about it except for the troops housed within. Granted, they'll be more likely to surrender—something imperial men are notoriously bad about doing—if the fort is compromised from within, but..."

"It may be a practice run for taking the Imperial Barracks."

"Oh. Good point. The Barracks are on a rocky hilltop, so the borer makes even more sense. Too bad we can't just shoo Heroncrest along and send him straight to harass Ravido."

Sicarius pointed at a conglomeration of tents on the other side of the vehicle clearing, all well lit. "That may be the command area we seek."

"It's busy." Sespian waved toward the soldiers coming and going. "I see a lot of pins with officer rank too. People who'll recognize you even if you're wearing a uniform and carrying a water jug."

"You're worried about them recognizing *me*? My face isn't on the currency."

A hair-raising howl floated across the fields, cutting off whatever Sespian's reply might have been. Sicarius's humor evaporated; there was no mistaking that eerie cry for anything except the otherworldly. It sounded as if the source were miles away, but with the muffling effect of the snow, it could be much closer.

"We should hurry," he said. "This way."

Sespian didn't object. He followed closely and didn't ask questions when Sicarius diverted into the vehicle area. Guards stood at the corners of the clearing, but the towering lorries and trampers provided cover.

The flap of one of the mechanics' tents stirred, and two soldiers walked out. Their route would take them straight toward Sicarius and Sespian. For a moment, Sicarius thought about testing their disguises, but the soldiers might wonder why someone was hunting for water amongst the vehicles. He chose a different option.

After tapping Sespian's arm to ensure he was paying attention, Sicarius set the water jug in the shadow of a tire, then slithered under a lorry. Sespian joined him, and they remained silent as the two sets of boots crunched through the snow two feet away. Instead of continuing to some destination, the pair of soldiers stopped at the front of the lorry. A soft rasp sounded, then the scent of burning tobacco reached Sicarius's nose. They'd be there a while. He tapped Sespian again, then crawled toward the opposite end of the lorry. Instead of rising, he chose a route that continued beneath the vehicles, using them for cover as he drew closer to the command area.

Perhaps fifteen feet away from the largest tent, he had to stop. The row of lorries had ended, and he was looking at the

gangly legs of a steam tramper; two of the towering vehicles were parked side by side. Sicarius eased into a crouch, intending to slip between those legs and head straight for the tent. But, as Sespian had pointed out, there were numerous soldiers coming and going. In addition, the trampers were in full view of a guard at the corner of the vehicle area.

Sicarius eyed the boxy metal bodies above the pillar-like legs. Cannons stuck out of raised portholes on the side, not dissimilarly to an imperial warship on the high seas. The top of the body would be flat, aside from a gunner's turret.

"This way," he breathed to Sespian.

When the guard had his head turned, Sicarius darted to the closest leg. He climbed up it, his sensitive fingers finding handholds on the icy metal. Cold snow waited on the top. He slid his fingers beneath it to grasp the edge, so he could swing his legs up. He dropped to his belly and gripped Sespian's arm as soon as it was close enough. Sicarius pulled him over the edge. Staying low, he crossed to the opposite side. Again waiting for the guard's head to be turned, he leaped the five-foot gap between the two trampers, landing lightly in the snow on the opposite one. Sespian followed, landing almost as easily.

"Good," Sicarius whispered. Though speaking wasn't wise, it seemed important to let Sespian know that he approved of his efforts.

They dropped to their bellies on the top of the tramper, the cold snow pressing against their parkas. They squirmed to the edge closest to the large tent. Two flags were thrust into the ground on either side of the entrance. From across the vehicle clearing, Sicarius hadn't been able to make out the patterns on the material, but he could see them now: the crossed swords on a blue background—the empire's flag—and a gold pick crossed over a musket and powder horn—the Damark Satrapy's flag. Lord Heroncrest did indeed govern that northern region.

Sicarius slipped out his black dagger. He would listen for what intelligence might be had, but he intended to eliminate Heroncrest that night, cutting out this thorn before it embedded

itself more deeply and festered. He thought of sending Sespian away, making some pretense of going back to check on something, but he doubted that'd spare any harsh feelings. No, he'd simply do what he intended, no lies, no excuses.

"That's the command tent, right?" Sespian whispered.

He scooted closer to the edge, shoulder to shoulder with Sicarius. Touching. It was the first time Sicarius could remember Sespian coming that close of his own volition. He rubbed his thumb against the side of his dagger. Killing Heroncrest... It'd put distance between him and his son again.

Regrettable, but Sespian would be better served by a quick resolution to the succession.

A captain trailed by a private carrying a notebook hustled for the command tent. He ducked inside without a word, but voices started up soon after.

"News, Captain Bearovic?" It was an older man's voice, General Heroncrest, Sicarius guessed, though he'd never heard the man speak and couldn't be positive.

"Yes, sir. Our intelligence men have reported back. Ravido Marblecrest is still in the Imperial Barracks and has approximately two thousand troops within the walls there and another fifteen thousand maintaining the peace in the city. So far, they're not openly attacking your men, and nobody's that concerned about Flintcrest's forces on the other side of the lake, but there have been isolated incidents between factions. There have also been a few altercations with civilians, university students mostly, who liked Emperor Sespian's progressive policies. They're causing trouble, demanding to know what really happened to him. They're pointing out that nobody's seen his body."

Sespian's head lifted. "I have supporters?" he whispered, a speculative note to his tone. Perhaps he was thinking he could make an appearance at the University and try to find men to back him there. But the young academic pups would be slaughtered if they tried to cross swords with soldiers.

"Because his body was incinerated in a train wreck," Heroncrest snapped.

"Are we certain about that, sir?" the captain asked. "We only have Marblecrest's word, right? And he's apparently being fed information by that gaggle of women."

Sespian leaned closer to Sicarius to whisper, "It's good that Ravido's colleagues don't seem to respect him or his alliance. We just have to prove that I'm the better option."

"And eliminate the Forge threat," Sicarius responded. "As powerful as that coalition is, it won't matter if anyone else supports Ravido or not."

"True, I hope Amaranthe's plan works."

"As do I," Sicarius said, though he cared more about her surviving the scheme than taking down Forge. He should be with her, not skulking around here. What would Heroncrest or Ridgecrest matter if Amaranthe was right and Forge *had* brought the *Behemoth* here, intending to use its weapons?

"If Forge says he's dead, he's dead," Heroncrest said. "Or he will be soon. Even in my northern satrapy, my family has had interactions with the leader of that organization in the last couple of years. They have an inconceivable amount of money at their disposal, and they have... other inconceivable powers too."

"Magic?"

"I'm not sure exactly what it is. But I've seen an impressive demonstration of power."

Sicarius wondered what else Forge might command aside from the flying vessel. He doubted they'd shown that to Ravido Marblecrest's rivals. Maybe they'd sought to cow Heroncrest, though, to warn him away from making a bid for the throne. He thought of the incineration cubes, imagining some aide of Heroncrest's burned alive before his eyes.

"My intelligence team has been following the newspapers," the captain said, "and there have been several horribly mutilated bodies found in the last few days. Similar to some slayings that occurred in the city last winter. Some have suggested the makarovi have been brought over from Mangdorian territory. Others say some magical beast."

"Forge's power... what was demonstrated for me, isn't anything like that. It's very... tidy."

"The cubes?" Sespian whispered.

"Possibly," Sicarius replied.

"Some people are suggesting the Nurians might be behind the slayings," the captain said.

"Of course they'd want to control the Turgonian throne too," Heroncrest said. "This is a massive once-in-countless-generations prize that's available. It's hard to believe they could have gotten people over here so quickly though. Unless they had advance warning."

"Or were planning an attack anyway."

Heroncrest grunted.

"Regardless," the captain continued, "tensions are thick in the city, and my reports suggest we can expect an escalation. It could get very bloody very soon. Also, word is getting out that we're camped out here too, though neither Flintcrest nor Marblecrest has started marshaling forces. It's possible they plan to let Ridgecrest deal with us on his own. If he can."

The wind shifted, refreshing the scent of cigarette smoke in the air. Sicarius lifted his head. No, the wind hadn't shifted. Someone who was smoking was coming closer. The guard in sight hadn't lit anything—Sicarius had been keeping an eye on him as well as the rest of the area while the officers spoke. He turned an ear toward the core of the vehicle lot, suspecting the pair of soldiers they'd passed earlier. Yes, the crunch of boots on frozen leaf litter came from that direction.

"...over here," one of the soldiers said.

A couple of young mechanics shouldn't have business in the command tent, but they were heading down the aisle in that direction. They'd pass beneath Sicarius and Sespian's tramper.

Sicarius touched Sespian's shoulder and wriggled back so his head wouldn't be visible if someone walked below them. When Sespian pushed away from the side to follow, a few clumps of snow were brushed over the edge. Sicarius hoped nobody was close enough to see or pay attention to the fresh lumps on the ground.

"...need it tonight?" one man asked.

"Sarge'll be mad if I don't have it at morning formation."

"Who is that?" called the guard at the corner of the clearing.

"Privates Tuller and Wardivk. Left my ammo belt in the tramper."

Sicarius pulled farther back from the edge and knelt. He probed the snow and found the hinges of the roof hatch. Careful to keep his head out of the guard's line of sight, he maneuvered about so he'd be behind those hinges, should the lid lift. If the soldiers entered this particular tramper to retrieve the missing belt, they *shouldn't* have any reason to stick their heads up there, but one had to be prepared.

He caught Sespian watching him and noting the knife in his hand. He'd drawn it to deal with Heroncrest—the officers were still talking in the tent—but felt the need to justify himself under that solemn gaze. An odd feeling. He'd rarely worried about justifications before. Under Hollowcrest and Raumesys, killing had been the norm not the anomaly.

The hinges of the belly hatch whined as they opened. Sicarius couldn't have said anything to Sespian if he'd wished it, not with the soldiers scant feet below.

"Better oil that in the morning," one said.

"The hinges are just cold. So am I. Whose blighted idea was it to lay siege to a fort in the winter?"

"Ssh, the general's tent is right over there, you dolt."

Thunks and clanks sounded as one of the men unfolded the drop-down ladder and climbed inside the tramper. Sicarius's hearing told him the other remained below—he was the one smoking. The smell of burning tobacco mingled with the pervasive coal scent in the air.

Sespian pointed at the roof hatch and spread his arms, palms up, silently asking what the plan was if the soldier opened it. He pointed to Sicarius's dagger and shook his head once, emphatically.

Out of habit, Sicarius signed, *I won't kill him*, though there wasn't enough ambient light for Sespian to read the gestures. So long as he got the gist.

A clunk sounded right below them, followed by a string of

curses. "Need a lantern," the muffled voice said from within.

Still poised to attack if needed, Sicarius waited while the soldier searched for his missing item inside and kept an eye—and ear—on the rest of the camp. Sespian returned his attention to the tent, no doubt trying to pick out more information for Ridgecrest. Aside from the discovery of the tunnel-boring equipment, they hadn't learned much that they hadn't already known or guessed.

It wasn't words, however, that reached Sicarius's ear, causing him to jerk his head up. A distant shout of surprise came from the rear of the camp. It wasn't from the direction where they'd left the cable, so it couldn't be related to that.

The surprised shout turned to a shriek of pain. Cries of, "Get back!" conflicted with orders to, "Help him!"

Nearby tent flaps were thrust back, and soldiers streamed out buckling ammo belts as they balanced rifles and lanterns in their arms.

Sicarius gripped Sespian's arm. "We need to get back to the fort."

Sespian turned wide eyes toward him. "The soul construct?"

Another cry of pain sounded, this one closer and on a direct path inward from the first cries.

"It's coming for you," Sicarius said.

* * *

Amaranthe didn't think she'd let any of her alarm over the announcement that Ms. Worgavic was on the way show on her face, but Books stepped forward and nudged her arm.

"You said this wouldn't take long and that I'd be allowed to begin my research of the current socio-political climate in the capital for the paper I'm writing. These times of upheaval must be documented. Yet—" Books tilted his head toward the women, "—it's been delay after delay. First we had to endure the blockade and the questioning from the soldiers, now this. Perhaps we could return to the boarding house and come back tomorrow, when the process can be expedited."

He was trying to give her a way to walk away from the yacht club before Ms. Worgavic showed up, but Amaranthe didn't want to leave. That would mean abandoning their plan entirely. What she needed was a ride down before Worgavic returned. She supposed it was too much to hope that her old teacher would get her shoe caught in a sewer drain, trip and fall, and be run over by a trolley.

"You're staying at a boarding house?" the middle-aged Forge woman asked. "When your parents' home is only a few miles up the hill?"

Alarm flashed in Books's eyes. He'd said the wrong thing, and he knew it.

"I'll be visiting them most certainly," Amaranthe said smoothly, "but the last I'd heard, Mother had turned my old room into a study. After being absent for so long, I wouldn't wish to intrude upon them. I doubt Retta is staying with them either."

Retta blanched and touched her eyepatch. "No."

Amaranthe patted Books's arm. "I understand your concerns, but we needn't rush. As I've told you, you'll have a firsthand view of the changing of emperors and the rise of a new power if you simply remain with me. My colleagues are spearheading the movement."

Books was searching her eyes, probably trying to figure out if she wanted him to continue arguing so she could pretend to eventually give in or if she truly wanted him to drop it.

"I'm hungry," Akstyr said. "Do we really have to wait for this *pomak*?"

That was one of the Kendorian words Books had taught Amaranthe—a derogatory term that translated to scavenger fish. She hadn't realized Akstyr had been paying attention. Books didn't seem as surprised—he gave Akstyr an amused and almost fond look.

"That had better mean venerable and wise gentlewoman," one of the Forge people said.

"Something of that nature," Books said.

"I can pilot them out if they want to go now," Retta said. "It

won't take that long, then I can come back for Ms. Worgavic and the rest of you. I'm quite eager to show my sister around the... ship." The steady gaze she gave Amaranthe as she spoke suggested she was more interested in throttling her for details of her scheme rather than offering tours. "As some of you know, I've been wanting to show her the work *I've* been doing as well." Bitterness laced the statement, a true one, Amaranthe sensed. Retta wanted to show her sister that, though she'd always been in her shadow when they'd been children, she was now reading the language of, and manipulating tools from, an advanced and utterly foreign race, something few people in the world could claim.

Amaranthe kept her face neutral. She didn't know how the real Suan would respond or how much she knew about the *Behemoth*, if anything.

"Ms. Worgavic won't appreciate a delay if she returns and our little tug isn't here," one of the younger women said, lips pursing.

Tug? More like a submarine—it had to be.

"You can blame me. I don't mind." Amaranthe waved her hand airily. "We've known each other for years."

"Yes, I understand you were one of her students back when she taught math."

"Actually, she taught economics," Amaranthe said, not certain if this was another test or if the woman simply didn't remember. "But, yes, I was a student at Mildawn."

"Ah, economics, of course." The woman nodded and pointed two fingers at Retta. "Fine, take her out."

Good. Amaranthe gave the women a curtsey and a "Thank you," and turned for the door. She didn't want to delay, not when Worgavic might come in at any moment.

"Not them," the woman said as Books and Akstyr started to follow.

Amaranthe froze. "Pardon?"

"Our new... yacht is not for outsiders. They can wait for you at the boarding house."

Amaranthe took a moment to make sure none of the panic clutching at her heart reflected on her face, then turned toward the table again. "These aren't outsiders. They're my advisers and my allies. I've known them for a long time, and we've been through a great deal together."

"Perhaps they can be invited dow—out at a later time, but not now. You'll understand when you see the yacht. Tell her, Retta."

Amaranthe met Retta's eyes, hoping for some support.

Retta licked her lips, glanced at the others, then nodded. "We can't let strangers down. For our safety and theirs. They might not be ready for... the truth."

Books snorted. Akstyr looked intrigued. They were both interested in seeing the inside of that craft, if for different reasons. Their curiosity aside, Amaranthe had reasons of her own for wanting them. Not only would they be necessary for coming up with a plan on how to take over or break the *Behemoth* somehow, but she'd need them to help her sneak or fight her way to the engine or navigation room, or whatever the craft had, the place of power and control. More than that, she needed... them. There at her back. Helping her and lending support in case... in case... cursed ancestors, she couldn't face that place alone. Not again.

"I'm sure they can handle it," Amaranthe said, shocked that her words came out calmly without terrified squeaks punctuating the words. "For Turgonians, they're quite ecumenical."

"*No*," the middle-aged woman said.

Retta shook her head once, minutely, a silent message in the gesture: Give up this fight. You won't win.

"The guards will escort them out," one of the younger women said. "You can meet up with them again in the city tomorrow."

"Very well," Amaranthe said and struggled to keep a lid on the pot of desperation trying to boil over inside of her. She'd never hyperventilated in her life. She wasn't going to start now. She hoped.

CHAPTER 13

"**B**LOODY BEARS, WHY'S IT COMING FOR *ME*?"
Sespian whispered. "You're the one who's
irked the world."

Sicarius, scanning their surroundings, didn't answer. He'd
picked an escape route when they first climbed onto the tramper,
but with so many soldiers thundering out of their tents now, their
lanterns burning away the shadows, there weren't any obvious
paths out of camp. Any direction that he and Sespian ran, they'd
be seen. They'd have to risk it and hope their uniforms and the
soldiers' distraction camouflaged them sufficiently.

"I'm sorry," Sespian said. "I didn't mean that I want it to kill
you. I just..." He shrugged.

Sicarius hadn't been offended. Besides, it'd kill both of them
if it found them together. "We'll go back this way, between the
vehicles, then south. Don't worry about being seen. Cut across
the field and back to the fort. If we get separated or there's not
time to reach the walls, meet up at the water tower."

"I understand."

The shouts were everywhere now, then a screech of utter
pain rose above them. It couldn't be more than a hundred
meters away.

Sicarius rose to both feet, intending to leap down. At that
second, the hatch flew open. Sespian had been crossing the
roof, following Sicarius, and the metal lid thudded into the side
of his knee. His leg buckled, and, in the slick snow, his other
foot lost purchase. He dropped hard with a pained grunt.

Sicarius grabbed Sespian's arm to pull him to his feet.

"Blasted ore, what's—" The soldier, head and torso rising from the hole, whirled toward them. As he turned, he lifted a lantern, and he got a good look at Sicarius's face.

He dropped back inside, lunging for something. Sicarius had succeeded in helping Sespian up and pushed him toward the edge.

"Can you climb down?"

"Yes, I'm fine. Just—"

The soldier's head popped out again along with a hand holding a pistol. Sicarius had expected it and was already moving. Before the weapon came to bear on him, he'd closed the distance, and his fingers latched around the man's wrist. Sicarius pulled the arm, forcing the soldier off balance and feinted at his eyes with his dagger. The man tried to yank back, but Sicarius held his wrist fast.

"Don't!" Sespian blurted, fooled by the feint.

Sicarius had already reversed the blade, and it was the hilt he drove into the sensitive flesh between the soldier's nose and mouth. Tears sprang to his eyes, and the pistol dropped into the snow. The man stumbled on whatever he was standing on, and disappeared below, thumping his head against the rim of the hole as he fell. Sicarius kicked the hatch shut.

He sensed the approach of danger, of a Science-crafted entity in the same heartbeat as Sespian shouted, "Look out!"

Instincts blaring, Sicarius flung himself to his belly and rolled sideways. There wasn't enough room on the roof for the maneuver, and he dropped over the edge. Before his head descended below the level of the roof, he spotted the dark hulking form landing, snow flying as it struck down, claws screeching as they attempted to brake by digging into metal.

Like a cat, Sicarius twisted in the air, landing feet-first to the ground. Someone was sprinting out from beneath the tramper and toward the tents. At first, he thought it was Sespian, fleeing the wrong way, but the bright red tip of a burning cigarette clenched in the man's teeth stopped him. It was the second soldier. Where was Sespian? There. He'd jumped down, too,

and must have yanked the soldier's rifle from his hands, for he waited by the front leg of the tramper, the stock of the weapon pressed against his shoulder, the barrel pointed upward. He was ready to fight, ready to shoot the creature when it leaped off the tramper.

"Mortal weapons can't hurt it." Sicarius lunged, grabbing Sespian's arm, intending to propel him toward the vehicles and the escape route they'd planned.

Snow dropping from the roof of tramper warned him a split second before the soul construct sailed off the roof, its massive form bigger than four people combined. It landed between the vehicles, twisting to face them.

Sicarius turned the push into a pull. "This way."

They'd have to escape in another direction.

Sespian fired before obeying. Even though Sicarius was pulling him off balance, the rifle ball hammered into the huge dog-like head, striking between the eyes. It bounced off with all the effectiveness of hail striking a cement sidewalk.

Sespian might have stood there, stunned, for a moment, but Sicarius grabbed him about the waist and hoisted him onto his shoulder. That elicited a startled squawk and a protest of, "Put me down!" but Sicarius didn't pay attention. He sprinted toward the tents, knowing that creature could catch them in a heartbeat. He couldn't run away as fast as he'd like, as soldiers were forming into squads around the vehicle clearing. One rank had dropped to a knee, preparing rifles to fire. He would have to plow through them and hope they gave way.

As Sicarius approached, one hand gripping his black dagger, one hand holding Sespian in place, General Heroncrest strode out of the command tent. With knives bristling from his belt and a cutlass and pistol in his hands, he was ready for a fight. He'd come out behind the first three squads of soldiers, and he faced the trampers right away. His eyes widened, not with recognition of Sicarius but at what was *behind* Sicarius.

"First squad, prepare to fire," a sergeant commanded.

With more reason than ever to get out of the way, Sicarius

jumped onto a rock and leaped over the row of kneeling soldiers as well as the squad standing behind. Because of the extra weight on his shoulder, he wouldn't have cleared that second row, but they saw him coming and stumbled out of the way. He landed not three feet from Heroncrest.

"Private! Where are you going?" The general stepped into Sicarius's path and held out his cutlass, blade showing, to further block him.

"Wounded man," Sicarius barked.

"*Wounded?*" Sespian blurted, voice full of indignation.

"Fire!" the nearby sergeant commanded.

Sicarius glanced back. Two dozen rifles boomed at once, stinging the air with black powder smoke and pelting the massive hound-shaped creature as it bounded toward them. It didn't falter one iota under the fire. It leaped into the air, outstretched paws broader than snowshoes, long fangs gleaming in the lantern light.

Knowing it was leaping for him—and Sespian—Sicarius didn't hesitate. He kicked the cutlass out of the general's hand. When Heroncrest cursed and grabbed, trying to prevent him from running past, Sicarius lashed out with his boot again, this time hooking it around the general's leg, banging the heel into the back of his knee. As he was crumpling, Sicarius rammed his shoulder into Heroncrest's back, shoving him toward the flying construct.

Without waiting to see what happened, Sicarius sprinted around the tent corner, racing past soldiers pounding in the other direction. Despite the chaos, he heard the sound of the creature landing, Science-enhanced claws shredding into clothing and flesh, bearing the general to the ground. A pain-choked cry of, "Get it off, get it off!" arose, only to be cut off by another round of rifles firing.

Hoping the creature was distracted for a few seconds, Sicarius raced toward the edge of the camp, Sespian bumping and cursing on his shoulder.

"Let me—oomph!—down," he said. "I'm done trying to shoot it, I—argh, watch the branches!—I swear."

More gunfire erupted behind them. Not far enough behind for Sicarius's liking, but he thought he had a second to spare to set down Sespian. They'd travel faster on four legs instead of two.

"I'm sorry I didn't—" Sespian stopped when he was plopped to the ground.

"Later," Sicarius said. "Go!"

He waved his knife for emphasis, and Sespian sped off in front of him. They sprinted around tents and lorries, dodging men every step of the way. Despite the gunshots and screams of pain echoing through the camp, the soldiers ran *toward* the chaos. It was a testament to their training, or perhaps an indicator of their ignorance in regard to the mental sciences.

Sicarius let Sespian stay in the lead so he could keep an eye on him, but when Sespian veered to the southeast instead of directly south, a route that would take them to the fort, Sicarius objected.

"You're off course. Urgot's straight ahead."

"I'm going to the cable," Sespian called over his shoulder without slowing. "We can climb back to the tower that way."

Sicarius understood Sespian's vision right away, but was skeptical it was the right choice. "That'll be a long hard climb with gravity and your body weight slowing you down." He knew he could make it, but doubted Sespian had endured enough upper-body training to earn the required stamina and strength. "And with the time it takes, the creature will catch up with us—we'll be stuck on top of the tower with no chance of making it to the fort. Better to sprint across the field."

"It might catch us then. We'd be helpless out there." Sespian almost crashed into a pair of men pushing coal-filled wheelbarrows through the snow toward a steam ram. They must be preparing the bigger machinery to fight the construct. Good idea, but it'd be too late to help those the creature was chasing...

Sicarius leaped over the wheelbarrows even as Sespian darted around the soldiers.

"The climb—" he started.

"I can make it, no trouble." Though he was panting, his cap had fallen off, and blood flowing from a cut near his eye, Sespian threw a grin at Sicarius. "Unless you're too old to handle it!"

"*Old.*" Sicarius said in his flattest tone. *He* wasn't panting.

"You're agreeing that you're old?"

"I'm experienced."

Shouts and a crash sounded, followed by a shriek of pain. It was the wheelbarrow men being knocked over and injured. Or killed. Sespian knew it too, and the humor vanished from his face. He lengthened his stride and reached the base of the pine tree a blink before Sicarius. He led the climb, scurrying up much faster than he'd climbed down, ducking and weaving around the proliferation of branches radiating from the trunk. Clumps of snow fell in his wake, many landing on Sicarius's head and shoulders, but he wasn't about to complain, not with a monster tracking them.

"Sorry," Sespian whispered down after knocking free a particularly large clump. "I should be more careful. If we're not rattling the branches, there's a chance that oversized hound will run past our tree and not realize where we've gone for a while."

"Unlikely." Listening as he climbed, Sicarius could hear the crunch of heavy paws on snow. Not only had the construct already arrived, but it was circling the pine, walking slowly, considering it.

"You're not the optimistic sort, are you?" Sespian asked.

Something slammed into the base of the tree. This time more than a couple of clumps of snow detached themselves—a small avalanche dumped to the ground.

"Not when evidence promises there's no reason to be so," Sicarius responded.

Sespian's boots came into view, and he stopped climbing. The trunk had narrowed, the girth of the branches dwindling. They must have reached the harpoon.

"It's my first soul construct," Sespian said. "It's possible I'm underestimating it."

"Yes."

"I'm sorry I shot at it under the tramper. I should have taken your word for it that our weapons wouldn't work." As he spoke, Sespian wriggled out onto a branch near the cable. "I'm apologizing a lot tonight, aren't I?"

"Young people rarely believe or heed the advice of their elders." Sicarius wondered when he'd grown old enough to be considered someone's elder. "Should you correct that mentality sooner than your peers, you may live longer than many of them."

The tree shuddered again.

"I'd settle for living through the night." Sespian tugged on a pair of mittens. "Can that thing knock over trees?"

"Yes."

"Of course, it can. We better both go at once then." Sespian waved to the cable. "Think it'll hold our combined weight?"

Thick snowflakes still fell in the field, obscuring the view of the water tower and the fort beyond. Sicarius could only see a few meters of the cable, but noted that an inch of snow had come to rest upon it in the time they had been exploring.

"You go first." Sicarius shook off as much snow as he could, knowing that, across a hundred meters, it'd add weight. The cable remained as taut as when he'd originally tied it, though, and it budged little. "I'll wait as long as I can before following you."

"Right."

Sespian wriggled out farther on the branch until it bowed under his weight, then grabbed the cable with both hands. Though he was aware of shouts coming from all directions as men sought to pinpoint the creature's location, Sicarius never took his gaze from his son. The cable sloped upward toward the tower on the hill. He feared Sespian was underestimating the effort the climb would take and didn't know if it'd be better to be right beside him, to catch him if his grip gave out, or to wait in the tree, ensuring the harpoon didn't slip out of the trunk.

Chewing sounds arose from below. The soul construct had remembered how it'd felled the last tree. Sicarius might not have time to wait.

"Go now, if you're going to do it," he said.

"Right," Sespian said again and took a deep breath.

The shadows masked his face, but Sicarius sensed the concern there as Sespian gazed at the cable angling upward into the snowy night. Hands gripping it, he rotated onto his back and swung his legs up to hook over it as well. The harpoon creaked where it stuck out of the trunk.

Sespian gulped, but, dangling like a pig on a spit, he began his journey, inching up the cable and away from the tree.

"Over here!" a soldier yelled nearby.

"Don't get close. It eviscerated Yankowic and Drakar. Wait for the engineers to get the vehicles running. We'll crush the slagging bastard."

Unlikely, Sicarius thought, his gaze locked on Sespian. The soul construct was too fast to be pinned by lorries. It'd take something more akin to Amaranthe's old plan to destroy it—or at least render it immobile. He should have been creating a trap for it instead of planning a spy mission.

The pine tree shivered, shedding more snow from its branches. More gnashing came from below. Sicarius tried to guess how long his perch would remain upright—and holding the cable aloft—then estimated how long it would take him to make the climb to the water tower. The night carried sounds of vehicles clanking into motion and hisses of escaping steam. The soldiers *might* distract the creature, adding time to the tree's life.

Sespian had disappeared into the curtain of snow. Sicarius wrapped a hand around the cable, trying to judge how far up the line he had gone. He couldn't tell, but quivers traveled through the braided steel. Sespian was still on it.

Another shudder, this one the biggest yet, coursed through the tree. Wood snapped somewhere within the trunk. Sicarius eyed the harpoon. It was already quivering from Sespian's movements farther up the cable. He didn't think it'd support both of their body weights for long. The chewing sounds from below continued, though, and he didn't have another choice.

Eschewing mittens, he gripped the cable in both hands, preferring the naked feel of it against his calloused palms. He

swung his legs over it and climbed, head twisted to watch the ground as he skimmed up the line.

A steam ram and tramper came into view, angling toward the tree. He envisioned inept soldiers missing the soul construct and knocking over the tree. In spots near the tower, the fall was close to a hundred feet. Six inches of powder wasn't *that* insulating.

The snow was lessening, and even from twenty feet away, Sicarius saw the construct back away from the tree, a dark shape against the white ground. It turned toward the approaching vehicles. Good, it would take a couple moments for it to deal with them. But then the misshapen hound head swiveled toward the field, its fat snout testing the air. A pair of crimson eyes focused on Sicarius, then shifted a couple of degrees higher. Toward Sespian.

Sicarius forced himself to keep climbing, to remain calm, though concern thrummed through his limbs. For so much of his life, he'd had little difficulty turning off his emotions— he'd never cared that much whether he lived or died, beyond a vague desire to complete missions and survive challenging circumstances. But Sespian had been safe within the walls of the Barracks then.

"It's coming," Sicarius called when the construct leaped away from the tree, its paws churning snow as it raced across the field. Rifle shots pelted the snow as well, and he acknowledged the vulnerability of his position. He was more than fifty feet above the ground at that point.

"Let it go," someone in the camp barked. "It looks like it wants to be Ridgecrest's problem now."

Not Ridgecrest, Sicarius thought as the creature slowed to a stop below him. Almost like a real dog, it sat on its haunches and tilted its head. Without warning it sprang, trying to reach him with that maw full of daggers. It didn't come close before dropping back to the ground. Maybe it'd thought it could startle him into letting go. Not likely.

The beast sniffed the air a couple more times, then trotted toward the water tower. And Sespian. If Sespian had truly

doubted whether he and Sicarius shared blood, the construct's confusion between the two of them ought to prove the link. The hound could smell their blood. It knew.

Sicarius continued up the cable at a steady pace. The upward angle added to the challenge, but his hardened muscles and palms had no trouble with the climb—he'd trained his whole life doing similar maneuvers. He noticed an increased tremor in the cable, though, and caught the sounds of panting coming from ahead. Sespian was young and lean, but he *hadn't* trained for this sort of event. Sicarius picked out his dark form and the outline of the water tower beyond.

One of Sespian's boots slipped, and Sicarius froze, hands clenched around the cable. If Sespian fell... he was too far away to do a cursed thing about it. The feeling of helplessness that weakened his limbs was unfamiliar. And unpleasant.

Analyze later, he told himself and returned to climbing. If he could get close enough, he could catch Sespian if he slipped.

Sespian had stopped. Resting and gathering himself? Or was he too tired to continue? Even without the upward slope, holding one's weight from a cable became a challenging task after a time.

"We're close," Sicarius called, intending to sound encouraging, but his voice came out hoarse, and he didn't know if Sespian heard it. He cleared his throat and tried again. "Keep going. You can rest on top of the tower."

"Thanks," Sespian called back. "I hadn't thought of that."

"It is difficult for me to know when you're being sarcastic." Sicarius climbed closer. A few more meters, and he'd be close enough to grab Sespian if he fell.

"Maybe you're not as *experienced* as you thought."

The light tone didn't hide that his forearms were quivering. Sicarius could feel the vibrations through the cable. A tremor ran through it next, and he thought Sespian's legs might have slipped off. But they were still hooked over the cable. No, that tremor had come up from below. From the harpoon.

Sicarius glanced over his shoulder at the eighty-foot drop

and the soul construct waiting below. If the harpoon gave way now...

"Is that what I think it is?" Sespian whispered.

"No."

Sicarius drew close enough to touch Sespian, though he chose not to, not wanting to startle him. It was enough that he could grab his son if the situation demanded it. Except, the back of his mind said, if the cable fell, their proximity to each other wouldn't matter....

"Continue up," he ordered, then, realizing the order came out harshly, tried to soften his voice when he added, "I'll catch you if you slip."

"This climb is a little longer and harder than I realized," Sespian admitted, though he started moving again as he spoke, forcing one trembling arm then the other to pull his body weight up the slope. His leg slipped again, and Sicarius's hand twitched toward it. Sespian growled and flung the deadened limb back up. The cable trembled in the aftermath of the move, and Sicarius glanced back toward the harpoon. The snow had dwindled further, and he could see the outline of the trees and tents now, along with the lights of the encampment. They were too far away to see the harpoon though.

"Is this not tiring you out at *all*?" Sespian asked as he inched closer to the tower.

"It is moderately wearying."

"What's that mean? You could only hold yourself up here for twelve hours instead of your usual twenty-four?"

This time Sicarius was certain of the sarcasm and attempted to reply in a humorous manner. "No more than five or six, I should think." Perhaps talking would distract Sespian from the ache in his forearms and the deadness in his legs.

Sespian grunted.

Down below, the construct snarled and paced. They'd come to the base of the hill. Another twenty meters, and they'd reach the top of the tower.

Sespian paused again, grimacing as he lifted one hand, then

the other to flex his fingers. He glowered up at the edge of the water tank. "Almost there," he muttered. "You can do this."

The construct jogged up to the crown of the hill. It was closer to them there than it had been at any spot during the journey, and Sicarius watched it intently. It paced back and forth, trying to find the closest possible point. The muscles in its haunches bunched, but it didn't yet leap. It must know it'd only get one chance before Sespian climbed out of range again.

Sespian saw it and moved his arms faster. Sicarius was on the verge of telling him not to hurry so much that he made a mistake and slipped. But the creature jumped.

Sicarius yanked a throwing knife out of his arm sheath and hurled it at one of the beast's crimson eyes. It didn't even blink. When the construct reached the apex of its jump several feet below, he thought they were safe, that it wouldn't reach Sespian, but one long powerful paw lashed out, claws angling toward Sespian's back.

Sicarius dropped his legs, twisting in the air to kick at that paw. He connected, deflecting the claws, but the cable abruptly went limp. A thunderous snap echoed from the tree line. It wasn't the harpoon that had slipped free, came a useless thought from the back of his mind as he and Sespian fell; the entire pine had broken off at the base.

Their weight carried them downward like a pendulum, sweeping them between two pillars of the tower. Sespian held on, trying to climb up even as the wind whistled past their ears. Sicarius was lower on the cable, and he had to tuck in his legs to keep them from striking the earth. He held on by one hand as they swung, pulling out another throwing knife with the other. The soul construct's leap had carried it to the bottom of the hill, but it had already spun about, and it was charging up the slope toward them. Though he knew the effort useless, he hurled the blade. It was all he could do.

The knife spun true, cutting into the gaping fang-filled mouth. It lodged in the maw like a toothpick gone awry, and the construct paused to shake its head, trying to spit it out.

"Climb," Sicarius ordered. He was relieved Sespian had kept his grip on the line, but they weren't out of danger yet.

"Trying," Sespian growled. "Can you make this thing stop swinging?"

Before he'd finished the sentence, the cable, which had carried them beneath the tower and out the other side, reached the end of its path and jerked to a halt. Sespian's grip slipped and he cursed as he skidded several feet before catching himself. His boots were in Sicarius's face.

Sicarius gave a shove with his free hand, ordering, "Climb!" again, more insistently this time.

Already, the soul construct had flung the knife from its mouth and was bounding up the slope again. As the cable reversed its path, swinging back under the tower, the creature reached the crown of the hill. Encouraged by Sicarius's order—or death's approach—Sespian found reserves in his muscles and he raced up the cable. Sicarius started up, too, but the construct leaped into the air, again targeting Sespian.

Sicarius whipped his legs backward, then hurled them forward and up, trying to catch the creature in the chest. He did, his heels slamming against the broad torso, but even with the momentum, his blow barely diverted the six-hundred pound monster. It was like kicking a mountain, and it did nothing except jar his knees. Sespian had seen the construct leaping, though, and he'd yanked his legs up to his chin. Perhaps Sicarius had distracted it an iota, for the beast sailed past without managing more than a swat of the claws.

That swat, however, cut through the cable below Sespian. Sicarius plummeted to the ground.

Though surprised, he found his feet and landed in a crouch in the snow, immediately jumping for the nearest tower support. He didn't see the construct land on the edge of the hill, but he heard it thump down, and that sound was incentive enough to send him up the metal post in scant heartbeats.

The creature howled, a frustrated edge to the sound, and hurled itself against the support. Sicarius was already climbing

onto the snow-covered beam above. He wouldn't pronounce them safe yet, but the steel posts set in concrete should be harder to bite into than a tree trunk.

Eyes rounder than marbles, Sespian lay on the beam, his legs and arms wrapped around it. "What took you so long?" he asked.

Sicarius studied him, concerned by the manic edge to his tone.

"It was a joke," Sespian said, taking a few breaths. "You know, because you're not slow." He must not have seen what he wanted in Sicarius's face for he added, "Never mind."

"I understood." Sicarius thought to explain that, after a lifetime of maintaining a facade over his thoughts, it took conscious effort for him to let his expression change, but the creature was prowling below, testing the posts. He stood up. There was more to do before they were safe.

"Thanks for saving me from painful mauling and certain death. I'd probably try to hug you if I weren't so busy groping this beam right now." Sespian peered over his shoulder. His knees were clenched around the steel so tightly he was in danger of losing feeling in his nerves. "I'm not quite sure I can let go either."

Sicarius bent and offered him a hand. "You would be permitted."

Sespian stared at the hand. "To what?"

"Hug me." Sicarius knew it'd been a joke—or an utter-relief-at-not-being-dead outburst, but he made the offer in case Sespian should ever be so moved in the future.

"Oh. Uhm, I'm not really someone who..." Sespian offered an embarrassed shrug, but he did accept the proffered hand. "But good to know I'd be allowed."

Sicarius pulled him to his feet, steadying him when his legs, doubtlessly exhausted from the climb, threatened to buckle.

When Sespian regained his balance, the corner of his mouth quirked up. "Do many people try? To hug you?"

"Few. Usually women."

"Ah. Amaranthe." Sespian's face grew wistful, though it seemed accepting as well.

"Infrequently." Sicarius headed for the ladder leading to the top of the tower.

"Really? If a girl was inclined to hug me, I'd encourage her to do it frequently."

"I am not good at... encouragement." Sicarius climbed the ladder and found the harpoon launcher where he'd left it.

"I've noticed," Sespian said, reaching the top behind him. "It's easy though. You spread your arms like this and give a girl your most inviting smile. Do you... have an inviting smile?"

"No."

"Any sort of smile at all?"

"No."

"I can see where you'd have a problem then," Sespian said.

A boom sounded at the nearest corner of the fort. An instant later, a startled yowl came from below. Sicarius lunged to the edge of the water tank in time to see the soul construct fly out from under the tower and down the hill. It tumbled to a stop at the end of the slope, taking a moment to recover. It shook itself like a wet dog and sat on its haunches.

"Reinforcements." Sespian pumped his fist.

A hundred-odd meters away, atop Fort Urgot's closest wall, a cannon bled black smoke into the air. Grim-faced men lined the parapet, rifles in hand. Others reloaded the cannon while someone cranked the elevation, bringing the weapon up to aim at the top of the tower. At Sicarius.

Sespian's fist drooped. "Or perhaps not."

CHAPTER 14

A FTER HER PREVIOUS ADVENTURES ON THE BOTTOMS OF lakes, the novelty of traveling underwater had worn off, but Amaranthe still flinched at each creak and groan that emanated from the tiny submarine's hull. On the other side of its convex glass viewing port, fish flitted away as the craft descended, its exterior lamps sending a beam of light into the dark water.

She sat shoulder-to-shoulder with Retta in the tiny navigation compartment while two guards loomed behind their seats. There was only a few feet of cargo space behind them in front of a bulkhead with a hatchway in it. Amaranthe hadn't seen beyond it, but Retta had waved in that direction and said, "engine room," when they'd first entered. Given the overall size of the submarine—most of the lavatories on Mokath Ridge had larger footprints—she could see why the Forge women had called it a "tug." She didn't see anything magical about it, and it had a Turgonian feel with steel construction, pipes running along the bulkheads, and levers and gauges similar to what she'd seen on imperial ships.

"Where did you get this vessel?" Amaranthe asked. She *wanted* to ask about everything that had happened since she'd last seen Retta and, oh, how do you go about blowing up the *Behemoth* too, thank you very much, but the guards might find those questions a tad suspicious.

The frown Retta gave her suggested she'd said something wrong anyway. "This is one of the ones *you* purchased on the Kyatt Islands."

Oops. "Oh, is it? I handled all of the paperwork in town and didn't get a full tour of the crafts." There, that sounded plausible, didn't it? How much information could the guards have been given anyway?

Retta nodded slightly. Right answer.

"They're more Turgonian than I'd realized." Amaranthe probably ought to keep her mouth shut for the rest of the trip, but she didn't know if she'd get a chance to be alone with Retta in the *Behemoth* either. The Forge women hadn't seemed to trust her fully—maybe they knew Retta had helped Amaranthe escape back down south. These guards might be permanent attachments to her ore cart.

"It's to be expected, since all of the submarines in the world today—and, as you know, there aren't many—are based on Admiral Starcrest's designs."

That "as you know" made Amaranthe pause. Suan had probably been the one trotting around the world, shopping for Forge's imports. A warning not to ask for more details on this subject? Probably.

"I can't believe he's still alive," one of the guards whispered in an awe-struck tone.

Thus far, both of the men had been too busy looming menacingly to speak, and this declaration surprised Amaranthe. The guard, previously the image of gruff professionalism, sounded like a wistful youth, lamenting that he'd never met the admiral. Not all that surprising, she supposed. Even Sicarius, who respected few people, could quote Starcrest's books on military strategies and tactics and had admitted to reading a few of the "based on real events" but largely fictional Starcrest novels as a boy.

"What's he like?" the guard asked Amaranthe.

"Er?"

"Didn't you meet him when you were on the Kyatt Islands?"

"No, I understand he's very busy with..." Work? Family? Nude sunbathing on the beach? How was Amaranthe supposed to know? Along with most of the rest of the populace, she'd

thought he was dead until recently. That'd always been the official Turgonian statement, that he'd been killed in the Western Sea Conflict more than twenty years earlier. Unlike Sicarius, and apparently every other male in the empire, she'd never studied the man's work either; she'd gone to business school, not a military academy, after all.

"He's quite devoted to his family," Retta said. "That's kept him busy, and he's taken on a number of subaquatic engineering projects for the Polytechnic's research division, to help further underwater exploration around the islands and abroad. Now that the children are older, I understand he and his wife have been off-island, investigating ancient ruins and mysteries."

The wife, that was the linguistics specialist Sicarius had met in those tunnels, wasn't it? The one who'd originally decoded the language of the *Behemoth*. Amaranthe hoped she wasn't involved with Forge in any way, but hadn't Retta said she'd learned the language on the Kyatt Islands? What if Forge had the wife—and maybe Starcrest too—tucked into a back pocket?

"That must be why you didn't meet them when you were there," Retta finished, her eyebrow twitching ever so slightly.

She thought Amaranthe should shut her mouth and stop chancing discovery, too, but maybe it was better to learn this information here, in front of guards who couldn't be fully knowledgeable about who and what "Suan" was supposed to mean to the Forge organization, rather than later when talking to some high-up official.

"Yes, that sounds right." Amaranthe gave Retta an eyebrow twitch of her own, wishing she could mentally convey the suggestion that this would be a good place to relay information in some oblique manner that the guards wouldn't see through. Too bad Retta wasn't a true telepath. As far as Amaranthe knew, it had only been some Made tool that had allowed their minds to link and share memories.

"It's fortunate that you were able to get a hold of so many of their submarines," Retta said. Maybe she read minds after all, or could decipher twitchy eyebrows. "Though Admiral Starcrest

gave out the plans to his original submarine to all the major governments in the world, no one has yet melded Turgonian metallurgy and engineering technology with practitioner-crafted power supplies the way the Kyattese have."

The guards shifted at this mention of practitioners. Amaranthe wondered what she'd see if she opened the hatch in the back. Some flashing ball floating in the air, thrumming with energy? The submarine had leveled off and Retta was steering it along the lake bottom. The *Behemoth* should be in sight soon. If the guards had been down here before, they must have seen it, at least on the outside, and have some idea of what it might do. Maybe the idea of advanced ancient technology alarmed them less than that of magic-slinging contemporaries.

"I had to work hard to make that deal," Amaranthe said, hoping for more details. Anything she could learn about Suan's background could only help.

"Oh, yes, I'm sure it was quite difficult finding the right person to bribe in the Kyattese government," Retta said, "especially with all that Forge money to throw about."

Amaranthe was trying to decide whether to respond to that— it sounded like a comment directed at the real Suan, rather than her—when a thump came from the rear of the craft.

"What was that?" one of the guards blurted.

"Did something hit us?" the second asked.

"I don't think so." Retta considered the gauges, then peered through the viewing window.

Nothing except seaweed and silt-covered rock lay within the light's influence, though Amaranthe had the impression of a presence ahead of them, something denser and blacker than the deep dark water around it.

"It came from inside," the first guard, the one who'd spoken of Admiral Starcrest, said.

"What if something broke?" The second man shifted uneasily, his fingers tightening on the back of Amaranthe's chair. "I heard... They said if a tank or a seam or something ruptures, the boat could implode, and we'd all die horribly."

A second thump came, identical to the first.

"I'll check on it," Retta said.

She rose halfway out of her chair, but Amaranthe stopped her with a hand to the arm. "We're getting close to our destination, aren't we?" she asked, hoping nobody would remember that she wasn't supposed to know anything about their destination. "I think you should stay in the pilot's chair." She tried to give Retta a significant look. She had a hunch about those noises back there.

Retta glanced out the viewing area again. "You're right. I can see the *Ortarh Ortak* now." She eased back into the seat. "Valter, will you check please?"

"I don't know anything about these boats," the second guard said, his fingers like talons where they gripped the chair. "Something could be broken, and I'd never know it."

"Just open the hatch and describe what you see." Retta flicked a couple of controls. The black shape ahead was growing more pronounced, something that spread for hundreds of meters in either direction. Amaranthe hadn't been imagining it; they were approaching the *Behemoth*. She surreptitiously wiped a palm on her dress.

"I'll go," the Starcrest enthusiast said when his comrade didn't move.

The other guard, Valter, was dealing with sweaty palms of his own as he stared at the seams of the hull, the whites of his eyes visible all the way around the irises. It seemed unsporting to attack such a man, but if Amaranthe's guess about those thumps was right, she wouldn't hesitate.

The first guard reached the hatch and spun a wheel to open it. She twisted in her seat, readying herself. The guard stepped through the hatchway and peered to his left. A pair of legs swung down from above, wrapping about his neck. Someone else yanked the cutlass, knife, and baton from his belt holders. The neck grip kept the guard from hollering anything, but Valter heard the scuffles and thuds. He whirled about, yanking out his own sword.

Before he'd taken more than two steps, Amaranthe vaulted out of her chair and onto his back. She wrapped one arm around his neck, locking it with the other to apply pressure. At the same time, she clasped her legs around his waist, so he wouldn't be able to shake her off. The hem of the dress restricted her movement, and she almost didn't get the position she needed. Fortunately, he was more worried about her grip on his neck and she had time to readjust her legs for a better hold.

The guard grabbed her arms, trying to break the lock, but she'd practiced with Sicarius and knew to keep her grip so tight that he couldn't thrust his fingers between her arm and his neck. He flung a hand behind his head, trying to smash her with his fist. His knuckles brushed her temple, but she buried her face in the back of his neck, making it hard for him to do any damage, and kept applying pressure. His struggles would grow feeble once his air supply dwindled.

The guard wasn't ready to give in yet though. He turned his back to the hull and drove her into the unyielding metal. The blow jarred Amaranthe from teeth to toes. She might have released him to pursue another attack strategy, but Akstyr stepped out of the engine room and pointed a dagger at the man's nose.

"Stop thrashing around out here, or I'll carve out your tonsils." Akstyr sneered. "By going through your nostrils."

The man stared at him for a moment, then passed out, plummeting to the deck like a felled tree. Amaranthe released him and rolled away.

"Do you find it difficult to make people believe your menacing threats when your robe is open like that?" Books stepped through the hatchway and waved at Akstyr's askew attire.

"No." Akstyr scowled and tugged the flap over to cover up things Amaranthe hadn't wanted to see. It seemed robes weren't much better than dresses for fighting in. "He paid attention, didn't he?"

"Because his face was purple and he couldn't breathe, I believe," Books said. "Also, his eyes were a little glassy, so I'm not sure he saw more than the knife."

"What are you people *doing* down here?" Retta alternated between glowering at Books and Akstyr and looking through the viewing window. They'd rounded a curve in the Behemoth's massive dome-shaped body, and a white light had come into sight, a stark contrast to the dark water and the black sides of the craft. "My assistant is going to be inside, manning the controls so we can dock, and there's always at least two guards in that room. Strangers can't *stroll* inside."

"Ah, but we're not strangers." Books bent and unbuttoned the green uniform jacket of the unconscious guard, dusted it off, then held it aloft. "We're employees in the—" he eyed a patch on the sleeve, "—Brackenshaft Armed and Armored Protection Coalition. Goodness, what a pretentious name to refer to uneducated louts with pointy sticks."

Amaranthe smiled, pleased and relieved that her men had found a way on, though she knew it meant that the guards who had been escorting them out of the building were probably tied up in a closet somewhere. She'd originally envisioned having a few days to get to know her way around the *Behemoth* and interact with Forge people, maybe gathering crucial insider information before enacting a plan to destroy the craft. Now, they'd be lucky if they had until dawn before their identities were discovered.

Retta growled again, apparently neither pleased *nor* relieved by Books and Akstyr's appearance. "What are you planning to do down here, Lokdon? I went along with this against all the voices in my head telling me it was crazy, and—you haven't done anything to my sister, have you?"

"No, of course not. Though she is in town, so I did have to send someone to detain her."

"What do you mean by *detain*?"

"Escort her to a secret facility for holding until such time as we've completed our mission," Amaranthe said. That didn't sound so bad, did it?

"You mean you *kidnapped* her?"

"Technically, that word might be appropriate," Amaranthe admitted.

Books might have snorted, though it was difficult to tell with that shirt pulled over his head. Akstyr had shucked his robe and was bent over the unconscious guard in the engine room, removing the man's clothing, his bare buttocks thrust through the hatchway as he did so. Retta, still manning the controls and checking their progress out the front window, did a double glance—one might call it a gape—when she noticed this display of nudity. Amaranthe rubbed her face. This wasn't the way she'd imagined this trip going.

"What *mission* are you planning to complete?" Retta asked when she recovered from the spectacle behind her.

"We intend to make sure Ravido Marblecrest doesn't succeed in his coup," Amaranthe said, "and to do that, we need to ensure Forge doesn't have any secret super powerful technology to call upon to aid him. The money and advanced firearms they've supplied are already giving him too much of an advantage. I assume they're willing to use that huge black craft if they need to?"

"They don't wish to reveal it," Retta said, "but they may use it or elements to ensure their agenda. They believe Ravido has enough to fight down mundane opposition, but one of the other potential candidates has Nurian allies with him. Assassins and wizards."

Amaranthe didn't like the way she'd pluralized wizards. "We've met one of the assassins and a soul construct. Which general has these foreign friends?" She thought of the army surrounding Fort Urgot. At that very moment, Sicarius and the others might be trapped inside by those troops. She trusted his preternatural skills to keep him safe from guns and muscles— and Maldynado, Basilard, and Sespian were capable as well— but a practitioner? Maybe *multiple* practitioners? Ones strong enough to summon soul constructs? Even Sicarius had been smashed to the floor by Arbitan Losk's power, and there'd been luck involved in the man's defeat.

"Flintcrest," Retta said.

Good. Mancrest had said Heroncrest was the one with the

fort surrounded. With luck, Amaranthe could get the whole team back together before anyone came up against practitioners. "Neither Ravido, Heroncrest, or Flintcrest is an acceptable candidate," she said. "Sespian Savarsin is alive and well and wants the throne, and we think he's the best bet for a peaceful and prosperous empire."

"Ah." Books had dressed in everything except socks and shoes, and he held one of those socks aloft now in a gesture of protest. "That's not *precisely* what we want, at least not what I wrote up. A democratic election open to all educated members of the populace should determin—"

"Not now, Books." Amaranthe made a cutting off motion with her hand, then turned that gesture into a quick series of signs, spelling the last word out since Basilard's language didn't have many terms yet for discussing governments: *Let's keep it simple for those we're recruiting; not everybody is ready for a new Turgonian paradigm.*

Retta was piloting the submarine closer to the light and didn't seem to see, but her uncovered eye was tight, her face tense. "I don't care who's on the throne. I just want the freedom to study the *Ortarh Ortak* and other artifacts from this civilization, and now that Forge is suspicious of me, I want to get away from them. That's been true for a while, as you know and used to your advantage." She skewered Amaranthe with her gaze.

"I meant what I said about helping you escape if I could," Amaranthe said. "I'm back now."

"You're here to use me again because you want to kick Forge in the balls."

Though it was clear Retta was irritated, Akstyr snickered and nodded his approval of this language. He and Books had changed into the uniforms and tied up the guards in the back. They'd shut the hatch and taken their places behind the navigation seats.

"Yes," Amaranthe said, figuring honesty was all that had a chance of working, "I want to use you. I was hoping you'd vouch for me here, but I can help you escape Forge too. Just leave with us after we—"

"After you what? What do you think you're doing to my craft?" She pointed toward the *Behemoth* and the light, almost blinding in its intensity as they drew closer.

Amaranthe paused. "*Your* craft?"

"I'm the one who's been studying it for years. And for years before that, I was studying the language. It's the most complex thing you've ever seen. And the *Ortarh Ortak?* There're a million things it can do, but I've only been allowed to focus on piloting it, landing it, and shooting things."

"Shooting?" Books murmured to Akstyr. "Is that what they call it when they raze an entire swamp, lighting fire to thousands of acres of wilderness, and blowing a dirigible out of the sky?"

Amaranthe started to speak, but Retta cut her off. "Yes, it can damage things, and it's very powerful, but there are facilities on here, technologies, that could be used for good too. For healing people and making items to improve life. A few years back, Professor Komitopis found a science lab in underwater ruins off the Nurian coast that was left by this civilization. Among other things, it can instantly fertilize and alter soil composition to favor whatever crops you wish. Something like that could end hunger forever."

Books and Akstyr were sharing dubious looks, and Amaranthe agreed with the sentiment. Even if she hadn't been there for the razing of the swamp and the blowing up of the dirigible, she could see more uses for evil than for good with this technology. Humans couldn't be trusted with this kind of power.

"Has Professor Komitopis seen this craft?" Amaranthe asked casually, though her mind had leaped back to her earlier thought. What if Starcrest and his wife knew about the *Behemoth* and supported the research of it? Had Komitopis trained Retta herself?

"No." Retta scowled down at the controls. "Everyone high up in Forge has agreed that it has to be kept secret from outsiders. I didn't know anything about it until Ms. Worgavic called me back from my classes on the Kyatt Islands. After a couple of years at their Polytechnic, I'd been selected for the tiny, secret

program that studies this technology. The professors were very select about who they allowed in, and I thought it was my grades that won me entrance, but it turns out that Ms. Worgavic had a hand in things all along."

Amaranthe nodded. She'd suspected as much when she first spoke with Retta. She doubted that those Forge high-ups would keep the craft a secret forever, though, not if it could be used to secure the throne and the rest of their goals.

"Where did you get that medallion?" Retta asked out of nowhere.

Amaranthe almost blurted a, "Huh?" but remembered how Retta had noticed it up above. "We randomly picked it out as part of the costume." At least Amaranthe thought it had been random. She met Books's eyes.

He shrugged and signed, *They're very popular in Kendor. They sell them to tourists at all the ports.*

"It looks like…" Retta cleared her throat. "When we were girls, Da used to go away on trips out of the empire. It's what first got us interested in world history and other cultures. Once he brought back a medallion like that. I adored it, but he gave me some candies and gave *it* to Suan. She always got what I wanted."

"Well, here." Amaranthe removed it and handed it to Retta with a smile. She knew she was trying too hard to win this woman's favor, but the jewelry meant nothing to her and if there was a chance it would mean something to Retta… "You can wear it later when we take you to meet her, and you can gloat about how she got kidnapped and you didn't. I bet she didn't want that."

Retta snorted and waved her hand, as if she'd push the medallion away, but it snagged her eye for a moment, and, with a mulish set to her chin, she took it and put it on. "Maybe I will."

A clank reverberated through the submarine, the hull shuddering.

"What was that?" Akstyr asked.

Retta's hands flew over the controls. "Sorry, I wasn't paying attention. We're here. We have to dock now."

She steered the craft into the source of the light, and another clank and shudder coursed through the submarine. Amaranthe thought they'd struck something at first, but some sort of arms had stretched out to clamp onto their craft. That was her guess anyway. The bright light obscured the details, and she couldn't stare through the viewport for long.

Retta released the controls. They were still moving, being pulled into some bay by those arms.

Amaranthe sensed her heart speeding up. Not only did she have to face those soulless black corridors again, but she wasn't sure Retta wouldn't step out of the submarine and turn them over to the guards.

Amaranthe leaned closer to her, dropping her elbows to rest on her knees. Last chance to make sure Retta was on their side. "We don't have to destroy the craft," she whispered. "I just want to make sure Forge doesn't have access to it. If it was... I don't know, buried under the ice in the South Pole, it wouldn't be a problem. Only those who knew it was there could go and study it, a long way from all the major governments of the world."

Books watched Amaranthe steadily as she spoke, a question behind his creased brow. Maybe he was wondering if she meant what she said. She wasn't sure. At the moment, she wouldn't be above prevarications to ensure Retta worked with them.

Retta didn't respond to the words though. She was either concentrating on the gauges... or ignoring Amaranthe.

A final shudder ran through the submarine as it came to rest on something solid. Gurgles sounded on the other side of the hull—water being drained from a holding chamber?

Retta rose from her chair and headed for the hatch on the side. "We can go out now."

Akstyr's fingers flew: *Do we stop her?*

Books also watched Amaranthe for an answer.

Yes, she thought, no, I have no idea. Outwardly, all she did was sign, *No.*

* * *

Sicarius crouched, making himself a smaller target for the soldier at the cannon. Out of the corner of his eye, he gauged the distance to the side of the water tank. If he could leap over the edge fast enough and catch the beam as he fell...

Sespian took a step forward and removed his cap. "We're on your side," he called across the hundred-meter gap.

"The armbands," Sicarius said. Though the snow wasn't falling as heavily as before, it still obscured the view, and the men might have a hard time seeing Sespian's face and identifying him. The broad blue cloth strips tied to his and Sicarius's sleeves were another matter.

Sespian removed his as he continued shouting to the men on the wall. "General Ridgecrest sent us out to spy. He'll thank you if you check before shooting us. We do, however, appreciating you trying to blow up that ugly mutt that was chasing us."

As if it knew it was being discussed, the construct stood and loped away. The cannonball hadn't damaged it any more than rifles and daggers had, but it was done with the attack. Perhaps it knew it couldn't reach Sespian now—or perhaps it thought Sespian might be taken care of by other means. Sicarius stared at the men manning the cannon, his jaw set, his eyes hard.

"The general did *not* send a murdering criminal out to spy for him." One of the soldiers, a young lieutenant perhaps, pointed at Sicarius.

Someone over there must have a spyglass and be able to recognize faces after all.

"Actually, he did," Sespian responded. "On my suggestion. If you didn't notice, I'm Sespian Savarsin, and though my authority is somewhat debatable right now, I've been working with General Ridgecrest since last night."

"The emperor is dead," came the response.

"I guess they didn't notice the guest at Ridgecrest's side for half of the day," Sespian muttered. "Armies, the shield arm is always oblivious to what the sword arm is doing." He raised his voice to the officer. "My death was a lie. Why don't you go talk to Ridgecrest? See if he approves of you blowing up the water tower I'm standing on. I wouldn't wish for you to be punished."

The officer muttered something to the cannon crew. Maybe he was wondering if they could shoot Sicarius while leaving Sespian upright. A lowly officer would find the idea of approaching General Ridgecrest intimidating—indeed, in the army, he'd be expected to report to his captain instead, and only eventually, after word had filtered through the chain of command, would he find out Ridgecrest's response.

"Come over here." Sicarius gripped Sespian's arm and pointed to the edge. "You can shout at them from *behind* the water tank."

Sespian grumbled under his breath, something about how those soldiers would have believed *Amaranthe* if she were making the same arguments, but he allowed himself to be guided toward the edge. "I can't believe there aren't at least rumors floating around the fort about me being alive."

"You had your hood up all day, and Ridgecrest has probably told his closest men that there better *not* be rumors, not until he's made his decision."

"What else can we try? They don't look like they're in the mood to let us shoot a harpoon and tightrope walk to the wall."

Sicarius, gaze riveted to the officer and the cannon team, didn't respond. In his peripheral vision, he observed the rest of the wall and the men in the watchtowers. When the officer said a single word and nodded once, he saw it.

"Down," he barked.

Flattening to their stomachs might have been enough, but he wouldn't risk it, not with his son at his side. He gripped Sespian's arm and pulled him over the edge.

They weren't on the side of the tank with the ladder, so there was nothing to grab onto as they fell. Sespian blurted a startled, "What's wrong with—" before the boom of the cannon drowned him out.

Using his free arm, Sicarius caught the beam before they could zip past it. Between the fall and Sespian's extra weight, even his best attempt to soften the landing couldn't keep it from being jarring, and he wasn't surprised at the flash of agony in

his shoulder. The joint popped out of socket, the feeling—and sound—unmistakable. He hung on though, mentally clamping down on the pain as he swung Sespian up to catch the beam. When he'd locked on with both hands, Sicarius pulled himself up.

After ensuring they weren't in anyone's line of sight, he bent his wounded arm, keeping the elbow by his side, and rotated the limb until he could push the shoulder back into joint.

Sespian had been eyeing the sky in the direction the cannonball had gone—when it hadn't thudded into Sicarius, it'd sailed across the field and into the trees—but he turned at the crunching noise and grimaced. "I can't believe I'm related to you."

"Does that mean you won't proffer a hug this time?" Sicarius gave his arm an experimental rotation and found the range sufficient.

Sespian gaped at him for a moment, then snorted. "I don't know. Did you just save my life again, or were you the target?"

"The cannon was aimed at me. I agree with your earlier assessment that funambulation is unlikely for either of us."

"Fu...nam...bu..." Sespian shook his head, then laughed. It wasn't a snort this time, but an unabashed laugh.

Odd that Sicarius struggled to elicit humor in others when he attempted to do so, but in mere speaking could inadvertently have a humorous effect. Perhaps this was why Hollowcrest had always insisted he keep his mouth shut unless he was replying to a question.

Sespian brushed at the corner of one eye. "I'm beginning to think my own childhood social awkwardness may have had less to do with a solitary, peerless upbringing and more to do with hereditary tendencies."

Sicarius wasn't sure how to respond to that, but these acknowledgments that Sespian believed they did indeed share blood pleased him. "If they will not allow us inside, perhaps we should use the remaining night to sneak past Heroncrest's army and return to the city." And Amaranthe, he thought, if she hadn't already left for her mission.

"No," Sespian said. "They need to know about the tunnel-boring equipment. Once Ridgecrest hears we're out here, he'll let us back in."

"He'll let *you* back in. He'd prefer I not be around." But Sicarius wouldn't leave Sespian, not as long as that creature was out there. Although...

He gazed across the field at the great paw prints left in the snow. With a trail like that, it would be easy to track. Sneaking through Heroncrest's camp would be difficult with everyone up and alert now, but he'd managed such feats before. If he went alone, there'd be less likelihood of being caught. If he could find the construct and eliminate its owner, there'd be one less trouble to deal with. But, as they'd seen with Arbitan Losk, the wizard who'd animated the last construct, killing the creator wouldn't necessarily stop the beast or alter its mission.

"What are you thinking about?" Sespian asked.

"Tracking. Traps."

Sespian eyed the trail of churned snow. "Now? Instead of going back in? Don't you ever eat or sleep?"

"I have rations with me."

Sespian winced. "Not those meat bars again."

"I do not require that you eat them, though you would find them nutritionally superior to many other offerings."

"Oh, I'm sure of it. Anything that tastes that awful *has* to be good for you. Listen—" Sespian waved toward the fort, "—come inside with me. We'll talk to Ridgecrest together. He should know that you're openly helping him. Everyone knows you as this notorious bloodthirsty assassin who's slain countless soldiers, enforcers, and more than a few warrior-caste men in prominent positions. I'm never going to be able to give you a job on the staff if you don't change a few people's minds about your nature."

Sicarius didn't see how his reputation mattered at the moment, but the thought that Sespian might want him on the staff pleased him. "Have I changed *your* mind?" If so, he wondered if it was a result of Sespian spending time with him or more a matter of

Amaranthe speaking on his behalf. Or perhaps reading his files in Hollowcrest's office had made a difference.

"It's... possible you're not as utterly evil and loathsome as I thought."

"I see." One probably shouldn't find such a dubious accolade amusing, but Sicarius did so anyway. "My employability can be discussed further once the succession is solidified. For now, there's little I can do inside, whereas I can be hunting the soul construct—and its creator—on the outside. Ridgecrest doesn't seem to be a threat to you at this time. Nor has the soul construct shown an inclination toward entering the fort. You should be relatively safe in there."

"Until Heroncrest decides to launch an attack," Sespian said grimly.

Was he truly worried about surviving such an event? Or was it possible he didn't wish Sicarius to leave his side? Or, if not that, maybe he worried that Sicarius would die if he went hunting for wizard's beasts. No, he was reading too much into a simple statement.

"It's unlikely they'll breach the walls quickly," Sicarius said. "If they start shooting, duck. Faster than you did with the cannonball."

Sespian propped a fist on his hip. "I knew that cannonball wasn't aimed at me."

"You may find it easier to go in through the front gate. I'll disappear before light comes." Sicarius took a few steps along the beam, intending to check on the soldiers—he didn't *think* they'd blow up their own water tower in an attempt to kill him, but he wouldn't be dumbfounded if they were discussing the repercussions now.

But they weren't discussing anything. Most of the men who'd been lined up along the parapet, pointing rifles or manning artillery, had disappeared. Only the soldiers in the watchtower remained, and one of them was facing the door.

"What happened?" Sespian peered around the opposite side of the tank. "Something more interesting going on inside?"

Sicarius couldn't imagine what, though he did detect a number of distant shouts coming from the fort. Was it possible the tunnel borer had already plowed through the earth and come up inside? He had little experience with such machines, but it seemed too soon.

"Is that smoke?" Sespian asked.

There were furnaces and stoves burning inside numerous houses and buildings within the fort walls, so smoke was natural, but there *did* seem to be a thicker plume rising from one side. It was difficult to tell against the cloudy night sky, but Sicarius caught the scent of burning wood. The furnaces and stoves would be burning coal.

Two more figures strode into view on the parapet, both wearing military fatigues. They had familiar forms and gaits.

"Uhm, that soldier's hair is too long," Sespian said. "And that one's awfully short for a Turgonian. Those wouldn't be your friends, by chance, would they?"

Maldynado and Basilard strolled up to the corner guard tower and knocked on the door. It opened. Maldynado pointed at the water tower and said something. When the soldier stuck his head out to look, Basilard grabbed his wrist and pulled him off balance at the same time as Maldynado kicked the back of his knees. While Basilard finished subduing him, Maldynado rushed inside. The second soldier's head disappeared from the window.

"Yes, those *must* be friends of yours," Sespian said dryly.

Basilard faced the water tower and waved. It was too far to read hand signs, but Sicarius understood. They'd cleared the way. They'd probably lit one of the officer's houses on fire. Not Ridgecrest's, one hoped.

Sespian was already climbing to the top of the tank. He had the harpoon launcher in hand by the time Sicarius joined him. Sespian tied off the end of the cable, then, with surprising accuracy, shot the weapon, sending the harpoon sailing around a lightning rod on the top of the guard tower.

"Funambulating time," he said with a wink.

"You go." Again, Sicarius eyed the trail in the snow. "Stay with Maldynado and Basilard. They'll protect you."

The harpoon launcher drooped in Sespian's hands. He looked like he might argue, make another objection, but Sicarius lifted his hand to forestall it. They'd discussed this enough. He gripped Sespian's arm briefly, then slid down the ladder to the beam, and finally down a post to the ground. He headed into the night to track the soul construct.

CHAPTER 15

As Amaranthe headed for the submarine hatch and the voluminous black chamber beyond Retta, she second-guessed herself. Maybe she shouldn't have let Books and Akstyr change into the guard uniforms. Not only did they fit poorly—Akstyr and Books were both tall and lanky, rather than thick and burly—but surely any guards they encountered down here would be familiar with all of their colleagues working this gig. On the other hand, they wouldn't have known that the woman above had vetoed Amaranthe/Suan's attempt to bring her comrades along. Amaranthe might have walked in with them in their original costumes. Of course, disallowing visitors might be a Forge-wide policy. Maybe she would get lucky, and there wouldn't be any guards on duty. It was getting late after all, wasn't it?

The submarine hadn't docked so much as been sucked all the way into a cargo bay, the "wall" closing behind it, and now it dripped water from its hull, forming puddles. When Amaranthe ducked through the hatchway and stepped into the chamber, she had to squint and blink at the day-bright light emanating from the walls and from a ceiling thirty feet above her head. More than the light disconcerted her. Those featureless inky walls and the disproportionate architecture—they brought back memories. Walking through corridors, being smashed into a wall by Pike, being picked up by a mechanical claw and locked onto that table, spending hours under the man's knife, being helpless to escape any of it...

A hand gripped her shoulder. Books.

Amaranthe licked her lips and tried to draw strength from his presence. She wasn't alone this time, and Pike was dead.

The rest of the men on the *Behemoth* hadn't shared his fate, however, and a number of guards were waiting. So much for her hope that there wouldn't be any. Not only were they there, but there were more than Retta had led her to expect. Ten men, lined up in two squads, stood a couple of meters away from the submarine hatch, their hands clasped behind their backs, crossbows slung over their shoulders and swords at their belts.

Amaranthe's fingers itched. Books and Akstyr carried the subdued guards' rifles, but she still had nothing more than a knife.

"Uh, hello?" Retta lifted a hand toward the waiting squads. No, she hadn't lied; she truly hadn't expected this many men.

Amaranthe stood in front of the hatchway, trying to block the men's views of Books and Akstyr's faces. Difficult given that they were almost a foot taller than she. Wisely, they hung back in the shadows of the hatchway, keeping their heads ducked.

"We've two days off," the highest-ranking guard said. "Captain Wricket said you might be able to take us back up, ma'am."

Amaranthe barely heard him. She was staring at a pair of men in black fatigues standing by a wide cargo door on the far side of the chamber. They clasped repeating rifles in their arms, making the guards with crossbows seem lackluster in comparison. Stolid, humorless expressions stamped their faces, faces that she recognized. They were two of Pike's people. She feared they'd see through her flimsy costume and recognize her straight away.

"I certainly can," Retta said, "but I was going to show my sister around first. We've been waiting a long time for her to join us."

Every set of eyes in the chamber swiveled toward Amaranthe. It was all she could do not to bare her teeth at Retta for drawing their attention. Were those two guards by the door squinting at her with suspicion? Or did they naturally look that constipated?

She didn't know if she should say something—would Suan deign to speak to the hired help?

"Where's Neeth?" someone asked from the side.

The submarine body had blocked the view of a control station set into the wall and the person who sat at it. The woman stood and joined them, peering at Retta, then studying Amaranthe. Tight gray curls cupped her head, and spectacles thicker than bottle bottoms framed inquiring brown eyes. She must have been in her seventies, but her step was springy, her curiosity almost palpable.

"We waited for her, but she hadn't arrived yet, so I decided to make two trips," Retta said. "Ah, Suan? This is Mia, my assistant."

"Your assistant?"

Mia's lips quirked with wry amusement. "You retire from your old career and begin a new one, and they make you start all over at the bottom. I do not, however, fetch her tea or flatcakes."

"I'll remember that," Amaranthe said, instantly liking the woman and hoping she wouldn't be forced to do anything untoward to her.

"She's a fast learner and is almost as adept as deciphering the runes as I am." Retta sighed, and Amaranthe sensed more bitterness than fondness in the exhalation.

Mia didn't seem to notice. She grasped Amaranthe's forearm. "Suan, I'm glad you're here. I've heard much about you."

Uh oh. Amaranthe hoped there wouldn't be further tests. At least this wasn't an old colleague.

One of the men at the door murmured something to the other.

"Perhaps we can share a meal later?" Amaranthe asked. "I'm weary from my weeks of travel. Retta, can you show me to a room before leaving to take these fellows back up?" More precisely, Amaranthe wanted a tour of the *Behemoth*, a better one than she'd had last time, including the navigation room or engine room or whatever the equivalent was.

"Who are you two?" one of the guards in the first squad asked.

Amaranthe stifled a wince, knowing before she turned that someone was addressing Books and Akstyr.

"Cafron and Vinks," Books said. "We're new."

"New? And you got this assignment? Nobody but Lettodjot's most trusted men have gotten to come down here. There's no chance you'd—"

Amaranthe was trying to decide if she should attempt to talk her way out of the situation or simply accept that they'd have to fight when the speaker's belt unclasped and his trousers descended. In fact, that happened to every man standing in the squads. Still lurking in the shadows, Akstyr had his eyes shut, grinning like a boy pawing open Winterfest gifts.

His distraction wouldn't startle the guards for long. Amaranthe had to act. She rejected the idea of using Mia for a shield and lunged for the closest of the startled guards instead.

"What happened?" one was blurting, bent over and yanking up his trousers.

"It's magic, you idiots," came a yell from the door. "Get them!"

A rifle fired. If Amaranthe hadn't already been moving, the bullet might have slammed into her chest. As it was, it ricocheted off the hull. Retta and Mia lunged between the control station and the submarine, hiding behind its bulk.

Amaranthe snatched the crossbow off the back of the closest man who was struggling with his trousers, elbowing him in the gut to buy a second to pluck out bolts as well, then jumped behind the nose of the submarine with the other two women. More shots fired from the soldiers, all aimed in her direction. She didn't know whether to take it personally or assume they weren't shooting at Books and Akstyr because their own men were in the way. Either way, the submarine and the wall behind her took the brutality for her, though one bullet did ricochet off the control station and bounce into their cove. Retta screamed. She'd been hit. Cursed ancestors, this wasn't how things were supposed to go.

Amaranthe leaned out and loosed a quarrel toward the doorway. It skipped harmlessly off the wall. The two soldiers had moved. They'd run into the room, each dropping to one

knee, rifles pressed into their shoulders. They fired as soon as they saw her.

She ducked behind the submarine again. Metal clashed to her right, near the open hatch. In her peripheral vision, she'd glimpsed the mass of green security uniforms descending on the submarine. Books and Akstyr had retreated inside. Given that only one person could attack at a time through the narrow entryway, they ought to be able to hold their own. Amaranthe on the other hand... Those soldiers were definitely after her.

"Stop drawing their fire," Retta snarled, her voice thick with pain. She was clenching her shoulder. Blood soaked her blouse and seeped between her fingers.

"Emperor's warts, I'm sorry," Amaranthe said, reloading her crossbow. It could hold two quarrels at a time. She'd pay all the money in Sespian's secret stash for one of those repeating rifles just then. "Where'd your assistant go?"

Retta jerked her head to the left, then winced, doubtlessly wishing she hadn't. If one followed the control wall to the end, there was a tall narrow door there. It was a good fifty feet away. Mia must have trusted that the soldiers wouldn't shoot her. Amaranthe didn't have that luxury. She checked to the right, thinking she might run around the submarine and surprise her attackers by appearing on the other side, but it had been parked too close to the hull. That barrier must have become permeable to allow their entry, but it appeared solid now.

"They're coming," Books yelled over the twang of crossbows and the screeches of swords.

Amaranthe dropped to her belly, hoping the soldiers would expect her to pop out at her regular height. Crossbow leading, she stuck her head around the corner.

The soldiers must have been racing toward her and stopped at Books's shout, for they were closer but on one knee again, prepared to shoot. When they saw her, they had to drop their rifles to adjust for her new position. She fired a bolt and ducked back.

A rifle boomed, the bullet clanging off the hull a hair from where Amaranthe's eyes had been. The noise rang in her ears like a bell. She didn't know if she'd struck her target or not. A new round of growling and cursing came from behind her. She was glad Retta didn't have a weapon; at this point, she must be ready to stick a dagger between Amaranthe's shoulder blades.

Retta could always shove you out into the soldiers' line of sight, Amaranthe thought.

Another shot fired, the bullet caroming off the wall behind them. Neither Retta nor Amaranthe had been exposing any body parts at which to aim, so Amaranthe guessed it was meant as a distraction. She leaped to her feet, the butt of the crossbow jammed into the pit of her shoulder and stepped back.

As another shot fired, causing Retta to bury her head under her arms, a black form somersaulted around the nose of the submarine. She'd expected someone on his feet to charge their hiding spot, but reacted immediately, lowering her aim.

The soldier unfurled, a throwing knife in his hand. Amaranthe pulled the trigger, then dropped to the floor, hoping to evade the blade. It clattered off the hull above her. She grabbed the knife and scrambled to her feet, ready for a close quarters fight if that was what the soldier wanted. But he'd never risen from the floor. Her quarrel protruded from his neck and he only had time to utter one gurgled word.

"What'd you say?" Amaranthe asked.

He pitched sideways and didn't move again.

"Bitch," Retta snarled, one hand clamped to her shoulder again.

"Was that his word or are you cursing me?" Amaranthe didn't have any more quarrels for the crossbow so she eased back to the nose of the submarine with the throwing knife in one hand and her own dagger in the other.

Retta panted, trying to control the pain. "Both."

"Let me finish dealing with these men, and we'll take care of your shoulder."

Amaranthe peeked around the corner, ready to jerk her head back if she caught sight of anyone aiming at her. There was at

least one more soldier and all those green-uniformed guards as well. "Or perhaps not," she murmured, taking in the carnage littering the floor around the submarine hatch. The black-clad man was dead, a crossbow bolt protruding from one eye. She gulped. Her first wild shot from her belly had done that?

Most of the guards were down as well. That hadn't been her doing. Two of the men had either fled or made it into the submarine, but the clangs and grunts of battle had faded.

Not lowering her weapons, she eased around the nose of the submarine and headed for the hatch. Half of the guards' trousers were about their ankles. What had been amusing with the gang thugs on the docks failed to stir her humor now, not when the recipients of the pranks were dead with cut throats or bullets in their backs. Somehow Amaranthe doubted the soldiers had intentionally shot their own allies and suspected Akstyr's hand had been in that as well.

She couldn't chastise him though; his tactics had saved them all from being captured. Or worse.

Knowing they might not have much time before reinforcements came, she picked her way to the hatch. Books stood inside, cast-aside rifles on the deck, daggers in his hands, the blades dripping blood onto the threshold. A dead guard lay at his feet, and he was staring at the other bodies, his expression somewhere between shock and horror.

Amaranthe gripped his arm. "We have to go."

Akstyr slipped past Books, bumping his elbow. Books didn't seem to notice.

"All dead?" Akstyr asked.

"Yes, but I think some got away." Amaranthe pointed at the doorway. "Can you help Retta, please? We need her to help us figure out... everything, and she's injured."

Akstyr shrugged. "Sure."

Amaranthe rooted about for weapons. There were crossbows and rifles aplenty; ammunition was another matter. The guards must not have anticipated a big battle on their way to shore leave, for nobody was carrying extra, at least in the first few belt pouches she checked.

Books dropped the daggers and wiped his hands on his trousers more times than was necessary. "You should bring Sicarius along when you need people..." He swallowed. "Dispatched. This isn't... I don't..."

"I know." Amaranthe was reluctant to abandon her search before finding ammunition, but she couldn't let Books fall apart. She guided him out of the hatchway while hoping the size of the *Behemoth* meant it would take a few moments for those men to find help. "I keep waiting to get smart enough to figure out how to avoid killing people on our quest to save the empire. I sense we're not doing something right."

It wasn't an appropriate time to joke—she'd simply meant to distract him—and Books's scowl informed her of the fact. "Remember our discussion on prudence earlier this year?"

That hadn't been it, eh? "You're the one who jumped the guards up there and in the submarine, ensuring we'd run into trouble tonight," Amaranthe pointed out, then wished she hadn't.

Books flinched.

"Sorry," she said. "I know you came to help me. This was all my plan, and it's all my fault. As usual."

She picked up the daggers Books had dropped, wiped them off, and handed them to him. She wished he'd say she was being too hard on herself, but he didn't.

"More men coming," Retta said through gritted teeth. She'd slumped into the chair at the control station, but rose after making the announcement, nearly tumbling into Akstyr's arms.

He caught her and they headed for the door Mia had used.

"How soon?" Amaranthe let Books go, thinking to resume her hunt for ammunition.

"Now."

Amaranthe cursed, abandoning her search. Frustrated, she dropped the empty crossbow she'd been holding and jogged after the others. "That door? The way your assistant went? Are you sure that's wise?"

"The guards don't know the back corridors as well," Retta said, "and we can get to the core from there. It's a control room of sorts."

Or Retta could lead them right to Mia and a trap. She had more reason than ever to be annoyed with Amaranthe now.

"I don't have much choice now but to help you." Retta hissed when a misstep jarred her shoulder. "Mia will let everyone know I was working with you. I—"

Footfalls pounded the floor in the corridor outside the bay.

"All right," Amaranthe whispered, hustling her comrades toward the alternate exit—it was their only other choice. "Go, go," she urged, all too aware that having an injured party member would slow them down.

Retta and Akstyr passed into the corridor first, and Amaranthe and Books lunged over the threshold just as a squad of soldiers burst into the bay. More of Pike's men.

"There!" one cried, spotting Amaranthe and Books.

"They saw us, Retta," Amaranthe barked. "Can you shut this door? Lock it?"

Retta stumbled back to them and waved her hand on one side of it, high up. That section of smooth black wall looked no different than any other along the corridor, but four enigmatic runes flared to life, glowing crimson. Amaranthe pulled her dagger out, prepared to throw it at the first soldier who ran into sight. Retta pushed in one of the symbols and twisted it. Two soldiers appeared, rifles raised, ready to shoot. The door slid down. A dozen weapons fired, but the bullets were barely audible, soft *tinks* as they struck.

"It's locked?" Amaranthe asked as her team ran away.

"For now."

Amaranthe didn't find that encouraging.

* * *

Sicarius jogged across the snowy field, following the soul construct's tracks, staying downwind as much as possible. He left his own tracks in the half foot of fresh powder, something he noted with displeasure, though there was no way to avoid it. As it was, the inches of soft snow were slowing his gait. He thought of places along the western side of the lake where he might acquire snowshoes. It would depend on how much longer he needed to follow the tracks and where they led. He'd slipped through Heroncrest's camp and out the other side without being seen, partially thanks to his stealth and partially thanks to the death and disarray the creature had left in its wake. It should have made the soldiers more alert, Sicarius thought, chastising them for the ease with which he'd passed unnoticed between tents and under vehicles, even as he accepted that the situation had been advantageous for him.

Now, with night still blanketing the fields, he searched for lights on the horizon, listened for sounds, and sniffed the air for the fresh blood that stained the construct's paws. Twice it had veered toward farmhouses to kill, not caring whether its victim were man, woman, or child. Sicarius hadn't caught sight of it yet and didn't want to—if he drew that close, it would smell him and begin its chase anew. He wanted to follow it to its home, to its master. With dawn only two hours away, it should be heading in that direction now.

The snow had stopped, and a few stars peered between the clouds overhead. With the increased visibility, he made out a lantern burning a half mile away, somewhere near the lakeshore. He pulled up his mental map of the area. That ought to be the ice cutting camp he and Amaranthe had visited for a mission the year before, the only one that claimed permanent dwellings and housed machinery outside of the city. Sicarius would have to deviate from the construct's path to visit it, but it might be worth it. Following the creature wasn't enough; he had to come up with a way to kill it, or at least render it permanently unable to move. So long as it was out there, he and Sespian would both be vulnerable to an attack, one that might come when they were distracted by another battle. He could see his own death coming that way, but more, he could see Sespian's. To lose him, after all of this effort to protect him and after they were finally exchanging... banter, as Amaranthe would call it, would be—he clenched his jaw—unacceptable.

Sicarius veered toward the camp. It wouldn't take long to

survey, and it was probably not a bad idea to come later to the soul construct's destination, when its master assumed there'd be no retaliation for the night's activities.

Even with the snow slowing his pace, he covered the half mile in a couple of minutes, and reached the outskirts of the camp. The light came from a single guiding lantern posted near a concrete dock that stretched a quarter mile into the lake. Numerous cabins and sheds dotted the banks, along with a metal machine shop with vehicles parked outside it. Sicarius eyed a crane and large lorries, some for carrying heavy loads of ice and others with winches and cutting equipment for removing the blocks in the first place. Currently, only a few feet of ice edged the lake, but, in another month, dozens of people would fill the camp and they'd be working around the clock. For now, only a couple of the cabins showed signs of occupation, early laborers sent out to ready the site.

Sicarius passed a snow-covered stack of beams, materials for a new building, and picked a lock on the machine shop. Inside, workbenches, a smithy, and welding tools took up a large chunk of the area. After a moment considering everything, he left, trotting back across the field to find the trail again. He hadn't spotted any cement mixers or convenient already-dug pits that would let him reenact Amaranthe's first soul-construct trap, but perhaps he could construct one of his own in that machine shop. He mulled over ideas as he followed the tracks, now angling to the southwest and away from the lake.

He was surprised at how far the creature had traveled to terrorize him and Sespian. Fort Urgot was five miles outside of the city, and he judged he'd gone another nine or ten, meaning the construct had made a thirty-mile roundtrip to hunt Sespian near the factory two days earlier. Of course, with those long and tireless legs, it could traverse a great distance in a short time. As more miles passed beneath him, and dawn drew closer, he started to doubt his thoughts of laying a trap at the ice-harvesting camp; only he or Sespian would work for bait—and Sespian was out of the question—but how would he lead the construct all the way back there without being caught himself? It could run far faster than he.

The smell of smoke reached Sicarius's nose. Someone's morning cook fire, or a sign that he neared a larger encampment? Numerous species of wood burned, and he caught a few whiffs of coal as well. Yes, the odors represented more than a single home's hearth, and there were no towns out this way, only farmlands and some rolling hills to the southwest. Hills that might, he wagered, hide an army camp, at least from a distance. They were a couple of miles from the nearest major road, and the railway tracks were farther yet.

Sicarius veered away from the soul construct's tracks, so he could circle around the area where his nose told him the camp lay without being seen—or smelled. Night was relinquishing its hold as dawn brightened the clouds in the eastern sky, and perimeter guards would pick out an approaching figure. He didn't know if they knew a soul construct lived in their midst or if it was being kept hidden. If the latter, those enormous footprints would cause quite a stir.

As Sicarius skirted the foothills, he heard and smelled more signs of a large force camped within the draws and valleys—the scents of eggs and flatbread cooking mingled with the smoke smells, and here and there the tops of tents or trampers poked above the ridges.

He approached the camp from the far side with higher, rockier hills at his back. He had to scramble over and around the granite boulders and dells of the area, but he found a few trees that had escaped loggers' axes by growing from inhospitable slopes, many quite sheer. He scrambled up a fir, using its needle-filled boughs for camouflage, until he had a view of the entire camp. The way the tents and vehicles meandered along the valley floors and walls made it hard to calculate numbers, but he guessed the force as large as Heroncrest's. In addition, it must have at least one practitioner.

The Nurians had a distinct culture, often wearing attire Turgonians would find outrageously flamboyant—though

perhaps Maldynado would not feel that way—and Sicarius thought a brightly colored tent might mark their spot, but only the green canvas of portable army dwellings dotted the valleys. He did spot an army-issue medium near the rear of the western edge of the camp. There was nothing notable about it except for the fact that all the soldiers coming out of their tents to attend their morning ablutions were avoiding the spot. Exactly what one would expect from Turgonians aware of a wizard in their midst. The tent had room for a few people to sleep in it—or a couple of people and a huge soul construct. It was also possible that the creature was sleeping in some cave in the hills. That seemed more likely than it strolling amongst a thousand tents filled with Turgonian soldiers. Sicarius would prefer to deal with the construct independently of its creator anyway. He hadn't picked up the tracks again yet on this side of the camp, but he hadn't circled the entire area yet.

He was about to drop down from his tree perch when the front flap of the tent he'd been watching stirred. A figure in cloth shoes and green and blue silks stepped out, a thick fur-trimmed jacket the man's only concession to the cold. Silver hair fell halfway down his back, and his yellow-bronze skin was creased with age, though nothing about his erect posture and alert black eyes suggested senescence.

Sicarius thought to slip out his spyglass for a better look—he'd like to try for a glimpse inside the tent to see if more Nurians occupied the cots or if the soul construct might be there—but that silver-haired head turned in his direction.

He hadn't moved or done anything that might have drawn someone's gaze in his direction, and more than a hundred meters separated his tree from the Nurian's tent. Further, branches and needles camouflaged his position. It didn't matter. Through some percipience or another, the man sensed his presence and continued to stare in his direction.

An eerie howl echoed from some valley in the hills, the sound stirring the hairs on the back of Sicarius's neck even though he ought to be familiar with it by now. Coming here

before he'd laid a trap may have been unwise. He'd assumed the practitioner wouldn't send the beast out during the day, but that may have been a fatal assumption. It was a long run back to the water tower outside of Fort Urgot.

The tent flap stirred again, and a second man stepped out, this one fit and young and wearing a scimitar at his waist, with a bow and quiver slung over his shoulder. It might have been another wizard hunter brought along to act as an assassin, but Sicarius suspected it was a bodyguard. When the younger man asked a question, drawing the practitioner's attention for a moment, Sicarius dropped from the branches. He was running before his feet alighted in the snow. He'd learned what he'd hoped to learn, but, with his presence being detected, he might not have time to do anything with his knowledge. He ran anyway.

CHAPTER 16

"How much farther?" Amaranthe whispered as the sounds of footfalls faded. "You don't look well."

Retta crouched beside her in the alcove, with Books and Akstyr pressed in behind them. They'd used Akstyr's guard jacket to fashion a bandage for her, but she must have torn something anew during the last scurry for cover, for fresh blood dampened her hand. Her face was Kendorian pale.

"Not far." Retta leaned her head against the wall. "We've been 'not far' for an hour. We're just having trouble finding an unblocked route to our destination."

"I've noticed."

"Mia must have guessed where we're going, and she's directing troops to hunt in the area."

"Their hunting is proving oddly effective," Books said. "We keep seeing the same men. It's as if they know right where we are." The look he directed at Amaranthe held some extra meaning. Maybe he thought Retta was giving away their position somehow.

She shrugged back at him. Striking out on their own wasn't an option. At this point, Amaranthe was completely lost. They were depending wholly on Retta to lead them to the control room. Or anywhere for that matter. If she passed out from blood loss, Amaranthe feared they could wander for days and not find their way out.

"They do know where we are," Retta said bluntly. "There are ways to track humans in here."

"Do we need to set up a diversion?" Books asked. "Draw the guards off so you two can get in?"

"Just what *we* are you volunteering for that?" Akstyr asked. "I've been shot at enough tonight."

Not for the first time, Amaranthe wished she'd brought Sicarius along. He could handle the guards. Given time, he could probably hunt down everyone on the craft. Much more desirable than being hunted themselves. She hoped Sespian appreciated the use of her men.

"There's one more route we can try," Retta said. "This way."

She wiped her moist hand and led them back into the maze. A few fresh droplets of blood splashed to the floor.

"Is there a first-aid kit in that control room?" Amaranthe asked. "Maybe we should stop somewhere to patch up your wound."

"Yes," Retta said.

Books and Akstyr shrugged when Amaranthe looked their way, wondering which of her questions Retta had been responding to. So long as she didn't lead them back to the room with that crate and operating table. Pike might have left some of his salves in there, but Amaranthe shuddered at the idea of going in there to retrieve them.

Something floated out of an intersecting aisle ahead of them, a black cube. It rotated in their direction, a glowing red hole on the front, burning into one's soul like a hot iron. Amaranthe flattened herself to the wall.

"Hairy donkey dung," Akstyr whispered, and he and Books did the same.

"Not again," Books said. "Run?"

The cube floated toward them.

"Just step aside," Retta said.

"It'll try to flambé us," Akstyr blurted.

"No, I reworked their operating instructions early on." Retta stepped out of its way, and the cube drifted past without pausing. "They don't vaporize humans any more."

"One we met in your underwater base did," Amaranthe said.

"Those weren't from the *Ortarh Ortak.*"

"Just how many stashes of advanced technology does Forge have?"

"Enough," Retta said.

"How comforting." Books still sucked in his gut and pressed every inch of his back to the wall as the cube passed.

It paused, and Amaranthe tensed. A fine red beam shot out of the orifice, angling toward the floor. Something flashed, and smoke wafted up, then the cube moved on.

"What's it doing?" Akstyr asked.

"Cleaning up my blood." Retta grimaced.

"We should have brought more weapons." Amaranthe flicked a finger at the dagger on her belt, lamenting the pile of crossbows and rifles they'd left in front of the submarine—not that they'd do anything against that cube. "Real spies would have figured out how to sneak aboard with more than dinner knives."

"I assumed you had the explosives in your purse." Books waved at the satchel she had managed to retain throughout the night.

"I thought someone might search it. I only brought things a normal woman from the well-to-do business class might carry around."

"Such as pens, ledgers, and abacuses?"

"Cosmetics, lotions, and breath mints," Amaranthe said. "And adhesive for my fake nose."

"Well-to-do businesswomen sound much like regular women," Books said. "Regular women with prostheses anyway."

"Maldynado may have thrown some... additional items in there too. I couldn't figure out why it was so heavy this morning until I located a cedar candle inside." She'd left it on the desk in her office, wondering if Sicarius would find the supposedly "stamina enhancing" scent amusing when they finally got to stand guard together. "Maldynado believes a woman should always be prepared in case she stumbles into some handsome stranger's bed."

"That dolt has a singular mind. A good-hearted one though." Books sighed. "I suppose I should tell him that someday."

"Yes, you should."

"Does your team always talk this much in enemy territory?" Retta led them up a ramp.

"Only when it takes five hours to get from one side of that enemy territory to another," Amaranthe said, then regretted the whining. She wasn't the one with a bullet in her shoulder.

"That's not true," Akstyr said. "Maldynado talks all the time, no matter where we are."

"We're almost there." Retta rounded a bend and stopped at a dead end.

Terse shouts sounded in the distance, orders being given.

"Wrong turn?" Books asked.

"No." Retta lifted her uninjured arm and pressed her hand against the wall a foot above her head.

Runes similar to those at the other door flared into existence. Retta pressed three in a particular order. So smoothly Amaranthe didn't realize it at first, the floor lifted. She turned, checking back the way they'd come, but a wall had formed out of nothing behind them. They were stuck—trapped—within a box.

Nothing inimical, Amaranthe told herself. It was just a steam lift. Without the steam.

Retta slumped against the wall and hissed, her face tired and pained. "You can't die from a shoulder wound, can you?" So far she'd been brave, fearless in fact, but there was an uncertain quaver to her voice now.

"No," Amaranthe said.

"Sure you can," Akstyr said. "It can get infected and your arm can rot off and then you'd be climbing onto your own funeral logs."

"Ssh." Amaranthe elbowed him and told Retta, "That won't happen."

Retta stared bleakly at him.

Amaranthe didn't sense the lift coming to a stop, but what had originally been the dead end wall disappeared, crimson runes and all, between one eye blink and the next. The wall behind them opened up as well.

They walked into... what had Retta called it? The core?

Glowing images floated in the air all over the chamber they entered, some globe-shaped, some squares and rectangles, and some shapes there was no name for, at least in Turgonian. They all hovered above head level. Amaranthe didn't see any consoles, or levers, or gauges or anything else she would associate with a control room. In fact, there wasn't anything except those glowing images. Some contained three-dimensional maps while others showed more of those strange runes and still others contained... schematics was the only word she could think of, though they were so complex that she didn't know if her concept of the term applied.

"Magnificent," Books whispered, stepping up to a globe-shaped image with blues, greens, tans, and whites. Even at his six-and-a-half feet, he had to tilt his head back to look at it. "Is this the world?"

"Our world, yes." After poking at one of the images, Retta had shambled to a blank section of wall. She touched it with her blood-smeared palm. A rectangular structure the size of a train car slid out of it. She touched something on the side and a tall door opened. "There are thousands of worlds in there. I've looked at some. It's hard to imagine they exist. Or existed. According to Professor Komitopis, the race that built the *Ortarh Ortak* was here more than fifty thousand years ago. Our ancestors were running around in spears and loincloths when this civilization came here to experiment on us." Retta stood on her tiptoes to pull something off a shelf.

Amaranthe rushed over to help, figuring Retta meant to patch her wound.

"There are... other worlds?" Books cleared his throat. "I mean, I know there are other planets in our solar system and that some of them have moons and such, but would they actually be hospitable enough to visit if one could? I've read that Kyattese astronomers surmise that other planets are placed too close or too far from the sun to be habitable by any form of life as we know it." He eyed the chamber about them.

"Later, Books." Amaranthe made a cutting-off motion with her hand, though if there were some way to send this craft to another planet altogether... that'd be an excellent way to keep Forge from mucking around with it. "Retta, what can I do to help? Can that box heal you somehow?"

Retta was tapping a series of symbols on the side of an object she'd pulled out; these were ice blue and smaller than those from the lift. "Yes. I'm not sure what it'll do with the bullet, but hold it against my wound. It should knit the hole."

"I think the bullet went out the other side. There's blood saturating the back of your shoulder too."

"Joy."

As directed, Amaranthe held the box to Retta's wound. She nearly dropped it when the flat surface transformed before her eyes, curving to mold into the contours of Retta's shoulder.

"Stop that." Books swatted Akstyr on the arm.

Akstyr was poking and prodding at the floating images. "These are brilliant. I don't sense them at all. They're not Made, and they don't even have a feeling about them like physical objects. If not for my eyes seeing them, I wouldn't believe they existed."

"This place is intriguing," Books admitted, though he was keeping his hands clasped behind his back.

"Can they hurt anything by touching things?" Amaranthe asked.

"Probably not." Retta's eyes were closed, and she was leaning against the wall, letting the object do... whatever it was doing.

"Can we steer the craft off the lake bottom from here?" Amaranthe was careful not to call it the *Behemoth*. Retta seemed inordinately fond of the technological monstrosity and might not appreciate the sobriquet.

"Yes, but I need to know where you want to go."

Where indeed? Destroying the craft was still at the top of Amaranthe's thoughts, but Retta wasn't going to go along with that. She couldn't imagine landing the *Behemoth* anywhere within fifty miles of the city. Even if there weren't the problem of explaining it to the populace, she didn't want a two-day hike to return to Sicarius, Sespian, and the others.

"Perhaps we could leave it here," Books said, "but coerce its occupants to abandon ship. We could then sink the submarines that are capable of reaching this depth. In the time it would take someone to repair the submarines or build new ones, we should have resolved the political situation in the capital."

The pained expression on Retta's face had faded as the healing tool mended her shoulder, but a new pinched frown arose at Books's suggestion. "There are only a handful of submarines docked in the *Ortarh Ortak*. Not enough for everyone onboard to escape at once if something happened to... motivate them to do so."

"Do they have to escape?" Akstyr asked.

Amaranthe and Retta glared. Books elbowed him.

"What? I'm being practical. I mean, these are all our enemies in one spot, aren't they? We could get rid of them all and stop having to worry about them." Akstyr snapped his fingers and pointed at Retta, oblivious to her glare. "You could fiddle with those floating boxes again, so they go back to incinerating people. But not us. We should get out of here before that starts. Can that happen?"

"No," Amaranthe said even as Books and Retta roared the same word.

"Those are my colleagues," Retta added.

"They poked your eye out," Akstyr said.

"That was Pike, that sadistic miscreant. Nobody else here would do something like this. They're my colleagues, some of them are even friends." Retta tore the device away from her shoulder and thumped it against the wall. "I don't know why I'm even helping you people."

"Because," Amaranthe said, stepping in front of Retta, capturing her gaze, "you know Forge is going about this the wrong way. They don't want to vanquish the warrior caste; they want to replace it. But we're going to instate a new government, one that's fair for everyone, giving every person a chance to live freely and pursue their dreams." She wondered if she sounded like a madwoman when she raved about tossing out

old governments like dishwater and plopping new ones down as if it'd be a simple task.

Out of the corner of her eye, Amaranthe saw Books clear his throat and raise a finger. For at least the third time that night, she made her cutting-off motion at him. She knew his ideal government was more about allowing equality for *educated* people and probably didn't mention the words pursuing dreams, but she hadn't read his opus yet, and this had to be close enough for the moment. It had to convince Retta to calm down and stay with them.

"I thought you wanted Sespian back on the throne," Retta said.

"That's a stopgap measure. He's agreed to change the government once he's there." Actually, she hadn't brought it up yet, but he'd be open to it surely. Careful, girl, she told herself, you're starting to sound grandiose again. Maybe madwoman was an appropriate label. "He'll step down. He's not a power monger, and he knows he won't be popular with the people with an assassin for a father."

"What do you want me to do then?" Retta spread an arm toward the floating images.

"Get us out of the lake and set this craft down somewhere out of sight of the population centers," Amaranthe said.

"How will we get back to town?" Books asked.

"There's a small independent craft—several actually, but we've only verified that one works," Retta said. "They're the equivalent of lifeboats."

"How far can they go?"

"I don't believe they were designed for travel between planets, merely for short range trips, short range by these people's standards that is."

Amaranthe blinked. "So they can go anywhere in the world?"

"That should be the case, yes."

"How long would the trip take?"

"It would depend on the distance to be traveled, but from what I've seen of the one lifeboat's speed capabilities, perhaps an hour from one side of the world to the other."

Now it was Books's turn to blink in astonishment. "That would mean it'd travel faster than the speed of sound."

"Yes." Retta smirked and mouthed something that might have been, "Boom."

"Then we can simply take the *Behe*—this craft to the South Pole, drop it off, ride back in the lifeboat, and return for dinner, right?" Amaranthe's mind boggled at the idea, but Retta shrugged and nodded, as if this were some workaday concept.

Thunks sounded beneath them—from the direction of the lift, Amaranthe realized, though the mechanism had disappeared back into the featureless black floor after it delivered them.

"I think someone knows we're here," Akstyr said.

"It was only a matter of time." Retta slumped, breaking Amaranthe's gaze.

Amaranthe backed away. She didn't know if she'd won Retta over or simply made her question herself further. "Is the floor... uhm, locked?"

"Yes. There are several entrances, but I secured them when we first entered." She waved toward the floating image she'd touched before moving to the cabinet.

"So we're safe to do what we want in here?" Amaranthe asked.

"Mia will find a way past my locks before long."

Amaranthe had been afraid of that. She gripped Retta's uninjured arm. "The South Pole. Park this on top of a glacier, then we'll take the lifeboat back here, and you can drop us off then... do whatever you wish. Go get the rest of your old Kyattese friends and take them down to study it. So long as Forge can't bring it back here." Amaranthe hadn't figured out yet what she'd do with all the Forge people who were on board now, inadvertent prisoners if they traveled to the other end of the world. And then there was that Mia. On the chance that she could also steer this craft, she'd need to be captured and taken... Where? She didn't know. Amaranthe massaged her forehead, willing away an oncoming headache. Her eyes were gritty, and everything was too complicated. She made a mental rude gesture at the long-gone race that had deposited their monstrous technology on her world.

"Very well," Retta said. She'd apparently been wrestling with complicated thoughts of her own. At least they came up in Amaranthe's favor. "This will take time."

More bangs sounded from under the floor.

"How *much* time?" Books asked.

"You may want to start thinking of delaying tactics."

Amaranthe shared his groan. She didn't think having Akstyr mentally pull people's trousers down was going to be sufficient this time.

* * *

Full daylight had come by the time Sicarius returned to the ice camp. Heavy clouds had drifted back in, and tiny flakes, more hail than snow, tumbled from the sky, bouncing off his shoulders and pelting his cheeks. A few sturdy fishing boats floated out in the center of the lake, and he thought of Amaranthe. Was she even now hundreds of feet below the surface, sneaking about in the Forge craft? Or was she back in the factory, waiting for him to return before she delved into enemy territory? He liked to think so, but he doubted it. He'd been gone too long.

Once he breached the boundary of the ice camp, Sicarius headed for the machine shop. A single stream of black smoke wafted from the chimney. The workers must have started their day. Good. He planned to requisition their help. His welding skills were limited, and he would need something as sturdy as a mountain to trap and hold the soul construct.

Before heading to the building, he took a closer look at the vehicles lined up in the parking area. The wind had been blowing that morning, and snowdrifts a couple of feet high nuzzled the tires on one side, but the lorries were in otherwise good condition. He glanced back the way he had come, noting his tracks across the white field. He didn't see anyone on the stark, flat landscape, not yet, but the snow would make his trail easy to follow. The practitioner might alert the soldiers to Sicarius's morning spying, or he might choose to handle it himself. Neither the Nurian nor the soul construct would be

appealing enemies to battle, not when he'd had so little time
to prepare.

On the chance that he might need to flee, he climbed into
the cab of one of the bigger lorries and shoveled coal into the
furnace. He'd keep it stoked throughout the day. The practitioner
he could outrun on foot, but the soul construct? There was no
chance. The lorry *might* be able to outpace it, though the snow
blanketing the roads would likely slow the machine down more
than the creature.

Nobody came out while Sicarius was building up the fire in
the furnace. Once the gauges promised readiness, he headed for
the machine shop, pausing again to eye the stack of steel beams
along an outside wall. They might be sturdy enough for his
needs, especially if the camp also had thick sheet metal.

"Might," he repeated aloud. He seemed to be using that word
a lot.

Finding the back door unlocked, Sicarius slipped into the
one-room building, where the heat and the chatter of two men
met him. Articulating arms and oversized cutting tools littered
benches and worktables. The men, both bearded and brawny,
with sleeves rolled up to their elbows, were building up the
fire in the furnace. Sicarius padded across a floor littered with
sawdust, stray nuts, bolts, and screws, and bits of coal, then
stopped behind the pair.

"I require your assistance."

Both men spun about in surprise, one dropping his shovel
and the other clenching his like a club. Amaranthe would have
given them a friendly greeting and figured out a way helping
her would help them, but Sicarius lacked the patience for social
pleasantries. He lacked time as well.

"You're Sircareius," one of the men said.

"Sicarius," the second corrected, nudging his comrade with
an elbow.

"Yes." In other circumstances, Sicarius might not have
responded to a statement of the obvious, but if they knew of his
reputation, they might be less inclined to offer resistance and
more inclined to follow his orders. Swiftly.

"You helped the boss last winter," the second speaker said. "You and that girl. Lokdon, wasn't it? She was nice."

"Isn't he an assassin?"

"Yes, but he was on our side that night when... well, the boss said not to talk about it, but we all would have died if not for him and his friend." He wiped his rough coal-smeared hands on his trousers and stuck one out toward Sicarius. "I'm Wodic. This is Mederak."

Sicarius walked to the closest workbench while keeping the men in his peripheral vision. He believed them innocuous, but one didn't survive years of having a million-ranmya bounty on one's head by putting beliefs ahead of vigilance. For men like these, such money would change their lives.

"I require a steel trap approximately eight by eight by eight feet joined with the strongest welds possible. It will have two hatches, one on the top and a smaller one on the bottom or side. The walls must be thick enough to withstand the pressure of—" Sicarius noticed the men staring blankly at him. One, Wodic, still had his hand out. "Here. I will draw it."

Wodic looked down at his hand, shrugged, and walked over to the table.

"He wants us to use the boss's materials for her new holding warehouse?" Mederak whispered to his comrade while Sicarius was drawing.

"Ssh, it'll be all right. We'll tell her it's for Ms. Lokdon. She won't object. Not after the..." Wodic lowered his voice. "Not after the mare-cats and that... that evil spirit thing. Did you hear about that?"

"Just stories."

"They're true," Wodic said.

Sicarius finished his drawing without comment. It seemed odd that these men were willing to help him without the application of threats, but he was not surprised Amaranthe had left that feeling of indebtedness behind. She certainly had a knack for winning over allies. Not all of them remembered her so fondly later on, when the heat of the moment passed, but the situation had turned out in these people's favor.

"Here." Sicarius pushed the sketch in front of the two men. "It must be assembled outside, so it can be moved."

"Moved where?"

"Into the lake."

Wodic and Mederak scratched their heads. "The lake?"

"The obvious trap does not catch the fox." Sicarius realized he'd quoted one of Basilard's grandfather's sayings. In this case, it was apt. "It must be assembled today."

"*Today*?" Mederak blurted.

Still rubbing his head, Wodic stared at the sketch. "I don't know if that's possible, Mr. Sicarius. There's just us two and our driver out here this week. Until the ice freezes—"

"It will be done today," Sicarius repeated. "I will assist you."

They looked him over. Yes, his black clothing was adorned with knives rather than smith's tools, but he was a capable worker.

"All of our lives depend on it," Sicarius said.

They considered the sketch again, perhaps for the first time considering *why* Sicarius might need such a trap.

"Today's good," Mederak said at the same time as Wodic said, "We can do today."

CHAPTER 17

A MARANTHE ALTERNATED BETWEEN YAWNING AND nibbling on her pinkie nail while Akstyr paced around the section of floor that hid the lift. She'd lost all sense of time, but they'd been locked in the control room long enough to share some of Sicarius's travel bars. Retta had known where to find potable water, though the secret cabinets could not, alas, supply more appealing meals. Amaranthe was too anxious to digest properly anyway.

Retta, her shoulder healed, was moving from floating map to schematic to knot of runes, portions of the three-dimensional images brightening or pulsing when she touched them. Hands clasped behind his back, Books walked behind her, watching her every finger swipe. The knocks and clunks had stopped emanating from below, but every now and then Amaranthe heard a scrape or a thump; people were moving around down there, probably with their weapons drawn as they waited for the assistant to figure out a way to let them charge inside.

"How long will it take to get the *Behe*—the *Ortarh Ortak* moving?" Amaranthe asked.

"We're getting close," Retta said. "Perhaps an hour now."

"An *hour*?" Akstyr asked. "Hasn't it already been four or five days?"

"Not quite *that* long," Amaranthe said, though she commiserated with the sentiment.

Retta had been poking images for a long time. Even a giant boiler could be heated and a steam engine brought to readiness in less time than this was taking.

"A course must be entered into the navigation system, the engines must be brought on line, the current human population density around the lake must be calculated so we can leave the area in a way that we're least likely to be seen, and..." Retta frowned as a blue blip on the image in front of her pulsed and a couple of runes formed in the air. "The civilization that created the *Ortarh Ortak* would have had an entire crew of people working in this room. That we—*I*—have been able to get it working at all is amazing."

"Yes, sorry, continue on, please. We'll keep our mouths shut." Amaranthe wasn't going to argue about Retta's amazingness, not at this point, though she lifted a hand to stop Books the next time he drew near. She lowered her voice to ask, "Now that you've been watching her, do you think you could operate the craft if something happened?" She tilted her head toward Retta.

The South Pole plan was workable, she supposed, but she'd still feel better if this thing was forever buried somewhere that people couldn't find it, especially Forge people. With the money that organization had, arranging an expedition to the other side of the world to continue research would be entirely feasible.

"Dear ancestors, no," Books said. "She'd have to instruct me on the language and how to operate everything. Right now, it's a miasma of confusion. The utter alienness of it... I'm sure it'd take months, if not years. Were I to attempt to pilot it, or even open a door, I'd be like a lizard beating its tail against levers on a control panel, hoping for the best."

Akstyr snickered, but paused mid-laugh. "Something's happening down below. I can feel—they're getting ready."

At that second, a square of the floor rose.

Books and Akstyr leaped back, landing in crouches, their daggers ready. Amaranthe jumped on top of the moving square. The ceiling was so high she could barely see it up there, and she didn't think the lift had risen that far when it delivered her team to the room.

"Retta," Amaranthe blurted as a rifle poked through the growing opening between the top of the lift and the rest of the floor. "Door lock's broken!"

Amaranthe dropped to her belly and snatched the barrel of the rifle. She tried to rip it from its owner's hands, but, though obviously surprised, the man didn't let go. She did, however, pull it far enough out to reveal the hand holding the bottom of the barrel. She swiped at it with her dagger, drawing blood. The owner cursed and let go. This time, she succeeded in pulling the rifle away, but three more took its place.

Books and Akstyr, in far more vulnerable positions, ran to the sides of the lift, trying to use them for cover. With it being open on the front and the back, that was a challenge. Gunshots rang out.

"Cursed Mia." Retta left her work and darted for one of the image banks that displayed internal maps. The lift halted, halfway up, but it didn't go back down.

Still on her stomach, Amaranthe risked scooting close to the edge, lining the side of her body up parallel with it. Holding the rifle in one hand, her finger curled around the trigger, she lowered the barrel and angled it to shoot inside. The long weapon was heavy and awkward to wield that way, and someone grabbed the end. She fired, and whoever had it let go. Amaranthe yanked the weapon away, rolling onto her back.

"That's not going to work," she muttered.

More shots were fired. Two of the men climbed out of the lift and burst into view. They knew Amaranthe was on top, and one promptly turned, a rifle raised in her direction. If she'd still been on that side of the lift, she would have been an easy target, but she'd rolled to the back edge. She lowered her head over the side and fired into the guards who remained below. Yes, gentlemen, she thought grimly. Your lift is open on two sides.

Abruptly, her perch descended. Amaranthe nearly dropped the rifle.

"Get out, get out, it's going back down!" someone inside yelled.

Gunshots continued to fire, and more than one shout of pain arose. Amaranthe didn't think the cries came from her men, but they were outgunned, and there was nothing to hide behind in

the control room. Those translucent floating images did nothing to stop bullets.

Amaranthe moved back to the front of the lift and bashed the butt of the rifle down on a man trying to climb out. At the same time, she searched for Books and Akstyr, and the two guards who'd already leaped out. One was fighting with Books, using the rifle like a club, while Books defended with his dagger. The other had his rifle raised, pointed at Akstyr's chest.

Amaranthe jerked her own rifle back up, trying to ready another round in time to help him, but even though the firearms held more ammunition than a regular muzzle-loaded weapon, she'd run out with the random shots she'd been firing. Fearing she'd be too late, she dropped the rifle and lifted her dagger to throw. But the guard hadn't fired. He was standing there, aiming, and nothing more.

"Are you holding him, Akstyr?" Amaranthe asked.

He didn't have his hand outstretched in the usual manner. The rifle twitched a few times, then was pulled out of the man's grip. It floated over to Akstyr and he caught it with a firm nod. The guard never moved.

"I'll take that for a yes," Amaranthe said.

A clunk sounded, a rifle hitting the floor. Books had disarmed his opponent.

The lift disappeared back into the floor and Amaranthe jogged over to join her men. "Let's tie these two up." She waved toward the cabinet, figuring there had to be something useful in there. At the least, they might be able to close it and shut the guards inside.

"I've locked it again for now," Retta said, returning to the image she'd been manipulating before the lift rose, "but I'm sure she'll keep trying. There are other entrances to this room too."

"Lovely." Books eyed the distant walls, each of which probably held a door, though who could tell on those featureless facades? "What happens when they're better prepared and split their forces, so they can charge us on multiple fronts?"

Indeed, Amaranthe thought. That last group hadn't been

prepared. After waiting so long, they might have been caught by surprise when the lift started rising.

"We have rifles and more bullets at least," Akstyr said.

He had opted for tying the guards up with their own trousers, then shoving them into the cabinet. He'd relieved them of their belts and ammo pouches. A yawn stretched his lips, and black bags nestled beneath his eyes. Sweat dampened his shirt as well, a reminder that his mental science gifts didn't come without effort. He was more efficient at them than he had been a year ago, but they taxed him nonetheless.

"Thank you, Akstyr." Amaranthe nodded her approval toward him, then dropped her chin in her hand, mulling.

"We should all stand around Retta," Books said, "and if they attempt to come in, we'll shoot from there. Protecting her is the most important thing. If we don't..." He frowned at Amaranthe. "You look like you're scheming."

"Do I? How can you tell?"

"You're wearing your harbinger-of-trouble face."

"Hm, Sicarius calls it that too."

Books blinked. "He says harbinger of trouble?"

"No, he shortens it to trouble." Amaranthe smiled. "He lacks your gift for verbosity."

She said it to tease him, but Books nodded seriously. "Yes. Regrettable."

"What're we going to do?" Akstyr asked.

"I was thinking that a small sortie out of the control room might be advisable," Amaranthe said.

"A sortie?" Books asked. "There're only three of us. Doesn't a sortie require more people?"

"You and I will go, and Akstyr will stay here to guard Retta."

"That's fewer people, not more," Books said.

"Yes, thank you for confirming the math for me." Amaranthe hated to disturb Retta while her fingers were flying about in preparations, but risked asking, "Is there a way to see where your assistant is located?"

"She'll be three floors up in the auxiliary control room."

Retta sidled over to the image displaying the interior map, where blue dots floated between lines. People and walls, Amaranthe realized. At the moment, the view was focused on the knot of guards in the lift, but Retta manipulated the picture, and it enlarged, showing more of the corridors around the control room along with levels above and below it. An orange dot came into view, along with two blue ones. "That'll be her and two guards."

"If we can kidnap her, there'd be nobody else on board who can operate the craft, right?" Amaranthe studied the map, trying to find a route to the auxiliary room that didn't require going past the guards in the lift. "Did you say there were other exits out of here?"

"Here and here." Retta pointed at two perforated lines. One had a cluster of blue dots in front of it, but the other door appeared unblocked.

"I think I've got the route memorized," Amaranthe said after a moment, then lifted her eyebrows to ask if Books had done the same, in case they were separated.

He sighed and muttered, "Sortie," but nodded.

"Akstyr, you're in charge of defenses here." Amaranthe clapped him on the back. "If you see any blue dots wandering onto this route—" she traced the path she and Books would take, "—we'd appreciate it if you tormented them a little. Trousers around the ankles would be fine." She guessed that took less effort than some of his other tricks.

"You don't ask for much, do you?" Akstyr brushed his fingers through hair damp with sweat, pausing to frown anew at the shortness of his locks.

"With luck, nobody will cross paths with us," Amaranthe said. "If you get bored, you could also keep those people in the lift uncomfortable, so they're less prepared to attack if a door opens. I imagine they're wearing a wide variety of undergarments that they'd like to model for each other."

"I can't believe you're encouraging that behavior," Books murmured as they checked their rifles, stuffed cartridges into their pockets, and headed for the secret door the map had indicated.

"You don't approve?" Amaranthe asked. "It's better than killing, isn't it?"

"You won't be laughing if he decides to try the gag on you someday."

"Those are the risks you must accept when you step into the role of leadership."

* * *

By the time noon approached, the pieces of Sicarius's trap were laid out on the flat bank above the dock. If not for a clock inside the shop, it would have been difficult to guess the hour. Snow was falling again, more inches accumulating on the fields beyond the camp, and the sun had not been seen all day. The temperature had dropped as well, and the ice edging the lake seemed to expand outward with every hour. Sicarius was watching it, knowing his plan hinged on immersing the trap in the water, not under a frozen sheet.

Steam hissed as the arm of a crane lifted and moved one of the heavy walls of the incipient box. The other two machinists operated welding tools powered by the engine of a second vehicle. Sicarius had been directing the placement of the beams and sheets, but he paused to gaze out at the field. It was one of many scans he'd been making of the area. He hadn't sensed anything otherworldly, such as he might feel if the soul construct approached, but something kept plucking at his senses, a discordant twang on a harp.

The camp was being watched. He was certain of it.

The area had long ago been logged, so the white fields should have left few hiding places, but there were always dips and rises in seemingly flat land, and the falling snow limited visibility to a quarter mile or so. Further, someone might approach along the waterline, using the clumps of brown vegetation thrusting out of the drifts for camouflage.

"I think we'll make it by dusk, Mr. Sicarius," Wodic said,

his voice muffled by the welding helmet he wore. The glass faceplate didn't hide his eyes—and the concern in them as he glanced up from his work. "What is it you think'll come?"

Though Sicarius knew his own face betrayed nothing of his thoughts, the men must have noticed his frequent surveys of the surrounding land. Normally, he wouldn't have shared anything with the workers—he required them to complete this task, nothing more—but because they had a loose relationship with Amaranthe, he felt more disposed toward them than he would in other circumstances.

"General Flintcrest has brought a Nurian wizard with him to support his bid for the throne," Sicarius said.

"That ore-stealing traitor," Wodic growled. "That's his camp out there, isn't it? We've known about it, but the soldiers haven't bothered us yet, so we've been staying out of their way. Mederak went to town yesterday, though, and he said Fort Urgot is surrounded. Is that Flintcrest?"

"Heroncrest." Sicarius directed the crane operator to pick up another beam to reinforce the tee weld Wodic was finishing.

"Them officers are all over the place with their troops," Wodic grumbled. "Can't even go into town for a swig of applejack without them stopping to question you, like you're some foreign mongrel, not a loyal imperial subject who's lived here his whole life."

"Continue welding," Sicarius said. "We must finish this as quickly as possible. The wizard has summoned a creature that is hunting the nights." He thought about mentioning Sespian, but did not know if these men cared one way or another who was on the throne. "It is hunting loyal imperial subjects." They ought to be concerned about their own lives if nothing else.

Sicarius thought the workers might be skeptical about wizards and magical creatures, but Wodic must have seen enough to believe in such things, for he only said, "We've heard it out hunting the last few nights. We stayed locked up tight in the cabin with the thickest walls. I don't care how much I had to water the bushes, I wasn't going outside before morning."

A flash of movement drew Sicarius's eye, and he spun toward the source, his black dagger finding its way into his hand. He didn't see anything except snow falling about one of the cabins on the edge of the camp. A clump of powder dropped from the roof, plopping into a drift below. In other places as well, clumps fell from the roofs as more snow accumulated above the eaves. It *might* have been what had drawn his attention. Sicarius didn't sheathe the dagger.

"What is it?" Wodic lifted the faceplate of his helmet.

"Continue working," Sicarius said, then jogged toward the cabin.

He veered around it, approaching the corner where he'd seen that movement from the opposite side. He slowed his steps, compressing the snow underfoot as softly as possible, making no sound as he drew near. Before he poked his head around the corner, he stopped to listen and sniff the breeze. He also touched his fingers to the chinked log wall, trusting he'd feel it if someone bumped against the cabin on the other side. The smoke from the steam crane tainted the air, making it difficult to pick up lesser scents, and its clanking and hissing also may have smothered lesser sounds, but Sicarius felt something. A faint scrape that traveled through the logs.

Without sheathing the dagger, he pulled out a throwing knife from the trio sheathed on his right forearm. He could throw with equal accuracy with both hands, and he was prepared to loose the blade with his left as he peeked around the corner. Nobody was there.

Sicarius immediately looked up—roofs were a viable place from which to launch an attack. There wasn't anybody up there either, but a few trickles of powder whispered down from the edge. Using the eaves for cover in case an attack came from above, he eased toward the other corner, eyeing the ground as he approached. Footprints marked the snow, two sets of footprints. Their owners had come from the direction of the southern shoreline. The prints indicated soft shoes with soles that curved up at the edges, hand-made moccasins rather than the more common boots of the Turgonian people. Kendorians or Nurians had such footwear, and the latter was more likely given the situation.

The footprints showed that the people—men he guessed from the depth of the marks, each around his weight—had stopped at the wall, then jumped up. His first guess had been correct.

Something plucked at his senses again. This time, it did have an otherworldly taint to it. The wizard? The signature was faint. People using Made tools, perhaps. He thought of the man with the scimitar who'd been speaking to the practitioner.

Sicarius sheathed the black dagger and, keeping the throwing knife in hand, jumped and caught the gutter. Snow pattered against his face, but he ignored it, pulling his eyes over the edge. He was prepared to release the grip and drop down in an instant, but the roof was empty of everything except snow. And footprints.

He followed the apex of the sloping roof to the other side. According to the tracks, the intruders had leaped off the roof, but the paths below were packed with dozens of bootprints as well as the heavy tire treads from the vehicles that had driven to the dock. Picking out a fresh trail would be difficult.

Sicarius crouched on the edge of the roof, scanning the camp and again testing the air for some telltale scent. By this point, he wasn't surprised that he didn't see the intruders. They were either very good, or they had some trinket that bent the light waves around them, rendering them invisible. But if he could determine their goal, he could guess their location.

Kill him? No, they were avoiding him.

The working men had to be the target, Sicarius decided—it would be obvious to a Nurian observer that he was fashioning a trap for the soul construct, and as the wizard's employees, they'd want to stop that.

He hopped down from the cabin, watching Wodic and Mederak, as well as the crane operator, for any sign of alarm as he approached. Hard at work, they might not notice an attacker until a blade was slipping between their ribs. Sicarius

also watched the snow around the trap, hoping he'd catch the indentation of a footprint as it was being made in a patch of soft powder.

If it were he, he'd stand back and shoot arrows into the laborers from afar. The Nurian he'd seen in the army camp had been wearing a bow. But Sicarius returned to the workers without anyone being attacked. Maybe the Nurians believed time was on their side, thanks to their camouflage. Or maybe they believed destroying the trap—or keeping it from being completed—was the priority, thus ensuring nobody else from the capital could come out and complete the work. Already, the bottom and three sides were attached, the walls standing erect in the air, and his sketch was on the seat next to the crane operator, so someone could theoretically finish the task.

The crane.

Without it, nobody would be able to move the trap once it was finished. On land, it'd never fool the soul construct.

Sicarius ran around the steel walls, using them to hide his approach, and scooped up an armful of snow on his way to the crane's cab. The scent of blood flooded his nostrils. Before he bounded up the side of the vehicle, he knew what he'd find. The driver was slumped in his seat, head lolled back, blood gushing from his slashed throat.

Sicarius hurled the armful of snow. For an instant, the powder outlined a figure gripping the crane controls, preparing to steer the vehicle into the lake. It reacted instantly, spinning toward him, but he was already leaping for the invisible person, his dagger in hand. Whatever device protected the intruder, it compensated for the thrown snow, and the white outline disappeared. But Sicarius had already closed the distance and caught a fistful of clothing, part of a fur cloak. He'd intended to grab the man's arm, to pull him off balance, and slip his dagger into the lung, but the Nurian recovered and backed away too quickly. The noisy vehicle drowned out sounds, so Sicarius couldn't hear the rustle of clothing that might have signified an attack, and only the tug at the cloak and his familiarity with

Nurian combat styles prepared him for the jab-straight-punch combination that was typical.

He blocked both, one-handed, sight unseen. Before his opponent could add a hook, he glided to the side, pulling on the cloak with his free hand and adding a leg sweep to further distract the man. As fast as Sicarius's movements were, the Nurian might have countered effectively, but he bumped into one of the control levers. The crane lurched forward, and the cab floor jerked beneath them. This time Sicarius succeeded in grabbing the invisible man's arm and forcing it up. He slipped his dagger in beneath it.

As the intruder cried out, Sicarius's nose caught a whiff of a hard-boiled egg on someone's breath. It was the only warning he received. Pulling his dagger out of the first man's torso, Sicarius dropped to the floor. He threw the weapon even as he rolled for the opening on the opposite side of the cab. A moist thunk sounded—metal driving into flesh. Hard.

He came to his feet, facing into the cab, a throwing knife in hand. Both men were still invisible, so he made his best guess and hurled the second weapon. It halted in mid-air and disappeared. They'd both landed, but not accurately enough, for a thump sounded, someone jumping down into the snow.

Sicarius ran to the side of the cab, tempted to leap out in pursuit, but if he were in the other man's place, he'd pause down there to throw a knife of his own. Instead of exposing himself, he used the frame of the vehicle to hide his body and watched the ground for newly forming footprints. Again the oft-trampled snow made it hard to spot them, but droplets of blood gave away the intruder.

Several new droplets fell, and Sicarius, envisioning the throwing motion that might have caused it, ducked behind the frame. A blade appeared in midair, then clanged off the metal, an inch from his eyes. Before it clattered to the floor of the cab, he was hurling his own knife. Again, it disappeared behind that field of invisibility, but this time a pained gasp sounded, and something heavy flopped to the ground. More than droplets stained the snow now.

Sicarius checked both men to make sure they were dead before cleaning off his knives and sheathing them. He was aware of Wodic and Mederak standing a few meters away, gaping, but did not say anything until he'd walked a perimeter of the camp, ensuring no other new sets of tracks had appeared.

"There *is* a wizard." Mederak nudged one of the invisible bodies with his boot.

"Mr. Sicarius wouldn't lie." Wodic had climbed into the cab to check on the driver. He shook his head and muttered something to himself. "We'll have to tell his family and see if they want to do a funeral pyre out here or—"

"Tomorrow," Sicarius said. "We must finish the trap before dark, or we'll have a much bigger problem than invisible Nurian bodyguards." In truth, he didn't know if they *had* until dark. Just because he'd only encountered the soul constructs at night or dawn in the past didn't prove they couldn't travel during the day.

Mederak's gaze drifted toward the lake, in the direction of the city. "Not getting paid for this," he muttered, too low for most people to hear, but Sicarius had good ears. "Better to—"

Wodic thumped him on the back, silencing him. "We're with you," he told Sicarius.

It was odd to have this stranger's loyalty. Oh, he understood it was due to his and Amaranthe's actions the winter before, but she wasn't here, and the man was still willing to give that loyalty to Sicarius. Few ever had unless it'd been out of fear or a desire to fawn, that too usually having a fear component. This fellow simply seemed to believe he owed a favor.

"Let's get this last side up and the top on." Sicarius waved to the partially assembled trap. "I'll operate the crane."

As he climbed up into the cab, a boom drifted across the lake, and he paused, cocking an ear.

"What was that?" Wodic rotated around, trying to locate the source.

"The wizard?" Mederak asked in a tone that said he'd rather chew his foot off than have that be the case.

"No," Sicarius said. Distance and the snow made it hard to pinpoint the source, but his trained ears knew it had come from the north. When gunshots started seconds later—a *lot* of gunshots—he knew he hadn't been mistaken. "It's Fort Urgot. Heroncrest's army is attacking."

Sicarius closed his eyes. Now Sespian was in danger from more than the soul construct.

CHAPTER 18

"THIS IS THE RIGHT CORRIDOR, ISN'T IT?" Amaranthe whispered.

"Yes," Books said. "I believe so."

Amaranthe wished he hadn't voiced the addendum. They'd both memorized the map before leaving the control room, but the three-dimensional, multilevel display had been a different type of cartography than they were accustomed to, and all the tunnels looked the same. She and Books walked shoulder-to-shoulder, passing identical tall, narrow doors with identical runes that brightened into visibility when one of them drew close.

"I am certain we're on the correct floor," Books added.

Good, that narrowed the searchable area down to twenty or thirty million square feet. "The entrance was at the end of a dead-end corridor, I remember that at least."

"There's an intersection," Books said as they rounded a curve. "I believe we go left."

"Which left? There are three of them. And two rights. These people weren't into simple."

"That I could have told you after a second of looking at their language."

"They must never have heard that old saying," Amaranthe said, "about any dolt being capable of complicating matters and true genius lying in making a thing simple." She herself struggled to keep her plans simple. That probably said something about her, but she didn't want to examine it too closely.

"Most likely not, since they visited our world tens of thousands of years before Scribe Ilya Yaro of the South Gaolas wrote that platitude."

"Good point."

With her finger on the trigger of one of the acquired rifles, Amaranthe eased her head around the corner and peered down each corridor before committing herself. They hadn't seen anyone since they'd left the control room floor, but if Mia had guards with her, they couldn't assume all the hallways would be empty. Further, a familiarity to this intersection nagged at her senses. Had she passed through it on her way into or out of the *Behemoth* the last time? She couldn't remember; the only events that were distinct in her mind from that week were ones she wished she could forget.

"I think it's *that* left." Books pointed to the closest one.

Amaranthe led the way, passing several widely spaced doors before stopping a few meters in front of the one at the end. A wave of apprehension washed over her. She'd been in that exact spot before, she was certain of it. Books passed her, heading to the last door, but she couldn't seem to move her feet. She looked left, then right, then left again.

"Hm," Books said from the end of the corridor, "perhaps we should have arranged for Retta to open it for us." He waved his hand, and runes lit up beside the door, but he'd have to press or twist or dance naked enticingly in front of one in the right way before they'd be let inside.

"I don't think this is the right hall." Amaranthe put a hand on the smooth, cold wall, trying to control her breathing. All these corridors looked the same—why was she so sure she'd been down this one before?

"I was watching her open the cabinets," Books mused, his back to Amaranthe. He didn't seem to have heard her. "I think she pushed this rune in and twisted it." His fingers moved as he spoke, gestures mimicking words.

The door slid open. Books stepped inside, his rifle at the ready. A sick feeling weighed down Amaranthe's stomach, but she rushed after him. If he was right and this was the correct room, he would need help handling the guards.

As soon as she crossed the threshold, though, she knew it

wasn't the right spot. She clenched her eyes shut, but it was too late: she'd already seen the surgeon's table, the articulating tool that could swing down from the ceiling, and that blasted crate was still there too.

"I guess it was the other left," Books said and turned around. He halted. "Are you... Amaranthe, what is it?"

Amaranthe barely saw him. She'd opened her eyes, but only to focus on the floor. She'd lowered to a crouch, hand braced against the wall as memories of her time spent on that table and in that crate washed over her.

She tried to push them away—logically, she knew that what had happened was past now—but they refused to be cast aside. They were as vivid in her mind as if she were living the moments again.

A hand came to rest on her shoulder. "Amaranthe?"

She shook her head. She couldn't look up, couldn't risk seeing that cursed table again.

Books lifted her to her feet and turn her around. She stumbled, but he didn't let her fall. Back in the corridor, he fiddled with the runes until the door shut. Amaranthe wanted more finality than that; she wanted that whole room burnt to the ground. No, the whole cursed vessel.

"I assume you have some familiarity with that chamber." Books's consoling pat on her shoulder was awkward. He probably couldn't tell if she'd want a hug or to be left alone. "Shall we try the next corridor?" he asked.

Yes, moving on with the mission. That was a good idea. If only Amaranthe could lift her eyes and get her feet to move. "I just need a moment," she croaked.

"Of course."

Amaranthe focused on the tip of her rifle, not because it had any curative qualities—hardly that—but it was an object in the present, something to fixate on long enough to clear her head.

"As long as we're bringing up old platitudes," Books said, "perhaps I should remind you that the strongest, finest metals are created through the heating and hammering of raw ore."

Amaranthe felt more like slag than fine metal at the moment, but she'd managed to bring her mind back to the present, and she didn't want to dwell on that room any longer. "Let's just check that other hallway, eh?"

Later she'd thank him for being there, but she felt foolish for falling apart and wanted to put some distance between herself and the moment.

Books let his hand drop from her shoulder, and he led the way back to the intersection and into the other corridor. "Ready?" he asked before touching the runes that lit up.

Amaranthe took a deep breath and lifted the rifle to her shoulder. "Ready."

Books replicated the twisting of the rune. Nothing happened. He tried again, but the door didn't open.

"That's the same thing I did for the other one," he said. "She must have locked it somehow."

"Makes sense. I wouldn't want rabid gunmen charging in behind me while I was working." Amaranthe debating how far knocking might get them while Books tried a couple of the other runes.

Without warning, the door slid sideways, disappearing into the wall. Amaranthe didn't know whether Books had stumbled onto the unlocking mechanism of if Retta was watching their progress and had done something, but she charged in without waiting for those inside to figure out they had visitors. Books ran in beside her.

Earlier, there might have been two guards represented by the blips on the image, but there were four inside now, two by the door, and two by Mia who was poking and prodding at a wall full of diagrams.

Amaranthe shot the closest guard before he could bring his own weapon to bear, aiming at his thigh instead of his heart. Without waiting to make sure she'd hit him, she aimed for a second, one of the men by Mia. As soon as she fired, she dropped to one knee, knowing the other guards would be targeting her by then too. Good choice, for a bullet soon zipped over her head. Another clanged off the wall beside Books.

Similar to the control room, the chamber had no furniture and nothing to hide behind. Though she felt cowardly doing so, Amaranthe grabbed the closest man, the one she'd shot in the leg, and used him for cover while she lined up her next target. His high-pitched curses in her ear made her regret the choice. Before she could shoot again, Books, who had already disarmed the other door guard, charged toward Mia's second protector. The guard focused on him instead of Amaranthe. She took advantage, firing for a third time, and the bullet slammed into his knee. His scream shattered the air as surely as his kneecap shattered in his leg. She grimaced, wishing for a more humanitarian method, but at least the guards were alive. Perhaps later, they could be treated with that healing device Retta had used.

For now, all Amaranthe did was grab the rifle from the man by the door, then jog toward Mia. With both of her guards writhing on the floor, the woman should have spun back to face her attackers or, even smarter, raced off to escape again, but Books had to grab her arms and drag her away from her work.

"Unhand me, you benighted vandal," she cried.

"Benighted?" Books managed to look indignant while he was gripping the woman beneath her armpits and dancing to avoid having his foot stomped on. "I assure you I'm neither benighted *nor* a vandal."

Amaranthe kicked the rifle away from the last guard on the floor, the one whose kneecap she'd destroyed. She wished there was a way to lock everybody in the room, rather than worrying about tying up another group. Maybe they could—

"Look out," Books barked.

Amaranthe lunged to the side. A shot fired. Bewildered, she glanced about. She'd collected all the rifles.

One of the guards by the door had risen to one knee. Blood saturated his trouser leg, but he had a pistol pointed at Books, smoke wafting from the barrel. Amaranthe didn't know if he had another shot in the weapon, but she wasn't going to risk it. Without thinking, she lifted her own rifle and fired. This time, the bullet took him in the chest, and he tumbled backward, the pistol dropping from his fingers.

"Books." Amaranthe spun around, lowering her weapon. "Are you—"

She swallowed. Seventy-year-old Mia, spectacles still perched on her nose, was staring down at her chest, at the spreading bloodstain on her white blouse. Books was cursing under his breath and blinking rapidly.

"Dear ancestors, I didn't mean to use her for a *shield*," he said, voice cracking on the last word.

Amaranthe slumped. She thought to say, "She chose her side," to alleviate some of Books's guilt, but she couldn't. She felt it herself. She'd come here to kidnap the woman, not kill her. If she'd shot to kill the guards in the first place, instead of trying to injure them, this wouldn't have happened. No, she told herself, rubbing her face, it'd just be someone else dead.

Books carefully lowered the woman to the floor.

"Sorry, Books. Let's... get back to Akstyr and Retta. They may need us. It's been—"

The floor vibrated slightly beneath Amaranthe. She braced herself, but that subtle sensation, a faint pulse, was all that came.

"Are we rising?" Books asked.

"We must be." Amaranthe pointed to the door, intending to say, "Let's go," again but Books held up a hand.

"Before we leave, you should know... she said something right before I pulled her away from the controls."

"What was it?" Amaranthe asked.

"A triumphant little, 'Hah.'"

She groaned. That couldn't be good.

* * *

Wind skidded across the fields, driving snow sideways to gather against the northern walls of the log cabins and the machine shop. Darkness was settling on the lake, and Sicarius pointed and gestured, guiding Wodic, who'd taken his place in the crane, to pick up the completed trap. Mederak waited at the base of the

dock, a brush in one hand and a paint tin in another. He wasn't watching the crane; his gaze was focused on the cabin where they'd put the dead man.

Gunshots and artillery fire continued to ring out from the direction of Fort Urgot. It'd been going on all afternoon, and Sicarius itched to go check on it—to check on Sespian.

Soon, he told himself. He had to complete this task first. Or die trying.

"Where are we putting it?" Wodic called once he'd hooked the trap. When he lifted it a few inches off the ground, the crane's long metal arm shuddered under the weight.

Sicarius had wanted it sturdy enough to contain the soul construct, but he worried they wouldn't be able to carry it to its destination. Best not to dawdle, and for more reasons than the coming night.

"In the water." Sicarius pointed at the dock, glad its concrete surface was reinforced with thick pilings. It was *meant* to be driven on by lorries laden with heavy loads of ice, not cranes carrying multiple-ton steel traps. He'd done a few mental calculations, but he wasn't entirely certain it wouldn't collapse when the crane drove out upon it.

"*In* the water? Are you sure?"

"It has to be hidden so the creature won't see it." Sicarius pointed again, more firmly. He didn't care to discuss his plan with these people, not when he was already doubting it himself. Maybe he should have gone to the city for concrete, had these two dig a pit, and attempted to reenact the one strategy he knew had halted a construct. Too late now. "Go. I'll tell you where to release it."

Once the crane was in motion, Sicarius jogged onto the dock ahead of it, eyeing the dark water on either side, trying to judge the depth. He also kept an ear toward the camp behind them. By now, the practitioner knew his men weren't returning. He'd send the soul construct or have another attack ready. Or perhaps he'd come himself.

The dock trembled beneath the weight of the advancing

crane, the pilings groaning in protest. In the cab, Wodic's face was tight and tense.

"There." Sicarius pointed to the right of the dock. "Set it down there."

His selected spot was just forward of the encroaching film of ice stretching out from the shoreline. If the temperature dropped much more after dusk… He shook his head. He'd have to find the creature quickly, that was all. By midnight, his trap could be beneath an inch of ice. If that happened, it'd be useless.

Despite the cold, sweat dripped down Wodic's face as he manipulated the controls, slowly swinging the crane off-center, out over the water.

"Keep it close to the dock," Sicarius said, imagining himself running this way at a not-so-future point.

Gesturing with his hands for guidance, he had Wodic lower the trap through the ice and into the water, inch by inch. At one point, he made Wodic halt to open a hatch on the side. It had been sealing a hole less than two feet wide in one of the walls. To the men's bemusement, he'd already tested it, ensuring he could squirm out through it. He was counting on it being too small for the soul construct to do the same. A larger hatch over a bigger hole in the top was already open, this one spring-loaded to shut easily once a latch on the outside was thrown. Getting to the latch before the prey could escape… That would be a challenge. Especially at night. In freezing water.

This was your idea, Sicarius told himself.

He gave away nothing of his spinning thoughts as he stood on the dock, arms crossed over his chest, watching the huge steel block disappear beneath the waves. He made note of how far the crane hook descended beneath the surface before the trap hit the bottom. Less than three feet. Good. The water hid the hatch and the entire trap, but it wouldn't be far to swim, so long as he found it swiftly.

Sicarius waved for Wodic to back the crane away, then called, "Mederak," as soon as the dock was clear.

The man jogged out with the paint can. Sicarius pointed and

Mederak made a red circle on the dock. In the fading light, the color appeared similar to blood.

"What now?" Mederak licked his lips and eyed the dead man's cabin again.

"I suggest you and your comrade either go back to the city or lock yourself in that machine shop for the night."

Mederak nodded vigorously as if he'd been contemplating the same thing. "The city sounds good."

He jogged back into the camp, left the paint tin in the snow, and headed for the vehicle lot. Sicarius watched to make sure he didn't try to take the lorry he'd kept fired up all day.

"Do you need help with the trapping, Mr. Sicarius?" Wodic asked after he released the pent-up steam in the crane and climbed down.

"No. Go with your comrade."

"How're you going to get it to jump off the dock and swim in there?"

"It will be following bait."

Wodic glanced at Mederak's back. "Human bait?"

"Yes, but there are only two people whose blood it's interested in." Technically, it only wanted Sespian, as far as Sicarius knew, but it had trouble telling them apart. "I am one of them."

"Oh. Are you sure—"

"Yes. Leave."

Sicarius strode through the camp, stopping only to grab a pair of snowshoes out of one of the cabins, then jogged to the waiting lorry. All he had to do now was find the construct and lead it back here, assuming he could do so without it catching him. The snow lay deeper on the field now, and he didn't know if the vehicle would be able to outrun the creature even on the best road. But it would be better than running—floundering—across the snow on foot. Or so he believed.

CHAPTER 19

A MARANTHE WOULD HAVE SPRINTED BACK TO THE control room, but she and Books had to be careful not to get turned around in the black maze. If they became lost, who knew if they'd ever find their way out again?

She was letting him lead and almost crashed into his back when the word, "Hurry!" flashed into her mind, along with an image of fire. It was so intense that she gasped and stumbled in surprise, throwing a hand against the wall to catch herself.

"What is it?" Books asked.

"Akstyr, I think." Amaranthe couldn't imagine anyone else hurling mental images into her mind, though she hadn't known he could do that. "Go, he needs our help."

She raced after Books, trying to shake the image out of her head. Someday, when they had the leisure to discuss such things, she'd let Akstyr know he could tone down his warnings. Books turned left at a five-way intersection and up a thankfully familiar ramp. It rose two stories, then deposited them at the back of the control room, at the hidden door they'd left through earlier. This time it wasn't open.

Amaranthe thumped her fist against it while Books tried to tease runes out of the wall. Neither method was effective.

"Akstyr?" she called. "Retta? Can you let us in?"

From somewhere up the corridor came the sounds of heavy footfalls. Amaranthe didn't think they belonged to Akstyr or Retta.

"This way," Books said. "I think I can find the other entrance."

Too bad he hadn't left out the "I think" part of that statement.

Amaranthe followed him regardless. She'd done her best to memorize the map, too, and thought she'd know if he took a wrong turn. Sure, she thought, and that's why you got lost and visited your own personal torture chamber.

They ran around a corner and skidded to a halt, arms flailing, the smooth floors denying traction. A single one-foot-wide black cube floated down the corridor toward them. The small circular orifice on its front flared to life as soon as they appeared.

"Back, back," Amaranthe cried, though Books needed no urging.

As soon as they found their footing, they leaped around the corner again. A streak of crimson light pierced the air where they'd been. Amaranthe peeked back around the corner long enough to fire at the cube. She doubted a rifle could damage it, but maybe it'd deter it for a time, convince it to float down some other intersection.

As soon as she fired, a second red beam shot out, this one catching her bullet in its path. A tiny wisp of smoke was the only proof it had existed.

There was no time to gawk. That orifice was lighting up again. She ducked back into the corridor, sprinting to catch up with Books. A male voice screamed somewhere in the maze of corridors, a scream of absolute pain. Akstyr?

Amaranthe gulped, afraid she'd be too late to help. She and Books raced back the way they'd come. Facing guards would be far better than being incinerated by machines.

They passed the locked door and raced down a long stretch, rounding another bend. Once again, they were forced to halt in a rush. Two bodies lay sprawled on the deck ahead while two cubes hovered over them, steady beams lancing through the air, burning into flesh, bone, and organs. Amaranthe gagged at the sight—and the stench—but didn't hesitate to turn around. Books was staring, so she grabbed his arm to make sure he turned too. Though the cubes hadn't noticed them—or they had but wouldn't bother with them until they finished their current... jobs—Amaranthe wouldn't count on that lasting.

"They're killing their own people," Books rasped.

Better than Akstyr, Amaranthe thought. "I don't think any of us are *their* people, not the cubes' anyway. Mia must have changed them back to what they originally were. Maybe she didn't know what would happen exactly. The guards' deaths could have been accidental." She jerked her thumb over her shoulder.

"What a way to die."

Amaranthe couldn't disagree, though it was faster than a lot of ways. She and Books ran back to a ramp they'd passed. This time, she checked for cubes before stepping out.

"If we go down a level, think we could find that lift back up?" Amaranthe asked. They didn't have many options. "Maybe it's unguarded now." Or maybe those guards would be busy dealing with that wall of flame Akstyr had shown her. What machine or wizard had shown up to cause *that*?

"Yes."

Books wasn't so eager to charge into the lead this time, and they ran side-by-side down the ramp. On the lower floor, they reached the dead-end corridor without barreling into any more cubes—or guards. Did that mean the men had already breached the control room?

Amaranthe and Books stopped, and he prodded the symbols into existence, repeating the combination Retta had pressed. The lift started to rise, but halted with a lurch. The entire craft lurched.

"Did we hit something?" Amaranthe pictured underwater wrecks, then imagined the lake iced over. What if colder weather had come in, sealing them below? But surely the *Behemoth* would be powerful enough to break through a couple of inches of ice.

"I don't know." As Books spoke, the lift started rising again.

Amaranthe readied the rifle, anticipating a chamber full of guards.

Instead, the lift reached the control room, and a wall of fire blazed before them, pouring heat. Amaranthe jerked her arm up

to shield her eyes from the intense light and her face from the sweltering air. Smoke filled her eyes and nostrils. She squinted, trying to locate friends and enemies.

A body in a black uniform lay on the floor, the lower half sticking out of the curtain of flames. A rifle had fallen next to him, the wooden stock charred to black.

"Emperor's warts," Books bit out, "this whole place is made from metal. What could be burning?"

Besides the bodies? Amaranthe didn't say it out loud. Too morbid.

"Akstyr?" she called, worried about giving their position away if there were guards inside, but—she stared at the charred body—it might be too late for it to matter.

"Come around the wall," came Akstyr's strained voice from the other side of the fire.

The wall? The wall of flames?

Amaranthe trotted down its length, though the intensity of the heat made her want to scurry out of the room as fast as possible. She imagined her arm hairs singeing and shrinking away. At first, she'd thought the flames stretched from one wall to another, but there was a gap of a few feet at one end. She stepped through and found Akstyr kneeling on the floor, one arm down, supporting his body weight, the other outstretched toward the fiery curtain. Sweat bathed his face and stained his clothes. His eyes were red and bleary when they focused on Amaranthe.

She took a step toward him, but halted, noticing black shapes in her peripheral vision. One of the other doors was open—the one that had been locked earlier—and two cubes hovered on the threshold.

"Blasted dead ancestors." Reflexively, Amaranthe jerked her rifle up, though her mind knew it'd be useless.

"It's all right." Akstyr grimaced. "Well, not really, but they're staying there for now. Something about the heat."

"They sense that it's akin to their own output and believe other cubes are already cleaning the mess inside." Retta didn't

glance at them as she spoke. She stood behind Akstyr, between two floating images, the only ones remaining in the room.

Behind *her*, smoke poured from perforations in the black wall. That view arrested Amaranthe's eyes even more than the flames or the cubes. She hadn't thought *anything* could destroy that impervious material.

"The cubes did that?" Originally, Amaranthe had attributed the smoke to the flames, but this was coming from within the wall, something damaged.

"Yes." Retta's fingers flew as she manipulated... whatever it was she could manipulate through those images. "They're not supposed to inflict damage on their environment, just the debris, as they think of us and everything else, within it. Mia altered them somehow. In trying to send them after us, she may have doomed us all."

The *Behemoth* lurched again, this time the floor—the entire room—tilted five degrees. The cubes in the doorway didn't react. They remained floating on a level plane while everything around them shifted. Amaranthe wished they'd shift themselves out of the control room completely.

"You didn't... bring her back?" Retta glanced around.

"Uh, no. Her own men shot her. Inadvertently."

Retta's eyes narrowed. "Unfortunate."

Yes. Especially if she was the only one who could return the cubes to their nonaggressive state.

"Why aren't you putting the wall over there?" Amaranthe asked Akstyr, avoiding Retta's hard glare. "In front of those two in the doorway?"

Akstyr's exhausted head tilt made her regret being picky, but maybe he could make it smaller if he moved it, and maintaining it would require less effort. He could block the door, nothing else.

"There were some coming out of the lift too." Akstyr's arm was still extended toward the wall, though it was drooping, even the fingers. He couldn't maintain that effort much longer. "This kept them fooled from both directions."

"Are we out of the lake yet?" Books asked.

Yes, best to figure out how to do something with the *Behemoth*, so they could make their escape before Akstyr's will gave out and those cubes swarmed inside.

"Almost," Retta said, "but I don't know if I can steer us anywhere. The engines are behind that wall." She waved to the smoke. "I'm sure we're not irrevocably damaged—according to the documentation I read, the *Ortarh Ortak* can repair itself automatically, so long as it has time to—"

"Where're those lifeboats you mentioned?" Amaranthe didn't care about the cursed thing's ability to regenerate itself. If anything she'd prefer it to crash and explode so nobody could tinker with it ever again, so long as she and her men escaped first.

The irked expression Retta gave her was almost as heated as Akstyr's wall, but she twitched her finger a few times, and an image popped into existence beside Books and Amaranthe. It was the map of the interior again. Green pinpricks of light appeared at irregular intervals all over the schematic.

Books pointed. "That one's right above us. Is there ceiling access?"

Amaranthe couldn't imagine how a "lifeboat" could be located in the center of the ship—most of the green dots were along the perimeter—but maybe there was a tube it could travel through to escape.

"No." Retta waved toward the door where the cubes hovered. "You have to go back out, around, and up."

"Of course you do," Books said.

"I can't hold this much longer," Akstyr whispered. He dropped all the way to the floor and lay crumpled on his side, only that one arm still raised.

Amaranthe knelt beside him. "Can I do anything to help? Do you need water?" He looked like a man who'd run twenty miles through a desert.

"Just get me out of here so I don't have to maintain it any more. Please."

Amaranthe swallowed. She didn't think she'd ever heard

him say please. It had to be a testament to how close he was to pitching over the edge of the precipice.

Shots rang out from the direction of the lift.

"Down," Amaranthe cried even as she flung herself to the floor beside Akstyr.

Bullets ricocheted off the walls. Many bullets. The flames had blinded them to the newcomers' arrival, but Amaranthe cursed herself for having been caught unaware. Keeping her head to the floor, she searched all about, as if some hiding spot might have appeared in the room in the time she and Books had been gone. It hadn't. Retta remained standing, sweat streaming from her temples as she continued to work the floating controls.

"Those cabinets," Amaranthe said. "Books, can you open them?"

A shot fired, this time from their side. Flat on his stomach, Books had wriggled to the closest wall, and had the rifle trained in the direction of the lift. He hadn't heard her request. She grimaced, not certain if returning fire was a good idea or not. It would let those on the other side of the flames know exactly where her people were. Still hunkered by Akstyr, she didn't want to draw fire. His eyes were glassy, distant. She wasn't certain he knew people were shooting at them.

Without warning, the curtain of fire dropped.

"Akstyr," she blurted. She couldn't blame him for getting tired, but this wasn't the time to drop the only camouflage they had.

"It wasn't me," he whispered back. "Someone made me drop it."

"Huh?"

Four guards had charged out of the lift, each facing a different direction, each with a rifle poised and ready. Two women stood on the pad behind them. One was Ms. Worgavic—emperor's warts, who'd driven her down here?—but the other was the bigger concern at the moment. A tattooed woman in a buckskin dress stood beside her, eyes half-lidded in intense thought as she gazed about her.

"Drop your weapons," the lead guard ordered.

Outnumbered or not, Amaranthe wasn't keen to obey. If she hadn't been beside Akstyr, uncertain whether he could move to flee or protect himself, she would have fired back and sprinted for those cabinets.

"The cubes!" Books barked.

Cursed ancestors, she'd forgotten about them. With the flames gone, they'd decided to float into the room.

"Bring back the fire," Amaranthe called toward Worgavic and the shaman. "They're targeting everybody, your people too!"

She grabbed Akstyr and pulled him toward Books and the wall farthest from the door, hoping the guards would be too busy looking at the cubes to worry about shooting people getting out of the way. And if her team was farther from the cubes than the other group, they'd go over there first, right? Maybe.

"Retta," Amaranthe hissed. "This way."

"I've almost got it fixed," Retta said, her fingers still flying. "We've broken the surface of the lake. We either have to—"

"Shoot them," Ms. Worgavic said, her words icy as they cut over the rest of the voices in the room, "then get back in the lift before those things get over here."

Shoot *them*? The torturing hadn't been bad enough? As the guards swung their firearms toward them, Amaranthe whipped up her own rifle in response. She wouldn't get all of them, but if she could get Ms. Worgavic...

"Akstyr," Books whispered. "Do something!"

"I can't."

Amaranthe fired. The bullet should have taken Ms. Worgavic in the chest, but it bounced off some invisible shield. She wanted to clench her fist and shake it in frustration, but three other rifles were coming to bear on her. She buried her head under her arms, knowing it wouldn't be enough.

Several men yelped, then something clattered to the floor. Their weapons?

"Nice," Books said, "you did that right, Akstyr?"

"Made them too hot to hold, yes, but—"

A shriek came, a far greater cry of pain than the previous yells. The cubes had closed on the party by the lift, and two beams streaked out, one catching a man too busy trying to pick up his dropped rifle to react in time. The shaman frowned at the deadly floating devices and lifted her hands.

Amaranthe jumped to her feet. "Let's get out of here while they're distracted. Retta, time to go." She took a step in that direction—she'd pick Retta up and fling her over her shoulder if she had to.

Before she finished her step, a huge cone of fire shot from the lift, from the shaman's outstretched arms. Her eyes seemed to glow red, reflecting the wicked orange light. The flames engulfed the cubes, but they spanned half the room and also engulfed—

A feminine scream of sheer terror and pain came from the center of the inferno. Retta.

Amaranthe lunged in that direction, as if she could do something, pull the other woman out of the flames, but heat blasted against her face. She couldn't get close. A hand clamped around her arm, Books pulling her back. Akstyr was slumped against the wall, his arm up as a ward against the heat. They were on the edge of the inferno, the route to the doors blocked by a curtain of flames. All Amaranthe could do was plaster her back to the wall alongside Books and Akstyr and wait.

Retta's screams stopped, and Amaranthe clenched her eyes shut. All she'd done here was get people killed.

Someone else screamed—one of the guards?

"It's not working!"

"They're still coming!"

Akstyr wiped his face and muttered, "Didn't do it right."

In a wink, the flames vanished.

The lift, along with Ms. Worgavic and the shaman, had disappeared. The bodies of the guards littered the floor in their wake.

Undamaged, the two cubes still floated in the air, incinerating the dead men.

"Not again," Books whispered, staring.

Amaranthe's own stare was in the other direction, toward the charred unrecognizable woman lying on the floor, limbs twisted and unmoving. She opened her mouth, a self-pitying, "Why?" forming—why couldn't any of her plans ever work out without people getting killed, and why couldn't she learn to stop putting others in these situations?—but Akstyr poked her and shoved Books.

"Lifeboat, right? We gotta go."

Amaranthe pushed away from the wall—and her condemning thoughts, leaving them to haunt her later, along with all the others. "Yes."

They sprinted across the room, angling for the closest door.

"Who's going to pilot that lifeboat?" Books asked.

Amaranthe would have answered—not that she *had* an answer—but the movement of the cubes caught her eye. She thought they'd have time to make it through the door, that the cleaning artifacts would finish incinerating the bodies before chasing after her team, but they were, as one, already floating after them.

* * *

Full darkness descended on the snowy field as Sicarius drove across it, the lorry bumping and slipping on the fresh powder. The big vehicle performed acceptably, given that there was no road beneath it. He had chosen a direct path toward the army camp, hoping the trip back would go more quickly if he could retrace the trail broken by his own tires. If things went as planned, he wouldn't be able to afford any delays on that return trip.

The snow had stopped, with dusk bringing a clearer sky, so he hadn't lit the exterior lanterns on the lorry. Had he done so, the camp's roving guards would have seen the lorry from a mile away. The only thing he wanted seeing him was the soul construct.

He approached the camp from the north, knowing he'd be

upwind of the creature. If it was still in the hills behind the tents, its otherworldly senses ought to be able to smell him from miles off. Sicarius eyed the stars coming out above. It might have already left to hunt, bypassing the ice camp and traveling straight to Fort Urgot, straight to Sespian.

Stay with the plan, he told himself. If he didn't find the creature in the camp, he'd drive to the fort. He couldn't hear the booms and cracks of the battle raging there, not over the rumble of the lorry and the hisses of escaping steam, but he knew the fighting was still going on—he'd heard cannons cracking before leaving the lake. That *should* mean the walls hadn't been breached yet.

A mile and a half away from General Flintcrest's camp, Sicarius stopped the lorry. He dared not drive the vehicle any closer. Even without the lanterns to alert the soldiers, its noise would carry over the flat field. He might already be too close, but he dared not park farther away, not when he had to outrun the soul construct, make it back to the lorry, and drive all the way back to the ice camp before it caught up to him. That trap would be for naught if he couldn't reach it.

Before jumping out of the lorry, Sicarius added coal to the furnace, ensuring the boiler would be hot and ready when he returned. Outside, away from the heat of the cab, the frosty air wrapped around him. The temperature had dropped at least fifteen degrees with the disappearance of the clouds; it'd be a cold night to throw himself into the lake.

He licked his finger and tested the wind. Yes, it was blowing his scent toward the camp.

Sicarius jogged a couple hundred meters away from the lorry and crouched, listening for telltale howls in the night. Nothing stirred. With the vehicle stopped, it wasn't making noise, and he could hear a few clanks and shouts from the camp.

He stood, deciding he'd have to go closer. Before he took a step, the first eerie howl drifted across the plain. Sicarius turned around, unease slithering into his stomach. The sound hadn't come from the camp, but from the northeast. The soul construct

was between him and Fort Urgot somewhere. It was either on its way, or it was returning. If it was on its way... he had to divert it. Unfortunately, his plans to make sure he was upwind of the camp now meant he was downwind of the creature. It might catch his scent anyway, but he couldn't count on it.

Sicarius ran back to the lorry and jumped into the cab. Another howl drifted down from the northeast, audible over the firing of weapons beyond it. He turned the vehicle in the direction of Fort Urgot and watched the field ahead. Maybe he should have stopped long enough to light the lamps, but, no, he'd have an easier time picking out that dark shape on the white snow without flames dulling his night vision. In the back of his mind, he admitted that he might not make it back to the lake if he waited until he was close enough to see it. It couldn't be helped. He couldn't let it hunt Sespian, especially not tonight, when he, Maldynado, and Basilard would be distracted by the battle.

Ears and eyes straining, Sicarius bumped over the uneven snow, urging the lorry to travel faster, willing the soul construct to catch his scent and turn away from the fort. The howls had stopped, or they'd moved too far away to hear.

He glanced toward the odometer, judging the distance to Fort Urgot. In that heartbeat that his eyes weren't focused on the field ahead of him, the soul construct appeared out of the darkness. It was bounding across the snow toward him.

He'd survived too many near-death experiences to react with some thoughtless yank of the controls that would have made the vehicle skid in the snow. He carefully turned around, angling toward the lake. Only when he was facing in the right direction did he urge the lorry to its maximum speed.

Snow churned and flew up from the tires, some of it finding its way into the cab, pelting Sicarius. He alternated between watching the route ahead—the packed path he'd carefully made on his way to Flintcrest's camp was two miles to the south now and useless—and glancing out of the cab, tracking the construct's progress.

Its powerful legs pumped, propelling it through the snow in

great leaps, each one eating meters of earth. The fresh powder didn't deter it at all. As Sicarius had feared, even with the lorry at full speed, the creature was gaining on him.

A wheel found a rut hidden beneath the snow, and the vehicle lurched. The rest of the wheels skidded, and it swerved, catching another rut. Sicarius kept his balance in the rocking cab, but the jolts reminded him to keep his gaze on the field. Driving at night, at top speed, in the snow was asking for—

A chilling screech, more like the undulating cries of coyotes than the wail of a wolf, cut through his thoughts, raising the hairs on his arms. There was exhilaration in that unnatural baying, the delight of the hunt. Strange how some creature summoned into existence by a practitioner could feel the same exuberance as a flesh-and-blood beast.

The lake came into sight ahead, but the ice camp wasn't on the horizon yet. Sicarius estimated it four or five miles away. He was making good time, despite the bumping jolts of the lorry racing too fast over a field that wasn't nearly as flat as it looked, but he didn't know if it was good enough.

The undulating cry came again, closer this time. Sicarius glanced behind the cab but didn't see the creature.

A thump sounded, something striking the vehicle. No, something *landing* on the vehicle. Claws scraped at the cab above Sicarius's head followed by an ear-splitting squeal of metal. What was it doing? Tearing off the top of the smokestack?

He turned left, then right, trying to swerve with enough force to throw the creature free. More metal squealed, as if claws were digging in, trying to find purchase to keep its massive body aboard.

A paw swiped in from the open side of the cab. Without taking his hands from the controls, Sicarius dropped into a squat so deep his butt smacked the floor. The claws swept in, tearing his cap from his head. Another centimeter, and he would have lost his scalp.

Before the paw retracted, Sicarius shoved at the levers again. This time the vehicle turned so violently, the wheels lost

LINDSAY BUROKER

all traction on the snow, and it skidded several feet, the back end spinning in the opposite direction. Sicarius grabbed at the brake bar above his head. Steam screeched like an injured beast as it was released into the night. The brakes caught more fully than he expected, and a lurch jolted the vehicle, nearly pitching him through the windshield.

The construct flew from the roof, its giant hound-like form rolling sideways several times when it hit the snow.

Sicarius urged the vehicle into motion again. The creature's roll was slowing, but it hadn't recovered yet. He steamed right toward it.

The beast found its feet, but didn't leap out of the way fast enough. The lorry pummeled into its backside, sending it spinning again.

Doubting he'd done more than surprise it, Sicarius turned back toward the lake, pushing for maximum speed again. An ominous *clink-thunk* started in the engine, and the cab shuddered with each revolution of the wheels. Finally, the camp came into sight, a few dark buildings and cabins against the white snow. There were no lamps burning behind the shutters. The men must have heeded his warning to flee.

Sicarius glanced behind him again, hoping the soul construct might have taken a few moments to recover, but it wasn't more than fifty meters back, its legs pumping to gain ground.

Without slowing, he ran the lorry all the way to the bank, jumping free of the cab before it plunged over the edge. Ice shattered beneath its mass, but, before it continued far, it struck a submerged piling or boulder, resulting in a crash that must have been heard in Fort Urgot.

When Sicarius landed, he was already running. As he turned onto the dock, the construct came into sight, tearing around the corner of a building so fast that its paws slipped on the ice and snow. The slip scarcely slowed it down. In one mighty jump, it leaped onto the concrete dock, twisting in the air so it wouldn't overshoot its target. All four paws touched down, and it bounded after Sicarius.

The red circle painted on the concrete was barely visible under the starlight, and he almost overran his own target. He dove off the right side of the dock, arrowing into the water. Its grasp was so cold, so icy, that the shock pelted his body like a hammer striking an anvil. But he knew he couldn't hesitate, not for a heartbeat, or he was dead.

His knuckles smashed into steel. The trap, no the hatch. Good. He found the opening and squirmed through it.

The creature smashed into the surface of the water above him. A wave of force propelled him into the trap so hard, he rammed into the bottom. He righted himself and started to swim for the opening on the side, but he paused. What if the construct had landed on the open hatch, slamming it shut instead of swimming in as Sicarius had planned?

He peered upward, trying to see through the inky blackness of the steel-walled trap. The water outside and the sky above were nearly as dark, but he did make out the opening in the ceiling, then the darkness as something blotted out the light. There. It was coming.

Sicarius stroked for the hole in the side. He didn't want to dart out too quickly, before the construct committed to entering, but if he waited too long, the thing would simply—

Claws raked into his calf, and pain surged up his leg. Sicarius clamped down on the feeling, not letting it stir panic, but it urged him to make a quick escape. He grabbed the lip of the hole and yanked himself out, twisting in the water to grab the hatch on the side. Numbness from the icy lake was already creeping into his extremities, and his fingers fumbled uncharacteristically. He slammed the covering shut, but it took precious time to secure the latch.

Worried the soul construct would have already seen the trap for what it was, Sicarius darted up to the top, angling straight for the other hatch. The cursed darkness made it impossible to see inside the steel cube—was the creature still inside? Had it already escaped? Maybe it waited right behind him, ready to gnash down on his skull.

Sicarius threw the hatch shut regardless. Except it didn't close. It caught on something. A paw. The soul construct was in there. Good. But it was trying to get out. Not good.

Another paw batted at the hatch from below. In the water, Sicarius lacked leverage. He wouldn't be able to hold the lid shut once the creature threw some effort into escaping—it must not have quite figured out the situation yet. Sicarius lifted the hatch and hammered it down. He couldn't hurt the construct, but maybe it'd be startled enough to yank its paw back. If he could get the cover shut, he could throw the latch.

The paw didn't budge. In the freezing blackness, Sicarius didn't see it, but he sensed it sweep out, its claws scraping against the steel as they raked about, trying to catch him. Once more he lifted the lid and hammered it down again, trying to grind the hatch shut, to convince the creature to pull its claw back. His leg burned, and his air was running out.

More pressure pushed against the hatch. He'd have to let go, try something else. But what?

A boom thundered, the sound powerful even under water. The force nearly threw him off the hatch, but he kept his grip with his hands, though his legs were flung to the other side. The trap lurched, and the paw disappeared back inside. Sicarius hurried to take advantage, hammering the hatch shut one more time. This time metal clanged against metal. He threw the three latches designed to secure the door against tremendous force. And hoped they'd be enough.

Sicarius swam for the surface. He'd no more than popped up when a burning piece of wreckage splatted into the water, not three inches from his eyes. He blinked up at the sky, not certain if more would pour down, and not knowing at first what could have exploded.

Oh, he realized, as he swam for the dock. The lorry. He snorted and pulled himself out of the water. The smoldering wreck in the shallows was still spitting burning coal and shrapnel into the night. Amaranthe would be proud.

A stiff gust of wind battered at Sicarius's damp clothing.

He needed to strip and find a place to warm up, or he'd be in danger of losing digits—maybe more—but he had one more task to complete.

He raced to the base of the dock and around the building to find the crane. He'd stoked the furnace before he'd left, and it didn't take much to stir the coals to life. The water in the boiler was still hot, and it held enough steam to drive the crane down the dock and out to the red paint. He maneuvered the arm with numb, shaking hands, trying to find the hook in the top of the trap by feel. His legs were numb, too, and when he tried to wriggle his toes in his boots, he couldn't feel them. Blood as well as water ran down his leg.

Sicarius finally found the hook, and lifted the trap out of the water. Numb hands or not, he could feel the reverberations as the construct flung itself against the steel walls of its new cage. As soon as it cleared the water, Sicarius maneuvered the vehicle toward the end of the dock. He drove it as far as he could, then swung the crane back and forth a couple of times. The cables creaked and the crane groaned beneath the weight, but he managed to use the momentum to release the trap at the right time, hurling it into deeper water. With luck, the construct would remain down there for a very long time. He'd have to deal with the practitioner to ensure nobody would find it and release it any time soon, but not tonight. He gazed north over the placid black waters of the lake, toward Fort Urgot. The sky was brighter there, an indication of all the lanterns and perhaps fires burning in that direction.

He hopped out of the crane, intending to run all the way to the fort, but a massive gush of water sounded behind him. He whirled back toward the end of the dock... and stared. A massive dome shape was rising from the lake, its body blocking the entire view of the city on the opposite shoreline.

The Behemoth.

Amaranthe. Sicarius swallowed. Was she on it? Was she the reason it was coming out of the water? Or had Forge chosen this moment, when the city was all indoors, staying out of the cold

night, to move the craft? Maybe they'd captured Amaranthe and decided they had to run before someone else came down after them.

Sicarius had never seen the *Behemoth* lift off, and he didn't know what to expect, but the craft had an unanticipated wobble to it. It lurched, half of it dipping back toward the water, then recovered. He backed up, feeling vulnerable on the dock. But the craft wasn't heading his way. It continued to climb until he could see the city lights again beneath it. He thought it would keep going, disappearing into the starry night, but it lurched again, one side dipping.

Then it plummeted, not back into the lake, but downward at an angle. His breath froze. A northward angle. Toward Fort Urgot.

* * *

Amaranthe didn't waste words as they raced through the corridors. She simply ran, Books and Akstyr pounding after her, and they veered onto the nearest ramp leading up. Reaching this lifeboat wouldn't be enough. They'd have to figure out how to get inside and how to fly away. Or swim away. Or... who knew? She had no idea if the *Behemoth* was in the air, on land, or in the water. The blasted thing could at least have a window here or there.

"That should be it." Books pointed to a short dead end.

Amaranthe raced to the far wall.

Akstyr hesitated in the intersection. "Are you sure? Those cubes are right behind us. We'll be trapped if we get stuck down there."

"Books?" Amaranthe waved uselessly at the wall.

"Oh, I see. I'm the expert here now." He tapped about, trying to illuminate the runes that should be there somewhere.

"You've opened two doors to my none. That makes you a downright professional."

Books found the runes, this time on the left instead of on the right and in more of an orange color.

"Uh oh." Amaranthe didn't recognize any of them.

"Cubes are in sight," Akstyr called from the intersection.

"Blighted ancestors," she said, "we'll have to run, try another lifeboat. If we can find it."

Books tapped one of the runes and pushed in and turned another. A door slid upward. "It's the same pattern as was on that cabinet she opened," he said.

Thank his ancestors for paying attention.

"Is it safe in there?" Akstyr asked, then yelped and raced toward them. "It had better be!"

A horizontal crimson beam burned through the air in the intersection behind him. Akstyr darted through the doorway and into a dark cubby without stopping to check inside. With few other options, Amaranthe and Books jumped in after him. For all she could see, they might have jumped into a cider barrel without so much as an unstoppered bunghole to illuminate the interior. The only light came from outside, from the door still yawning open.

"Uh, we might want to close that," Akstyr said.

"I'm trying." Books was patting all around the opening.

The floor tilted again, down to the left, then quickly back to the right. Were they flying? Or floating on the surface of the lake? Amaranthe wished she knew.

The cubes appeared in the intersection.

"Not good." Amaranthe lifted her rifle.

They rotated slowly, their crimson orifices coming into view. It'd be useless, but she shot at one. What else could she do?

The cubes didn't bother incinerating her bullet this time. It simply clanged off the front of one, and it ignored it. They floated closer, the holes glowing in preparation.

"There's nothing in here," Books cried, desperation in his voice, something that'd often accompanied his words in tight situations early on. They were perfectly justified this time. "I can't find it anywhere."

"Take cover," Amaranthe said, shooting again.

As if there were cover. She flattened herself against one

wall, while Books leaned against the other, but their chamber was so tiny, there were only a couple of inches of wall on either side of the door. Akstyr had fallen to the floor.

"Too tired," he groaned.

Amaranthe almost grabbed him, but he had as much cover down there as she did. The first beam lanced out, slicing through the air in the center of the doorway. It bit into the metal or whatever comprised the front of their supposed lifeboat. Smoke filled the air.

A second beam joined the first, and they started moving, one beam to the left, toward Books, and one toward the right, toward Amaranthe. She patted about on the wall, hoping to find a weapon or controls for the door. Anything, cursed ancestors, anything.

The beam inched closer. She dropped to the floor beside Akstyr.

"I don't know who designed a lifeboat without a door that closes, but it's a severe design flaw," she growled.

Inevitably the cubes drew closer, and the beam lowered toward the floor, toward Akstyr and toward her. From her back, Amaranthe fired one more time, uselessly.

Her bullet landed, not with a clang, but with a concussive boom. The force of the explosion threw her into the air so hard and so high that she struck the ceiling. Or maybe that was the wall—the entire chamber seemed to flip onto its side. Pain bludgeoned her like a locomotive, her hip and her arm pounding into one wall, and then she hit another wall as the world spun again. Had she somehow blown up one of the cubes? How could such a small object contain such an explosive force?

Cries of surprise and pain came from Books and Akstyr, too, and the lights in the hallway went out. Everything went out. Or maybe the door had finally shut. Amaranthe couldn't see a thing.

The world stopped moving, and she dropped one final time, hitting the floor with her other hip. She groaned and had no more than lifted her head—though what good that movement would

do just then, she didn't know—when a soft thrum ran through the chamber. There was a brief surge—acceleration?—and then a wan gray light entered the chamber.

After the darkness, even the weak illumination made Amaranthe blink, shielding her eyes with her hand. When her vision came into focus, she found herself staring through her fingers at a starry night sky.

"We're outside?" she asked.

A stupid question, she supposed, but she was so disoriented that she couldn't figure out what had happened. Amaranthe tried to sit up, to gauge her injuries. She didn't think she'd broken anything, but in the morning she'd have lumps bigger than those love apples Maldynado was always talking about.

"Books?" She touched a dark form beneath her, and then the other. "Akstyr?"

They weren't moving. Everyone was crumpled on the floor, their limbs entangled in the confined space. Amaranthe's earlier assessment, comparing the space to a cider keg, wasn't that far off. The rounded walls didn't possess any visible instruments or gauges, though the front had disappeared, replaced by a window of some sort. A translucent barrier, might be a better term, as nothing so familiar as glass shielded them from the outside. She remembered escaping through a similar door the last time she'd left the *Behemoth* and wondered if that would become the new exit. The old door, the one through which they'd entered this "lifeboat" was sealed shut.

Amaranthe disentangled herself from Books and Akstyr. She was alarmed that neither was moving, but curiosity prompted her to check the view first, to see if she could see more than the stars. What if... She gulped. What if the *Behemoth* had spit them out on some trajectory that would take them to the South Pole? Or, dear ancestors, another world?

On hands and knees, she crept as close as she dared—she had no idea if she could fall out, but had no wish to chance it.

Snow and rocks and trees blurred past below them, *far* below.

The only other time she'd been airborne had been on that

dirigible, and they hadn't been this high, nor had they been traveling so quickly.

"Books," Amaranthe rasped. She picked out cliffs and canyons below, then a river that disappeared almost as soon as it had appeared. They were flying over mountains. That meant they'd already left the capital and the farmlands around the lake behind. "You'll want to see this."

Before he stirred or she could prod him, the speed at which the terrain was passing below slowed down. A queasy empty feeling came over Amaranthe. Had she eaten recently, she might have thrown up. Was the ground getting closer?

It took a moment for the truth to dawn. They'd reached whatever apogee they'd been hurled toward and were descending.

"Never mind," Amaranthe squeaked. "You may want to stay unconscious for this."

She refused to accept that either of them could be worse than unconscious. Though if their lifeboat didn't have a means to soften the landing, they'd *all* be worse than unconscious. The smoke that tainted the air, burning her eyes and her nostrils, wasn't reassuring. Maybe whatever means this craft had of landing safely had been destroyed.

Indeed, they were picking up speed. Not lateral speed this time, but vertical speed. Dropping like a rock, came the unwelcome phrase from the back of her mind. It was the last fully formed thought she managed.

She stared, terror rising within her as the rocks and trees and snow drew closer and closer. She patted around the walls, frantic to find some control, something that could slow their descent, but the smooth featureless interior of the craft offered nothing. Lastly, she dropped to her knees, curled into a ball, and flung her arms over her head.

The window disappeared with a hiss and pop. More smoke flowed into the cabin, and blackness dropped over the craft.

CHAPTER 20

S ICARIUS COULDN'T FEEL HIS FINGERS OR HIS FEET. Numbness made him stumble as he ran through the snow along the lake. Blood dotted the tracks he left, but he barely noticed. He didn't care. He couldn't tear his eyes from the dark horizon.

There should have been lights, fires, sparks from weapons, but blackness lay ahead. In the aftermath of the *Behemoth*'s crash, the night had grown utterly silent. Not so much as an owl hooted from the bare icicle-draped branches of the trees lining the running path. The air stank of more kinds of smoke than his nose could identify—burning trees, and coal, and black powder, but more alien scents too. And blood. The scent of blood lingered amongst it all.

Through no conscious awareness of his own, Sicarius's pace slowed when he reached the end of the trees, the scant trees that remained standing. The *Behemoth* had mowed down all the ones by the lake on its inbound trajectory; the closest ones had been topped, such as a logger might do, with only the tips of the trunks torn off, but the ones farther in had been knocked to the snow in their entirety. Wreckage, wood, and bodies littered the white fields. The tents that had housed the invaders were all flattened. And the fort...

Sicarius stumbled to a stop, his legs numb from more than the icy cold that encroached upon his extremities. Aside from one crumbling corner of the wall, Fort Urgot was gone. It had been completely and utterly flattened beneath the massive black dome of the *Behemoth*. One side of the craft was buried meters

into the earth, while the far side merely lay upon the snow, but that great weight... There was no sign of the buildings, the defenses, or the *people* who had been inside the fort when it hit.

Images of Maldynado and Basilard and Sespian flashed through his mind, with Sespian being in the forefront. Sespian shooting down the cable into the enemy camp. Sespian smiling and explaining how to encourage a girl. Sespian sleeping in his bed as a boy, charcoal sticks and a sketchpad scattered all about the blankets.

Sicarius closed his eyes and swallowed hard. He willed his legs to carry him forward. There was a chance...

Maybe Sespian had been out on the field, fighting hand-to-hand with the invaders, or maybe he'd seen the *Behemoth* coming and there'd been time to run away.

Sicarius scoffed. Run away. Right. Once it had risen from the lake, the craft had taken less than five seconds to plummet across the water and crash.

He ran to its side anyway, his legs carrying him over and around countless bodies in the snow. Some had died from the fighting, but others must have been flung through the air as a result of the crash, mangled like the tents and like so many of those trees.

As he passed, Sicarius glanced at each face, checking to make sure. He didn't recognize any of them as soldiers from within the fort. These men all wore blue armbands. He ran a full circle around the crashed vessel, just in case... but, no. Nobody inside the fort had made it out.

Sespian was gone.

He halted, shoulders slumping, and stared at the ground. He'd never gotten a chance to... They'd barely started to... His chin drooped to his chest. How was he supposed to—

Someone coughed, the noise loud against the silence that had descended upon the battleground. Sicarius located the source. A man had appeared in the side of the *Behemoth*, seemingly stepping out of the hull of the ship ten feet above the ground. He slid down the side to land in a ridge of snow pushed up

around the bottom. A second person, a woman this time, stuck her head out of the black wall, hiked up her skirts and followed the same route.

Sicarius pulled out his black dagger and strode toward the invisible escape hatch. The tangled thoughts that stampeded into his mind were hard to follow, and it was more some buried primitive instinct that guided him than intellect. That monstrosity had killed Sespian, and he was going to kill those who had brought it here. And if Amaranthe was in there, he'd find her.

She *must* be in there, he realized. Her plan... this was because of her plan.

He shied away from the idea of blaming her for this, for Sespian's death. *She* hadn't brought this abomination to Stumps. Whatever plan she'd enacted, she'd been trying to help Sespian. He'd find her in there and bring her out. If he'd lost Sespian... Sicarius's fingers tightened on the hilt of his dagger. Amaranthe was all he had left.

Though he strode toward the *Behemoth* without worrying about stealth, the man and woman never saw him coming. Sicarius slit their throats and ran up the smooth, curved wall, a feat some would have found impossible. He didn't think about it. His eyes were focused on his targets, nothing else. He slashed the throat of another man trying to escape the vessel, a guard in a black uniform that reminded him of Pike. The thought filled him with cold fury that propelled him through the intangible wall and into a cargo bay.

Numerous guards were inside, rushing to evacuate. Sicarius cut down several before the others knew he was there, but then rifles were being brought to bear. In another situation, *any* other situation, he would have spied before crashing inside, made sure no one would spot him, but he was too numb to care about his own safety. Now his only defense was to sprint, slashing and cutting and ducking and somersaulting to throw off his opponents and draw closer to his enemies.

Rifles fired, and crossbows twanged. A bullet slammed into

his side. He threw a dagger, taking the shooter in the throat. Another bullet clipped his temple before he finished off the room. He paused only long enough to collect his thrown knives, then ran for the corridor. He was being reckless, ridiculously so, but he didn't know how much time he had. What if Amaranthe had been captured and some maniac held a knife to her throat, ready to kill her for causing the *Behemoth* to rise from the lake?

He couldn't lose her *and* Sespian. He couldn't.

As he'd long ago been trained to do, Sicarius shunted off the part of his mind that acknowledged pain, locking it away to deal with later. He had never been inside the craft before, and wouldn't have had any idea of which way to go in the maze, but he used the fleeing people and the shouts and calls to evacuate to lead him deeper inside. Wherever they were coming from... it was where he wanted to go.

At the end of a long corridor, two women turned around a corner and came into his sight. Sicarius kept running, though he recognized the significance of one's buckskin dress and tattoos. He threw a knife, hoping to distract the shaman, but the long hallway gave her time to react. She raised a hand, and an invisible force deflected the blade into a wall before it reached her. Her hand remained up, and her eyes narrowed with focus. The other woman didn't carry an obvious weapon, but she stopped behind the shaman, uttering a command.

A side corridor opened up halfway between him and them, and he sprinted for it even as he braced himself for an attack. If it was a mental assault, he *might* be able to block it.

As soon as the first flame sparked into existence, Sicarius knew he couldn't fight it; he had no way to defend against physical Science, except by avoiding it. He sprinted and dove into a roll for the intersection. As he twisted to angle around the corner, he loosed a second throwing knife. The impudence cost him, and fire engulfed his arm. A split second later, he rounded the corner, the wall blocking him from further damage, and he raced off, batted out the flames on his sleeve. The scent of seared flesh rose from the burned fabric and blackened skin.

Another wound to worry about later. He threw himself around the next nearest intersection, but stopped there, peering back the way he'd come to see if the women followed.

They charged past without more than a glance down his corridor. Abandon the mission, abandon this craft, their harried expressions said. Sicarius wondered, not for the first time since he'd run in, if the crew feared the *Behemoth* was going to explode, much like that lorry had earlier in the night.

Sicarius ran back toward the main corridor, intending to return to his earlier route—if those women were amongst those in charge, they might have come from dealing with Amaranthe. He gritted his teeth, hating the images that came to mind at the words "dealing with."

Before he reached the main corridor again, a black cube floated into view. Between one step and the next, Sicarius halted, dropping into a crouch. No wonder the women had looked harried.

Poised on the balls of his feet, he waited, ready to flee again if needed. The cube continued on after its original prey. After a few seconds passed, Sicarius ventured back into the intersection. He was in time to see the cube disappear around the corner back the way he'd come. For a moment, he imagined a fleet of those things floating into the city, incinerating every man, woman, and child they came across, but his concern for Amaranthe leaped back to the forefront of his mind.

Still following the women's route of origin, he turned into a dead-end corridor. He'd seen a few of those dead ends twenty years earlier, in those ancient tunnels, and he knew there could be doors even in spots where they weren't apparent. He touched the wall when he reached it, and symbols flared to life. He'd seen them before, too—had watched Professor Komitopis open numerous doors. Though years had passed, many of those events from that strange mission were indelibly imprinted on his mind, and he found the right combination on the first try.

It wasn't a door, but a lift, and the floor rose, carrying him to a new level. He waited in a ready stance, a dagger in each hand,

but the room he entered was empty of the living. The air smelled of charred flesh and blood, though, and he stepped off the lift and around the bodies of guards. Another body lay facedown on the floor on the opposite side of a room, the skin and clothing burned off, features seared past the point of recognition, though it was a feminine form. Something under its torso glinted, and a sick sense of dread made Sicarius's belly quiver as he glanced at his own raw arm, remembering the shaman's power. What if Amaranthe had been trying to control the vessel and that woman with the shaman... had been determined that she not?

Sicarius sheathed his daggers, or maybe he dropped them—he was barely thinking—and walked forward. Slowly. If the craft was about to explode, he wasn't sure he cared.

He tried to kneel by the form, but his legs gave out—whether from his injures or loss of blood or frostbite, he didn't know—and he tumbled to the floor. From his knees, he rolled over the body. The flesh was still warm, blood and pus oozing from cracks, but the eyes and face had been burned away, and the chest no longer rose and fell. The garments, too, had fallen to ashes, and the only thing that remained was a silver chain and medallion, the slitted eyes of a Kendorian lizard staring up at him. The medallion Amaranthe had been wearing as part of her costume.

Sicarius didn't know how long he sat there, but his blood was pooling on the floor, a lot of it. If he wanted to live, he ought to bandage his wounds. He rubbed his face with a shaking hand, not sure he cared any more. About living. For so long Sespian had given him purpose, something to work to protect, a reason to be in the world. And then Amaranthe, though he'd done so little to encourage her, had insinuated herself into his life, and he'd had another reason to be, another reason to think the world might grow more interesting later on. And now...?

He found himself lying on his back, moisture—blood—seeping through his shirt as he stared at the black ceiling high above. He'd long suspected the world would be a better place

without him in it. Maybe this was some sort of cosmic fate, finally catching up with him for all he'd done.

A soft whisper of sound reached his ears. More out of reflex than because it mattered, Sicarius turned his head toward the lift. He was too numb to react with surprise or fear or pain when a solitary man walked onto the floor.

Hands clasped behind his back, the silver-haired Nurian practitioner strode across the room, his vibrant robes flowing about him, his weathered face grim. He stopped a few feet away and stared down at Sicarius.

A fitting end, Sicarius thought. His wounds might not have been enough to finish him, but the practitioner could ensure his death.

"You have been nettlesome," the man said in his native tongue.

Yes, Sicarius thought, *I have.* "Then end it," he whispered in Nurian.

A single silver eyebrow rose. "Oh, I don't think so. You've robbed me of my bodyguard and my beast of burden when my mission here is far from complete. I will need another to fill those roles."

The words percolated slowly through Sicarius's battered mind, and it wasn't until the wizard removed his hands from behind his back that their meaning sank in. He lifted an exotic opal between thumb and forefinger, its black, orange, and greens arresting even before he murmured something under his breath, and the stone began to glow. The practitioner lowered it to Sicarius's temple, pressing it against the skin. It was warm. More, it caused a strange tingle to run straight into his brain.

Sicarius should have lifted his arm, should have knocked that stone away, but either the practitioner or the loss of blood kept his limbs from responding. Instead the tingle grew hotter and more intense, as if the opal were burning its way into the side of his head. Abruptly the fire went out, and a quenching relief flared from the stone.

"It is done." The practitioner nodded. "You are mine now."

Through no intent of his own, Sicarius felt his gaze being pulled to the side until he stared into the other man's deep brown eyes, eyes as dark and inscrutable as his own.

"You will obey me," the practitioner said. "Understood?"

Against his wishes, Sicarius whispered, "I will obey."

THE END

ALSO BY THE AUTHOR

The Emperor's Edge Universe

Novels
The Emperor's Edge, Book 1
Dark Currents, Book 2
Deadly Games, Book 3
Conspiracy, Book 4
Blood and Betrayal, Book 5
Forged in Blood I, Book 6
Forged in Blood II, Book 7
Encrypted
Decrypted

Short Stories And Novellas
Ice Cracker II (and other short stories)
The Assassin's Curse
Beneath the Surface

THE FLASH GOLD CHRONICLES

Flash Gold
Hunted
Peacemaker

THE GOBLIN BROTHERS ADVENTURES

5052624R00225

Printed in Germany
by Amazon Distribution
GmbH, Leipzig